THE OTHER WRITING

*For Rebecca —
with admiration &
friendship

Fondly,
[signature]
16.IX.93*

DJELAL KADIR

THE OTHER WRITING

*Postcolonial Essays
in Latin America's Writing Culture*

PURDUE UNIVERSITY PRESS
West Lafayette, Indiana

Copyright ©1993 by Purdue Research Foundation.

All rights reserved. Unless permission is granted, this material shall not be copied, reproduced, or coded for reproduction by any electrical, mechanical, or chemical processes, or combination thereof, now known or later developed.

97 96 95 94 93   5 4 3 2 1

Design by Cheryl Payne

Printed in the United States of America

The paper used in this publication meets the minimum requirements of the American National Standard for Permanence of Paper for Printed Library Materials Z39.48-1984. ∞

LIBRARY OF CONGRESS CATALOGING-IN-PUBLICATION DATA

Kadir, Djelal.
    The other writing : postcolonial essays in Latin America's writing culture / by Djelal Kadir.
        p.   cm.
    Includes bibliographical references and index.
    ISBN 1-55753-031-9 (cloth : alk. paper). —
  ISBN 1-55753-032-7 (pbk. : alk. paper)
    1. Spanish American literature—History and criticism.
2. Difference (Psychology) in literature. I. Title.
PQ7081.K33 1993
860.9'98—dc20				92-27622
						CIP

For Aixé

The red-plague rid you
For learning me your language!

Wm. Shakespeare, *The Tempest,*
1.2.363–64

Contents

PREFACE — xi

ACKNOWLEDGMENTS — xv

INTRODUCTION
OTHERWISE READING AND WRITING — *1*

CHAPTER ONE
ORBIS TERTIUS: Colonial Discourse and Emergent Cultures — 17

CHAPTER TWO
SURVIVING THEORY — *31*

CHAPTER THREE
A SHORT PARABLE: Borges's Admonition to the Self-seeking Reader — 45

CHAPTER FOUR
ARBORESCENT PAZ, INTERLINEAL POETRY — 55

CHAPTER FIVE
FUENTES AND THE PROFANE SUBLIME
   History's Apostrophy — 73
   Parturient Scripture: Sterne Rejoyceings — 86

CHAPTER SIX

INTERSTITIAL GARCÍA MÁRQUEZ
   Between Milton and Tasso   *111*
   Between Inevitability and Life   *123*

CHAPTER SEVEN

SCATOLOGY, ESCHATOLOGY, PALIMPSEST: Vargas Llosa and the History of a Parricide   *137*

CHAPTER EIGHT

WRITING BEYOND THE BOOK: José Donoso Elsewhere
   Ghost House   *157*
   Next Door   *167*

CHAPTER NINE

A WOMAN'S PLACE: Gendered Histories of the Subaltern   *179*

EPILOGUE   *203*

NOTES   *207*

INDEX   *215*

Preface

These essays rehearse and, in doing so, assay the enabling conditions for reading and writing that our historical era has forged for itself. Forged enablements are inevitably problematic. At best they are the consensual, which is not to say unanimous, procedures that emerge from the clamor of an era's contention and factious conversations. At worst, and certainly so for literalists and votaries of resentment, such enablements are cultural caprices for being products of our human contingencies rather than immutable absolutes. In either case, only the most obdurate among us would persist at this hour in viewing the reading process and the signifying mechanisms of literature as anything but problematic. Every epoch has its pharisees who would proscribe all but the immediate meaningfulness of scripture, sacred or secular. And every epoch too would seem to find indispensable the wardens of culture's prison house who would relegate literature exclusively to a derived structure faithfully reflective of certain historical and economic determinations. This is especially so, and such expectations become most acute, when the literature in question belongs to "exotic" regions and other-world cultures through which cosmopolitan readers expect to be taken on tour, expectations that in some cases they might not entertain about their own literary tradition.

All this notwithstanding, in the final decade of the twentieth century, we generally recognize that reading and writing practices are problematic endeavors that rehearse possibilities, often obliquely and self-consciously, rather than proclaim truths or assert neat explanations. In this sense, there is a continuity, inevitably perhaps, between our reading practices and the writing endeavors of critically aware contemporary writers. And this is certainly the case with the writings read in the essays that follow. In this respect, the writers treated here have preselected themselves, so to speak, for a reading project that undertakes an examination of how literarily aware writers cope with the traditions of writing that circumscribe them. And like writers of any literary tradition, these authors anticipate as well the repercussions of being read, and they do so in highly textured, elaborately allusive, and relentlessly self-conscious ways. As such, they are engaging in the extreme. They engage us as readers, they engage the traditions in which they write, and they engage too the common ground of writing's history on which they explore and assert their own uncommon intervention. They are acutely aware, in other words, of their otherness as an inalienable function of their cultural and writerly identities.

Cultural and literary identities too are forged, forged in the heat of writing and reading, in the ways one writes oneself and the ways in which one is read. As with individual identities, the process is elaborately problematic, a relational exchange among differences and othernesses, internal and external, individual and multiple. Literary and cultural identities, then, are a function of difference in a network of intricate relations with fused edges and confused attributes. One should not expect, therefore, an otherness so other as to require that any critical reader venturing into such literary terrain become a tour guide pointing up natural sites and essential differences. By logical definition, difference cannot be domesticated into naturalized or essentialized, that is to say, reified, phenomena. Pardoning the tautology, difference is differential; which means, in effect, that it becomes identifiable on common ground. In the specific case of the authors and works discussed in the pages that follow, this is the common ground of the Western literary tradition. The differential here consists in how, by what strategies, literary devices, and authorial wiles these writers identify themselves with and against that common ground. The point is, of course, that unless one still subscribes to the marvelous guided tours of Sir John Mandeville and the miraculous wonders of Prester John's far-flung kingdom, our hypothetical Professor Kimosabe's concerns about the group uniqueness, cultural specificity, or representative status of these writers are mooted. It is no secret that these writers write in good measure to dispel the idealization, exoticism, and reductive cultural ghettoization to which they are subjected.

Preface

Even the late Medieval and early Renaissance tourist soon suspected that emergent wonders were expedient mechanisms of self-investment in the capital returns and commodity futures of utopia. And this is why we might do well to consider when dealing with what we are now given to calling "emergent literatures" that, in the cultural imbrications from which we derive our identity, whatever *emerges* becomes tantamount to what is being *merged*. In reading and writing selves and others, we inevitably provoke emergencies of mergers. Mergers are, of course, forms of incorporation. As in the corporate world, such embodied fusions can be friendly or hostile; they can occur by mutual consent or by leveraged muscling. What we perceive as emergent then is, in all likelihood, an inevitable target of our merging zeal and vesting interests. Cultural, like individual *identities*, emerge invariably as functional *entities* of our *id* which we prefix to them. This is why I go to such lengths in the Introduction and first two chapters of this book, the "id-" of the "-entities" that follow, if you wish, to point up the perils and prize of our reading practices before I actually move into the reading of these works, works which embody in their writing structures precisely the problems of reading and writing that our time has willy-nilly come into and has willed us.

I would have preferred, were it not for the practicality of descriptive titles, to have called this collection of essays "alternate readings in common places." Not necessarily because I offer alternative readings of these now or soon-to-be canonical and oft-read works. Perhaps I may well be doing this, too. But because I would wish to stress that the authors discussed here are laboring in the literary vineyard of a tradition which is common to them, to us, and to those mostly European and traditionally sanctioned writers and writings that these authors confront and evoke in their own works. They countenance this commonality alternately with ambivalence and self-differentiation, by way of equivocation and deferential ambiguity. Their confrontation is vexed and often vexing, albeit tempered by irony and subtle subterfuge. That is why the narrative trajectory, and even what we conventionally call plot, to say nothing of the language of these works, is often elliptical. These are works that presume mightily on the literacy of the reader in the Western tradition which they engage. I have made an effort to limn out that evocative cargo and the intricacies of its allusive web. I have

Preface

attempted a colloquy that resonates with the clamor and timbre of these writings, and I have tried to shun trivialization of their elaborate scaffoldings by avoiding, where possible, a falling into the anecdotal or into a reduction of their strategies to summary thematics or plot lines. The authors discussed here are by no means naive storytellers, and their tall tales carry within them elaborate telltale signs to which we have to respond with critical alertness, lest we be duped by the winking persiflage or ironic pathos in which they cloak their narratives.

Engaged in an essayistic enterprise, I have endeavored to keep the scholarly apparatus to a minimum. Some of the works discussed have received scant treatment, others have elaborate critical encrustations attached to their cultural and institutional life. Rather than harp and scrape on these, I have made a deliberate decision to evoke a sense of these writings in readings that resonate with the exigencies and knowing allusions embedded in the works themselves.

Finally, I should like to say a word about the language of this study and the circumstances implied by this book's epigraph. If the linguistic manners of the project seem overly scrupulous, it should be understood that the historically determined language protocols for a former British colonial subject and subaltern demand a more rigorous decorum. I am, after all, a guest in the house of English and in the hegemonic norms of its historical privilege.

Acknowledgments

My greatest debt is to the authors of the works discussed, with almost all of whom, at one time or another, I have had the pleasure of engaging in writerly conversation or in convivial dialogue on issues treated in these essays. I should like to acknowledge my gratitude to a number of colleagues and their institutions who elicited earlier versions of some of these chapters: to Wlad Godzich and the Humanities Center of the University of Minnesota; to the late and missed William Stafford, editor of *Modern Fiction Studies;* to René de Costa of the University of Chicago; to Ricardo Gutiérrez Mouat of Emory University; and to Steven Moore, editor of the *Review of Contemporary Fiction.*

I also would like to express my appreciation to a number of colleagues who have read versions of these essays or who have offered their moral support and the enlivening fruits of conviviality and conversation: Francine Masiello of the University of California, Berkeley; Rebecca West of the University of Chicago; Anthony Julian Tamburri and John Kirby of Purdue University; Alberto Moreiras of Duke University; Fred Gardaphé of Columbia College; Lucille Kerr of the University of Southern California; Peter Carravetta of Queens College, CUNY; Randolph Pope of Washington University, St. Louis; Ruth El-Saffar of the University of Illinois, Chicago. And, generally, I am grateful to those readers and colleagues—from the anxiety-laden in the East to the mellow in the West and the earnest in between—who have read and responded to my work, anonymously or otherwise. Needless to say, I stand responsible for the outcome. Finally, I should like to acknowledge with gratitude the unremitting professionalism of Margaret Hunt, managing editor of the Purdue University Press, and the diligence of the Press staff.

Introduction

OTHERWISE READING AND WRITING

To be other-wise means to be wakeful to the otherness within as well as mindful of the other as other.

Here, today, in the context of the world's most powerful hegemonic culture and in the final decade of the millennium, being other-wise is an ethical imperative. Surviving the barbarity within has always been much more difficult than holding the barbarians at bay. History, ancient and contemporary, has been most instructive in this regard in all human societies, including our own—always and especially our own—whatever and whichever our own culture may be.

Here, today, where culture and human value are daily reduced to bite-sized, fungible commodities in a futures market controlled by merchants of information, when the modes of cultural practice of greatest currency are founded on retrieval systems or on the epigonic nostalgia for recuperation via the skewed investment in such prefixes as *post-* and suffixes such as *-ism*, being wakeful to the wisdom of an other-wise conscience may be our only means to salvaging anything that resembles civility, which is to say a grace of intelligence that checks our innate predatory impulse.

Introduction

Here, today, at a juncture when we have finally begun to glimpse, if not as yet to admit, that culture is not exclusively a product for capitalization by the clever and quick who would free-market it as the fetish of privilege, it is imperative that we attend to each of our minimal acts of cultivation whose composite constitutes what we call a culture. We would do well to attend to our own performance with a degree of alertness to what simultaneously underlies and belies our self-salvaging acts in the name of cultured and culturing activity.

Here, today, in an age and place in which alertness and insight have to be self-conscious practices cloaked in reflexivity and suspicion, lest we be had or taken by those who would have us, in an age and place where the supreme value is accorded to the (self-)examined life otherwise not worth living, the other-wise have an obligation to keep reminding us that an unlived life may not be worth examining.

Here, today, where and when information and microknowledge become instantaneously televated to the status of wisdom by those whom one of their own (Fred Graham) has aptly called "blow-dry jerks," and where and when we speak of civic and academic leadership as forms of institutional modeling entrusted to entrepreneurial *role models* or human simulacra, it might be essential to suspect the clamorings for authenticity by those who otherwise covet the *roles* from which they have been cast.

Here, today, in our own institutional context, when and where reading and writing have become institutionalized by expediency into marketable packages to be pressed into the service of professional advancement, it might be well to consider the cultural repercussions of activities seemingly as innocuous as reading and writing.

Here, today, we cannot afford to read and write, and certainly not to publish, except as other-wise participants, because we still live and work in a worldly context in which respect for and decency toward otherness have to be legislated, litigated, and policed.

Reading and writing too are institutional acts that function within definite strictures of legitimacy. To begin a book with the impertinent tenacity of an anaphora that harps on our "here and today" could tend to disconcert our disciplinary safeguards aimed to keep the barbarians amongst us at bay so that we might tend to "heres and nows" of others with greater tranquility and with the safer equanimity of detachment. Suspicion of our

OTHERWISE READING AND WRITING

own barbarism notwithstanding, we are not wont to grant licit status or legitimacy to those who, by their ideological mien or linguistic demeanor, define themselves as gentiles to our chosen tribe. And the only reason we accede to such legitimation for literary works engaged in such barbaric gentility is because the peripeties of happenstance, or of the marketplace, have accorded such works canonical standing whereas, if we had no expedient need of their canonicity for our own institutional existence, we might have banished them at the gates of our disciplinary fortress. Such literary works are clearly pernicious when engaged on their own terms of otherness. They are to be domesticated, and that incorporation can only occur in the language and protocols which our self-serving equanimity and recuperative regimen have deemed appropriate. Any reading/writing interaction with these works via procedures other than those proven comforting to our professional interests and institutional advancements should most certainly be contained, if not outright excluded. Since their exclusion would redound to the detriment of our ecumenical reputation of open-mindedness and toleration, containment is the most expedient course, and the most effective means of containment consists in the inclusion of such undertakings as negative examples, or anti-values, whose obdurate otherness serves to reinforce the institutional legitimacy of ourselves and of our own. Having privileged our own grounds through such self-reinforcement, we are now in a position to incorporate the incorrigible and anachronistic others in our midst, appropriating their practices as unimpeachable evidence of our culture's dire predicament that makes us indispensable to its melioration, salvaging, and sanity. We thus authorize ourselves as the medicine men of cultural recuperation, prescribing our serums against the contaminants within and the barbarians without, against threatening otherness, endemic and exotic.

This is certainly one form of being other-wise. But it is a way of questionable wisdom. It is a way that allows us to read and write only ourselves, and, inasmuch as our self-consciousness or reflexivity permits us to read others, we are able to read them and write of them only as chimerical mutants of ourselves. Ultimately, in this form of being otherwise, we see nothing but our own permutations, the spectral refractions of our obsessions, the phantoms of our visions, the monstrous proliferations of our own unrecognized and, to us, unrecognizable otherness, the echoes

INTRODUCTION

of our barbarous yawp. Obsessed with singing ourselves, we succumb to our own din. Smug in our own multiplicity, self-contradictions, magnanimous pluralism, and grandeur, we become self-empowering, self-serving, and bilious. We then can only read and write with the literacy of a narrowly circumscribed alphabet, with a civility that recognizes no other civilization, in a culture that ends by cultivating nothing but arid ground. Most egregious of all, we lose our most humanizing quality, our sense of humor. And in taking ourselves so seriously, we necessarily preempt anyone else from doing so.

Self-consciousness to the exclusion of alterity is a neurotically righteous form of oblivion. Inasmuch as reading and writing are acts of love, such obliviousness leaves us incapable of loving any other except as ourselves. And self-love under such spectral circumspection is ultimately sickly. Reading and writing are acts of generosity. Generation and engenderment require love of the other as other, just as reading and writing demand a sentience to the difference in self and in the other, a wakefulness to the problematic nature of identity. In short, the generosity that attends our being other-wise requires a receptive awareness of alterity and, in texts, an alertness to rhetorical motives other than the ulterior that might threaten to usurp or displace us.

Otherness is not an absolute or a unique phenomenon. It certainly is not an exotic status to be romanticized or mythologized. In fact, otherness might be our greatest commonality. The significant thing to be remembered about otherness, then, is that some have the wherewithal to cast others as other and to enforce that status by dint of self-privilege and unmitigated authority. In that self-assertion, we run the danger of seeing ourselves as the genuine item and others as the aberrant version of our authenticity. Thus, the answer to the question, "What/who is the other writing?" would indicate that the other is you and it is I; it is your culture and mine, our culture to theirs and their culture to ours; it is we to ourselves, and it is the myriad of impediments and enablements that any writer with a vision and sensibility beyond his/her own pencil's end wrestles to accommodate, assuage, shoo away, engage with ambivalence and generosity, if not in fright or celebration.

When the other writes with a conscious wakefulness to the condition of otherness, writing becomes an alert form of reading, a reading that takes on

OTHERWISE READING AND WRITING

a political dimension. This is the politics of mediation within and between other(s). Under such conditions, the form and attitude of dealing can range from the adversative and factious to the conversative and ludic, from oedipal sublimity to ironic desublimation. In any case, one cannot make claims of hermeneutical mastery or strong interpretive representation for this form of reading by virtue of the fact that the writing and signifying practices that undergird and sustain it are knowingly partial, partially privileged, otherwise, and rhetorically engaged in negotiating a particular course vis-à-vis the other and the conditions of otherness.

When the other writes as other, the space of culture becomes charged with a certain intensity. This is the tension that results from an interventionist act that disputes hegemonic uniformity, disrupts homogeneous consensus, challenges self-privileging equanimity, and disconcerts the *terra firma* of a culture's territorial grounding. Such acts of intervention, whether precipitous and eruptive, or surreptitious and interruptive, can be properly termed "minor" or "minoritarian," after Deleuze's and Guattari's delineations on Kafka, to which I shall refer again in a later chapter.[1] The minority here does not necessarily imply ethnicity, race, age, gender, or numerical conditions, although any, or any combination, of these may well act as determinants for the manifestation of a minoritarian position. Otherness, in this sense, does not come between quotation marks or in demographic ratios; and to treat the question of the other in such literalist arithmetic is to reduce a human condition to anthropometry. Phrenology and craneometry have fallen sufficiently into suspicion for us to reinstitute them now in the guise of gender, race, and ethnicity as measurable determinants of peoples' humanity and as criteria for such a universally human condition as otherness. Political correctness must obviously be modulated by an ethic greater than expediency and the calculus of self-interest, especially since "P.C." whether uttered with good will or flung as invidious accusation, always runs the inevitable risk of being a Personal Calculator. *Minor* refers, really, to a political and cultural quotient that is more than gender- or ethnicity-specific. It addresses an otherness that brings the *status quo* as centered, as unquestioned, as unquestioning, and as unquestionable into question. A privileged discourse or master narrative is not founded necessarily on majority, though this condition could obtain; and claims to authority and privilege could well be made on such grounds, just as they

INTRODUCTION

could be made on the bases of claims of racial and ethnic superiority, gender privilege, ideological purity, economic and military prowess, or institutional rank. In all such instances, the claims of representational mastery and interpretive authority are predicated on the delegitimation of the other and, where total eradication of otherness proves unworkable (as it always would, even in solitude), self-authorizing rests on a derogation of alterity as aberrant of self. Nothing threatens such claims as much as the cultural economy of otherness because alterity interjects a wild card, an ideological indeterminacy that potentially remands any position and its claims to the periphery, dislocating territorialization from its privileged center, unmasking the discourse of self-justification, and disrupting the thread, the line of a dominant narrative.

Consistent with its volatility, its own disruptive inconstancy, the discursive act of an alterior writing, as a critical act on/of literature and cultural practice, proves doubly disquieting. It disorders by design and plays havoc by example, for it targets not only the other but also its own alterity, lest it replace the other as self-authorizing and privileged territoriality in displacing it. Thus, one senses an irrepressible impulse in the other writing to always be other, not only to its others, but to its own otherness, without privileging the conditions of "other" as ideological value or as self-serving narrative locus. Unremitting transvaluation and wakeful dislocation, *an alert nomadism,* then, are the optimum course to lead.

This, of course, is not a formula but a supple procedure by which writing (as mediate practice in/of a space of culture) proscribes self-privileging formulation or culture by prescription.[2] Culture should be characterized by what it makes (and what it makes possible) as much as by what it consumes (or subsumes of the other), by what it does (for itself and unto the other) as much as by its claims (what it claims to be, what claims it makes on the conditions and materiality of the other). Within a writing culture such as the one we live in, a culture of writing cannot do without a minor key, the key in which it must perform the mediative and conversative acts of reading, a reading with a sensitivity to a culture's contexts, history, tradition, and enabling conditions. The minor is the key that modulates sense, negotiates consensus, textures uniformity, refines sensibility, tones ethical impulse, and curtails self-aggrandizement at the other's expense, even if it does not altogether eradicate self-delusion.

OTHERWISE READING AND WRITING

I have chosen to put into practice the principles and procedures articulated here with the authors and texts discussed in this book for two reasons. If the first of these reasons be serendipitous, the second is surely compelling enough to be inevitable. The accidents of fate and history find me practicing my professorial trade as a teacher of literature primarily through the literary traditions of the Americas. This accidental outcome often disconcerts those bureaucratic wardens of ethnographic authenticity and cultural filiation who would question one's right to work within any literary tradition other than the one whose authors happen to have the same kind of names as one's own, and whose ethnicity, race, or gender corresponds to the onomastic list in the bibliography of that literary corpus.

This is a vengeful type of ethnocentrism and hegemonic circumscription that shades, in some notable cases, into ruthless opportunism and ultimately aims at an exclusive and proprietary limitation of cultural practices to the literary tradition that one happens to have been born into.[3] Such exclusionary proprietariness speaks of a form of tribal filiation whose rationale once justified mythical pasts, hereditary monarchies, patrician orders, old-boy networks, and, most recently, the baleful process termed "ethnic cleansing." It is also a symptom of a profound sense of insecurity about one's own self-worth and about the merits of "one's own" cultural patrimony deemed less than worthy of the attention of someone with a name or ethnic background seemingly so alien.

Ultimately, however, the astonishment, condescension, suspicion, and often outright aggression expressed toward those "aliens" who would pursue an intellectual and scholarly interest in the culture and literary tradition of a region such as Latin America or the United States are symptomatic of a profound sense of uncertainty toward the realm of otherness, internal or external. The Cuban novelist and professional iconoclast Guillermo Cabrera Infante, queried once by the Spanish press about his engagements with the national language of the Spaniards, quipped that the Spanish language is too important to be left to the Spaniards. And in this sense, the second reason for my choosing to deal with Spanish-American texts in demonstrating what I mean by reading and writing other-wise has to do with this compelling encounter between the cultural web of these texts and the historical inheritance of an other literary tradition. I discover that these texts dramatize in eloquent ways the question of otherness. Their

INTRODUCTION

dramatization of this issue is clearly not in the story line or plot of their tale necessarily, although this too becomes poignantly real in the treatment of ideologies in writers as diverse as Fuentes and Vargas Llosa, or of issues such as exile as, for example, in José Donoso, or the politics of gender, as in Diamela Eltit. The most dramatic treatment of otherness in these texts is where the composition of the texts is most deliberate, i.e., in the writing, and in the writing in the writing. These are texts, in other words, that demonstrate a highly developed awareness of the otherness within them, an otherness due to a particular history of colonization and displacement, and to the inherited layerings on which their own edifice restlessly wends its scripture; the otherness, in other words, imposed on their history by historical accidents and the wiles of human self-interest; and the otherness these authors feel within their own practices as readers of a scripture that writes itself through them, whether they wish to be its willing hosts or not.

Like the reading and writing culture of Anglo America, Spanish America's literary culture engages most often and most virulently its ancestral other. This is the European tradition, a tradition at once other and inalienable from the American contexts of culture and literary practices, by which I mean both reading *and* writing practices, since many of these works teach us most eloquently how to read, how to read them, and how to read with the ethical sensitivity I have referred to as characteristic of being other-wise. Many treatises in sociology, history, political science, and literary genealogy have dealt with the shape and the issues of this confrontation. I do not minimize their significance. I only wish to do something other. I wish to read the writing as it writes with an alertness to alterity.

Works of literature are made word for word. I cannot claim such thoroughness in my reading of their procedures here. I do make an effort, however, to curtail the precipitous fall into the anecdotal, into the interpretive reduction of "what these works mean," or what sort of unequivocal ideological or political claims these authors are making for their subject or for their own cultural practices. As I say, these sorts of endeavors, some laudably thorough, conscientious, and informative, abound. My aim is to focus on something else: the writing as it writes. This does not mean I neglect the issues or the human realities involved. For a writer, and lest we forget that all of the authors discussed here are writers, the most compelling human reality is writing. Need one reiterate the obvious to those most

Otherwise Reading and Writing

concerned with reading and writing that reading and writing are also ways of life and ways of livelihood? This is something we often deny or forget, lest we be accused of making a living and living a life by less than altogether legitimate means. It is a form of self-denial that gives the lie to the life claims we make for the cultural realities of the works we study and of the ideas we espouse and supposedly live by. This too is a form of otherness that we often are reticent to countenance. If writing and its readings are not life, then we are all hypocritical phantoms purportedly examining a life worth living, even as we deny its legitimacy, a denial that turns us into ghastly revenants and subjects of a fraud we perpetrate on society.

Writing is real and a way of life, and these works press the point most emphatically, especially in the case of writers whose writings determine what geographical space they can occupy, whether native or exilic, and how they negotiate the institutional strictures that determine their way of life. That is why how they are read, and how their cultural contexts are construed, matter. For this reason, I dedicate the first two chapters of this book to statements, or position papers, that have to do with the ways in which these writing contexts are treated by those cultural centers that see themselves as the culture brokers in universal history's cultural stock exchange. All of the works discussed here confront the self-arrogating license of this cultural exchange. They do so by confronting the other within them, the other most often confronted in this case being the same as the tradition of that cultural hegemony that would *represent* them by characterizing them through certain forms of language or by speaking on their behalf. Representation is unavoidable anytime anyone endeavors to read, write, or speak of one self and certainly of the other. It is precisely for this reason that wakefulness to the other as other and to otherness is imperative.

The works dealt with in this study, then, are expressive forms of a confrontation. This confrontation emanates from a locus that is removed from the "mainstream" and that militates for the maintenance and respect of that distance, even while that "mainstream" forms part of the very confrontation's genealogy. If the European inheritance constitutes a center, or the illusion of a metropolitan paradigm, the works discussed here intervene from the "periphery" to contend as marginal other and to contest

INTRODUCTION

the privileged grounds of the "matrix" or "center." As I have noted, this is indeed a political engagement, and the politics of contention in this writing are, in large measure, the politics of reading and of writing itself. We could say that the dramatization of this contest takes place in the writing, and writing, in addition to its own institutional status as a form of cultural practice, becomes a functional allegory for the phenomenon of otherness.

I am disinclined to claim for these works and for their authors the status of being representative. Otherness, by definition, cannot represent except by contrariety and contradistinction. Alterity as representative entails a paradox and, while paradoxes are neither alien nor anathema to or in these texts, to reduce them to that status simply would be to impoverish the creative and imaginative ways by which they unmask the condition of those unsuspectingly duped by paradoxes. These works and these authors merit fully to be accepted on a par with any context of world literature rather than being subjected to the apartheid designations of a neocolonialist discourse that would have them controlled as representative alterities, confined to "homelands" and culturally occupied territories from where they display their exotic peculiarities as "Third-World" phenomena or as quaint specimens of a geography's magical realisms relegated to the status of aberrant exempla of a particular ideological franchise conditioned by local peripeties. These works and these authors already know themselves to be from where they are. And they do have a full sense of their ambivalent relationship to wherever they may not be from. To appreciate that difference, we must read them in the light of the criteria and concerns they themselves display in their own processes as writing, rather than plot them exclusively on this or that ideological grid to assuage our conscience or perplexity.

We obviously cannot help but read as who we are and according to determinations that condition our modes of apperception and appreciation. Thoughtless and uncritical capitulation to such utter determinism, however, is a form of abdication of any responsibility for our own acts and cultural practices. Conditions of production and enablements of practice are inevitable strictures, but unquestioned and unquestioning procedures on our part are tantamount to willful obliviousness to our own potential alternatives as well as to the alterities we take as the object of our actions. Because of this caveat, which I view as ethically indispensable, I deliberately have shunned the edification of, or adherence to, a uniform "theory" or a sustained system and superstructure for the phenomenon of otherness. Such an overarching construct would only lead into the very conditions of homogeneity, uniformity, self-authorizing ideology, colonization, and hegemonic usurpation that I am trying to question. Such "theoretical integration" may yield, for some, a comforting quotient of sustaining cogency and edifying order. But the texts discussed in this study teach us that this type of systematicity as reassuring sustenance is a pabulum more prone to enslave than to liberate, and that such secure edifications build enclosures of mind and cloisters of visions rather than opening up to imaginative tolerance of pluralities and their differences.

Like overarching theories, representation, or the role of being representative, intrusively compromises alterity; it razes difference into proprietary and dictatorial sameness, into presumptive privilege that presumes on the other with impunity. To represent, unless it be an act that is conditioned by an ethical impulse of the other-wise or that ensues from common consent and mutuality, means to claim the authority to speak for, and to displace and usurp, the other. Even with such ethical conditioning, of course, the violence of representation as suppositious and presumptive is not assuaged, just mitigated. But even this modicum of restraint is better than the wholesale violence of an oblivious incursion. A critic's designation of this or that work or author as representative entails presumptions no less pernicious. Rather than imperiously self-authorizing one's own cognitive constructs at the other's expense, it would be best to read and open up to a reading in a way that minimizes compromising the existence of the other as much as possible. In order to do as much, we need to recognize otherness, *ours included,* as a shared condition that does not deem the other expendable or as the unproblematic object of appropriation, theoretical or otherwise. In such recognition, hopefully one learns to curtail the impulse to privilege as absolute the criteria and determinations of one's own otherness.

In their writing, the texts discussed here share in this precognition. They also share in the ability to discern, often ironically, the fact that their otherness inevitably and ambivalently blends with the alterity of their targeted other. Yet—and this too they have in common—these are texts that do not come unhinged in the confrontational movement of approximation and retraction, of intervention and supervention. The ambivalent and

INTRODUCTION

often ambiguous forays of these writings into and between alterities unmask our own acts of reading, the implications of our interpretive intervention upon their textual and cultural space. In their engagement of the "dominant," Europe-centered literary tradition that also forms part of their genealogy, these works highlight, in dramatic fashion, the dynamics of the economy of otherness. An *economy* refers, by etymological definition, to certain house rules. The texts discussed here foreground the problem of not entirely belonging to the house, yet being subject and often subjected to its rules, to its domesticity and irrepressible impetus for domestication. In this sense, these works share the predicament that any one of us has to countenance within our own institutional economy or domesticity, anyone, that is, who would venture to question or transgress the rules of the Home Office by offering anything not already tried, presanctioned, and found unthreatening.

The essays that follow could be taken as various demonstrations of the form of cultural practice advanced by the foregoing discussion. I should like to say a word about the ways in which I have endeavored to put into practice the tenets of reading and writing otherwise that I have articulated here.

Chapters One and Two comprise an affidavit of sorts. They could be called a monitory statement on our languages of reading and writing about the cultures and literatures of the other. The remaining essays constitute an engagement with/in certain acts of writing. I must reiterate that these are not representative of the practices of writing's alterity in a particular region. Rather, I view the works discussed in the ensuing chapters as exemplary ways in which these authors, each in his or her own way, deal with the question of otherness in writing and in the traditions of writing's history. I proceed in a way that endeavors to show how we can adhere to the scruples articulated in this Introduction and in the first two chapters. In the process, hopefully, we can see how the writing practices of a number of writers overtly dealing in/with writing convoke us to certain reading and writing practices of our own as "professors of literature," practices that could sharpen our receptivity and enlarge our generosity, even as they curtail our hubris through modes of allegory and winking subterfuge.

I address first the question of our language vis-à-vis the cultural conditions of the other in an attempt to show up the self-privileging entailments that are embedded in the very vocabulary we use in speaking of

OTHERWISE READING AND WRITING

cultures other than our own. Then, in Chapter Two, I engage the problem of theory, the aversions it awakens, its inherent difficulties, and its inevitability, despite the resistances to it and within it. Given theory's inevitable role in anything we do, I attempt to explore the possibilities of theory along the lines I have been delineating here as reading and writing practice.

What bridges these initial chapters to those that follow is a manner of reading, an approach, if you will, that endeavors to demonstrate by example the possibilities of averting a fall, willy-nilly, into reading practices of a postcolonial era that is always on the verge of shading into a neocolonial cultural hegemony by dint of certain practices and theoretical investments. What I choose to focus on, then, are certain writing strategies devised by the authors discussed here to hold such an outcome at bay.

Accordingly, in the third chapter, I consider a brief allegory from Jorge Luis Borges, an admonitory fable of reading and its hazards, especially for the self-seeking who would wish to see nothing and no other but their own likeness in anything they read. I take Borges's tale as an antihermeneutic parable that dramatizes the dangers for a hubris with an impulse for mastery in interpretation and in specular representation. As usual, Borges does his job with admirable economy. His is an irreducible terseness not to be dilated unduly, lest its allegory turn on the exegete.

Chapter Four focuses on a self-avowed critical writer whose scripture irremediably moves beyond his claims. Octavio Paz's latest collection of poetry, *Arbol adentro* (1987), is yet another instance, an acute manifestation at that, of a poetic discourse whose writing invites its own otherness to resonate between the verses. This book is Paz's encomium to poetic tradition and a celebration of human links and historical circumstances that have engendered and nurtured the poet's vocation. Nonetheless, the scriptor's expansive generosity takes him, inexorably, beyond the genealogical emplotment of his itinerary. As a mature poet, the 1990 Nobel laureate is not blind to the impetus that interjects writing's differential and equivocal otherness into the domesticity of poetic form, thereby disrupting the circumscription, the *hortus conclusus,* of a cultivated landscape. This insight finds Paz exploring and being led by the poetic potential of that indomitable disjunction and its alterities.

The two-part chapter on Carlos Fuentes explores the desublimation of the Romantic Sublime, a recuperation of an earthly, human art from a supernatural ethos. In the first part, I trace the profane sublime, as opposed

Introduction

to the numenous or transcendental sublimity of the eighteenth and nineteenth centuries, to the suspected natural father of the sublime, Longinus, and I examine Fuentes's deliberate appropriation and accommodation of Longinian sublimity in *Terra Nostra.* The profane sublime, I argue, functions as a historical, situated, contingent limner of a human worldliness, as opposed to linking us to metaphysical other-worldliness. The otherness engendered by this sublime is a scriptive, narrative otherness that issues from sublimity as rhetorical, rather than ideological, art, as *techne,* rather than mystified epistemology.

In his novel *Cristóbal Nonato (Christopher Unborn),* discussed in the second part of this fifth chapter, Fuentes presses the possibilities of the profane sublime even further. Whereas *Terra Nostra* thematizes Longinian/Stoic sublimity, in *Christopher Unborn* we actually witness that theme in practice as writing strategy. The temporality of the sublime is pushed to the edge of time, to the liminal, as opposed to subliminal, verge of "being." Like Laurence Sterne and James Joyce, whom he incorporates into his novel's ventriloquy, Fuentes tropes, in a manner both writerly and risible, "being" into "becoming," and becoming turns into a linguistically unfolding bio-logical and bio-graphical process of conception and gestation. In the process, Fuentes articulates a deliberate, and ironically literal, minoritarian position, a revolutionary course that engages tradition and the discursive, as well as political, determinations that operate in the cultural possibilities (and impossibilities) of a postcolonial society under the shadow and "in the backyard," as we are wont to say north of the Rio Grande, of a neocolonial hegemonic power.

Chapter Six also has two parts to it. In the first, Gabriel García Márquez's *One Hundred Years of Solitude* is read as interstitial scripture that places itself in that unstable space between ideological plenitude and catastrophe. I read this novel, now elevated and firmly planted on sacral ground, not as privileged scripture but as telltale trace of the other writing alluded to in the work, the differential writing that survives the solemnity of prophetic voice by dint of specular exacerbation and ironic wryness turned against two of the most sacred cows of Europe's providentialist foundations (Tasso and Milton) that would subsume its writing into their hallowed parentheses.

The second part of this García Márquez chapter focuses on *Love in the Time of Cholera,* particularly on that threshold which the novel identifies as a pivotal crossing in its scripture: "The Arcade of the Scribes," where writing circulates as commodity and as love's instrumentality. Writing as cipher of love ironizes the sentimental tradition, irreverently flouting the amatory scripture through ludic hyperbole, an intervention that tries to recoup both love and writing from banality and melodramatic bathos. The arena or theater for this irreverent sally is that graphic space which lies between *inevitability* and *life,* the opening and final words, respectively, of García Márquez's novel.

Chapter Seven is devoted to the Peruvian Mario Vargas Llosa and the antithetical scripture of *The War of the End of the World.* The novel could be read as a titanic oedipal allegory for Vargas Llosa's autobiography vis-à-vis his ideological precursor, dramatized in the novel and in contemporary Peruvian politics, the Brazilian Euclides da Cunha. I shun that psychologistic enterprise and instead focus on the novel's demystifying project, aimed primarily at the ideological investment of positivist progressivism in Latin America. The totalizing title of the novel is deliberately misleading; the force of that irony, which today haunts the former presidential candidate Vargas Llosa himself, is aimed as much at the author's own oft-declared project for a "total novel" as it is at his precursor's mystification with Europe's religion of progress proffered as a panacea to the ills of the New World.

The eighth chapter, also bipartite, is devoted to the Chilean José Donoso and to two key novels from his considerable corpus. *The Obscene Bird of Night,* a pivotal work that catapults Donoso into canonical standing, *pace* the countercanonical scripture of the novel, and *El jardín de al lado* (*The Garden Next Door*), a chronicle of writing's futility as writing's salvaging from *Néant.* The first part of the chapter discusses *The Obscene Bird of Night* as a transitional and transgressive way-station, a house of writing deliberately read through the window of Emily Dickinson's "house fairer than prose" and the marvelous permutations writing can take in and turn out.

Like *The Obscene Bird of Night* and many of the works discussed here, *The Garden Next Door,* more than a garden, is a "dark wood" where writing labors to constitute a book but, in the process, differentiates itself into other than the book it leaves behind as *graft,* as both graphic insertion etched unto the scriptive corpus of a culture, and as ex-tortion, as a "twisting out" that disconcerts and violates the privileged complacency of

INTRODUCTION

a sanctioned scene of writing. The place of writing, Donoso's novel seems to tell us, is the unrelentingly displaced other space, next door, perennially exilic, like the Joyce, Eliot, Mann, and Cavafis whom Donoso convokes at the heart of his novel. In their circuitous itineraries, the characters of this novel act also as allegorical figures for the writing practices by which they are grafted, dispossessed and inscribed into baneful history, then turned out to history's exilic wandering as other to its story, as alterity to its "facts," as irrepressible *altereffect* of the official script.

I have suggested variously that otherness, or "the other" as such, is not an absolute phenomenon but a relational exchange. It certainly is not an alienable phenomenon that occupies an unbreachably separate locus. Otherness is part of identity—personal, cultural, national—and its conditions of existence as other reside in difference, in the ways it is differentiated from same and from self. The condition of the other in this sense, then, depends on how the dominant and self-empowered dispose of and are disposed toward what is perceived as other. The Chilean novelist and filmmaker Diamela Eltit chronicles for us baneful alterity as a dominant culture's subaltern. Her focus is on society's dispossessed other and, most emphatically, on the dominant patriarchy's gender-determined otherness. Eltit's work is a dramatic indictment of the chronic patriarchal hegemony that sentences women to a destiny of embodying society's historical experience and to serving as the corporate repository of the historical record, of cultural memory and its enduring patrimony. In this final chapter, I attempt to discern and decipher Eltit's female agon and her personification as an allegory of a national crisis and a hemispheric fate, of a political order's disenfranchised but indispensable subaltern.

CHAPTER ONE

ORBIS TERTIUS
Colonial Discourse and Emergent Cultures

You come from a world that soon will exist.
—Madame de Staël to Fray Servando Teresa de Mier

The seemingly innocuous phrase "emergent literatures" or, in a more inclusive version, "emergent cultures," is the focus of this chapter. I aim to subject this figure to a semantic parsing with an eye to ferreting out the ideological claims that enfranchise its political authority as a discursive move and representational narrative. An epistemological skepticism of heterodox persuasion informs my procedure. In this spirit, I should like to persuade you to read with me the performative repercussions of a problematics of representation whose willful exercise entails the deliberate vocabulary of culture, state, and emergency. There is an etymological wheel that underwrites culture. It is the tautological wheel of self-legitimation and self-justifying circular reasoning. Some have called this the wheel of fortune, and fortunes have been made throughout history in the expropriation of cultures other than one's own. Let us examine these self-validating formations that crystallize around words to palliate their instrumentality in historical contexts, formations that inevitably mask self-interest through linguistic screens and circumspect locutions.

Culture, by its radical Greek definition, consists in the circulation of a particular ideological currency, and the nature of this currency is

CHAPTER ONE

conditioned and constituted by language, that most efficacious and at the same time self-betraying commodity of culture. When one's semantic horizon for the notion of culture is in tendentious disharmony with what circulates, an empyrean distance in the name of "disinterestedness" and a diction tinged with righteous valuation conjoin with the notion of culture, as, for example, in Matthew Arnold's binary "Culture and Anarchy." When, on the other hand, one harkens to more heterodox and more problematic linkages between culture and its currency, a more repercussive and more highly textured conjunction obtains, as in Arnold's antithetical successor Raymond Williams's "Culture and Society." In either case, a hyperconsciousness of language becomes paramount; a consciousness that renders culture and its currency hierarchical and hieratic in the first instance, and heterodox and iconoclastic in the second.

In Arnold's case, then, the contending resonances of language and its equivocations become occulted behind a screen of authority and the supposed transparency of the univocal where things are seen as they "really are." In the case exemplified by Williams, on the other hand, things are more problematic than they seem and the reaching after an adequation of language to the world yields to contextualized specificities of culture that confound verbal transparency and linguistic constancy. I suspect this is why Williams's enterprise engendered the necessity of its own lexicon, which, in keeping with his insight into the volatility of words and of language, Williams insists on calling a "vocabulary" rather than a "dictionary." I am referring to *Key Words: A Vocabulary of Culture and Society.*[1] As Williams tells us in his introduction to *Key Words,* this compilation originally formed part of *Culture and Society,* which was published some twenty years earlier. (The intervening time is due to an editorial interdiction that proscribed the joint publication of the original project and its key. As we all know to some degree, publishers, the present publisher excepted, of course, are generally less interested in words than they are in books, and any connection between the two may often be a bothersome necessity.) Arnold's *classicism manqué* notwithstanding, Williams betrays a better understanding of the classical filiation between culture and the etymological wheel, that is, a keener appreciation of the relationship between the Greek *kúklos*—the epistemic currencies that society authorizes for circulation—and the constitutive acts of that rotative encirclement which comprise culture. That is why, I would venture to say, Williams places the vocabulary of his own apperception of culture into published circulation, well aware of that key's delimited and localized "universality" by virtue of language's semantic mutability and culture's protean inconstancy.

It is in the spirit of this transgressive and historicist philology that I approach the lexical and discursive complex connoted by the binomials "emergent literatures" and "emergent cultures." And I should clarify, too, at this juncture my use of the term *discursive*. I employ the term in a limited and two-tiered sense: (1) an interested deployment of language and (2) a deployment of language that betrays its own resistance, its own duplicitous otherness to itself and to its putative audience. We traditionally characterize the first of these—interested deployment of language—as *rhetoric,* more specifically, the rhetoric of persuasion, and the second as *deixis,* or language pointing to its own difficulty of being other than what it articulates. This, too, is ultimately a form of rhetoric. Rather than a rhetoric of persuasion, however, we might call it a rhetoric of assuasion, language that seeks to assuage its own difficulty through its ostentation. In both instances, the strategy of this discourse is political and politic in that twofold Greek sense of diplomacy.

As a discursive formation, the figure "emergent literatures" or "emergent cultures" is necessarily value-laden and thus carries, implicitly, an interpretive charge. In this sense, too, it implicates its discursivity in the political; for interpretation, our modern philosophical tradition teaches us, is inextricably mired in the realm of the political. In part two, chapters twenty-six and twenty-nine of his *Leviathan,* Hobbes has no qualms about subordinating interpretation to the demands of the state. Nietzsche, on the other hand, in the preface and first two essays of *The Genealogy of Morals,* privileges interpretation over politics, rendering the interpretive activity as the form that the will to power takes in its intellectual and artistic manifestation. Not surprisingly, Kant, in the eighth section of *On History* and in his essay "The Strife of the Faculties," occupied a more conciliatory middle ground between these two poles by portraying the interpretive project as an act of mediation between the people and the head of state. It is not until the nascent discriminations of a positivist ethos that an institutional divorce between interpretation and politics is sought. Max Weber, in this sense, is exemplary. His essay "Science and Vocation" renders interpretation a science, and politics an altogether separate domain.

CHAPTER ONE

A good deal of our intellectual activity still carries on under the aegis of this mystification and its velleities of scientificism, as the heterodox diagnoses of Michel de Certeau perceptively disclose.[2] Our postpositivist critical discernments have always sought to unveil the inevitably specular necessity of an interactive implication between the politics of rhetoric and the rhetoric of politics. One thinks of Kenneth Burke in this regard, and of a more recent Weber, Samuel, whose incisive delineations between institutional functioning and the acts of instituting represent a latest chapter in the history of this discernment.[3] Weber's scansion of another sensibility on the political and conflictive rhetoric of interpretation, Fredric Jameson's, becomes suggestively revealing.[4] Weber's de-definition of Jameson's "political unconscious" reminds us that what circulates in the name of culture (political or otherwise) has an inexorable situatedness, a habitation that circumscribes the many turns and circulation of the *kúklos* within a cultivated space of discourse and ideology, to which Weber assigns the shorthand term "institution."

We might amplify that a discursive habitation entails and is entailed, in turn, by a habitual space, an indwelling, inhabited and tilled, that reaches and tends that other root of culture's etymological tree: the *colonia*. This semantic nexus that finds *culture* and *colony* radically entwined may well be a reflective formation in which certain political and textual practices are lexically inscribed. This may well comprise, in other words, a case of a semantic radical configuration inhabited by a complex of historical determinacies with rhetorical force and historical density. One could test the plausibility of such a theoretical formulation by merely asking how many cultures since classical antiquity that have had a conscious idea of the notion of culture, and a sense of their own cultural development, have or have not had a colonial phase. Should this be begging the question, the issue could be examined from a venue of rhetorical performance, of discursive practice and narrative production. I shall devote a good part of the remainder of this chapter to such an exploration.

Culture as indwelling, that is as *colony,* underwrites a textual discourse of its own domesticity. The performative and productive parameters of this habitat might constantly shift, as might the provisional constructs of its discursive performance. Those parameters, as margins which define that dwelling's inscriptive legitimacy as interiority, necessarily possess and are possessed of an exteriority, of a (t)exterior, as Michel de Certeau would have it—of an institutional formulation that rests on certain *de*stitutional acts, as Samuel Weber might have said. In this sense, all cultural discourse, or simply *culture,* comprises and is comprised by a *colonia* and colonial entailments.

Cultural deliberation is a loaded issue, a matter of weights and measures that assays its own density and measures its own dimensions oppositionally: in the opposition of elements within and in opposition to the space without its own habitation. When focused reflectively on its own situatedness, culture's discourse betrays a maximal ostentation of its own otherness, its performance's nonidentity to "itself." When that performance aims at a target without, there *would seem to be* a coalescence of internal difference into uniformity. De Certeau exposes this circumstance of internal falling into formation as "representation (becoming) itself the means by which the real conditions of its own production are camouflaged" (206). The external other is seized on, or *colonized,* as a substitute for discourse's interior differential otherness. I say there would only *seem* to be an attainment of such gathering of self into self-identity, a seeming that de Certeau characterizes as "camouflage," because the process is self-betraying and more suggestively problematic, as we shall see in short order. If cultural deliberation is in itself so problematic, it is no less so when it makes the external other the object of its practice. Deliberation implies by definition a hefty bill of lading, a ponderous act, a weighty charge, an assessment of value, in short, a valuation as productive of a bill of goods as it is instrumental in the (re-)cognition and construal of those goods themselves. As such, deliberation is necessarily reductionist and reifying; it circumscribes and construes; it loads the dice and dices to measure; it settles the unsettled; it tames motion into stasis; maneuvers fluctuations to a stand; it shifts the shiftless into *a state.*

Deliberation, we could say, functions as an instrument for the cult of *the state;* and, in this sense, state and culture, which often would appear to be antithetical, become, in fact, mutually reinforcing. So much more so when deliberation is explicitly and willfully yoked to culture, as in "cultural deliberations." In this configuration, the dictates of the language paradigm betray all that is controlling in affiliative discourse and its inter-dictions: Lexically inscribed within this semantic calculus already is the inescapable determination that *cultural* deliberation amounts to a colonization of the

CHAPTER ONE

deliberated other, whether event or phenomenon. And the discourse of this deliberation is tantamount to a would-be self-validating discourse of cultural hegemony, were it not for the permeability of its "camouflage," for the irremediable interdiction of its own performance that proscribes its (self-)determination into a self-identity. This discursive curtailment or subversion notwithstanding, and certainly so where it is illusively occluded behind the veil of uncritical forgetfulness or deliberate ignorance, we do live in a purported "postcolonial" epoch inexorably practicing a neocolonial discourse.

Inasmuch as the radical ambiguities of our language, the duplicitous otherness in our discourse, the ambivalent ethos of our rhetorical and interpretive practices, and the unsettling settlements (or deliberations) of our representational productions bedevil a performance that would self-validate and universalize our discursive claims and their politics, we scurry to the two-faced folds, to the redoubled pleats of a face-saving diplomacy that still and already comprises an axiomatic field. Under scrutiny's pressures, this diplomatic duplicity exposes our paradoxical stand with no place, our utopical status, except as constituted by an illogic of power—rhetorical and otherwise. In our differential self-apperception, we engage in a displacement of self unto the other, a displacement that disposes the other into unsituatedness by banishing him/her from our commonplaces. This, in short, is the underlying significance of the figure encoded with the cataclysmic resonances of the apocalyptic and the eschatological as *The Third World* and with a sense of sublime volatility as *emergent cultures*.

These code terms are cultural statements, however contrived, that state and impute a state to the other, however paradoxical that stasis as "emergent" might be. These codes entail a linguistic practice, one that implies an interpretive theory of culture, one that is predicated on geopolitical delineations in which the object of contention is culture as projected by a set of interested ideological criteria. These code terms reflect a cultural diplomacy, in the Greek sense of this duplicitous ambivalence, that in this context imputes a configuration, a meaning that, as an interpretation of culture, folds back to reflect back meaningfully on a culture of interpretation. As such, these statements and cultural encodations ultimately may reveal more about the culture and discourse that deploys them than they disclose about their putative object. They may tell us more, that is, about the alarm, the dire conundrums, and the urgent antinomies of a Eurocentric culture's state of emergency than they might about the *emergent state,* if the catachresis be allowed, of the other, of the *Orbis Tertius* and its culture. I shall elaborate on how this disclosure plays itself out, displays and betrays the strategies of a discursive performance and its instrumentalities of representation of the other, by mapping the semantic and cultural formations of the term "emergent."

The term *emergent* is a "key word," in the sense imparted to this phrase by Raymond Williams. Its use in our critical discourse may seem pallid enough when applied to cultures that are "emerging" into independent political status, or statehood, from a past of imperial domination. Underlying the banality of such usage, however, is a conceptual determinant whose interstices allow an insight into more shadowy cultural recesses that authorize certain connotations and empower a rhetorical (by which I mean interpretive and political) discourse. The usage functions as a reduction that authorizes one's discourse on the other's condition and conditions of possibility. In this sense, the phrase *emergent cultures* serves the instrumentality of a superscription for a master narrative applied to a cultural process. It functions much in the way of that cultural cornerstone that Cornelius Castoriadis termed the "imaginary," by which the renegade Marxist—vindicated of late by history—means, among other things, that interpretive space where society seeks the necessary complement to its order.[5] The usage operates, too, as a mimetic strategy in that not so innocent signification of mimesis worrisome to Plato which Wlad Godzich coaxes out in his afterword to Samuel Weber's already mentioned *Institution and Interpretation,* that is, *mimesis* as a productive performance capable of creating otherness and, thereby, melting the distinction between real and apparent into undecidability. If we trace the lexical career of the term *emergent* to its broader cultural network, focusing first on the juncture that straddles the cognitive and the physical sciences, we can appreciate how the phrase *emergent cultures* functions in the ways I have referred to here. In the process—and incidentally—we might be reminded, as well, of how the "sciences," which Max Weber privileged as his preferred "vocation" to the exclusion of politics, are not so alienable from the rhetoric of interpretation and its political entailments.

CHAPTER ONE

"Emergence" in the sciences is functionally synonymous with an epistemological wild card in philosophy. That is, it refers to particulars which are not subsumable under a universal principle or system. It is associated with a confounding degree of complexity that short-circuits formal explanatory procedures within closed systems of conventional understanding. For the biologist, "emergence" describes the bursting onto the scene of a qualitatively different phenomenon at a specific stage of organization—an appearance, Emerson might have said, "by the stairway of surprise" ("Merlin, I"). In physics, "emergence" is a bedeviling surprise yoked to complexity and makes inordinate demands bordering on the poetic. Ilya Prigogine, winner of the 1977 Nobel Prize for chemistry and known as "the poet of thermodynamics," has gone so far as to impute a purposive principle to emergent complexity, a principle which would appear to go contrary to the notion of entropy that obtains in the science of thermodynamics. He sees complexity as an ever-increasing eventuality that befalls open systems, which, being in a state far from equilibrium or maximum entropy, arrive at an improbable and highly complex structure through fluctuations. If they should reach critical size, these fluctuations stabilize into what he calls an "equifinal state"—something akin, perhaps, to the ambiguities of otherness and the equivocal in language. The occurrence of these structures depends on the distance from equilibrium, that is, the rate and amount of exchange of matter and energy with the surroundings, with exchange and equilibrium displaying an inverse ratio. Further away from equilibrium, probability theory breaks down. Nonetheless, laws of physics in this context may become processes of construction and organization, and, thus, nonequilibrium does not preclude the possibility of some sort of order in open systems.

John von Neuman, of atomic bomb fame, is also associated with emergencies, and, in fact, in the history of modern science his name is readily identified with the mathematical problem of emergence. He saw "emergence" in terms of complexity that required a different order of theory based on probabilistic logic because of the paradoxical and critical properties that characterize the complex and its potential for compounding and producing complexities greater than itself.

And, finally, it was the notion of "emergence" that led to the now-famous Kurt Gödel incompleteness theorem in logic and mathematics: If a logical system is consistent in its logic, the theorem goes, it can never circumscribe itself by proofs of truth or falsity, since it can never step outside to a "metasystem" or globalized integrity that does not entail the expanded predicament of the original system, and, thus, complete definition is impossible.

I rehearse this brief excursus on "emergent properties" in scientific discourse in order to educe the cultural implications that may obtain in the transference of the notion of "emergence" as a key term among our shared body of words from the area of science to the broader arena of cultural criticism. What the various scientific concerns with the concept of "emergence" consistently reveal is that emergent properties tax and often outrun the capacity of scientific logic and systematicity and that cognitive adequation is strained to the point of having to switch at a critical juncture from the apodictic to the metaphoric, from a "literal" arithmetic to a figurative mathematics, from a topology of logical explanation to a tropology of probabilistic and paradoxical speculation.

A fruitful consideration of a semantic bridge that connects the physical sciences with what we fancifully know as the human sciences might focus on the classical notion of *anomie,* which Emile Durkheim resuscitated for modern social theory. If we qualify the semantic charge of the term and bracket the dire social implications with which Durkheim infused the word, we arrive at a functional analogue of "emergence" in cultural criticism. For what we glean is a critical point of normativity whose precepts founder and for which the classical measure of *adequatio intellectus et rei* becomes highly problematic, if not ambivalently mooted. At this juncture, as with the physical sciences, the discourse of cultural criticism must willfully brook its difficulty by some discursive, which is to say rhetorical, interpretive, and, therefore, political transformation that *forges* (in the double sense of this equivoque) an *adequatio* for very pragmatic ends.

I believe that such a move underwrites the deployment of the notion and rhetoric of "emergence" in the cultural deliberations on the other. In this sense, the superscription "emergent cultures" or "emergent literatures" is a revealing code term that betrays an institutional act as much as it is a representational ploy, a strategy of domestication of complex volatility, a strong move for an interpretive reduction. I would suggest, in other words, that recourse to such a superscription is tantamount to the instituting of a functional instrumentality that simultaneously abets a dominant position, an empyrean posture, if you will, and serves to contain the "anomies"

CHAPTER ONE

of the other, paradoxically enough, within a state of emergency. The "anomies of the other," of course, is a cognitive construct, a figured fiction of a cultural context, just as "emergent properties" are reflective of a system of description or explanation for which such properties prove to be an overload and inordinately complex. Complexity, like anomie, in other words, describes not the condition of the object of discourse necessarily; rather it reflects on the enabling conditions of the subject's discursive possibilities. In this sense, the figure "emergent cultures" or "emergent literatures" tells us something about the agency and conditions of its construction. And within the cultural context that has spawned this figure, I suggest that we might licitly remand the "wildness," volatility, and indeterminate character of what is "emergent" or in "emergency" to the startling and indomitable *sublime,* a cultural "imaginary" (in Castoriadis's sense mentioned previously) that has had an astonishing career in our history of astonishments.

I should like to propose the possibility that Eurocentric discourse's belated investment in the *emergent* amounts to a reinvestment in what Edmund Burke sought to exorcize from political consciousness in the late eighteenth century with his *Reflections on the Revolution in France,* thereby setting off a chain reaction that saw the sublime sublimated into the beautiful. The deployment of notions such as "magical realism" in the critical valuations of Latin American and other postcolonial letters, for example, may be symptomatic of this reinvestment. I should like to propose, in other words, that the incantatory shibboleth "emergent cultures" may spell the reinstatement of a cultural sublime that begs for domestication, the instatement of a history to peoples "who have none," the imposition of a manageable order where none is to be found except as volatility and surprising complexity. I am not unawake to the traditional and much-debated equation of sublimity with nature. The rendering of the other in terms of sublimity may well be a strategy of naturalizing the other. The fact that the nature/culture dichotomy has been mooted by controversy, that "nature" is no longer viewed simply as what is given in all its awesomeness, but that it also is tantamount to what and how it is taken with all our astonishment, does not change the implications of the sublime for a discourse on the other. It only augments complexity, of the other and of its attempted representations. I speak of a "cultural sublime" in the context of this "un-natural naturalization." I see, then, a repoliticization of the sublime, or a sublimation of the political wild card into culture's "political unconscious." Fredric Jameson's enterprise may be most exemplary in this regard. I defer to Samuel Weber's incisive discussion on this point and I stick, instead, to what I glimpse as a compelling avatar of a cultural sublime by way of "emergence" and emergent properties. I wish to consider, too, the implications of this franchise for a discursive epistemology that takes the other as its object.

The question for cultural criticism (as is the case for the physical and mathematical sciences) when faced with the surprise of the emergent or with the sublime is what and how we can know if, as Samuel Weber phrases it, "we are confronted by the unknown, the unusual or the unexpected, or in fact by anything that the concepts we have at our disposal are incapable of subsuming" (139)? Weber's words, which I trope here into interrogatory, could well be referring to "emergence." His ostensible topic is not "emergence," but what he is characterizing has the unmistakable marks of "emergent properties." Weber does end up having to face the sublime here. His focus is on the "ambivalent demarcations" that inhere in a cultural problematics of cognition and of epistemology within the institution of the humanities, "the confrontation of the particular, the unexpected, or the heterogeneous, of everything not yet subsumed by 'given' concepts" (140). This predicament, which echoes with the perplexities of "emergence," becomes explicitly yoked to the sublime through the invocation of Kant's preface to the *Critique,* where a distinction is made between "determinant judgment" and "reflective judgment." Here is Kant via Weber:

> Judgment in general is the faculty of thinking the particular as contained under the universal. If the universal (the rule, the principle, the law) be given, the judgment which subsumes the particular under it ... is determinant. But if only the particular be given for which the universal law has to be found, the judgment is merely reflective. (139)

Given this distinction, and given the indomitability of particulars such as emergent properties that cannot be "subsumed" under a universal principle of judgment, the ensuing judgment necessarily becomes *reflective* rather than *determinant.* As a result, cognition must confront a constitutive difficulty and the perplexity or embarrassment (*Verlegenheit*) of its vicissitudes. Here is Kant once more: "This perplexity about a principle presents itself mainly in those judgments that we call aesthetical, which concern the beautiful and the sublime of nature or of art" (140).

Here, then, I believe, we have a diagnosis of the difficulties in a cultural discourse that represents its object *as emergent* and, therefore, as unsubsumable. Instead of determining the other, instead of constituting the other as the object of a "determinant" judgment, that discourse ends up reflecting on the subject and on the relation of that agency to itself. In Kant's words, it comprises a judgment that takes "from and gives to itself." The other, in this case the "emergent culture," as the object of this cultural discourse becomes a differential or oppositional occasion for self-incorporation. It assumes and presumes on the other for purposes of self-naturalization, however reflective and self-conscious that "naturalness" may be. Othering, in short, becomes an instrumental and productive form of self-recuperation or "saming." In this sense, the discursive performance deployed against the other becomes a *forging* of a mirror for the cultural self. Thus, the figure of "emergent cultures" functions truly as "an imaginary" through which a society seeks the necessary complement to its order. But, of course, mirrors, forged or other-wise, are "other" as versions (inversions, perversions, diversions) of other and of self. They are, in other words, a fiction, an ambivalent and ambiguous identity; they are figures of equivocation and of duplicity. Under such *circumstances* (read: circulating stases, the states of *kúklos,* the predicaments of *culture*), what discourse, what rhetoric of judgment, or what judgment of interpretation will adjudicate those differential ambiguities without becoming preemptive and self-privileging? Who, indeed, is the "other" if othering or determination of the other in this sublime game is an aleatory pretext for "saming" the self that is not only *other* to the rest but is also reflectively other to an inescapable nonidentity, to an unsubsumable nonself?

These questions themselves are entangled, inexorably, in their own rhetoricity. I do not think, however, that they are merely "rhetorical questions." For as much as they may point to reason's paradoxical impasse, these questions are adjudicated nonetheless. And they are willfully adjudicated with a force that is commensurately paralogistic, or ill-logical, to the paradox they entail. The logic of these questions, we could say, is mooted by the imperious privilege of the dominant discourse that a particular culture assumes for its own practices. And we could say, furthermore, that a dominant discourse is a discourse of domination, whether its judgment be reflective or not, and that it musters the force of determination and of cognitive constituting, however illusive and illusionary its performance, not by dint of judgment but by the brawn of agonistic power, willful self-enablement, and pragmatic assertion.

As a cultural practice, such discourse camouflages an ideological prosopopoeia. In other words, its interpretive ploy, its encodation and representation of the other, comprise an illusion on the other's materiality that functions as a masked personification in a rhetorical figure. As such, its procedure is ambiguous and ambivalent, its rhetoric duplicitous and equivocal. It simultaneously affirms and negates the other's alterity; it incorporates and excludes; it appropriates and expropriates at once. It assumes on what it cannot subsume. It naturalizes the catachresis "emergent culture" and the oxymoron "emergent state" with paralogical and illusionary naturalness. This, clearly, is the *colonialist* thrust of the root verb *colere,* which, inextricably, also underwrites *culture.*

An equivocal historical pertinacity in Eurocentric discourse is rooted in the figure "emergent." Emergent cultures are emerging from a Eurocentered colonial past into a Eurocentered paradigm of cultural advancement: the other is othered into/unto us; we exclude it as other (we literally ex-merge it) to include it, teleologically and prospectively, into our sameness; we appropriated it as colony, expropriated it as former colony, to reappropriate it as cultural complement and reflective object. All this is not to say that Eurocentric cultural discourse is blind to its "blindness" here, or that it lacks insight into the duplicitous equivocations of its own practices. Yet, an inexorable streak or insurmountable current embedded in the very etymons of culture contravenes correction or even the desirability of it. Some sublime insight, a "political unconscious" more deeply rooted than blindness, places a premium on blindness's empowering potential. We could call it the blindness that is reflection's insight, or the obstinacy of a reflective impasse. Wlad Godzich, in his aforementioned afterword to Weber, suggests as much. "Reflecting upon blindness," he says, "forces thought into a reflective judgment about its own tortuous and discontinuous path, the very blindness of which consists in the fact that it has no guide to warn against its vagaries" (155).

CHAPTER ONE

In the circuitous itinerary of these vagaries, in its indomitable ferocity, its emergent properties, and sublime emergency, this reflective pertinacity seeks to complement its fictional mirror of fictions, not only within its own cultural texture but also outside it. If this pertinacity were to look back from its mirror of reflection to its reflected ambiguity and impossible identity, in that inter-diction it might discern a vocation that does not renounce its project of appropriation and comprehension of what it is constitutionally incapable of subsuming and comprehending except as other reflected into same. It might gain a gainsaying insight into its unrequited necessity to produce a simulacrum that substantiates the cultural conditions producing it, that legitimates the blindness of its enabling assumptions, that masks the partiality of its fictions with a camouflage of global integrity and wholesome privilege.

The writings we shall be examining in short order devise intricate mechanisms for reflecting back and, in the process, exposing the uncritical and presumptuous claims of such self-asserting and self-vesting cultural practices embedded in our acts of reading and in our characterizations of other peoples' cultures. Where such presumptive projections are inevitable, and to some degree they are indeed unavoidable, a number of the texts we shall be discussing show up this inevitability as part of their own makeup, as knowing difficulty that must be countenanced. In this respect, the texts discussed here create "emergencies" for the unsuspecting readers and for those cultural contexts that would presume a particular nature for them. As texts that provoke such emergencies, the works we shall be reading pertain to an "emergent literature" indeed. Unfortunately, this is not the commonly understood meaning of the phrase when used by Eurocentric and Anglo American contexts to project a novelty or belatedness on such literatures.

Before moving on to those writings, however, it is only appropriate that we examine the difficulties of such inevitability in our own procedures and in the theoretical and practical presuppositions with which we, as critical readers and members of a professional reading guild, are obliged to approach those texts and cultural contexts.

CHAPTER TWO

SURVIVING THEORY

> ... *impartiality-at-any-price is not unfrequently simply an unsubstantiated assertion of superiority.*
>
> —René Girard, Violence and the Sacred

Cultures that emerge from a protracted colonial past comprise traditions of accommodation that have assimilated numerous cultural discourses projected upon them. The problems of literary language and literary theory thus stand out starkly in such contexts, and it is from this vantage point that I should like to approach the question of theory and its survivability in the case of such overtly problematical literary traditions.

To speak of "postcolonial" cultures in terms of fiction and literary theory amounts to a tautology of sorts. I shall return to this observation. But first, I should like to retrace briefly the ground we are wont to impute, cavalierly at times, to theory, history, representation, and ethics. My sally, both speculative and specular, aims to be more pleading than chastening, more a conciliatory gesture than an indictment. Participation ultimately requires many parts, and my own must of necessity be partial. By partiality we should understand both a predicament of incompleteness and of unavoidable bias. A bias is by definition indispensable to any fabric and to any fabrication. Texture and conditioned texturing are what must save even the most unidimensional monolith, and circumspection in the face of that inevitability is ultimately the redeeming grace of even the most monadic

CHAPTER TWO

doxology, lest the lesson fall into orthodoxy, and speculation into dogma. A dogma is more wont to bark than see, and its irascibility precludes participation with mordant petulance. Speculation must have species recognition and some auto-recognizance. And, as we know, a dogma more often than not is deprived of that perspicacity.

Theory is what we have privileged as an alternative to dogma, and as a community of theoreticians we are heirs to a venerable legacy. Our guild is as ancient as our history unremitting. The Athenian *theoroi* originally were twenty-five in number. But history's inflationary spiral has wreaked havoc with that numerical economy as well. And as we are part of a New-World economy where, since the *Niña,* the *Pinta,* and the *Santa María,* the *Mayflower* and the *Arbella,* the indemnities for brazenness that some may call courage have rendered every man a *theoros,* or seer, it follows that every man and, at last, every woman, be blessed with the vatic powers of the theoretician. The most vexing question now becomes the ratio between the light of vision and the seemingly promiscuous proliferation of visions. But let me tactfully unpack my tropical haversack of self-suspecting strategy.

"I am unpacking my library. Yes, I am. The books are not yet on the shelves, not yet touched by the mild boredom of order."[1] So begins Walter Benjamin in what has now become a topical inheritance. His book of essays goes by the title of *Illuminations,* one that he himself sanctioned for a section of his *Schriften* posthumously published in 1961 and to which Hannah Arendt, in her 1969 American edition, remains faithful. *Illuminations* is a fitting title for the sundry reflections of a *theoros,* particularly a theoretician of Benjamin's stripe, one who had clear insight into that conventional link between theory and theistic vision. As a religious man and devotee of the book, he had an honesty in his dealings with books that enabled him to confess in the same essay with studied candor the spectral nature of his own praxis as a man of books speaking about books: "For such a man is speaking to you," he confesses, "and on closer scrutiny he proves to be speaking only about himself" (59). At the same time, however, Benjamin invokes that orphaned apothegm, adopted by posterity for the paternity of Horace: "Habent sua fata libelli," a kernel of wisdom about books having their own fates, but one whose own seed has been fated to remain libelously uncertain. Benjamin's ruminations comprise the soliloquy of a collector of books intended for our benefit. His confession thus is more than soliloquy, and his avid vocation is more than the métier of a mere collector. Just as he is engaged in dialogue through the misdirection of a spectral monologue, Benjamin ends by becoming "collected" into and subsumed as a recollection by the graphic objects of his acquisitive obsession:

> Of no one has less been expected, and no one has had greater sense of wellbeing than the man who has been able to carry on his disreputable existence in the mask of Spitzweg's "Bookworm." For inside him there are spirits, or at least little genii, which have seen to it that for a collector . . . ownership is the most intimate relationship that one can have to objects. Not that they come alive in him; it is he who lives in them. So I have erected one of his dwellings, with books as building stones, before you, and now he is going to disappear inside, as is only fitting. (67)

This fate of the man of books has varied Latin American intonations. One of the most obvious among them reads: "The world will be Tlön. I take no notice. I go on revising, in the quiet of days in the hotel at Adrogué, a tentative translation into Spanish, in the style of Quevedo, which I do not intend to see published, of Sir Thomas Browne's *Urn Burial*."[2] I use this predicament of the bookman's ineluctable entry into the edifice of books as entrée to unpacking my own prefiguration of a tropics for theory because the constitutive performance of a theoretical move is ultimately the reclamation of the reader's banished claims from the making of literature and the recouping of the collector's recollective power from an idealized institutionalization of the edifice of books that constitutes a tradition. To theorize on literature entails, in the final analysis, this dialectical interaction between subsumption and recovery, between intrusion and salvaging, between implosion and regurgitation to the periphery, between capitulation and recapitulation, or, in terms of Benjamin himself, between collection and recollection: "Every passion," avers Benjamin,

> borders on the chaotic, but the collector's passion borders on the passion of memories. More than that: the chance, the fate, that suffuse the past before my eyes are conspicuously present in the accustomed confusion of these books. For what else is this collection but a disorder to which habit has accommodated itself to such an extent that it can appear as order? (60)

CHAPTER TWO

If we use Benjamin's lexicon for a poetics of theory (and I use the phrase advisedly), we are to understand that theory, in its traditional denotation as orderly abstraction, as model metaphysics, as schema of fundamental principles, as systemic reflection that furnishes intelligibility to the desultory and to the chaotic, is an accustomed accommodation, a cohabiting with disorder that attains to orderliness in our habituation through a dialectical coexistence with it. We elevate that accommodation into suppositions and hypotheses that we deploy in our attempts to "make sense" of the world. What I should like to speculate is that literary theory may well consist, instead, in the breaking of that habit, by way of a dialectical engagement and interaction still, but one which does not resolve itself in the homogeneous merging of theoretical performance and the object of theory.

I should like to venture, that is, the possibility of theory as heterogeneous overture that does not implode into the representational concatenation that would erase the difference and contingencies of the particular and that does not render otherness into homogeneity and identity. In that participation, partiality would not become sanitized or compromised to the "ownership," however problematic, of the collector by the edifice of the collection or of the collection by the mastery of the collector. And the aphorism of questionable origin, "habent sua fata libelli," whether referring to books or to a cultural tradition, would retain its validity, not necessarily because those books or that tradition find their rebirth through us, but because, even if what Benjamin claims in this regard is true, we recognize and remain mindful that that rebirth is a "natural" and not a naturalized offspring, that is, a bastard (re)birth whose legitimacy is fugitive for being the fruit of a suspect conception and, therefore, resistant to domestication as appropriable object of our theoretical claims and their impetus for mastery. This way, in the perdurance of that differential intercourse, theory might be able to survive *and* remain survivable, as it well must, however problematically, so that intelligent reflection may carry on its enterprise and still retain the discrete alterity of a spectacle on which to reflect.

What sort of theory this may entail surely must have some relevance to the particulars of its spectacular object. In this sense, our acceptance of theory has no obligation to conform to the *theoria* of Athenian antiquity as tradition has fixed it. I suspect, and in one of his later essays ("Resistance to Theory") the late Paul de Man argues as much,[3] that some of our contemporaries' discomfiture with theory is rooted in the heterodox deviations of the kind of theory that I propose from the entailments of the classical *theoria*, not as it might have existed necessarily, but as subsequent accommodations have rendered it through the centuries. Etymology furnishes an index to how far we may have in fact strayed in our theoretical predicament from antiquity's theoretical strategy.

Classical theory is by definition inextricably linked to spectacle and the spectacular. It is both a mediate observation and a set of spectacles through which to contemplate the experiential and the speculative. For this reason, classical antiquity's dichotomy was not founded on a distinction between *theoria* and praxis, as the sixth book of Aristotle's *Nichomachean Ethics* makes quite clear. The antinomy to the practical was philosophical knowledge, a metaphysics if you will, and not the theoretical, which entailed practical ends of sanction and legitimation through the mechanism of collective accommodation, that is to say, through convention. The *theoria*, in this sense, was always plural and collective, and the *theoroi*, as official legates and observers, certified to having seen. Their certification legitimated what was socially deliberated. The *theoros* was a seer in the sense of observant and delegate to festivals of other city-states. Eventually, the task was to take on religious import as the *theoroi* became envoys to shrines and oracles, a turn that obscured the original purpose of the office. Thus, from sightseers the *theoroi* become seers of visions and eventually eponymous magistrates.

Originally, then, theoretical knowledge was founded on mediate understanding and not on reason. The yoking of reason to vision as religious experience and faith is, of course, a later development when rational instrumentality is called upon to support revealed truth and vice versa, as in the Thomistic assertion that nothing in faith is contrary to reason and, conversely, reason is an appropriate venue to the truths of faith. The spectacular character of *theoria* emerges clearly in the institution of the *theorika*, a form of state welfare for the attendance of spectacles whose emolument amounted to less than a pittance compared to what is commanded by the *theoroi* of celebrity status in our present institutions. Said to have been introduced by Pericles, the *theorika* consisted of two obols per individual and benefited primarily the poorer citizens of Athens by making it possible for them to attend theatrical performances.

What was held in contradistinction to *theoria* was not praxis but aesthetics. For although *theoria* attained a level of sanction by virtue of being

CHAPTER TWO

adjudicated contemplation, an understanding given legitimacy through the mediations of collective discourse, aesthetics, to the contrary, enjoyed no sanction because it was bound to a phenomenalism, to claims of seeing things as they naturally are, as the Greek verb *aísthesthai* (to perceive) and the nominative *aisthestá* (things perceptible to the senses) clearly signify. That potential imbued aesthetics with the possibility to abstract its claims into a philosophical formulation that may have been inconsistent with the one sanctioned by the system. The ontological pretension implicit in such phenomenalism, predictably enough, does become integrated as a philosophical formulation, and thus the status of aesthetics as a systematic part of our universalist philosophical tradition. That affiliation rests on the capacity of aesthetics to fuse articulated perception (linguistic or otherwise) with "natural reality," to confuse, that is, reference with phenomenalism, which is tantamount to a con-fusion that results in ideology. Plato himself was more than wary of this potential in aesthetics and moved against its sanctioning within the context of *theoria* and the institution of the *theorika*. I find that apprehension, a discomfiture that is founded not in this potential of aesthetics per se but in the question of who may be allowed to exercise that privilege inside the philosophical stronghold, in the *Laws* (700e–701a). Here is Plato, our primal philosophical ideologue, condemning simultaneously what he termed *theatrocratia* in *theoria* and *democratia* in politics. He is speaking here primarily of the spectacle or *theoria* of music:

> Our once silent audiences have found a voice, in the persuasion that they understand what is good and bad in art: the old "sovereignty of the best" in that sphere has given way to an evil "sovereignty of the audience" [*theatrocratia*] . . . no great harm would have been done, so long as the democracy was confined to art . . . but as things are with us, music has given occasion to a general conceit of knowledge and contempt for law and liberty has followed in their train.[4]

Aristotle, in his treatise on the *Constitution of Athens* (49.3), confirms that Plato's apprehensions were in fact realized.

Let us willfully misappropriate Plato's lexicon and trope his *theatrocratia* into *theorocratia*. In that paronomasia we will have captured the uneasy disposition of those threatened by the seeming proliferation of literary theory in our own day. I say seeming because literary theory is not as prevalent as some may perceive, particularly those who are provoked into uneasiness or vehement intolerance by that impression. What in fact has proliferated, in the name and guise of the would-be-banished claims of literary theory, are aesthetic ideologies, whether purely formalistic, if that is possible, or purely ethical and ideologically programmatic, should that also be a possibility. (And I follow de Man's problematic paideia on this point, fully aware of the risks involved in even invoking his name at this juncture in our befuddled cultural history. Intellectual honesty, where I am concerned, however, compels more than political expediency, lest we fall into the same trap that taints de Man's own memory.)

The larger portion of theory that parades as literary theory, then, consists of cultural and ideological philosophemes, reductive and formalistic, or ethical and religious, but in any case constructs and formulations that aspire naively (but not so innocuously) to representational determinacy or to hegemonic mastery by way of a misdirection that begs the question of determination. In short, the philosophical epistemology, that which Athenian *theoria* did not sanction and Plato admonished as "a general conceit of knowledge," has, in fact, become constituted as an aesthetic ideology that consolidated its hold in modern times through its reiteration in Alexander Gottlieb Baumgarten's philosophical rationalization of aesthetics as a system and in Immanuel Kant's metaphysical baptism and confirmation of Baumgarten. Since then, literary theory has, for the most part, functioned as a handmaiden, albeit problematic and often unruly, to philosophical discourse, even that Gallic miscellany of discourse that designated its philosophical mélange or potpourri as the "sciences of man."

If theory is to be speculative contemplation that reflects upon its object through a controlled, specular method that does not constitute or overdetermine that object, it must partake of a continuity between its procedure and the conditions of existence of what it is that it speculates or mirrors, keenly cognizant of the reflective distortion and permutations that accrue to its activity. The theoretical activity, that is, cannot be theoretical unless it purges itself (or compensates for determinacies it cannot withhold) of a priori determinants (philosophical, religious, ideological) that would compromise the discrete character of its object. We know, of course, that this is a naive and utopian desideratum, for by virtue of contemplating something,

CHAPTER TWO

or intending to do so, we do inexorably compromise its alterity, its own otherness. Reflection, specular or speculative, still entails a mode of representation. Such a qualification in essence admits of the impossibility of theory per se, but does it really amount to an admission to the impossibility of literary theory? One must concede that theory *as* an idealization of the philosophical tradition and as concomitant to aesthetic ideology may well preclude itself *as* theory under these conditions. And the remnants of the philosophical tradition within the literati among us impel many to militate against theory on these grounds or to acquiesce to literary theory with tolerance. Or, as de Man phrases it,

> literary theory may now well have become a legitimate concern of philosophy but it cannot be assimilated to it, either factually or theoretically. It contains a necessarily pragmatic moment that certainly weakens it as theory but that adds a subversive element of unpredictability and makes it something of a wild card in the serious game of the theoretical disciplines. (8)

We could rephrase that "necessarily pragmatic moment" that imbues the theory of literature with the proclivity for subverting theoretical fixity and "seriousness" with unpredictability as the necessity of a mobile speculation for a mobile spectacle. The constitutive element of literary discourse is language, a language that is figurative and, therefore, transgressive. As utterance, it has no obligation (or respects none) to the phenomenality of what it articulates. Free from the restraints of identity with the phenomena it articulates, that is, being neither Cratylian nor naively mimetic, the language of literature functions ultimately as paronomasia, a misnaming for which "correctness" remains a hypothetical and illusory impossibility. The relationship between the word and the thing signified is not phenomenal; rather, it is conventional, not unlike the conventionality of the collectively deliberated and sanctioned *theoria* of antiquity. In this sense, the spectacle of literature is ontologically unbound and, as de Man puts it, "epistemologically highly suspect and volatile" (10). If, then, there is to be a continuity between theory and its object, the theory of literature must necessarily partake of this volatility, of this transgressive dynamic, of this paronomasia and nonfixity of literature. If the language of literature is epistemologically suspect, then so does the metalanguage of literary theory need be "suspect."

<u>SURVIVING THEORY</u>

More importantly yet, it needs to be self-suspecting in the specular and speculative deployment of its strategies. A *modus loquendi* must reflect its *modus agendi,* and the agency of the critical theorist must proceed with the tact necessary to a rhetorical dimension of its activity that can withstand the problematic undoing of the cognitive and grammatical, of the systematicity of its strategies. In that suppleness, literary theory can maintain the necessary, albeit problematic, quotient of fidelity to its object and, in doing so, propitiate its own and its object's survivability. In the resilience to the tactical packing and unpacking of the spectacular apparatus it deploys, literary theory can mitigate the force of determinacies it would otherwise blindly inflict upon the otherness of the object of its speculation. In mediating its conceptual strategy with procedural tact, theory and its critical discourse mitigate the violence of its claims upon its contemplated object.

Not many literatures have been accorded such theoretical treatment. Least of all, the literature of what have been problematically designated as "Third-World" countries, among them the countries of Latin America, whose fictions I have opted to deal with in this study. On the contrary, as a literature that has been relegated to the margins and rendered as "other" vis-à-vis the literary tradition of Eurocentric cultural criteria, it becomes fair game for the specular projections of a self-privileging theoretical discourse and its ideological determinations. And yet, by dint of being in large measure the linguistic projection of a cultural discourse from the outside—a discourse that has sought self-validation in the mastery of the spectral other—Latin America, like other regions with protracted colonial histories, reflects starkly those pragmatic entailments that exacerbate the ideological grammar of cognitive formulations that make claims upon it. Thus, the empirical chastisement of would-be naturalizing structures of representation deployed against Latin America become unpredictably and irrepressibly rhetoricized as philosophical epistemologies. The result is the throwing of phenomenal correspondence between language and world, and of naive distinctions between fiction and reality, into a truly volatile epistemology that unmasks encroaching ideological aberrations. I do not claim that the resultant articulated culture is an absolute fiction, but it certainly has the marks of a self-mitigating supreme fiction that problematically absorbs and undoes programmatic absolutes. In this sense, Latin America has been

CHAPTER TWO

variously a pretext and a text that for five hundred years now has been generating a panoply of fictions about and from within itself. In this protracted cohabitation, fictionality (of fictions and of theories) and Latin America could be considered as functionally synonymous—if by fiction, that is, we understand an endemically multiple (con)text that stubbornly refuses domestication or reduction to a single meaning, to a universalizable canon, or to a generalizable schema that does not provoke contention among its interpreters and entrepreneurs.

From the beginning, itself a debatable point whenever it may have been, Latin America—then called, not so simply, the New World—has been the problematical "other" world to the world whose worldliness was forced to endure a most jarring encounter with the discovered "other."[5] The antipodal "Other World" to the world since its European delivery into Europe's consciousness, America congenitally becomes other to itself. Alien to its "deliverers," it would become alienated from itself through the chronic attempts to "naturalize" it, to render it viable and comprehensible to the economy of its discoverers' language, metaphysics, and commerce. From that problematic beginning to our own day, every hermeneutical constellation, interpretive machinery, and disinterested machination has been deployed in this attempt at domestication. And since that inception, Latin America has proved an incontinent continent. It leaks through every cognitive mold and ideological structure ever put upon it. Whether it be put upon by Genoese mariner, Spanish conquistador, papal missionary, English pirate, or Anglo American savior, Latin America inevitably has found a way to prove frustrating and indomitable. (I anticipate fully that my own critical diagnoses here are not exempted from that inevitability.)

Like the texts of Macondo's history in García Márquez's *One Hundred Years of Solitude,* Latin America's textured palimpsest finds a way to survive the (en)closures, nagging or cataclysmic, that would define and confine it within the space of the naturally comprehended: For Columbus's cosmological schema, it proved a cosmic error. The admiral died believing he had discovered the Indies. Time proved that he merely foundered on a stone of continental proportions in his path to the Orient. The conquistadors thought to have conquered a New World. They were conquered as much by its "docile" and bewildering quagmire in turn. The colonial imperialism of Counter-Reformation Spain thought to have found a pristine theater for the

SURVIVING THEORY

ideology of its pastoral mission. The animus of the tropics swallowed that dogmatic purity into a religious syncretism. Alexander von Humboldt sailed to substantiate his scientificist cosmos only to be confronted by an indomitable heterocosm. Positivist progressivism thought to have encountered a social geography blessed only with a future. It beached on the slippery ground of cyclicalist recurrence and revolutionary zeal. The econometric technocrat of modern efficacy seeks the machinery of bureaucratic management only to encounter the obduracy of satrapic personalism. Neoconservative fundamentalism seeks the surefooted political authority in militaristic paternalism only to find the ridicule and chagrin of death's ironic laughter and the inscrutable grimace of the living. The contemporary novelist has sought to exemplify a marvelous aesthetic only to be upstaged by a marvelous reality more magical on its own account than the magical realism of literary accounts.

The Great American Novel, sought in the literary alchemy of Anglo America like a philosopher's stone, is writ large in Latin America in continental space with an intricate plot of half a millennium's time. If by novel, that is, we mean a protean construct whose irrepressible turns yield unpredictable novelty and keep the plot energetically moving through gripping twists of open-ended drama. Within the context of this great American novel, Latin America's writers continue to forge their own textual world in unremitting dialogue with the text of the continental world about them and within them. As self-presentations of their own context, the enterprise of these fiction makers becomes thwarted by the intrusive otherness of this Other World that renders its fictions endlessly other to themselves. The dialectical relationship, this interchange between and within works and contexts, yields multiple fictions, a prodigious fictionality in which every assertion belies itself in becoming other than the intended object or formulation of its discourse. The stentorian voice of an ancestor frequently adopted from north of the Mexican border resonates in that multiplicity: "Do I contradict myself? I am large, I contain multitudes." Within the Latin context of America, Whitmanesque grandeur comes closer to the mean than to hyperbole. And within that ever-changing mean, the pertinacity of indomitableness operates as a deflective strategy that frustrates hegemonic attempts to naturalize or reduce the Latin American phenomena to a comprehended domesticity of representational discourse. If, that is, by

CHAPTER TWO

discourse we understand the strategic deployment of colonizing interests, of political power, of cultural subsumption, of historical representation, or of fictive transfiguration through the rhetorical operatives of a self-validating language of mastery veiled as euphemism. In the inadequacies wrought upon such discourses of hegemony, Latin America emerges as a survivalist or "residual" literary tradition, more so than an "emergent literature" in the condescending sense implicit in the euphuistic characterization of this tradition by the self-proclaimed "first-world" discourse examined in our previous chapter.

"Emergent" it is, indeed, but only in the sense that Latin American fictions have made a centuries-long vocation of the penchant for irrepressible emergencies. In view of the fact that the so-called First World is, for the most part, a parvenu to the scene of "culture," as it has come to be defined by the dominant centers of power themselves, it is not surprising that the euphemistic lexicon for characterizing literatures of regions such as Latin America, Africa, and the Indian subcontinent should ring with alarming emergency. Latin America's fictions are not naturally residual. They are residual as accidents of historical contingency that, if not natural, have certainly become institutional. American culture in the New World is in toto a "residual" historical entity—a culture of excess in a game of cosmological extra innings, if you will, that carries on postapocalyptically with eschatological fervor. Its apocalyptic demise was calculated as early as the prophetic arithmetic of its first calculator. In his *Book of Prophecies* (1501), Christopher Columbus reckoned that only 155 years remained before the End. That arithmetic would be seconded to the year on the providential abacus of New England's John Cotton (*An Exposition upon the Thirteenth Chapter of the Revelation* [1639]). It is suggestive in this regard to recall how many major Latin American novels of the past two decades, in addition to *One Hundred Years of Solitude* already mentioned, inscribe themselves as residual, as excess, or as survivor texts, of the apocalyptic cataclysm that befalls their novelistic world: José Donoso's *The Obscene Bird of Night,* Carlos Fuentes's *Terra Nostra,* Mario Vargas Llosa's *The War of the End of the World,* as we shall see in due course.

If Latin America's fictions constitute "a literature of foundations," as the Mexican essayist and poet Octavio Paz observes on various occasions,[6] it is a literature of *anxious* foundations, fully aware that its foundationalism is doomed to founder time and again on its own otherness to itself and as otherness that exacerbates and deflects formal and ideological attempts to naturalize and represent it. Any theoretical schema and critical reduction, whether foundationalist-ideological or truly critical and heterological, is bound to endure indeterminate and unpredictable chastisements when taking the fictions of Latin America as its target. Any overarching theory or philosophical ideology will inevitably find itself thwarted no less so than the chivalric quest of the conquistador, the utopian projection of the European Renaissance, the baroque redolence of the seventeenth century, or the postromantic positivism and its progressivist dream. Any hegemonic impulse of representation will find itself disposed to the ex-centricity of these fictions' ubiquitous dislocations to desultory margins.

The unsettled feeling with the "marginality" implicit in the designation "emergent literature" that emanates from European and Anglo American projects for and projections on Latin America will invariably reflect more on the anxieties of neocolonialist discourse faced with an indomitable object, as already discussed in the previous chapter. If there is a clearly identifiable constant in the fictions of Latin America that binds them as a tradition, it would have as its trademark this stubborn refusal to yield unconditionally and once and for all to thematic representation and institutional mastery. In this sense, their indomitableness also links them to the literatures of any number of other cultures.

Any theoretical ordering or critical project within this arena, then, requires a wakefulness, not for the sake of compensating for the deflections it might sustain but because of a mindful sensitivity that would allow the recalcitrant specificities of these fictions to make their rightful claims, in turn, on the claims that the theoretical-critical enterprise is making on and for them. In such a mutual engagement, a truly dialogical interchange, one in which the privileged potency above others is generosity, fiction and fictionality will have sustained and survived the theoretical agency and its critical discourse. In that imaginative heterogeneity of language and discourse, fiction itself will have moved to the fore, banishing the shadows of imperial pretensions and of recalcitrant self-idealization. Thus, our theoretical and critical task and the self-critical project of Latin America's fictions will have spectrally illumined each other as yet one more reflection of unfettered, that is to say heterodox and nonabsolute, fictionality. That fiction, then, will be one that intrinsically and constitutionally partakes (but not as mere verbalism or purely "mimetic" representation) of the continent's human and geographical realities in their accommodation of external and internal pressures of cultural discourses. In this critical generosity, then, our theoretical reflection and acts of reading will have been freed from the illusion that these fictions comprise, or need comprise, a homogeneous and fully comprehended whole. In the essays that follow, I shall engage in a series of readings that try to demonstrate the procedures articulated here.

CHAPTER THREE

A SHORT PARABLE
Borges's Admonition to the Self-seeking Reader

Within the economy of certain literary institutions, the politics of interpretation could be a deadly game. Borges's literary corpus emanates from a world context where the interpretation of politics often entails equally dire consequences. It should not surprise us, then, that this most notorious of Latin American writers should be dramatizing this predicament with the full force of its most foreboding and fatal consequences. Borges has often allegorized the ambivalent fate of reading and writing as an enterprise whose random contingencies could just as easily spell a saving grace—however deluded and illusionary—as a fatal blow, however indifferent and casual, but no less deadly for its matter-of-factness.

    As author, Borges demures on proprietary authority, often transferring that "privilege" to the reader, or allaying the dread of that awesome responsibility by allying his authorial activity with the interpretive acts of the reader, whose burden of responsibility traditionally has been taken as "less consequential," though, as the Borges plot often proves, no less ominous. If the author bequeaths, Borges appears to imply, the reader is the hermetic executor, the hermeneutical executioner, of the bequest. Borges's author, more often than not, warily wishes to forego proprietary

CHAPTER THREE

responsibility and its attendant consequences by re-leasing what he does not claim to have ever owned unto the desultoriness of the happenstance, unto inheritors of anonymity's randomness, that is, the unknown readers. The hermeneutical appropriator who would lay claim, that is, who would fool-heartily own up to an exclusive and improprietous appropriation, who would, in other words, reduce that bequest to a re-presentation in/of his/her own reflection, is surely exposing him/herself to consequences equally or perhaps more dire than those the wary author saw fit to avoid in his disclaiming bequest to unnamed "beneficiaries." The dramatic space where Borges has most often thematized this predicament lies, as he has mapped it, between the book and writing. The action of this drama consists in the suspenseful oscillation between the two, where the book translates as natural totality, as metaphysical absolute, as transcendental completion, as inappellable inscription and implacable law, on the one hand, and, on the other, writing as tentative and differential/deferential performance with provisional claims that abstain from the attempt to contain exhaustively writing's bequest within their own reflection.

Clearly, I am summarily rehearsing two alternate modes of interpretive activity that most vividly contend in the literary and philosophical institutions today, i.e., the veridic-univocal and the ludic-polysemic, the logocentric and the grammatological, the metaphysical and the differential. While Borges is often invoked as precursor in whom the debates of the contemporary critical institution have a franchise, the critical and exegetic work done is frequently not commensurate to the sweep of these often tendentious claims for/on Borges.

I should like to essay, on a minimal and modest scale, such a parsing with no intent at any proprietary or exhaustive representational claims. By way of such a tentative reading I hope to show how Borges's ludic casualness amounts to a critical reversal whose masterful persiflage spells an understated dramatization of the death sentence awaiting hermeneutical hubris when it would venture the attempt to contain writing within its interpretive and specular reflection. It is a Faustian plot with a Borgesian turn that juxtaposes, at the level of reading, as I have said, the paradigm of the book to the periphrastic pursuits of writing and reading as contingent activities. As in the best of Latin American writing, the pragmatic and political entailments are deftly sublimated in Borges. And one need not be a

A Short Parable

Michel Foucault to realize that in a context such as Latin America the extratextual realities, the torsions of "real-world" determinations, have traditionally been so pervasively deadly that a more subtle tact of textual formalization may well be the indispensable mask or ironic grimace that redeems literary/critical discourse from the heavy-handedness of apocalyptic overpoliticization. In this sense, we may yet learn to read Borges's cavalierly reactionary political assertions in the light and shadow of this necessarily misdirected and oblique narrative. Where the thrust of the Borgesian discourse may lie, in other words, may well be—as in the better part of Latin America's texts—in the implicit otherness of its understatement, in the tropical other writing in the writing. Latin America is not unique in this regard. As in most contexts where censorship, unbending normative imperatives, or institutional intolerance reign, forms of misdirection, ironic or otherwise, as well as textual circumspection have been the necessary recourse. Borges's lessons in reading, I venture to say, could well teach us to read accordingly.

The Borges text I shall try to track here is an incipient and factitious miscellany entitled "The Mirror of Ink" ("El espejo de tinta"). It first appeared in the periodical *Crítica* of Buenos Aires on 30 September 1933, and two years later it was strategically placed in an appendage aptly called "Etcetera" of that desultory congeries *Historia universal de la infamia* by the wily Borges.[1] The tale's anecdote is simple. Its allegory much less so: The implacably cruel ruler of the Sudan, Yaqub the Ailing, has plundered the country to satisfy the Egyptian tax-collectors. Yaqub dies "on the fourteenth day of the moon of Barmahat, in the year 1842." There are those who claim that the wizard Abd-er-Rahman al-Masmudi, either by poison or dagger, perpetrated that death. Our narrator has doubts about that claim. Since Yaqub was called the Ailing, "a natural death is more likely." We are told that Captain Richard F. Burton spoke to the wizard in 1853 and that our narrator *quotes* what was recounted to Burton: that the wizard's brother masterminded an unsuccessful conspiracy; that, as a result, his brother fell victim to the sword of the ruler's justice and the wizard suffered captivity; that the wizard is spared on promising to show Yaqub "shapes and appearances still more wonderful than those of the magic lantern"; that this display in a mirror of ink culminates in Yaqub's self-contemplation; that, finally, in that self-apperception, Yaqub witnesses his own execution by the

Chapter Three

hand of Abu Kir, the Court executioner who had dispatched the wizard's brother. In the spectral presence of his own countenance and of his execution, Yaqub tumbles to the floor dead.

Now "etcetera," as we have all been taught in our earlier school days, is a desideratum deployed to convince ourselves, if not others, that we know or command more than we actually do, and the ironic Borges turns that strategic datum, how consciously it is hard to determine, back on itself. He accomplishes that turn or deflection, deliberately or not, through an errancy that de-authorizes the pseudoknowledge immanent in the self-convinced insecurity of an *etceterum;* and, in doing so, he gives free play to the indeterminacy of "etcetera" as a rhetorical figure. The deferential depletion of self-certainty or conviction that ensues from the self-reassuring insecurity of this turn allows the author to err with a clean conscience, or, at least, with the more serviceable error that ensues from self-effacement as opposed to self-privileging conviction. And err he does, cunningly or naively. The ruse implicit in this sort of enabling power play has come to be one of the identifying marks of the Borgesian enterprise. One could venture the observation that Borges's project has consisted over the years in converting its own enterprise—writing—into the differential and cunningly diffident alterity or excrescence of a desultory *etceterum.* Through that ploy, allegorically dramatized—as we shall see presently—in "The Mirror of Ink," Borges has managed to attain the spectral other, the mirrored reversal, of an ironic depletion or de-authorization of the written sign and of authorial self-effacement. He has managed, that is, to convert, to divert, the furtive gesture of diffidence and its litotes into a posture (really an imposture) of authorial power, obtained as a dividend through an investment in the multivalent practices of reading.

The duality, the duplicity, the *di-vertissement* of this tactic comprises the identifying signature of "The Mirror of Ink." A title with a semantic overload, for if we associate "Ink" with the di-versionary and ambiguous enterprise of writing, "Mirror," the genitive alterity in the title, is already a surfeit term given to engendering multiple and supernumerary excess. In short, and at the very least, the title of this early Borges tale figures a pleonasm. Borges's avowed abhorrence of mirrors may well reside in his early precognition that his own activity as writer entails a mercurial, that is hermetic and hermeneutical, wizardry, a *spectral* self-presence with its

A Short Parable

attendant sleight of hand, its furtive gesture, fraudulent propriety, and incontinent kleptomania of abysmal citation. The measure of error in Borges's *etceterum,* therefore, is a measure of the writer's mercurial errancy, the furtive adventure of the thieving Mercury/Hermes, herald of gods and souls, of medicine and writing.

The mirrored or spectral mendacity of Borges here resides in the first, the predicative paragraph of this tale of infamy. As an early ruse, it establishes a precedent for what will have become in Borges an irrepressible constant: the apocryphal pre-text (or graphic pretext). Borges's attribution of this Egyptian tale of the wizard Abd-er-Rahman al-Masmudi and of the infamous Yaqub the Ailing to Richard Burton's *The Lake Regions of Central [Equatorial] Africa* has been detected as a false attribution by the tale's English translator, Norman Thomas di Giovanni.[2] Di Giovanni identifies the tale's origins, the elided pretext, in Edward William Lane's *Manners and Customs of the Modern Egyptians.* He tells us that "'The Mirror of Ink' has nothing whatever to do with Burton. It is pure, original Borges and gives the lie to the statement in the Preface to the first edition [of *Universal History of Infamy*] that 'As for the examples of magic that close this volume, I have no other rights to them than those of translator and reader.'" We must remember, however, that di Giovanni is himself a translator, in this instance the translator of a purported translator. And if these *tradittori* manage to dupe each other into compounded entanglement, surely we must guard against an extended entrapment that might ensnare us within the web of the scheme. How much more believable than Borges is di Giovanni here when he assures us of the authenticity of a "pure, original Borges"? At a more basic and problematic level, we might inquire, "Who, after all, is the referent of the preceding question?" before we seek to establish a "pure and original" specimen. I suppose we should be thankful that translators as such are neither critical readers nor logicians (they are at once less and hazardously more than that) and read them, as we must our own exegetical intervention, with the grain of salt that is their due.

Duped by Borges's seemingly optative stratagem, di Giovanni opts for the ready-made and, on the face of it, credible decoy and he settles with stripping the first veil. "The mirror of ink itself comes from Edward William Lane's *Manners and Customs of the Modern Egyptians,* one of Borges's favorite books. What is seen in that pool of ink is of Borges's own

CHAPTER THREE

invention, however, not Lane's." Di Giovanni's statement here reveals more than he himself might suspect. For Borges's *invention* is Borges's *invenio,* that is to say, what Borges *literally* comes upon. And while what he comes upon may not be in Lane, the possibility of its preexistence is not precluded, as di Giovanni would have us believe. What one translator may impute to another as a lie may well be the most assured "truth," like a positive magnetic field that ensues from two negative poles, or from a compounded fiction. Thus, when di Giovanni notes that Borges's statement in the preface to the first edition ("As for the examples of magic that close the volume, I have no other rights to them than those of translator and reader") belies itself, we can take di Giovanni's incredulity as we would an image that is righted by virtue of its reflection in redoubled mirrors—one of writerly ink and one of hermeneutical mercury.

But di Giovanni's putative addendum as corrective is tautologically excessive to the spectacle, for Borges's invention already comprises a pleonastic surfeit and, by dint of his spectral title's double "lie," Borges's declared role as translator and reader of the thaumaturgies that trail as miscellaneous "Etcetera" in his book masks a veiled truth. In the obliquity of that deflected "truth," Borges is, in fact, the translator, reader, and executor, albeit not solely of a misappropriation from Burton, nor exclusively of a datum from Lane. There is yet another Egyptian tale that Borges is interweaving, and hermetically delivering: an Egyptian *abecedarium scripturae* found in Plato, specifically in the *Phaedrus,* in the *Theaetetus,* and alluded to, as well, in other Platonic dialogues. Borges's citational *invenio* simultaneously educes and elides the graphic trace that lies embedded in Plato citationally, anagrammatically (in mirrored refraction) as the differential *pharmakos.* Insofar as Borges's tale is figured as a quote or as a citation—either through a ruse or a naiveté, with its self-differential falsities, half truths, and veiled potentialities—that tale figures as tautology, as abyssal citation of that which it cites. Tautological figuration, however, is ultimately self-presence, even if it be spectral, and the imminent danger in such plenitude or totalization is an unbounded hubris with all the marks of a fatal gesture. That violent eventuality, too, is emplotted into Borges's dramatic rendering of a Platonic citation. In this particular tale, the paroxysm devolves upon the sword of an executioner. Elsewhere in the Borges codex, it eventuates in ironic self-mockery and playful derision, as in the tautological plenitude of "El Aleph," for instance.

A Short Parable

In Plato's *Phaedrus,* writing is itself the object of tracing, clearly a redoubled and spectral undertaking. The invention of writing, traced to the Egyptian Theuth, is dubbed a *pharmakon.* Now, in our poststructuralist era, the term *pharmakon* as used to designate writing is untranslatable. In other words, it is immune to the mendacity or betrayal of univocal translation by virtue of the fact that it already "betrays" itself in its equivocations. That is, the chain of significations loosed by the term entail their own mutual reversibility, their mirrored inversion, and their virtual self-contradiction *without* interdicting or canceling each other. This is what we mean when we say that a term is "citational"; that the term becomes capable of quotation which "cites" other senses of itself in simultaneity. The exclusive rendering of such a term as only one of its significations becomes tantamount to the violence of catachresis, of misplacement, or to the mortal delusion entailed by the flat monody of a univocal reduction.

In "The Mirror of Ink" Borges simultaneously avoids these traps and dramatizes the foreboding dangers for those who would succumb to such temptation of normatively and righteously privileging *one* face of the *vultus mercurialis.* In my own reading of Borges here, you no doubt have noticed that I do not reduce Borges to interpreter or fabulist of Plato exclusively (as di Giovanni does with Lane). Both Burton and Lane persist, even as spectral "negatives," as mirror reflections, as differential alterities, as abysmal citations, even if they resonate in the guise of errancy, as ploy, or as naively wrought découpage. Reading, as Borges demonstrates through his obliquity, is no exclusionary exercise; because even what we might opt to exclude, in the mere rehearsal of that option, the "excluded" exerts a "determinacy," leaves a trace of otherness, a differential inscription, a graft, on the "included." Thus, what we do not care to recall or sanction haunts in our reticence, and, in this sense, what is left out persists.

The deferrent, citational spirit of this mutuality is precisely the necessary and irreducible virtue (the virtuality, as we would say in philosophy) of Plato's *pharmakos.* The Platonic dialogues conjugate the multifarious term *pharmakon* variously as charm, remedy, poison, recipe, drug, antidote, artificial tint. When, in the *Phaedrus,* Theuth, the divinity-inventor of writing, offers his invention to the Egyptian king Thamus as "Here, O King, . . . is a discipline that will make the Egyptians wiser and will improve their memories: both memory and instruction have found their recipe [*pharmakon*]" (274c–e, 275a–b), in his famous response King

CHAPTER THREE

Thamus inverts the utility of the "recipe," thus imbuing the *pharmakon* with its contrary signification—poison rather than remedy. Subsequently, the spectral *pharmakos* entails in its multifarious etymology the echoic significations of magician, wizard, poisoner, the propitiatory sacrifice expelled from the city for the community's purification, i.e., the scapegoat, that part of itself which the city turns out.

This complex chain of irreducible denotation becomes conflated into the intricate mesh of Borges's text. For the critical reader, for the student of writing, "The Mirror of Ink" becomes a recognition scene, a spectacular scene of writing. From the declarative title to the appellative coda, the reader, the executor-trustee of writing, is faced with the prismatic dispersal of the graphic looking glass. The mirror of the title is itself a *pharmakon*, since *tinta*, "ink," that artificial tincture, vital fluid of writing (or, as Borges puts it, that "specular water mirroring / the other blue within its bottomless sky" ["Los espejos," *La Nación*, 30 Aug. 1959]), is etymologically rooted in *pharmakon*.

The shimmering fragments sketched here from the *fata Borgiana* glimmer as citational prescription, as a grammatic spectacle, as a reading lesson in writing. The tale's wizard, Abd-er-Rahman al-Masmudi, "whose name may be translated as the 'Servant of the All-Merciful,'" is the steadfast ("al-Masmudi") servant of Theuth as much as, if not more than, of the God of the Arab Prophet, whom the citational allusion to Burton and the skewed elision of Lane overtly suggest. In this sense, al-Masmudi, the steadfast, the part of the wizard's name that goes unglossed in the tale, exhibits a more enduring loyalty to the ancient pharmacy that resonates in the epithet by which he is characterized: the wizard, *el hechicero,* the *pharmakos*—servant and avatar of Theuth, god of the *sentence,* written and executed, life-giving and life-taking. As in Plato's *Phaedrus,* he pleads before the king, offering the multiple *pharmakon* to the ailing Yaqub, promising "shapes and appearances more wonderful than those of the magic lantern." Cunningly, allusively, Borges's narrator beckons us *beyond* Burton, Lane, and the ruse of the *Arabian Nights* and its magic lantern, of which this tale too might be misread as an apocryphal *etceterum,* as a desultory and belated addendum. We are enjoined to witness the wonderful shapes and appearances conjured by the pharmacy of this *pharmakeus,* by its grafting *calamus,* incisive and ambivalent scissors, Venetian paper, the pharmaceu-

A Short Parable

tical inkhorn, the chafing dish with some live coals, coriander seeds, and an ounce of benzoin, in short, the perennial alchemy for smoke and mirrors.

In this necessarily minimal commentary I can only suggest, synoptically, the turns by which this alchemy figures an enabling fiction become a mirror to itself and a citation of writing's pharmacy. Within this trope of *pharmakos* as multifarious figure of writing, we recognize immediately in Borges's tale the fertile conjunction of inseminating calamus—the writing reed—and of the copulative/apocopeic scissors: instruments both in which the mirrored functions of life and death (remedy and poison) recoup each other as supplemental alterities. The written invocation, the epigrammatic or proleptic inscription within this tale's writing—the Koranic *sententia* "And we have removed from thee thy veil; and thy sight today is piercing"—becomes hauntingly meaningful. Our reader's discernment in this recognition scene of writing starkly obviates for us that crossing point, the threshold mediacy of these mirroring and mutually supplementing processes as acts of self-perception. Borges's cautionary advertence is clear: Interpretive speculations may well end up as self-reflective acts of overreaching for immediate and privileged self-presence as, for example, in the case of Yaqub the Ailing, whose very name and its Hebrew etymology (*Ya'aqôbh,* "he who takes by the heel or overreaches") point to overtaking and the dire consequences of such hubris.

Allegorically significant in this caveat is the mirror we hold up to writing: Reading and the crucial role of the reader as executor of writing's pharmaceutical alchemy, a role made critically acute in this Borges tale by way of an onomastic trope, through an ominous prosopopoeia. I am referring to Abu Kir, the Court *executioner* in the tale, in whose name and offices resonate the all-significant life-giving and life-taking powers of generation (*abu,* "father") and of readership, with *Kir* having, as it does, its root etymon in the Arabic *k'raa,* meaning "to read."

Through this nominal allegory, Borges convokes us to a reading lesson. The lesson becomes unmistakably urgent in the antithetical and supplementary juxtaposition of the story's two hermeneutical executors: the fated Yaqub the Ailing, whose reflection reaches after a mastered and mastering identity, an identical representation with his speculation—an autoscopy that reduces writing and its otherness, i.e., the mirror of ink, to the tantamount totality of/in his own hermeneutic likeness and spectral

CHAPTER THREE

reflection—and Abu Kir, the enigmatic Court executioner, whose dual name doubles back on his courtly function. As "father reader/of reading," he *carries on* writing's generic sentence, even as his offices require that he *carry out* (that he "throw the book" of) the Court's sententious law or nomos.

Borges's allegory of the reader, in short, would appear to anticipate by nearly half a century a kind of "reader-reception" theory whose hermeneutical enterprise would not enslave the text to the reader's willful strategy or ideological preferments, but, more accurately, function as a poetic theory that calls for a deferential criticism with the full array of its generative otherness and generosity of differentiation. In short, Borges points toward a "courtly reader" whose potency resides in hermeneutical "serving," as receptive host, rather than in a hermeneutic of interpretive mastery, of proprietary representation that levels otherness and its dialogic alterities. We cannot be unmindful, as no one could afford to be, of Borges's chastening admonition in our own acts of reading. I suggest we proceed accordingly through the pages that follow.

CHAPTER FOUR

ARBORESCENT PAZ, INTERLINEAL POETRY

> *La experiencia de la literatura es esencialmente la experiencia del otro.*
>
> —O. Paz, *Pasión crítica*

"The other constitutes us," notes Octavio Paz.[1] And the allegory of the reading lesson in the Borges of our previous chapter teaches us that to pretend to appropriate the other into our own image spells an eradication of otherness that inevitably translates into our own undoing.

As we have seen, Borges's allegory labors on the slippery ground of irony. Irony is, by definition, the double-edged instrument of otherness, the partitive device that sunders monisms and shatters the univocal into alterior multiplicity, into sundry resonances and altercations. Socrates domesticated irony's instrumentality into a pedagogical tool, and his disciple Plato sanctioned its possibilities by conferring philosophical highmindedness on irony's ends. Borges made a vocation of disporting with such sanctimony, recouping irony's potential for multifariousness from the philosopher's sobriety and the self-privileging orthodoxy of the metaphysician. And this is why for the steadfast ideologues and witless monodists of his time, Borges has proved as unsavory as Socrates did for the Sophists of his own epoch. Irony has always exacerbated otherness, and the other has been recapitulated into sameness, into less threatening, though deadly, oneness, most often through the expatiating sacrifice of the *eiron*. Borges,

Chapter Four

of course, made a habit of baiting the pharisees of his time, and he did so with a mischievousness that bordered on perversity. In a time and within a continent wracked by immeasurable human suffering, Borges's tenacious adherence to a detached aesthetic and its anachronistic proclamations has led many to indict his political ethics as abhorrent and led many others to view him as politically irrelevant, if not pernicious. Borges may well deserve such condemnation. But be that as it may, political oddities and ethical curiosities of a given epoch are no less instructive or any less reflective of the heterodoxies of that era and its local narratives.

Octavio Paz, though some fifteen years younger, may be Borges's most signaled contemporary (Borges was a "late bloomer," Paz brilliantly precocious). He may have been, as well, his most singular antagonist; not necessarily because the two held diametrically opposed views on literature and politics but precisely because of the relative absence of such polar contrariety. Borges himself often dramatized the uncanny coincidence, the ironic congruity between diametrical extremes and between those espousing such convictions (e.g., "The Theologians"). Paz has always cautioned against the dangers of unyielding adherence, even to the principle of nonadherence. Whereas Paz has managed, or at least has made a career-long attempt, to negotiate the capricious inconstancies of such a paradox, Borges, cannily perceptive of the paradoxical human predicaments he so often dramatized in scribal allegories, suffered an insurmountable blockage when it came to the transference of that allegorical insight to his own life practice. And, while he saw clearly that unbending agnosticism could itself constitute a religion, just as the most consummate ironist could be duped at some indeterminate turn by irony's implacable métier, he remained steadfast in his studied nonconformity, albeit to his own professions. At the end of the day, he proved no less pharisaic in his own constancy than the pharisees he unrelentingly taunted with glee, or at least with the twisted mask of a gleeful mannerism and the facade of unperturbable chivalrousness.

Writing, in the final analysis (on the hypothetical assumption that such finality could obtain), is a human activity, and the easiest way to sound foolish might be to claim any one human activity as tantamount to life. Like other mortals, writers must demonstrate or betray a humanity larger than their own activity or professions, lest they reductively delimit their own lives to the minimalism of a function or role within the script of an absurd theater authored and directed by some inscrutable and incomprehensible Scriptor. Our most extreme absurdists, our most Faustian modernists, like our most Stoic comedians of postmodernity, scream—mockingly, in earnest, or with irony—against such functional minimalism as a human fate. We are agons, whether in pathos or in derision. And the agonist's vocation, whether Luciferian or Hudibrastic, aspires for more than the acts and actions of that vocation, moved as such a vocation is by the necessity of insufficiency, by the desire (hedonistic or pious) that reaches beyond self-satisfaction and that is by definition unsatisfiable.

For more than half a century now, Octavio Paz, as poetic agon and as iconoclastic Jeremiah, has mediated for us that other space which lies between (and often belies) our acts and our humanity, between our actions and inhumanity. He has tried to chart the course of alternating currents that energize and liberate, that authorize and enslave. All the while, he has allowed for a permeability in the edifications of his own discourse, for a transparency in his own mask(s), for a contradiction to his own dictum, for yet one more otherness to his multiple oneness. Thus when he writes, "the other constitutes us," by the nature of that constitution we are to understand not a finished result but an interminable process that proscribes our finishing ourselves off in the self-satisfaction of our attainment, in the self-privilege of our precognition, in the self-righteousness of our ideas, in the narcissism of our reflection(s), or in the echo of our own words:

> Words turn into reflections, shadows and fog in rags. The "other" flutters and the landscape evaporates: we are before the sheet of paper, the table, the window anew. We perceive, almost as a sensation, our mortality. The experience of literature is, essentially, the experience of the other: the experience of the other that we are, the experience of the other that are the others, and the supreme experience: the other, the woman. But in all these experiences throbs, hidden, the *other* experience: the experience of death, the knowledge of ourselves to be mortal.[2]

We would be irredeemably remiss were we to understand the otherness Paz articulates simply in terms of a schematic reduction, of a dichotomous I and thou, of an existential binary and its illusionary optativity of either/or,

CHAPTER FOUR

or in terms of the historical progressivists' (whether metaphysical or materialist) dialectic of a now and a then. The intimations of our mortality are not reducible to an antiphonous duet intoned as the dirge of being and nothingness. Our mortifications are daily, but they are no more unrelenting than our sempiternal superventions. It is through the indomitable impulse of immortality and its scribal acts (supremely exemplified by Paz as writer and eloquently instantiated by Paz in the writing)—it is through this impulse and its attendant acts of insurrection that "we perceive, almost as a sensation," the certitude of our mortality. Yes, we are mortal as historical beings, says Paz, but our history is constituted by the perennial other, the countercurrent impetus of immortality. And if death as other constitutes us in turn, death is only made possible by virtue of life. For Paz, of course, death is not just an end line, a matter of eventual ultimacy, but an institutional warrant to be overcome through ruse, subversion, laughter, and critical verve in our cultural and political lives. Referring to the particular history of his own region, a reference that obviously has great potential and undeniable precedent for generalizability, Paz writes: "Our history is infested with strongmen, just as the waters of the Mexican Gulf with sharks, and our intellectual history with heretic-burning canons, with decapitating Jacobins, and Marxists with a jail warden's vocation."[3] The abdication of critical and self-critical heterodoxy to the orthodox monody of *any* ideology implies necessarily a capitulation to a mortality whose death in life, as history demonstrates, becomes fatal by contagion or by the deliberate transference of one's own death sentence unto the other. And the fatality of that projection is not merely a risk but all too often a ghastly reality of human disappearances, torture chambers, and mass graves.

Nor is Paz cavalier when it comes to the politics of gender. His reference to "the supreme experience" of the other as embodied in woman is not the flippant gesture of a chauvinist. Rather, it epitomizes Paz's urgent concern for difference, a concern that would have us be ever-mindful of the incommensurability of equality and identity. To fall into the latter in pursuit of the first translates into another form of capitulation of difference, into an abdication of otherness and the fateful aggravation of conditions one seeks to redress. Some two decades ago, in September 1970, Paz articulated as much in an interview with Rita Guibert at Cambridge University, where, at the time, he held the Simón Bolívar Chair of Latin American Literature:

ARBORESCENT PAZ, INTERLINEAL POETRY

> . . . equality doesn't mean identity, homogeneity . . . what distinguishes us is what unites us. We ought to conceive of society as an association of complementary opposites, the chief opposition being between masculine and feminine. I'll go further: I think that from the interplay of masculine and feminine a new and hitherto undreamed-of culture and creativity might arise. . . . When a society presents the masculine as its sole archetype, violence and distortion results . . . women have had to adapt themselves to this model; by masculinizing herself, woman has become deformed . . . Western civilization should be feminized. . . . Our men should be more feminine and our women more masculine. . . . The true revolution would consist of women imposing masculine and feminine archetypes on society, and men seeing ourselves in them.[4]

Difference, then, is the indispensable requisite that enlivens otherness—the necessary other, not necessarily of one's own truth but of one's necessity. In the history of Western culture, within and against which Paz often writes, such difference is a radical desire, suspect because it tends to question the historical impulse for sameness and identity, for homogenization and self-privileging, but a difference desired, nonetheless, because it may be the only deterrent to the centripetal impulse of territoriality and usurpation of the necessary other. Paz's is a scene of instruction from which we are to come away with a "poetic generosity," and by "poetic" we should understand not an idealized abstraction but an experiential mode of everyday living and the array of its pragmatic entailments. We are enjoined to dwell poetically, not merely within a philosophical dwelling as prescribed by Martin Heidegger in his discussion of Hölderlin[5] but with a self-critical capacity and a disposition beyond nostalgia (enablements countermanded by Heidegger's own historical, experiential life, *pace* his philosophical wisdom). Paz, then, would have us live a life, as he himself has exemplified, that critically opens up to difference, alterity, and the indispensable other.

Within the multiple alterities that constitute Paz himself, one cannot miss a continuity between political engagement and poetic practice. The critical differentiation that obtains in one carries into the other. In fact, Paz would more than likely look askance upon such schematization that would have the poet juxtaposed with the political man. "Yes," he would allow, "I

Chapter Four

am same and I am different." But we would have to understand that this is a constancy of "same" founded on otherness, on a vocation dedicated to life-enhancing criticism and difference, to the insurrectionist acts of immortality these make possible. In keeping with this monitory appreciation, Paz's poetry must be read in the spirit of a differential poetics that *it* makes possible by assuming such enabling conditions for its edifice and edification. Paz's scene of instruction, then, is a site of writing whose declared necessity makes it not a primal but an ever-alterior scene of transgression, a self-transgression that opens a breach in its fortitude, that parts its waters to allow a passage to the other within and to the other who might venture in from without. On this writing scene, we encounter a poetry whose verses point to the diversity between the furrows they occupy on the face of the page, between the masked facades of their impagination. And in this sense, too, Paz not only writes such poetry, but, as reader, he also teaches us to read accordingly. In a note he wrote on 12 April 1972 on the occasion of an art exhibition by the painter Adja Yunkers in Cambridge, Massachusetts, Paz lays out the alterior but simultaneous ways of the creative process, whether in painting or writing, or, inextricably, in reading. Paz's note is entitled "La invitación del espacio" and is deliberately echoic of another poet of spatial and ideological transgression whose sententia Paz cites in his commentary—"si l'on obéit à l'invitation de ce grand espace blanc" (Stéphane Mallarmé):

> Two attitudes: to re-cover the canvas, the wall, or the page with lines, colors, signs—configurations of our language; to discover in their nakedness lines, colors, signs—configurations of an other language. To tattoo space with our visions and obsessions; to heed what the empty wall says, to read the blank sheet of paper.[6]

But the creative artist, writer, or reader faces a paradoxical predicament in the sheer plenitude that belies the nakedness of wall, the emptiness of canvas, or the blankness of page that threatens to overwhelm with the abundance of possibilities. As Paz himself has often demonstrated, most dramatically in his simultaneously plural *Blanco*,[7] the two options he posits here become incrementally compounded with their own and with each other's otherness in the execution. The first, re-covery(ing), proves a palimpsestuous act whose transparencies betray indelible opacities of otherness with inalienable claims to simultaneous coexistence; and, the second, discovery, becomes at once an encounter with "configurations of an other language" *and* a confrontation with the critical reflection, an inverted mirror image of our countenance in the *vultus mercurialis* of the would-be blankness. The multifariousness in each of these options endures yet another compounding in the dilatory realization that the two options cannot be exercised in turn or discretely. A mutual implication in their alterities bedevils their duplicity into yet an other "in/mediation" and critical heterodoxy. The critical mediation, the discriminating intrusion, comprises necessarily a selectivity, a negotiated and provisional election. And the process itself chastens us in compensation for the inevitable curtailments of our critical mediations. In this sense, the artist's, writer's, reader's enterprise becomes a "via negativa." "But," notes Paz, "the *via negativa* is not passive. Criticism is a creative operation, the negation is active. An inversion of values: less becomes more" (*In/mediaciones*, 243).

In this economy of compensation where one must yield in order to harvest a yield, "asceticism, negation, criticism: all of these terms could be deceiving. The critical-creative operation assumes, alternatively, the form of convocation and of provocation. Convocation is a receptive disposition in the face of space; provocation is a transgression: a breach, a violation of space. Convocation and provocation are attitudes that insinuate themselves in the dialogue between contemplating and making" (*In/mediaciones*, 244–45). Let us hasten to bracket the alternative quality of Paz's pro-/con-vocation, for, in practice, these are not "alternative forms" but indivisibly enmeshed alterities. They are spatially superimposed and entwined, temporally simultaneous and comingled, as Paz's own work often illustrates. These are operations that function as fused coefficients, just as the horizons of critical subject and object of criticism fuse in the performance of "contemplation" and "making."

Contemplation is performative, and "making" is no less a contemplative exercise. Just so, "convocation" has no fewer provocative entailments. And within this myriad arena of contending otherness, acts of painting, writing, reading, and acts of political engagement become critical acts, that is, acts that mediate and differentiate. They are all implicated engagements of a poetic constellation, all committed to a *poesis,* a performance that *makes for* a particular social and cultural dwelling. Where does this

CHAPTER FOUR

dwelling occur? On what ground(s) does its dweller come to reside? What articulates dwelling into community? What poetic economy, that is, what "house rules," legitimate those binding articulations? These are critical questions whose responses require critical performance; which means, of course, that one cannot come to rest on a particular response that does not entail the germination of yet another coefficient, yet another act, yet one more alterity to compound the plurality of the heterocosm. To halt on a given response more than provisionally would be to arrest creative impulse, to petrify political will, to exchange poetic dwelling for ideological dungeon, to subsume otherness into oneness in fatal narcissism, to cannibalize the living in order to apprehend life.

Octavio Paz's career has been a relentless struggle and constant admonition against such monism, a moral struggle carried on through political actions, through his diagnoses of his country's history, and through his poetry.[8] A rebel by vocation, Paz has always been wary of revolutions and revolutionaries because of their inexorable penchant for falling into the monisms of self-justifying ideology. He has not winced from pointing to the history of Mexico's own revolution as a supreme example. His disdain for its institutionalization into a one-party system with an imperial presidency is as unremitting as his condemnation of what he refers to as "Stalinisms," whether of the left or of the right, whether in the satrapism of our "civilized" institutions or in the petty Caesarism of the Caribbean and of Central and South America. He has censured such terrorisms, whether perpetrated by the state or by the individual self-righteous, with equal vehemence.

The fall into such institutional or individual acts of immediation means reducing our historical existence to single-minded obsession, into a-historical abstraction of a metaphysics that dehumanizes and converts human dwelling from life-enhancing performance to deadening and deadly deformation: "If it is history and not metaphysics that defines the human, we shall have to displace the word *to be* [*ser*] from the center of our preoccupations and replace it with the word *between* [*entre*]" (*El ogro filantrópico,* 52). Paz's poetic persona and its moral force dwell, as he would have us do, in the interstices of this ambiguous threshold and its heterodox mediations. To "dwell poetically," then, means to dwell nomadically. "To be" [*ser*] must derive from an ontology of exception. Community, even an academic one, ought to imply the communing of differential alterities, its members bound by supple articulations, its economy responsive to the supple diversities of plurality, its cultural and political ecology resilient enough not only to withstand but also to engender a heterology capable of infusing orthodoxy's scleroses with heterodox vitality.

Ser [to be] is a sterile copula, *entre* [between] a prepositional convocation, but no less a provocative injunction whose imperative verbal urgency invites entry of/into the other. *A Tree Within*,[9] Paz's latest poetic collection, figures a passionate and compassionate invitation to partake of a tree of life, to dwell in the midst of a poetic genealogy, to commute between root and branch, between verse and obverse, in a commuting that commutes sentences of monomaniac judgment, and interdicts the *dicta* of a fixed idea, that banishes the claims of arborescent taxonomy and the inflexible order of its scansion tables. Paz's arbor is a dwelling to be entered and not an elemental tree by which to decline and parse historical existence and poetic filiation into the taxidermy of a prosaic grammar or a prosodic system. Divided into five parts, *A Tree Within* proffers a quintessential branching, an indexical handful ("un manojo") that reaches out with prolific roots from the seminal syllabary ("sílabas semillas") of its convocatory "Proema." The five parts of the volume are appropriately entitled "Sheaf" ("Gavilla"), "The Open Hand" ("La mano abierta"), "A Sun More Alive" ("Un sol más vivo"), "Seen and Said" ("Visto y dicho"), and "A Tree Within" ("Arbol adentro"), which includes the title poem. A germinal progression marks this titular unfolding, unmistakably, culminating in the fraternal credo of eros and solidarity of the final poem's declarative "Coda." This last poem, perhaps the finest in the collection, is fittingly entitled "Letter of Testimony" ("Carta de creencia").

Between proem and coda, Paz negotiates an intricate communion, an elaborate conversation with the dramatic personae of his poetic itinerary and its itinerant dwelling: Roman Jakobson, Matsuo Basho, Sor Juana Inés de la Cruz, Hsieh Lin-Yün, Kostas Papaioannou, Alberto Lacerda, Marcel Duchamp, San Juan de la Cruz, José Lezama Lima, John Donne, Joan Miró, Roberto Sebastian Matta, Chuang Tzu, and, among others, the myriad prosopopoeia that is Octavio Paz. It is a motley crew with which to take to sea, and its motliness is symptomatic of the multifarious syllabary that mans the poet's crossing: "se embarca en un barco de / papel y atraviesa, / durante cuarenta noches y cuarenta días, el mar de / la angustia nocturna y el pedregal de la angustia / diurna" ("boards a paper boat and crosses, / for forty nights and forty days, the night-sorrow sea and the day- / sorrow desert" [3; 7 in the original]). Casting off unto the lapidary and

CHAPTER FOUR

nocturnal wilderness of the white page, the poet's paper vessel must convey "the migrations of millions of verbs, wings and claws, seeds and hands; / the nouns, bony and full of roots, planted in the waves of language" ("las migraciones de miríadas de verbos, alas / y garras, semillas y manos; / los substantivos óseos y llenos de raíces, planta- / das en las ondulaciones del lenguaje").

Like its alluded scriptural prototype, Paz's is at once a spiritual and a historical, that is to say, a poetic pilgrimage that *makes* and *re-makes* its way within the echoic wilderness of spectral solitudes and between way stations of otherness, a passage through "la idolatría al yo y la execración al yo y la / disipación del yo; / la degollación de los epítetos, el entierro de los / espejos" ("the idolatry of the self and the desecration of the self and the dissipa- / tion of the self; / the beheading of epithets, the burial of mirrors"). There is a persistent and eerie other-worldliness to the worldly itinerary of this pilgrimage, a haunting precognition that any *ars vivendi,* as we have noted in Paz earlier, serves as perspicuity into our mortality, into life's inevitable other; art's insurrectionist acts shade into preparatory essay for an *ars moriendi.* The collection's final poem, "Carta de creencia" ("Letter of Testimony"), to which I have already referred, broaches the subject explicitly. Here it becomes clearer than ever that for Paz the art of life is an amatory art, an erotic commitment to the fullest extent. In the end, the question becomes "El arte de amar / ¿es el arte de morir?" ("The art of love / —is it the art of dying?" [153; 171 in the original]).

But to return to the "Proem" for a moment longer, we have there an insistent interment and vertiginous descent that hauntingly searches for the genealogical ascendancy of life's poetic dwelling, its versicles sifting down like particles of sand onto the desert-page, its restless resting place. The inward arborescence enciphered in the title, "A Tree Within," has at once a descendental rather than a transcendental trajectory. Thus, the triple "vertigo" of the proem's first couplet, each in affiliation with body, fortune, and death, that lead one, shut-eyed, to the edge of the precipice and to the early morning stroll in subaquatic gardens. Poetry as life, clearly, must embrace life's spectral other side: "A veces la poesía es el vértigo de los cuerpos y el / vértigo de la dicha y el vértigo de la muerte; / el paseo con los ojos cerrados al borde del despe- / ñadero y la verbena en los jardines submarinos" ("At times poetry is the vertigo of bodies and the vertigo of fortune and / the vertigo of death; / the walk with eyes closed along the

ARBORESCENT PAZ, INTERLINEAL POETRY

edge of the cliff, and the verbena / in submarine gardens" [Weinberger mistranslates "dicha" as "speech." I return the term to its original "fortune"]). At the end of this proemial overture and submersion, what remains is the unseen, the unheard, and the unspoken in life that now, in art, must comprise the rest of the book's commemorative multitude, which is comprised, in turn, by the parentheses of eros and an other life (or other lives) that bracket its genealogy. This is an eros of solidarity, an eros fraternally proffered rather than self-directed: "el amor a lo nunca visto y el amor a lo nunca oído / y el amor a lo nunca dicho: el amor al amor" ("love of the never seen, and love of the never heard / and love of the never said: love of love" [so thoroughly has Weinberger botched this coda of the "Proem" that I choose to ignore his rendering altogether here]). And this love disseminates itself in the italicized *"sílabas semillas"* scattered from the Proem's invocation into and between the verse furrows of the book's subsequent pages.

A spectral symmetry haunts in the ensuing syllabary that germinates from this seeding. As with the "Proem," the focus in the poems of this collection also falls on the liminal, on the wilderness of *entre* rather than on the domestic hegemony of *ser*. Take the first poem, for example. It is dedicated to Paz's friend Roman Jakobson and was occasioned by the distinguished linguist's death in 1982.[10] As an elegiac apostrophe, it addresses the activities that consumed Jakobson's peripatetic life, activities so intimately reflected in Paz's own. The poem meditates on the harvest of a long career that chose poetic dwelling as its vocation, a meditation on what remains after all is said and done. The poem is entitled "Decir: Hacer" ("To Say: To Do" [In the Weinberger translation not only is the title excised and substituted by the poem's first line, but the original poem, *en face,* is also stripped of its original title and given its first verse as heading!]). The prosody is intricate, and it keeps its semantic vigil through the doubled period—the colon—that hinges the verbal infinitives in the title. This simple punctuation mark would obviously mean much more than its conventional usage as convocatory aperture to exemplum, citation, or ratio to the signaled linguist Jakobson. At Jakobson's wake, one could say, Paz transforms the colon into a prosodic Jacob's ladder, a column on which he articulates the limbs and verbal extremities of a poetic edifice. It becomes quite clear that in this bipartite poem poetic vigil is tantamount to bifrontal wakefulness, an alert watch that turns on dia-critical hinges, now to the

Chapter Four

declarative inter-dictions of "decir," now to the conversative inter-actions of "hacer," to weave both terms into the watchful prosopopoeia of poetry's own masks. The anaphoric insistence and incremental repetition of the initial quartet yield their dialectical oscillation between alterities, at least provisionally, to the precarious constitution of poetry itself:

> Entre lo que veo y digo,
> entre lo que digo y callo,
> entre lo que callo y sueño,
> entre lo que sueño y olvido,
> la poesía. (11)

("Between what I see and what I say, / between what I say and what I keep silent, / between what I keep silent and what I dream, / between what I dream and what I forget: / poetry" [5].)

Provisional and precarious are characterizations that inevitably describe poetry's predicament in which the quatrain reaches its caesura; and poetry's interstitial genesis occupies a most fleeting position. Its locus proves a slippery ground on which poetry slides, slipping from the stanzaic shuttle of alterities that constitute it into the liminal betweenness of the predicates:

> Se desliza
> entre el sí y el no:
>   dice
> lo que callo,
>   calla
> lo que digo,
>   sueña
> lo que olvido.
>   No es un decir:
> es un hacer.
>   Es un hacer
> que es un decir.
>   La poesía
> se dice y se oye:
>   es real.
> Y apenas digo
>   *es real*,
> se disipa.
>   ¿Así es más real? (11–12)

("It slips / between yes and no, / says / what I keep silent, / keeps silent / what I say, / dreams / what I forget. / It is not speech / it is an act. / It is an act / of speech. / Poetry / speaks and listens: / it is real. / And as soon as I say / *it is real,* / it vanishes. / Is it then more real?")

The form of the poem itself follows the slippage, with the squared block of the initial quartet sliding into a ladder or step formation. The interactive terms of *hacer* ("to act") slide to the right of the margin; the declarative variants of *decir* ("to speak") hang plumb to the left. The poem, then, forms a stepladder that leads to dissolution and to the ontological querying of poetry's own reality at the foot of the poem's part one—"¿Así es más real?" ("Is it then more real?").

Dispelled as predicative declaration, as "saying/doing," in the dissipation of its reality, poetry re-turns, as it always does, in the second part of the poem to shuttle, once again, between alterities and, thus, to weave and unweave its graphic syllabary, its seminal inscription in the eye of the page and in the page of the eye:

>   Idea palpable,
>   palabra
>   impalpable:
>   la poesía
>   va y viene
>   entre lo que es
>   y lo que no es.
>   Teje reflejos
>   y los desteje.
>   La poesía
>   siembra ojos en la página,
>   siembra palabras en los ojos. (12)

("Tangible idea, / intangible word: / poetry / comes and goes / between what is / and what is not. / It weaves / and unweaves reflections. / Poetry / scatters eyes on a page / scatters words on our eyes" [7].)

Like our social commitments and political engagements, then, poetry is beheld but not arrested; it is beholding but not beholden. And poetry's own

CHAPTER FOUR

dwelling is in poetic intervals, on interlineal throughways, through nomadic way stations. Poetry's composition occurs as *poesis,* as "making" that traverses the composures of diction, a traversal through opaque verse and that opacity's ob-verse—white space—where poetic making ("hacer") and declarative deed ("decir") conjugate and converse as interlineal versification. But here, too, the resultant poem cannot, ought not, succumb to a static self-composure, to a self-identity, to the spectral narcissism of *ser* as ontological copula that binds and petrifies. True to poetry's vocation as a transgressive interaction, the poem must become an occasion for poetic dwelling as heterodox nomadism. In this sense, there is an uncanny and unmistakable consonance between poetry as occasion and occasional poetry in *A Tree Within.* For Paz's collection consists primarily of *vers de circonstance,* occasioned for the most part by the most implacable reminder of our fleeting nature, our inexorable nomadism, our mortality. *A Tree Within* is an extended elegy to poetry and poets, to poetic dwelling and its interstitial habitation between othernesses of temporality and poetic careers. This genealogy, this family tree, then, resonates as a multifarious conversation with and among limbs, members, radicals of a nomadic tribe ("gavilla" means this, too). *A Tree Within* becomes an occasion of communing in which poets (and readers) hear from one another, but they do so neither in echo, nor in spectral reflection. They remain, indeed, other to themselves as they do to each other, and nowhere is Paz more obvious and emphatic on this differential intermediation than in his elegiac apostrophe to the Cuban poet José Lezama Lima. "Refutación de los espejos" ("Refutation of Mirrors") is the title of the poem that commemorates Lezama's passing through the looking glass of Lezama's own words, emphatically intercalated into Paz's poem through italicization:

> Ya entraste en *el espejo que camina hacia nosotros,*
> el espejo vacío de la poesía,
>   *contradicción de las contradicciones,* ya estás en la
> casa de las semejanzas,
>   ya eres, a los pies del Uno, sin cesar de ser otro,
> idéntico a tí mismo. (52)

("You have now entered *the mirror that comes towards us,* / the empty mirror of poetry, / *contradiction of contradictions,* you are

already in the / house of similitudes, / already at the feet of the
One, you are, without ceasing to be other, / identical to yourself"
[My translation; the poem has mysteriously been rendered a
spectre altogether, alas, in the book's life in English.])

Paradoxical doxologist of the paradoxical, Lezama, perhaps more than
any other contemporary of Paz, elevated the vocation of poetic dwelling to
exquisite proliferation of alterities. America's "Poet Unbound," and unbounded, Lezama exemplified for Paz the poetic possibilities of shattering
all mirrors and loosing the myriad crystal fragments to pursue their magnetic constellations. His *Fragmentos a su Imán* reached Paz in xeroxed
manuscript form just after Lezama's death. In Lezama's poetry, Paz finds
an undeniable instance of freedom from the hubris of specular appropriation and mimetic representation, a freedom from narcissistic reflection that
in poetry translates into deadening self-seizure and in politics into deadly
ideology:

> Los espejos repiten el mundo pero tus ojos lo
> cambian: tus ojos son la crítica de los espejos: creo en
> tus ojos. (52)

("Mirrors reproduce the world but your eyes / transform it: your
eyes are the critique of mirrors: I believe / in your eyes.")

This is the unorthodox belief, an investment in *critical* speculation
rather than in reflection's dogmatic proprietariness, that has guided Paz's
mediations and crossings from otherness to otherness, a vocation of building invisible bridges that breach intangible and interminable facets: *"Un
puente, un gran puente, no se le ve"* ("A bridge, a great bridge, is not
visible")—Lezama's words that Octavio Paz had read fifty years earlier and
now incorporates into his commemorative poem. These are words Paz
clearly took to heart and, as he confesses:

> Desde entonces cruzo puentes que van de aquí
> a allá, de nunca a siempre,
> desde entonces, ingeniero de aire, construyo el
> puente inacabable entre lo inaudible y lo invisible. (50)

Chapter Four

("Since then, I cross bridges that go from here / to there, from never to always, / since then, engineer of the air, I construct the / interminable bridge between the unheard of and the invisible.")

And yet, as the fourth part of this five-part collection attests (it is entitled "Visto y Dicho"—"Seen and Said"), Paz's long career has been as much an exploration of visibilities—on canvas, stone, and screen, in museum and in archaeological monument—as it has been of language and its audible cadenza. Language and image and the graphic conjugation of the two form the lapidary elements that shore up the poet's bridges in the air, his poetic vocation of agon and Luciferian jester fading between mutabilities of apparitions and disappearances. Or, as Paz's apostrophe to Lezama reads:

> Tú dices que lo *lúdico es lo agónico* y yo digo que
> lo lúdico es lo lúcido y por eso,
>   en este juego de las apariciones y las desapariciones que jugamos sobre la tierra,
>   en este ensayo general del Fin del Mundo que es
> nuestro siglo, te veo . . . (50)

("You say that *the ludic is the agonic* and I say that / the ludic is the lucid and so, / in this game of apparitions and disappear- / ances we play on earth, / in the general rehearsal of the End of the World that is / our century, I see you . . .")

The nine poems dedicated to the visual arts in this fourth section all fade from visibility into temporality; the clausura of each punctuates a permutation, a transmigration, one could say, into fleeting apparition that dances into otherworldly diaphaneity. The climactic coda of the last of these poems draws the poet himself into its elemental house of haunted vigilance, where he goes on painting his poem in simultaneity with the painter's wakeful watch in the painting:

> hay que construir sobre este espacio inestable la
> casa de la mirada,
>   la casa de aire y de agua donde la música duerme,
> el fuego vela y pinta el poeta. (133)

("we must construct the house of glances over this dubious place, / the house of air and water where music sleeps, fire keeps watch, and / the poet paints" [113].)

The poet had already wrought his own invisibility, his own transmigration into apparition at the end of the collection's third part—"Y fui por un instante diáfano / viento que se detiene, / gira sobre sí mismo y se disipa" ("And I was, for a moment, diaphanous, / a wind that stops, / turns on itself and is gone" [85; 102 in original]). But the collection's title poem that opens the concluding part spells the poet's real *passion*. For it is here that the poet becomes consubstantial with poetry and his life becomes coincident with poetry's tree of life. Like Lezama's entry and passage through the looking glass of his words, Paz becomes at once the embodiment of the tree and its fertile ground, its radical uterine vessel and radical ("rhizomatic," as we would say in Greek) arborescence. The poet Paz and Paz the poetic persona conflate as never before. Poetic dwelling as life practice and the poem's own habitation (that "house fairer than prose," as Emily Dickinson would have it) now engage in communal convocation that beacons us to partake of the communion, for it is our partaking of it that enlivens its fire, animates its passion, and gives words to its silence.[11] And it is here that poetry dawns, in the betweenness of our otherness, in the fugal conjugation of our alterities:

>   Amanece
> en la noche del cuerpo.
> Allá adentro, en mi frente,
> el arbol habla.
>   Acércate, ¿lo oyes? (137)

("Day breaks / in the body's night. / There, within, inside my head, / the tree speaks. / Come closer—do you hear it?" [115].)

CHAPTER FIVE

FUENTES AND THE PROFANE SUBLIME

History's Apostrophe

Among today's Latin American writers Carlos Fuentes may well be the most elaborately articulate on the issue of fiction and history. As novelist and cultural critic, Fuentes incorporates the same critical and theoretical problems of history and fiction into the elaborate plots of his novels. His most ambitious project along these lines to date has to be *Terra Nostra*.[1] By focusing on *Terra Nostra,* I should like to elucidate some of the ways by which Fuentes appropriates, accommodates, and exploits the classical strategies of historical narration, poetic voice, and the problem of the narrator's own historical present in the act of presentation. As a poetic strategist, Fuentes is a centripetal gatherer who conflates the seemingly discrete elements of author, reader, narrator, and narrative into the historical occasion of tale telling. In that convocation he acknowledges a long tradition of poetics and historicism, making some of his key characters visitations of historical rhetors who return to haunt in the pages of his own

CHAPTER FIVE

works, uttering the same perplexed propositions that confounded them in their other lives and former avatars.

An *apostrophe* is a turning away, a *parabasis* a turning toward. In the first, authorial voice abandons privileged omniscience and impersonal narration to address someone, usually someone absent, directly. This results in rendering the absent individual present in the convocation. In Fuentes, the apostrophe is often directed at the reader, and the consequence of that appeal is the attenuation of distance between the narrating persona in the text and the putative reader outside the narration. The diminishment of this separation serves to make the reader part of the story and the reader's circumstance part of the tale's history. In the case of a novel like *Terra Nostra*, the effects of this strategy underwrite the plural possessive in the title, which overtly seeks to incorporate the reader into a family history.

The inclusion of the reader into a story that leaves no one out becomes akin to the ancient dramatist's manner of breaking down the formal barriers between the structured world in the play and the happenstance world of the audience. This maneuver is called *parabasis* and was commonly employed by the authors of Greek Old Comedy. The chorus would remove all masks and address the audience directly, usually on the author's behalf, on matters relating to the story in the production.

In *Terra Nostra* Fuentes makes use of these strategies and in the process manages to tell a tale that is also our tale—and to tell, too, about the tale's telling. Thus, like the bare-faced chorus of Greek Old Comedy, the author, pen in one hand, the mask in the other, with sanctimonious iconoclasm enjoins us to read history's tale as it might have been writ. History's tale, then, becomes the tale of history. In that specular procession, the self-manifestation of writing as mirrored reversal turns history's doxologies into pivoting palindromes, exposing its truths as a mask of constructivist discourse. Writing's own apostrophe, then, unmasks history's written homily, leaving it barefaced to speak to/of itself as plotted and plotting strategy.

Another way put, history's tale is the tale of history's writing, and writing's self-knowing imbues the historical tale with its own self-recognition as object and subject with concrete historicity. Fuentes's terrestrial family history, with the force of solidarity in the possessive of its title, then, is a poetic construct that "understands" itself poetically through the strategies of digression and apostrophe. In the historical plots it narrates, it forces history (by acting as its other and as its mirror) to understand itself historically. When a history, or any text, understands itself historically, it must abdicate any claim to universal truth, lest it be the time-bound, contingent truth of its own historicity. We shall see presently how this proposition unfolds in one of the versicles of *Terra Nostra.*

Before we embark on that exegesis, however, I should offer a word of caution. While some of the foregoing observations may well evoke, and with great justification given Fuentes's readings, the itinerary of post-Heideggerian hermeneutics,[2] lessons in reading specifically from the Hispanic tradition make more immediate claims on Fuentes's allegiances. I refer to undeniable precursors such as Unamuno, Ortega y Gasset, and, especially, Américo Castro. From Unamuno, Fuentes inherits a historical sensibility whose focus is on "the man of flesh and blood" rather than on abstractions, and whose historical perspicacity is modulated by "the tragic sense of life." From Ortega y Gasset, Fuentes, no doubt, learned to shun "being," or "essentialist metaphysics" and to look, instead, at the processes of becoming, to view history as constituted by acts, achievements, and the vicissitudes of becoming realized. Sartre, some years later, would distill this historical insight into the existentialist apothegm "existence precedes essence." Unamuno and Ortega conflate in Fuentes's most immediate precursor on historical understanding, Américo Castro. In Castro's accommodation, these historical theories are figured into the key metaphors of *vividura,* vital experience, and *morada vital,* dwelling place of life. The dynamic resonance in these metaphors is the register of stress, a register that led Américo Castro to read Hispanic history as "la edad conflictiva," "the conflictive age," and to view pluralism and multivocality as a salient trait of Spain's past. Rather than elevating a structural *center* or singular norm to the status of governing principle and proceeding to expatiate on history as the process of approximation and divergence from that locus, Américo Castro turns his historical gaze on disparates, on otherness, on the strife of contending alterities.

This gloss of immediate antecedents may help us understand the poetic strategies and discursive pronouncements deployed by Fuentes, particularly as they relate to that connubium between the poetics of literature and the poetics of history. As poet—and Fuentes is more prosodist than prosist—he, of course, skews the programmatic philosophies that may underlie and inform his enterprise, often twisting them into compensatory reversal, specular inversion, and metaphorical exacerbation. Poetic self-subterfuge, however, frequently represents another mode of affirmation, and the stratagems of misdirection cannot be read literally. Nor can we always accept the author's discursive pronouncements at face value. The quotient of authorial self-delusion is potentially as great as the ploys of a self-interested poetic operation. With these caveats in mind, we can proceed to elaborate on the claims of our overture.

I began by calling Fuentes a centripetal sensibility. The epithet must be qualified vigorously, even though it accurately describes the plots of his literary corpus. The vertiginous movement of Fuentes's narratives toward a center figures as overcompensation—as reaction formation, some would say—for a historically determinate *excentricity*. The eye of the narrative whirlwind is a ubiquitous pivot, analogous to the center of Pascal's sphere, and the historical determinacies of this ubiquity that circumscribes all centeredness are descried by Fuentes himself in his essay *La nueva novela hispanoamericana*.[3] This incisive study, barely one hundred pages long, encompasses the most significant figures of Latin America's contemporary fiction as well as the Spaniard Juan Goytisolo. While the insights offered by Fuentes are as acute as any critical statement on the new novel, the essay may be just as revealing as a self-diagnosis. In this sense it is truly an essay, as Montaigne would have us understand the term. In *La nueva novela hispanoamericana,* a critical discourse that I believe we should read as apostrophe in/on the author's own novelistic itinerary, Fuentes points to the oft-stated notion that Latin American literature is "ex-centric." It is so by virtue of belonging to an antipodal New World, by virtue of being written in an Old-World language that derives from a culture which itself is ex-centric to its European context. Ortega's patrimony resonates here, reminding us of his *Invertebrate Spain,* where Ortega, who had read deeply in Europe's historical canon—Renan, Nietzsche, Dilthey—echoes the Eurocentric shibboleth that Africa stops at the Pyrenees. Américo Castro resonates significantly here as well. Spain, he taught, is a conflictive plurality, alien to the European model of historical framing.

Fuentes offers us yet another indication that Latin America's maelstrom of discourse and deluge of language figure as a compensatory gesture. In a scene of writing as linguistically prodigious as Latin America, Fuentes discerns "the lack of a language," ("la falta de un lenguaje" [30]). Again, a cautionary aside: Though tempting, and even inviting when one considers Fuentes's familiarity with contemporary poetics and theoretical discourses, we cannot consign this absence to the *mythologie blanche* of Derridian grammatology. Nor can we claim without some qualification that the swirling tides of what we observe as linguistic prodigiousness figure a Heideggerian pilgrimage "on the way to language," in Heidegger's expectant phrase. Fuentes's discernment and self-diagnoses are more empirically radical, that is, more pragmatically rooted and, therefore, radically revisionary as opposed to metaphysically visionary.

And at this juncture, too, we need to ascertain, as does Fuentes, the conjugation of poetics and history: Splenetic de-nunciation as unmasking, as historical parabasis, constitutes a long tradition in Latin America that extends back to Bartolomé de las Casas, the Dominican friar who, in the sixteenth century, baptized the genre in the New World. But, in Fuentes and the new novel, *denunciación* can no longer be circumscribed simply as ideology's compensatory gesture of vitriolic garrulity. The rhetorical apostrophe as historic unmasking now surpasses the boundaries of denunciatory disclosure and emerges as *radical* supplement, not merely as release and ancillary completion but as critical and problematizing revisionism. Here is Fuentes's own characterization of this revisionary enterprise: ". . . the critical elaboration of all that remains unsaid in our long history of lies, silences, rhetorics, and academic complicities. To invent a language is to articulate all that history has kept silent. A continent of sacred texts, Latin America feels the urgency of a profanation that might give voice to four centuries of sequestered, marginal, and unknown language. The resurrection of lost language demands a diversity of verbal explorations that today is one of the signs of health of the Latin American novel" (30).

The urgent "profanation" of "sacred texts" by Fuentes and his fellow Latin American writers translates for Fuentes into the desecration of what he terms "the fatal univocality of our prose." Fuentes, no doubt, means historical as well as novelistic prose, as he indicates in this essay as well as in others, e.g., *Tiempo mexicano*[4] and *Cervantes o la crítica de la lectura*. That profanation becomes equivalent to what Fuentes calls, invoking Umberto Eco, "la apertura," an *overture,* an opening and an opening-up to *ambiguity*—another of his Américo Castro-inspired key terms. Overt

CHAPTER FIVE

profanation, then, entails the undoing of sacralized and petrified order, the sundering of immutable essentiality into the desultoriness of possibility. This decentering and demystification imply, too, the indefatigable destructuration of structure, that is, of the rhetoric of literary and historical discourse, into the contingency of event. Or, as Fuentes puts it in a citation from Paul Ricoeur, "the ceaseless conversion of structure into event, and of the latter into the former, within discourse" (33). The matrix of this operation, Fuentes tells us, is *la palabra,* "the word." *La palabra,* as any speaker of Spanish, particularly one with Mexican insight, might tell you, can carry out the duty of decentering operations that Fuentes would like it to, but it is also a most ambiguous, a most equivocal word in its own lexical right. *La palabra* is archeuphemism for all connotative contingencies that decorum dictates be euphemistic. Archcontingency of profane contingencies, then, Fuentes's choice of matrix for an iconoclastic project of profanation speaks to us of the experiential and vital antecedents of his historical and historiographic disposition. It reveals, too, the precursor poetics of his agon as poet/novelist.

Fuentes's poetic apostrophe in the homilies of *Terra Nostra* points unmistakably to a line of filiation that extends well beyond the binary reductions of structuralism and beyond the poststructuralist arithmetic of Paul Ricoeur invoked by Fuentes. It points to that long line of itinerant and timely contingency which we could call the profane sublime, an inheritance from Longinus (himself a forefather with an all too ambiguous and hotly debated identity), an inheritance that comes to Fuentes, I would speculate, through the mediation of Mexico's foremost classical philologist and Fuentes's teacher. I am referring to Alfonso Reyes, though I predicate my suspicion of his being an intermediary on circumstantial evidence rather than on unimpeachable proof. But we can claim with the certainty of textual corroboration that Longinian poetics figure prominently in the pages of *Terra Nostra.* That filiation obtains in the Stoic tesserae penned by Theodorus of Gadara, scriptor of Tiberius, whose chronicles haunt throughout this novel where he and his master dwell as characters.

The historical Theodorus of Gadara was a rhetor who had a great impact on Longinus. He was also the teacher of the historical Tiberius Caesar, on whom, alas, he must have had only a negligible influence.[5] Theodorus was the nemesis of Apollodorus of Pergamum, a "puritan" formalist whose rhetorical abacus would reach a paralyzing overload when pushed beyond the strictures of traditional rhetorical calculus: proem, narration, argumentation, peroration. We know Apollodorus's rigid propaedeutics and formalist orthodoxy through Quintilian. Theodorus of Gadara mounted the greatest challenge against this structural rigidity. The shape of their debate no doubt rings all too familiar in the institutional and critical discourses of our academy, which makes their contest as timely for us as it has been for historiographers and students of poetics of all ages. Rhetoric for Apollodorus is an *episteme,* a science, and the poetics of discourse is a matter of invariable structural rules. Theodorus, on the other hand, considers rhetoric an art, a *techne,* certainly with a canon, but one that has the necessary suppleness for accommodating contingency, otherness, variability of circumstance, and the timeliness of differing situations. Longinus dramatizes the antitheses for us in his treatise on The Sublime.

But Fuentes is too artful a Theodorian to appropriate these counter-postures with Manichean rigidity. He does personify the Apollodorus position by the trivial Cecilius. He himself articulates the *techne* of Theodorus. Longinus predicates sublimity not on sacred structure but on profane event. His key is *kairos,* a fundamental lexis of contingency and appropriateness. The semantic range of the Greek term may be as broad as the variabilities of timeliness it connotes.[6] A gloss that points toward the circumstantial, the opportune moment, the fit situation, may suffice for our purposes. I might mention just one more ploy in Longinus that wills its relevancy to Fuentes, as we shall see. I refer to the use of the direct, first-person address aimed at the second-person listener or reader, a second person ideally "present" in the narrative as ploy. The overt frame of Longinus's treatise is epistolary. He is ostensibly writing a letter rather than a treatise. In his periphrasis on the strategy of switching from the first-person narration to a second-person-singular address, Longinus points to the premier of historians, Herodotus, as the most admirable exemplum of that device.[7] With studied understatement, or sublime *meiosis,* Longinus calls his peripeteia a *digression.* Our more earthly poetics teaches us to recognize the procedure as an apostrophe.

The ways in which this timely sublime finds its apostrophic accommodation in *Terra Nostra* reveal another masterful Theodorian at work. Fuentes simultaneously dilates and intensifies the eventuation of historical

CHAPTER FIVE

structure into circumstantial timeliness and contingency. His strategy consists in undermining established historical order through a tactic of hypallage, a rapid exchange of traits that precipitates the conflation and superimposition of historical subjects. The extended frontiers attained through that ploy constitute the new perimeters of definition for the occasion. The result is the exacerbation of historicity to a point where history must become meaningful to itself in its own circumstance in order to justify its existence. This is another way of saying that history becomes metamorphosed into its own parabasis to speak to us directly, in the second person, as apostrophic discourse. Here is Theodorus in Fuentes's novel voicing the problematic circumstance of this historiographic strategy:

> A man like myself, who understands these things, must, nevertheless, choose between two attitudes as he writes history. Either history is merely the testimony of what we have seen and can thus corroborate, or it is the investigation of the immutable principles that determine these events. For the ancient Greek chroniclers, who lived in an unstable world, subject to invasions, civil wars, and natural catastrophes, the reaction was clear: history can concern itself only with what is permanent; only that which does not change can be known; what changes is not intelligible. Rome has inherited this concept, but has given it a practical purpose: history should be at the service of legitimacy and continuity; future chance must support the act of founding.[8]

Caught between the "immutable principles" that legitimate Roman order and the circumstantial events that chance has made coincident with his own time, Fuentes's Theodorus, like his historical prototype, opts for the contingent and timely over the legitimating formal structure of the timeless. "Before these truths and these disjunctions, I choose to be witness to the fatal chance represented by my master Tiberius" (689). Having decided to chronicle profane event rather than investigate sacred structure, Theodorus emplots his chronicle as an epistolary testimonial, oscillating between first-person narration and second-person-singular discourse. Thus, a rhetorical *techne* endowed by the historical Theodorus to the "kairoian" or profane, that is to say, time-bound sublime of Longinus, becomes reappropriated by Fuentes for his Theodorian persona in *Terra Nostra*. Here, once again, is the apostrophic periphrasis of Theodorus writing itself over its own writing:

FUENTES AND THE PROFANE SUBLIME

> I, Theodorus, the narrator of these events, have spent the night reflecting upon them, setting them down upon the papers you hold, or some day will hold, in your hands, reader, and in considering myself as I would consider another person: the third person objective narration; the second person of subjective narration; yes, Tiberius's second person, his observer and servant; and only now, in the seclusion of this cubicle filled with piles of paper . . . I can consider myself, in the solitude that is my spare autonomy, first person. I, the narrator. (687)

In this catachrestic hypallage, this strained exchange of subject, authorial persona becomes superannuated into the paper identity of a narrating voice. The predicament points to a fundamental problem: Whether a formal structure be sacred cipher, legitimating principle, or discursive episteme of rhetoric, its destructuring into event leads to the ultimate problem of the instrument of destructuration. At this problematic juncture, writing focuses most explicitly upon itself as *factor,* just as history's narrator "digresses," as other to himself, in order to voice his own mediating role. The event of history or the poetic event becomes entwined with the agency that mediates it for us, the addressed, second-person-singular reader. The liberation of event from structure may well set "the word" or the narrated historical act afloat to be experienced as circumstantial and "timely" incidence, or as *vividura,* in Américo Castro's idiom. But that transgression from a normative and immutable center into desultory variability implies another necessity, one that we could term the necessity of circumstantial entailment.

I suspect Fuentes's insight into this vital dimension, made necessary by variability of circumstance, is paramount in his poetic decision to render Theodorus of Gadara a Stoic outright. The necessity of the variable is certainly consonant with the Stoics' *eimarmeni,* translatable as fate or necessity, the *manifest* reason of God, knowable in nature as circumstantial wisdom, or that part of the divine reason which finds its manifestation in human reasoning. Stoic wisdom may be God-inspired, but it is worldly wisdom, subject to accommodations of human contingency and to one's self-apprehensions as knowing subject in the real world. *Kataleptikai fantasiai* is how the Stoa characterizes this concept of knowing, and the object of knowledge—whether historical event or poetic operation—becomes subject to the mediations of knowing and narrating in any given time and circumstance.[9] This inevitable mutability as the necessary consequence

CHAPTER FIVE

of poetic and historiographic mediation elicits from Theodorus one of the most suggestive parabases in Fuentes, one in which anyone putting pen to paper might easily share: "My stoic spirit dictates to my hedonistic hand the last words of these folios, and I say that in every good action what is praiseworthy is the effort; success is merely a question of chance" (698).

The historical Theodorus of Gadara lived during the epoch of ascendancy of the third Stoa, and, from what we know of his work, we can detect significant Stoic elements in his *techne*. But, in pointedly characterizing Theodorus as "stoic spirit with a hedonistic hand," I suspect that Fuentes conflates the fate of this Caesarean preceptor with the baneful circumstance of a later Caesar and his Stoic tutor: Nero and Seneca. Nero's artful decadence and lurid paranoia are visited upon Tiberius in the plots of Fuentes's novel, as is the emperor's irrepressible wish to see Rome succumb to all-consuming conflagration and dissolution, to the *ekpirosis* that early Stoic doctrine held to be a periodical occurrence, a doctrine that Nero no doubt usurped with perverse embellishment from his Córdoba-born Stoic teacher. Theodorus's cataleptic lucubrations evince the unmistakable tone of Seneca's confessional, valetudinarian ruminations in the *Epistulae morales*.[10] Seneca's remarks on literary style and authorial responsibility echo Theodorus's digressions on historical writing and narration. The epistolary form, with its putative, second-person-singular subject, certainly construes with the confessional appeals directed to us, the intended readers, by Theodorus.

The fictional transfiguration of these historic and historical personae ultimately constitutes a poetic strategy on Fuentes's part. The cloying apostrophes deployed through the novel's various writing characters (from among whom we can only discuss Theodorus on this occasion) at some point might be read as authorial ventriloquy. In the cunning eloquence of that artful mutism, we can read Fuentes's own circumlocution, his own authorial apostrophe as it relates to his own historical circumstance. At this level, Fuentes's predicament does not differ, poetically or historiographically speaking, from the predicament of his scriptor characters. The Stoic's nagging queries also assail Fuentes: How and how much can one know of one's own history when that knowing itself figures as a crucial movement in that history? The implacable force of the question proved fatal for Seneca. For the Theodorus in Fuentes's novel, it translates into stoic catalepsis and, ultimately, into random desultoriness. In a poignant insight that speaks so clearly of Seneca's tragic circumstance, Theodorus avers: "I know that my questions imply a temptation: that of acting, of intervening in the world of chance and placing my grain of sand upon the hazardous beach of events. If I succumb to it, I may lose my life without gaining glory" (689). Unlike Seneca, Theodorus only intervenes historiographically, a mediation that may not "change" historical events but certainly one whose discourse inevitably *makes* history, the generic history of *Terra Nostra*'s plot; for Theodorus's writings unfold in Fuentes's homily as mantic curse and dreadful prophecy. Thus, Theodorus writes his chronicle in triplicate, places each manuscript in a bottle, and consigns the three bottles to the indeterminate tides of the sea. Their recovery and reading is the writing that constitutes one of *Terra Nostra*'s narrative threads. In Seneca's suicide, so pointedly reminiscent of Athens's *pharmakos*, and in Theodorus's dissemination into randomness, perhaps we could glimpse an instructive parable that adumbrates our author's problematic circumstance.

Seneca's interventionist experience proved to be overreaching. His ambiguous role in the Pisonian conspiracy of A.D. 65 led to his excruciating death. As Tacitus tells us (*Annals*, 15.60), Seneca was denied the tablets on which to write his final testament. Fuentes's Theodorus, in one of his last testimonials on history, would appear to be redressing that privation as he offers what on that fateful occasion might have been denied to posterity: "The true history perhaps is not the story of events, or investigation of principles, but simply a farce of specters, an illusion procreating illusions, a mirage believing in its own substance" (699).

A pragmatic, experiential historicist in the mold of Américo Castro, Carlos Fuentes subsumes the historical postures rendered in his novel into poetic paraphrase. As Theodorian scriptor, he bears witness with a scrutinist's detachment. As iconoclastic paraphrast who would have history tied to human circumstance rather than sanctified in order to legitimate the sacral claims of overweening structures, Fuentes has not shrunk from discursive intervention. Aware that all historical claims are mediate, rhetorical events predicated on strategies of language and gesture, he has repeatedly questioned the sanctioning canons that would make vital circumstance and human event subservient to self-perpetuating historicopolitical order. In this sense, Fuentes's comments on the occasion of receiving the 1977 Rómulo Gallegos Prize for *Terra Nostra* could be read as an apostrophe on the apostrophes in that novel, an unmistakable instance

Chapter Five

of the destructuring of poetic structure into the eventfulness of experiential history. Fuentes averred on that occasion:

> In the final analysis, history too is an operation of language: we know of the past, and we shall know of the present whatever should survive of these, told or written.
>
> The history of Latin America seems to be represented by a mute gesticulator. We surmise, in the grimaces and blows of the orator, a clamor of grandiloquent speeches, proclamations and sermons, pious vows, veiled threats, unfulfilled promises, and trampled laws. . . . The gigantic task of contemporary Latin-American literature has consisted in giving a voice to the silences of our history, in countering the lies of our history with the truth, in appropriating to ourselves, with new words, the ancient past that belongs to us and inviting it to sit with us at the table of a present which, without that past, would be a rite of fasting. (I translate from the text of Fuentes's acceptance speech.)

The *repast* to which Fuentes convokes Latin America's contemporary writer all too often has proved a baneful banquet, fatal for some as it was for Seneca, cataleptic for the literary career of others. The tragic list is long, and the mock-Caesars have been and continue to be many. That sanguinary calculus is periphrastically figured into *Terra Nostra*'s family history as part of an awesome but all too earthly desultoriness. I refer to Tiberius's curse on the future inheritors of Rome, that is, the Latin countries: "And from this growing fragmentation let new wars be born resulting in multiplied and absurd frontiers dividing miniscule kingdoms ruled by less and less important Caesars" (694). Tiberius's curse, of course, is a backward projection. Its present actuality renders Tiberius an all too accurate seer, and his vision obviously has the vatic sublimity of his author's insight. What Tiberius foresees is what Fuentes sees, and the historical circumstance of that apperception is a tale that vindicates Tiberius's foresight with deadly accuracy. For what Fuentes tells is a tale of strife, a precarious human circumstance confronting ideological structures that prove much less than human in aspiring to transcend human contingency. If the sublimity of Classical tragedy issued from a confrontation between human circumstance and implacable fates ruled by transcendental and often-capricious deities, the profane sublime of modern history ensues from an unremitting contest between quotidian events of human survival and the self-enshrining idolatry of descendental structures seeking legitimacy through subterranean horrors.

The phantom presence of divine intervention in antiquity has found its modern counterpart in what Fuentes (on the same occasion of receiving the Rómulo Gallegos Prize) calls "the vampires that only prosper by night." In this sense, the homiletic *repast Terra Nostra* is simultaneously a banquet of family history and a ghost story. Its epigrams, particularly the first from Goya's *Los caprichos*—"What does that old spook want?"—make sure that we appreciate that fact. And when the scriptor Theodorus, whose master Tiberius Caesar is cursed with vampiric night vision, concludes that "true history perhaps is not the story of events, or investigation of principles, but simply a farce of specters, an illusion procreating illusions, a mirage believing in its own substance," his peroration is both haunted and haunting. Far from an attenuation of history into metaphysical illusoriness, symbolist absence, or academic exercise, Fuentes's ventriloquy darkly suggests what history proves to be: a deadly game. Certainly, if history is a *vividura,* a vital dwelling place, as Américo Castro would have it, its daily experience in most of Latin America is the *via dolorosa* that fulfills the curse of Fuentes's Tiberius Caesar.

I believe it was Friedrich Schlegel who characterized the historian as a *rückwärts gekehrter Prophet,* a prophet turned backwards. In *Terra Nostra*'s eschatological visions, Fuentes has gone Schlegel one better: He has turned his gaze backward to prophesy a future that is already our ambiguous present. Fuentes transforms historical structure into more than a *repast;* it becomes a movable feast of timely historicity—albeit an abominable feast, as we see even more explicitly in another narrative thread in *Terra Nostra.* That is the tragic plot of Spanish history and the historiographic tale of another scriptor—a fictionalized Miguel de Cervantes—on which I elaborate at great length in the final chapter of my *Questing Fictions* (Minnesota, 1986). Suffice it to say that neither history nor the plight of historiography fare any better in post–Imperial (post–Charles V) Spain than they did in post–Augustan Rome. And time only serves to exacerbate, through repetition, the baneful shape of history down to the apocalyptic year of the bimillennium, which is where Fuentes's novel begins and ends. That futuristic cataclysm harks back, once again, to the Stoic's *ekpirosis,* the periodic conflagration that changes the actors and the setting, but not the

CHAPTER FIVE

masks or tragic plots of history. In this regard, in a pointed periphrasis that is clearly aimed at two of modern historiography's greatest ideological programmers—Karl Marx and G. W. F. Hegel—Fuentes apostrophically characterizes the tale of history retraced by his own novel: "History was the same: tragedy then and farce now, farce first and then tragedy, you no longer know, it no longer matters . . . it was all a lie, the same crimes were repeated, the same errors, the same madness" (775).[11] Like the novel's ominous epigraph from W. B. Yeats's "Easter, 1916" ("Transformed utterly: / A terrible beauty is born"), Fuentes's peroration continues to hark to the profane voice of that sublime poet who records the terrible dangers that lurk in abandoning the timely human dimension in favor of overweening structure and ideology's mystified illusion, whether this be the ravished ideology of historical materialism or the ravishing materialist history of the freemarketeer.

Parturient Scripture: Sterne Rejoyceings

But, alas! . . . My Tristram's misfortunes began nine months before ever he came into the world.

—Life and Opinions of Tristram Shandy, Gentleman

I shall send these messages from my fleshly catacomb, I shall communicate with those who do not hear me and I shall be, like all minority, silenced authors, the rebellious voice, censured and silent in the face of the reigning languages, which are, not those of the other, not those that belong to us, but those of the majority.

—Christopher Unborn

If, as we have just seen in our discussion of *Terra Nostra*, Fuentes thematizes the profane sublime as the process of history, in his novel *Christopher Unborn*[12] he engages the time-bound process of historical sublimity as his own writing practice. In this regard, *Christopher Unborn* is tantamount to the linguistic performance of its own declarative acts and time-bound pronouncements. Or so one would expect, were it not for a delatory self-subterfuge scripted into the novel as an *altereffect*—of James Joyce coinage—that interdicts the commensurability of the work to its workings, of the book to its words. How this Fuentes novel undertakes such self-differentiation that makes it other to itself and that deliberately affiliates it with a scriptive genealogy extending from Cervantes through Laurence Sterne to James Joyce is what I aim to trace in this section. In the process, I hope to remark, as well, the political and polemical gestures that characterize, endemically, what I have already referred to as "minor literature" and what Fuentes's prenatal hero, in the epigraph above, ironically terms a language of "minority, silenced authors."

"A minor literature," Deleuze and Guattari tell us in their *Kafka: Toward a Minor Literature,* "doesn't come from a minor language; it is rather that which a minority constructs within a major language. But the first characteristic of minor literature in any case is that in it language is affected with a high coefficient of deterritorialization."[13] I shall take "minority" to mean in this context not necessarily, or solely, the ethnic or racial other, as is the case with Kafka the Czech Jew writing in German. Rather, I extend the designation to include a broader ideological and historical space of culture, a space-time where a people's *morada vital,* or "vital indwelling," has been "nomadized" from within and/or from without, by which I mean that its linguistic and ontological ground has been subjected to irremediable dislocations through colonial "de-terrants" that have deterred a colonized culture from its own course and means of unfolding and have deterritorialized the ground(s) on which such a process could *take place.*

Carlos Fuentes writes as a supreme exemplum of this "nomadic minority," and he does so with an implacable awareness that translates into splenetic hilarity. In the process, he deploys irony's subterfuge and writing's most subversive possibilities for deauthorizing messianic ideologies, nostalgic utopianism, and the language of colonial discourse, whether from the past or the present. It is telling, in this regard, that *Christopher Unborn* begins in a scatological "Kafkapulco" and wends its way to a ghastly laughter's "Karkajada" in the face of a Vietnam-style evangelical crusade from the north in the dismantled territories of what had been Mexican territory. I say what "had been" and I shall be saying what "will have been," because the fluid and heterodox reality in this novel's scripture figures as an unremitting oscillation between a past perfect of nostalgia (called

CHAPTER FIVE

romantic conservatism in the novel) and a future perfect of utopia and messianic delivery (referred to as Ayatollaism or Westering to Pacifica) that belie any possible perfectability.

In temporal terms, the story locates its events in the commemorative *annus mirabilis* of 1992. The narrative locus from which the tale emanates, in a manner tellingly reminiscent of Dickens's *David Copperfield,* is the prenatal memory of Christopher Palomar, as yet *no nato*—unborn—hence the novel's promissory and reflective temporal conjugations and verbal constructions. Christopher is conceived on the Epiphany (6 January) of 1992 in anticipation of his birth at zero hour on 12 October, "Día de la Raza," Columbus Day number 500, as a hopeful entry in a national contest of little Christophers. As the reader might anticipate, Fuentes's work abounds with genial gest(e): gesture, gestation, and ludigraphic gesticulation. The admonitory gestures of this expectancy and the uterine gestalt of genetic memory perform the ironic ventriloquy of this *opera genitabilis.*

Yet, this lightness of being has a density—historical and linguistic, ideological and nominal—that makes it unbearable, or one that can be borne only with the adversative bearing of a chiasmus, neither of whose terms is othered to exclusion. In the Heraclitan influx of this writing as conception and gesture, the multivalent promise and connotative value of acts of signification shade into one another, blending into a *chaosmos,* as Joyce would have it, that can never attain inalterable status or authorized stable place. The text, as a result, is perpetually rewoven. Its language unsettled, subjected to deliberate solecism and endless destructuration, it moves from dialectic to "polylectic" repercussion. The text's narrative under such conditions, rather than bearing a tale, bares its own bearing or performative gesture, which, of course, offers a tale in itself to those responsive to the text's invitation to a "ludic read" (133; "ludectura" in the original, 150), those addressed apostrophically throughout as "Elector" (impoverished to "Reader" in the English translation) as opposed to the type of readers caricatured in the novel (191–93, 200–201; 213–15, 222–23; the barb in these pages aims at the structuralist chic and the ideologically committed).

Thus, what the Irish minoritarian scripture of *Finnegans Wake* does to/ with the language of the English, Fuentes perpetrates on the Spanish language of his colonial patrimony as well as on the English of the evangelical empire to the north of Mexico. As with Joyce, Fuentes's iconoclastic verve is polyglotally subversive, with the target of its dismantling *razzia* shifting from any language(s) in particular to language as territorial grounding or as ontological substance, as *terra firma* or as *res proprius*. Joyce called this ironic desublimation in which even the most appropriate timeliness and situated adequation of the profane sublime feels seismic dislocation "the abnihilisation of the etym" (*FW* 353.22).[14] In the light of such radical deterritorialization, the slightest gesture, even the most conventional and circumstantial details come into sharp focus, begging the question of their own might-have-been-unproblematic status. In the case of *Christopher Unborn,* the very phenomenal existence of the book as an object triggers such considerations for "the Reader," for the *ludector* sensitized to the iconoclastic project of the text. And some of these considerations, by the way, are broached overtly in the narrative of the novel itself (e.g., 133; 150). If, for example, the conception and gestative life of the work is concomitant with the performance of its writing's enunciation, can the resultant object of/from the process, the book, still call itself *Christopher Unborn?* Christopher has been born by the end of the narration. If the narration has reached its natural end, an end beyond embryonic gestating, could it still term its object—its concomitant—*"Unborn"?* By conventional arithmetic and linguistic logic, no. But that it does so points to a deliberate catachresis, a studied non sequitur that betrays its own significance. This betrayal would suggest an unbreachable alterity between book as concretion, as reified completion, as a culturally institutionalized good, and writing as an indomitable, volatile, and uncontainable act unbound by/to the history, process, gestation, gesture of its own statements or end products, the *énoncés* of its enunciation. Writing's life, in other words, persists as alterior and ulterior coefficient in relation to its acts of signification and their by-products.

The book, then, leads a duplicitous existence, an equivocal life by virtue of being and not being the tantamount container of the writing purported to circum-scribe its contents. The convention of genre does not matter; it can be a novel or a history—"factual or fictual"—since the disjunction that obtains is not specific to generic class but is endemic to language and to writing. Joyce, again, betrayed a degree of characteristic hilarity and acuity when, in his punning manner, he alluded to *Finnegans*

CHAPTER FIVE

Wake in *Finnegans Wake* as an "authordux Book of Lief" (*FW* 425.20), with "orthodoxy" disrupted by the ducal intervention of an iconoclastic authorial intrusion. And the mythogenic authority of the Book of Lief, with capital privileges, is shattered by the exposure of the perjuring that gives the lie to its "Lief," that belies its genealogical and ontological truth. Laurence Sterne, too, echoes in this textual self-deauthorization, recalling the bottom line, the self-descriptive last sentence of Tristram Shandy's "Book of Lief": "A COCK & a BULL, said Yorick—And one of the best of its kind, I ever heard."[15] And Fuentes ironically echoes Sterne, in turn, with his own version of such a bottom line, that of the melic and sentimental Concha Toro, of her evolving persona and overripe person. "A CONCH & a BULL," Yorick no doubt would have it.

All this authorial winking brings up the further question of the name under the title *Christopher Unborn*. Is this "Carlos Fuentes" the "Carlos Fuentes" who will have figured on page 131 (149 in the original) as the author of a book "apocryphally entitled" *Christopher Unborn,* whose title obviously is a perfect homonym of the title of *our* novel? Does either "Carlos Fuentes" have any relation, other than homonymic, to the "Carlos Fuentes" of page 298 (324 in the original) of *our* novel (and maybe of the apocryphally entitled one as well) who, we read, will have been sixty-four years old in 1992 along with Shirley Temple and García Márquez?

And what are we to make of the publisher whose *sigilla* appear on the cover as advertence that the book has been published by Fondo de Cultura Económica, Mexico's has-been foremost publishing house? We are compelled to ask the question in view of the cultural and national *sfondamento*,[16] what the novel's narrative had chronicled as the foundering of its culture's fund of authorizing structures, the bottom falling out of its economy of foundations. Irony does not miss a blink at the fact that *Christopher Unborn* belongs to the "de-founded and de-funded" Fondo's *Tierra Firme* series! Heraclitus could have done no better had he been, as with Fuentes here, Joyce's or Sterne's avuncular accomplice in such mischievous punning. And, of course, the fact that the Xipe Totec, an avatar of Mexico's highest deity from the Maya classical period (A.D. 900–1200) on the book's original Mexican cover is owned by the Kimbell Art Museum of Fort Worth, Texas, with whose "authorization" he appears on this Mexican novel, is all too meaningful in terms of cultural expropriation, scriptural/

graphic reappropriation, and "re-authorization" from a deterritorialized locus of colonial displacement. One could only speculate that this too might well be another cover for the flayed deity that seasonally, sublimely, undergoes a change of skin in eloquent timeliness and placental "wrapture."

Proverbially, of course, we are not to judge a book by its cover. But conventional wisdom and literature's canonical conventions are precisely what have their cover blown by an unmasking scripture that brandishes its refusal to take cover in the decorum of authorized convention, and it does so, as already noted, by baring all that bears and is borne through its devices. Turning the cover, then, is not tantamount to turning a new page on revolutionary subterfuge. We transit, rather, to yet another phase of disporting with tradition's forms and the book-canon's etiquette. Fuentes does follow convention's protocols, but he does so with wile, with the conformity of a wily artificer who simultaneously complies and subverts, conforms with a ruse that holds a penetrating light to practices which convention has endowed with the privilege of being *pro forma* and with the authorization to pass unquestioned.

In this light, the vigilant reader will have found it impossible to blithely pass by the novel's dedication: "Naturally, to my mother and my children." ("Naturalmente, a mi madre y a mis hijos"). Its inscription, so natural, so obeisantly filial, so paternally obsequious, dedicates itself, as well, to conscripting, surreptitiously, an array of echoic insinuation that anticipates, proleptically, the myriad way-stations of the novel's itinerary. Naturally, this is all as naturally contrived as nature itself begins its cycle with insemination, the ostensible seed as etymon, as synecdochic microcosm that recapitulates nature itself, a dedicated beginning in which all subsequent peripety and radical dissemination is duly inscribed with expectant precision and sublime timeliness. "But, alas!" poor Tristram and Christopher might well exclaim, "the throwing of the seed, *ab ovum,* may differ little from Monsieur Mallarmé's hazarded dice!" Flung with full expectation of disporting with fickle contingency's spells and turns, Carlos Fuentes's inscription is hazarded in the hope that the putative *ludector* will design to follow suit and reJoyceingly venture into the "abnihilisation of the etym," and there recall the "etym's" own etymology, i.e., that *nature* is a nominal case predicated on the nascent action of birth(ing), borne by the light and lightness of being as incipient gesture, an ever-dawning *incipit* of *natura*

CHAPTER FIVE

naturans, a bearing in process whose dynamic performance has now become as natural as drawing life's breath.

And, no doubt, the inscription is hazarded with the confidence that the reader will not miss the elided Laius, the inseminating paternity oedipally secreted away from this primal scene. That elision, which invokes only maternity and progeny—"Naturally, to my [m]other and my children"—is executed with a finesse that makes the action seem second nature, almost. The sleight of hand, however, betrays its own dexterity, permitting the wakeful reader to grasp the phantasmal manifestation of at least one elided calamus whose graphic trace echoes as the ironic signature of the other amanuensis, one who inscribes his book's epigraphic overture with an equally echoic adverbial naturalness. That resonating absence reads: "Naturally, a manuscript." It is scripted by Eco, of course, and it germinates from his novel's epigrammatic seed into *The Name of the Rose.*

All of this graphic front matter—we could call it a promissory front—leads us to the "Prologue" and to the prologue's title page, which, of course, serves to protract and figures as an extension of the sinuated and "sintillating" foreplay. In this prolongation, this conceptual prolepsis in which prolegomena shade into Shandean paralipomena to undermine our canonical, readerly preconceptions, foreplay performs as novel conception ("and *vice versing,*" Shem Earwicker might pipe in). The performance is marked by unmistakable alacrity and agility, the "lightness" and "quickness" that Italo Calvino has willed to our next millennium as two of his six legacies.[17] This Shandean author of *Palomar*[18] is scripted into our novel in a poignant way, memorialized by Fuentes's narrator, who notes the coincidence of the Italian maestro's death in Siena with the killer earthquake in Mexico City on 19 September 1985 (39; 48). And, of course, Fuentes's hero carries the paternal surname of Palomar, surely a tribute to that perspicacious Palomar of Calvino's novel, who also has his novelistic inception on an Oceanic beach under the spell of an Edenic scene.

On the prologue's title page, Fuentes weds this agility to the profane sublime and its human timeliness, to the situatedness of experience in the vitality of becoming as dynamic process. The prologue is entitled "Prologue: I am Created" ("Prólogo: Yo soy creado"). The *nature* of this creation is overtly conditioned by the epigraph from Henri Bergson, one of the most articulate sensibilities of experiential sublimity, human life's *élan vital,* as he termed it, which animates ontology into process, being into becoming, centeredness into liminality. Fuentes's Bergson here reads: "The body is that part of our representation that is continuously being born." "Naturally," Mr. Eco might resound, "naturally." And the body in question is as much the palpable text stroked by the reading eye and the winking scriptor, as it is the love's body born of that desire which Christopher Palomar's priapic father declares "the most intimate, reactionary happiness" as he pants and blithers, slithering on the sand toward Christopher's supine mother-about-to-be, Edenically naked, except for her face, which is covered by a green tome that happens to be Plato's collected dialogues opened to the *Cratylus.*

Clearly, the novel's prologue is a textured and multivalent site where a primal scene of transgression conflates with a primal scene of writing, the two conjugated by/into a primal scene of instruction that refers to Edenic desire and to the endemic desire for a language of/for the world born into and borne by a family history and the familiar story of its multifarious romance (of the rose and of the name). In body and name, the generic tale is taken up and transformed into a song of innocence and experience, transported by Fuentes through historical counterappropriation of buggered *patria* (252–53; 276–77) and raped motherland (passim) to the embattled site of his native Mexico—land of departed but still-clamoring gods and seismic shifting ground: "'Mexico is a country of sad men and happy children,' said my father, Angel (twenty-four years old [*sic;* translation obviously ages one. Angel's age is twenty-two in the Spanish original]), at the instant of my creation." The angelic father at this creation betrays a Luciferian insight into history, a history of happy innocence and melancholy experience, an insight he is about to forego, overlook, and sublimate, driven by generic desire and engendering forgetfulness, possessed, as he says, by the most intimate reactionary happiness and its prehistoric, immemorial atavism.

Generic memory and historical knowledge—as usual with Fuentes plots—are the domain of the woman, who invariably remembers in generation and knows, too, that all knowledge, whether of past or future, is historical and commemorative. And—as in many such Fuentes plots— with the primal couple of this novel, too, man has a history he is prone to forget, while woman has none (52, 54; 61, 63, and passim). Yet, the only history that perdures is the one she knows or recalls. I suspect we can indeed extrapolate another minoritarian subplot of the other from this

CHAPTER FIVE

phenomenon, one based on gender as opposed to nationhood and colonial expropriation. One is hard put to placate the gnawing prescience that the generically usurped and historically dispossessed, like any alterity, is surely prone to hold on to whatever is left—the knowledge of loss, the private memory of (de)privation, and the public re-collection of official history's lapses and relapses. We shall return to this perennial issue more explicitly in the final chapter, "A Woman's Place," of this study.

Lapsarian is a decidedly apt characterization of the scene enacted by Angel the father and Angeles the mother on this paradisiacal shore of the Pacific Ocean in the shade of coconut palms and under the shadow of Plato's green tome. Lapsarian not in the sense of a fall from grace (too late for that already), but a falling into language—for Angel a language of desire uttered to the rhythm and frenzy, sense and nonsense, sound and fury of copulatory delirium, an oral and polyglotal ejaculation to complement the furor and release of what Walter Shandy refers to as the "animal spirits." For Angeles, the mother, falling into language is a falling into memory and into inter-rogation, a rogatory mediation of interstices where *her* history has been misplaced, between time(s), epochs, protocols, and trains of thought. Hers are interrogations that compel responses, even in the least opportune or least propitious moments (*"Pray my dear*, quoth my mother, *have you not forgot to wind up the clock?"* [*Tristram Shandy,* 1.1.35]).

From the narrative's first word, "Mexico," Christopher Palomar narrates himself, his "Book of Lief," into existence, narrating, naturally, the intercourse, linguistic and corporeal, of his (pro)creators. He narrates not only the articulation of their words and limbs, but also their soliloquies—mental and oral. Forged as much in the fever of loquacity as in the heat of fornication, Christopher Palomar becomes the consubstantial incarnation of his utterance. His enunciation, subsuming as it does the intercourse and interlocution of his conception, becomes the germinal word transmuted into flesh/text incarnate as bio/graphy. The ethereal, metaphysical sublime in the process of such genesis becomes profane sublimity, desublimated into the salt of the earth. Thus, the Platonic green tome with the seal of the National University of Mexico embossed on its cover—"THROUGH MY RACE SHALL SPEAK THE SPIRIT"—now bears the salty stain of the fornicating lovers' "Coppertonic sweat" (4; 11). And the idealist, historical vision of the university rector, José Vasconcelos, the intellectual guiding light of his epoch, the "teacher of the nation," who published Plato's dia-

FUENTES AND THE PROFANE SUBLIME

logues as part of the visionary program of Mexican nationhood in the post-revolutionary Mexico of the 1920s, now endures the ridicule of worldly history's perverse turns and intractable hazards. The utopian José Vasconcelos and the motto of the university seal both have their derisive inversion by the end of the prologue. The illustrious rector has his avatar in the avuncular tío Homero Fagoaga who flies over the copulating Angelic couple, defecating for fear of his life as he flees the guerrillas of the counterculture he dispossessed. As the scatological baptism of their conception rains on them, Angel and Angeles look up to see the celestial source of the effluence. The inverted motto now reads: "POR EL ESPIRITU HABLARA MI RAZA" (19. In the original Spanish, that is, for in the more hygienic English the inversion has faded into the invisibility of the Holy Ghost. It would have read, on what is page 11, "Through the Spirit my race shall speak."). Scatology and eschatology thus conflate into that effusion which is the outcome of the Spirit's teleological pilgrimage and end product of programmatic history's Hegelian progress.

So much for an ideal history in Mexico's institutionalization of its REVOLUTION (1910)—with capital privileges. In Fuentes's minoritarian book, that history figures as yet another "Book of Lief," this time of a collective, national "Lief" that petrified its revolution by grounding it on the mystified structure of a self-perpetuating and self-serving PRIvilege. (Fuentes is implacable in pointing up the absurdity of a nation's, his nation's, institutionalization of revolution into an apothecary's bottle as a potion for curing everything at all times. The PRI (Partido Revolucionario Institucional) for him has always been a paralogistic phenomenon founded on total obliviousness to the paradox it entails.) All of this cultural diagnosis and its not so implicit political critique is also embedded, synoptically, in the novel's prologue.

The prologue carries a semantic overload, certainly an ideological quotient, but also an aesthetic ideology, that is, the possibility of referring tautologically to itself, an ontological and epistemic self-ostentation. On that account, the *pro-logos* is an endorsement in favor of the word, rather than a tag to designate prefatory matter. "Prologue" as performative, in other words, might not merely be fulfilling the function of superscription for the text at the head of the novel. Rather, it might well be an "autograph," the subject of its topos, of this capitular text whose unfolding is chronicled under its name. Fuentes problematically suggests as much at one point as

CHAPTER FIVE

he verges on privileging language with a certain natural authority that places it beyond "political" ideology unto grounds of an aesthetic ideology: "the logic of the symbol does not express the experiment; it *is* the experiment. Language is the phenomenon, and the observation of the phenomenon changes its nature" (63; 72). Fuentes is paraphrasing Werner Heisenberg, to whose "uncertainty principle" he pays homage in his irreverent practice of deterritorialization. And while Fuentes borders the risk of territorializing language itself, the pragmatics of his iconoclasm and desublimation turn the verve of their irony on Fuentes's own language.

There is an implicit decentering mechanism in "minor literature" that targets its own potential self-privileging. The prologue, then, cannot be granted the self-engendering, tautological empowerment of its own practices, lest the word turn the conventionality and historicity of language into a naturalized system, into a natural necessity sanctioned by the nature of language itself. On that sort of ground a rose would be a rose, and the name would obtain inexorably, necessarily, *pro forma*. Then Cratylus would be vindicated in his naturalism, as would Gertrude Stein in her formality, and Hermogenes' conventionalism would be disproved, along with the rhetorical *techne,* the profane art and human contingency of Fuentes and Umberto Eco. In that eventuality, Angel, Christopher's libidinous father, would find his desire identical to his language, his *verba* identical to his *sperma,* his cantatory orality identical to his corporeal sensuality. But then he would have also found what proved impossible: the "suave patria" of Ramón López Velarde, found it not only in the word but outside the poem where he had gone searching.

National reality, in other words, would have imploded into a national and nationalist language, becoming consubstantial with its political and poetic rhetoric. Thus, Mexico's national history traced by the novel would have been entirely other. Rather, it would have *not* been "other" at all but would have been identical to the official language of its revolutionaries, rhetors, academicians, patriotic poets, even its novelists, and identical, in short, to the institutionalized discourses of its destiny. But, alas, Fuentes's novel and history's hazards demonstrate that the only identity or likeness in the course of the national becoming of the "suave patria" is a likeness to acts of its rhetorical destiny's betrayal, an identity only to the opportune and opportunistic turns, a mirror to the extortion of the patria's "impeccable

FUENTES AND THE PROFANE SUBLIME

and adamantine" purity, of its natural "identity to itself," as the poet of Angel's nostalgic search called it. But, while Angel inseminates Angeles in the aura of Ramón López Velarde's forgetful nostalgia and immemorial desire, Angeles conceives citing the *Cratylus,* impervious to the idealization of history and the naturalization of poetry and its language:

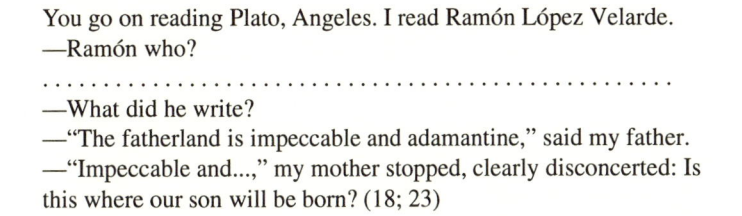

> You go on reading Plato, Angeles. I read Ramón López Velarde.
> —Ramón who?
> ....
> —What did he write?
> —"The fatherland is impeccable and adamantine," said my father.
> —"Impeccable and...," my mother stopped, clearly disconcerted: Is this where our son will be born? (18; 23)

The disconcerted interrogatory is one of three that Angeles persists in positing. In the previous two—What are we going to name the baby? What language will the baby speak?—Angeles betrayed an analogous suspicion of the naturalization of language, of nature's adverbial authorization and taken-for-granted privilege of whatever may be deemed to be "naturally" so. She is clearly not a Cratylian, though she read the *Cratylus.* Her triune inquiry threatens but does not manage to derail the single-minded course of Angel's enthusiastic "animal spirits." In her equally "multitrack mind" (5; 13), her triple train of thought is wary of what either nature or convention renders inevitable.

We can read in Angeles's attitude an allegory for the predicament of writing, for the fate of scripture as engendering agency and culture-bearing vessel. The *parabolic*—by which I mean both "symbolic" and "diabolic," gathering and sundering at once—lesson, which lies beside but never beyond the question, seems to me to be expressing the fact that those who must carry the geste, gesture, or gestation to term—terms of time and terms of language—are not wont to take the process for granted, especially whatever about it may be deemed natural or in the nature of things. For scripture as well as for maternity, nature, i.e.,birthing, begins with an articulate invasion of territoriality and eventuates in a dismemberment, an emptying out, that flushes onto-teleology and totalization into a partitive mood to pursue what is known to be irremediably unattainable but is ineluctably pursued nonetheless.

Chapter Five

And if I remarked earlier the feminine as agency of knowledge and as history's mindful bearer, I now find myself describing the viatic turns and vicissitudes of the historical process in terms correlative to the lesson of that lapsarian primal scene, at once transgressive, graphic, and instructive. This, at least, is how I feel compelled to read the gravid conjugation of Homer, Plato, and Xenophon in the prologue. And, as if such conflation did not distend sufficiently, or because it does so to such gravid excess, Fuentes adds the dilatory convocation of Sterne, Joyce, and López Velarde. As Shem Earwicker might quip, "Here Comes Everybody!"

If the first sentence of the prologue is attributed to the father, the second sentence extends beyond Mexican history to history's originary headwaters. It is uttered by Angeles, the mother-about-to-be: "Ocean, origin of the gods," a sighed utterance that intensifies further the father's apocalyptic longing for the climactic end-time in the impetus of his priapic desire. He turns Angeles's utterance into "coño origen de los dioses" (11, pruriently excised in the translation), as he crawls on his naked belly toward her. Her sigh also opens the floodgates of a Heraclitan river whose tributaries weave through the Western tradition's literary landscape and textual streams. Her commemorative, citational utterance floods the textual spring, the incipient fonts of this Fuentes novel, even as she flows lubriciously, orgasmically, to propitiate the generation of loquacious progeny (he is the one telling us all about it) and of the textual corpus that momentarily becomes the estuary and delta of all this loosed effluence.

Angeles's memorial utterance originates in the book covering her face. Literally under the spell and etymological spellings of the *Cratylus,* Angeles's citation conjures *Cratylus* 402b: "Oceanus, the origin of the gods,"[19] where Plato in turn is citing Homer, "Okéanos, from whom the gods arose."[20] Neither Plato's dialogue, nor Fuentes's novel, however, have theogony as their object. Rather, they both explore, *mutatis mutandis* (ineluctably), the nature of language and its relation to the world, to human kind's historical life. If the pattern of the Socratic dialogue is to undermine dialectically any definitive conclusion and to submit closure, instead, to the ruse of a *docta ignorantia,* the *Cratylus* is perhaps the most "genuinely," the least ironically inconclusive of Plato's dialogues. It is so, Socrates confesses, by virtue of the Heraclitan flux that inherently infuses language, the dialogue's topic of discussion, making the names of even the most venerable, mythologically sanctioned, culturally authorized ancestors synonymies of the Heraclitan influx and mutability. Socrates etymologizes with Hermogenes on the names of Cronus and Rhea, Oceanus and Tethys; all of them, he points out, bear names of streams. And by the end of the dialogue, in his attempt to mediate between Cratylus's position that names are naturally inherent and Hermogenes's claim that names are conventions of contingent circumstance, Socrates is forced to leave the issue open-ended, realizing that the Heraclitan flux infuses not only the topic but also the very terms of their discussion, obliging Socrates and Hermogenes to explore the etymology of the name of *name* itself (421a–c). *Onoma,* Socrates says, scans etymologically as a compression of *on ou zitima,* meaning "being for which there is a search" (421a). Related to the parsing of *name* is the etymology of truth (*aletheia*) and falsity (*pseudos*). Socrates insists that if *name* indicates a real existence for which there is seeking (*on ou masma*), *aletheia,* or truth, is also an agglomeration of seeking and motion—*thei ali,* "divine wandering" (421b). Falsehood, on the other hand, derives from stagnation, inaction, which compares to sleep, *eudein,* a word disguised to become falsehood by the addition of the letter *psi* as a prefix. Hermogenes, beside himself with excitement, is really carried away when Socrates points out to him the truth of the principle that being (*on*) is also moving (*ion*), and that not being, the cognate of falsehood—"it isn't so"—is likewise not going (*ouk-i-on*) (421c). In the end, then, being seekers of truth, Socrates, Cratylus, and Hermogenes must move on, keep trying to get somewhere, seeking after the names that are to be sought after by slipping definition, rather than alighting on a particular, decisive, authorized ground whose determinacy would, by definition, be a falsehood. Thus, Socrates defers to the Heraclitan flux, mutability, and indetermination or nonterminus.

Angeles, clearly far from being impervious to this Socratic paideia, is impregnated by its influx also on this thalassogenetic occasion on the shores of the Pacific Ocean. That is why, months later, in Mexico City, when she is employed by a division of the Ministry of Culture ("Secretaría de Cultura, Letras y Alfabetización, SECULEA"—the punned acronym in the original Spanish colloquially spells the false-passive mood, anonymous conjugation of the verb *culearse,* "to fornicate") to translate Shakespeare, to render him accessible to

CHAPTER FIVE

> proletarian neighborhoods (are there any other kind?) of D.F.
> DeeEff, DeFate, DeeForm, De Facto, Defecate, Dee Faculties
> her great success was the translation of *Hamlet:*
>
> 'To be or what?' ['Ser o qué?']
> But then she had to revise everything because perhaps she
> should have begun:
> 'To be here or not?' ['Estar o no'?]. (318; 345)

Even though the affected intellectuals of the post-punk Aztec-rock group Immanuel Can't fill the air with the din of their kant (*"The critique of reason puuure / For madnesss a sure cuuure"* ["La crítica de la razón púuuuura / Es el mejor remedio contra la locúuuuuura"]), Angeles maintains the presence of mind (always at least a triple train of thought) to change her hilarious translation of Hamlet's perennial ontological question from the essential verb *to be* (*ser*) to the locative, temporal, contingent, circumstantial ("and Heraclitan," Socrates would add) verb *to be* (*estar*): "Estar o no?"—which doesn't make it any less hysterical, naturally.

As I indicated already, there is an ample quotient of ReJoyceing in all this and, indeed, the last time Joyce conjured the Homeric notion cited by Socrates in the *Cratylus* was in *Finnegans Wake*. And it was a profanely sublime demythification, for "Oceanus, the origin of the gods" transmutes, diaphoretically, into "birth of an otion that was breeder to sweatoslaves" (309.12). There is little question about the *Wake*'s influence washing into Fuentes's scriptural Pacific shore, as we shall see more specifically. Joyce, of course, was as obsessed with Homer as Fuentes is, and the *locus classicus* for the Cratylian sententia can be found in the opening pages of the Telemachiad, the first episode of Joyce's *Ulysses*. And there, too, the Homeric mythos undergoes irreverent and scatological permutation: "The snotgreen sea. The scrotumtightening sea. *Epi oinapa ponton* [Over the wine-dark sea, *The Odyssey,* 2.420]. Ah, Dedalus, the Greeks. I must teach you. You must read them in the original. Thalatta! Thalatta! She is our great sweet mother."[21] In his characteristic display of brazen iconoclasm, Joyce conjoins Homer and Xenophon, thereby mitigating the epic sublime with a vehemently pragmatic desublimation. Xenophon's oft-uttered Thalatta! Thalatta! ("The Sea! The Sea!") connotes a bathetic end of Cyrus's *anabastic* expedition, in which Xenophon took part and chronicled in his *Anabasis*. Given the disastrous outcome of the expedition, the title itself resonates as a paradox, being as it is inadvertently ironic, and Joyce capitalizes on that irony to debunk epic heroism with impudent glee. Fuentes evidently follows suit, yoking, in the process, Homer to Xenophon via the *Cratylus*. While his irreverence may not be as shrill as Joyce's, Fuentes's irony is no less pointed for being more subtle: "you and I," Angeles tells Angel, " say 'sea' to refer to the 'sea,' but who knows what its real name is, the name the gods utter when they want to stir it up and say to themselves 'Thalassa. Thalassa. We come from the sea'" (5; 12). In this conflation, without anthropocentrically deifying humans, Fuentes humanizes the gods, imputing to them the Xenophonic utterance with its all-too-human pathos and paradoxical turns. (Xenophon's Attic double "t" is rendered into Athenian double "s" of Thalassa.)

But Angeles's question to Angel brings up another issue discussed in the *Cratylus,* one that concerns Homer, particularly in the *Iliad*. In book fourteen (line 291), Homer speaks of a bird "called 'khalkis' by the gods, by men 'kymindis.'" In book twenty (lines 73–74), he refers to a "mighty eddying river, / Xanthos to the Gods, to men Skamánder." The issue is language, as it is throughout Plato's *Cratylus,* and here the question of divine language versus human language specifically. Fuentes, in a persistent enterprise of destructuration and deauthorization of what is transcendent, mythical, and official, moves once again, through this section of the *Cratylus* (392a–393a) to press the historical, human dimension and to disprivilege the transcendent. We can only live human lives and with human language. As for the language of the gods and the differentiation that Homer is making in the *Iliad,* Fuentes would subscribe to Socrates' demuring, "Now, I think that this is beyond the understanding of you and me" (392b). But there is something within our purview, "the names of Hector's son [which] are more within the range of human faculties." Hermogenes remembers the lines (22.507), though he does not know which one Homer himself thought more correct, Scamandrius, which is what the Trojan women called the boy, or Astyanax, a name he was called by the Trojan men. Socrates queries Hermogenes: "And must not Homer have imagined the Trojans to be wiser than their wives?" To which Hermogenes replies, "To be sure." "Then," notes Socrates, "he must have thought Astyanax to be a more correct name for the boy than Scamandrius?" (392d). Hermogenes concurs and Socrates goes on to etymologize and demonstrate how "For he alone defended their city and long walls" (22.507)

CHAPTER FIVE

is a descriptive phrase of the etymons for Astyanax's name. Now, Fuentes subjects the time-honored wisdom of Socrates' and Hermogenes' discussion to an ironic subterfuge that foregrounds what for us and our time may almost be a commonplace, but for centuries since Plato has not been even an issue or, if it has been, has been subsumed and derogated by sanctioned wisdom, by official discourse. Here is Christopher's still spermatozoid narration, continuing where I stopped citing last:

> Blessed mother of mine: thank you for your multitrack mind—on one track you explain Plato; on another you fondle my father, while on a third you wonder why the baby must necessarily be a boy, why not a girl? And you say Thalassa, thalassa well named was Astyanax, the son of Hector. (5; 12–13)

What Angeles ironically pursues in her Platonic line of thought is the *Cratylus* 392–93, which we have just discussed. She is, in other words, explaining to the single-minded Angel, now utterly oblivious to everything except the fever in his testicles, the greater wisdom of the Trojan men, explaining how much more appropriate, according to Socrates, is the phallocentric language that has received its sempiternal sanction and natural authority since Father Homer's blessing. Angel's attention cannot be averted from his priapic fixation, from his enduring prowess and hardened privilege ("if you could only see how my Faulknerian chili pepper resists, it not only survives, it endures, it perdures, it's durable stuff" ["mi chile faulkneriano, no sólo dura, sobrevive, y no sólo perdura, es duro"—cf. "I believe that man will not merely endure: he will prevail," Wm. Faulkner, *Nobel Prize Speech,* 10 December 1950], 5; 13).

The irony, I should hope, is self-evident. Plato obviously never could have dreamed that he would have as reader and exegete of his dialogue on language not a Trojan man, not even a Trojan woman, but a Mexican woman with "no history," with only a circumstance all too distant in place and time, distantly reminiscent of yet another fallen Troy. Xenophon's interjection into this whole complex historicizes the epic mythos, and philosophical tradition has often juxtaposed Xenophon to his contemporary Plato in precisely such terms. Xenophon is consequential in this regard in more ways than one, and clearly Fuentes betrays an awareness of that significance. The *Anabasis* may be the first "historical" account written by someone on the losing side of the events historicized. Like Humpty

FUENTES AND THE PROFANE SUBLIME

Dumpty, what went up (*anabasis*) with Cyrus, came tumbling down (*katabasis*) along with Xenophon, and the latter's *Anabasis* is an attempt that we have come to identify with all the king's horses and all the king's men, not to speak of historians. Furthermore, Xenophon is known, too, for his *Cyropaedia,* a treatise on the rearing and education of leaders and statesmen, for which Cyrus the Elder serves as model hero. Interesting as it may be as a political treatise (it prompted Plato to counter with the *Laws*), the *Cyropaedia* offers a greater fascination to a novelist like Fuentes, as it did for Sterne, who emulated and satirized the work with Walter Shandy's interminable "Tristrapaedia," an obsession that led him to neglect the very Tristram he fathered while he pursued the composition of a treatise on how to raise and educate him.

What fascinates both Sterne and Fuentes, I believe, is the fact that the *Cyropaedia* may well be the first novel, since Xenophon employs the form of a historical romance. Originally considered a philosopher, as the historical events he narrated receded into the past, he was read as a historian. Now Xenophon could well be taken as a primal novelist. The eight volumes of the modern edition of the *Cyropaedia* figure as our first historical novel that discovered the possibilities of fictionalized biography. In a prologue such as the one devised by Fuentes for *Christopher Unborn,* it should not surprise anyone to encounter there the seminal conception not only of this novel but of the genre's own genesis. Xenophon, then, would have to head the list, as recapitulated prolegomenon, of that genealogy which Fuentes's novel charts for itself on page 134 (152 in the original), a genealogy whose congenital identifying mark has to be the circuitous waywardness, the dilatory wandering whose circumlocution and digressive restlessness seeks after the name—the *onoma, Cratylus*'s Socrates would say—that is a devious mirror to their seeking, a linguistic pursuit of language, a *scriptive pursuit* of scripture. Here is how Christopher Palomar characterizes the congenital trait of this family romance of family romances: "if the earth is round, why shouldn't a narrative also be round? A straight line is the longest distance between two words. But I know that I am calling in the desert and that the voice of history is always about to silence my voice" (189; 207).

The plaintive clamoring of Christopher's final sentence has proved groundless. History and its story may well be plotted on a linear trajectory, but history has never managed to leave behind its encirclements, spiral (Vico) or parabolic (Sterne). Nor has it managed to silence that elaborate

CHAPTER FIVE

circuitry's garrulous circumlocutions. If history is after a name for its trajectory, or if it pursues any motion worthy of claims to truth, then, Socrates would have to grant, history too must wander, seek, and *re-search* in keeping with its own circuitous etymon. That is why the genealogy which *Christopher Unborn* claims for itself consists of those works which literary history has seen fit to claim for itself despite their indomitable circum- and perverslocution, periphrases, and peripeteia that deride the very notion and grounds of canonicity. The list is to be found on page 134 (152 in the original), a page before the announcement in the limelight of emphatic characters that read, in the manner of Erasmus,

> *The Praise of Reading*
> *The Madness of Reading*

The proclamation is followed by a series of voices, an abbreviated cast from the family tree:

> Erasmus: Appearances are deceptive
> Don Quixote: Windmills are giants
> Tristram Shandy: Digressions are the sunshine of reading
> Jacques Le Fataliste: Let's talk about something else
> Christopher Unborn: Okay... (135; 153)

If I have dedicated what may seem a disproportionate part of my discussion to the ten-page prologue of this 563-page novel (in the original), it is because in its spiraling and parabolic circuitousness the novel enthusiastically *recapitulates* itself, by which we are to understand that it circles on (*not* back upon) its heady conception(s) and prologal headwaters, crossing, interpenetrating, and weaving into itself the incipient locus again and again. It does so not as *anabasis,* in other words, not as a heading upstream like Cyrus and Xenophon, and certainly not as *katabasis* like Humpty Cyrus and Dumpty Xenophon, but as a *parabasis,* which I discussed in the first part of this chapter with regard to *Terra Nostra* and the time-bound profane sublimity of parabastic history. Without unduly recapitulating myself, you will recall that at the head of the previous section of this chapter I characterized *parabasis* as a recourse employed to break down formal barriers between, on the one hand, the structured world of language, writing, discourse, play and, on the other hand, the happenstance, contingent, historical world and experience of the audience, reader, interlocutor. Through this recourse, for example, the author of Greek Old Comedy would recapitulate the historical life of the community that sustained the formal structure of his production *into* that production. He would do so by the destructuration of the comedy's form, by the de-authorization of its privileged territory. A common device for such transgression of form was the removal of the chorus's masks to address the audience directly on matters relating to the story and to the production. (Obviously at some point this recourse of unmasking itself became capitulated into the formality of structure by becoming established as *pro forma* procedure.)

Now, if a prologue traditionally serves to elucidate the conception of the work, Fuentes divulges that insight by sharing with us his readers, the *ludectores,* the conception's ploys and strategies not just discursively but *parabastically,* not just declaratively but through demonstration, so that the prologue does not speak to us of the novel's conception, but it conceives the novel and it does so as it unmasks its performance and procedures. However, Greek Old Comedy dates back a few years now, and a barefaced ruse is a ruse nonetheless and, like all time-honored procedures, a self-privileging one at that. We might say that a barefaced ruse is a ruse more than on the face of it. But this perspicacity, too, is divulged, as we have seen, in a self-directed irony by which writing reflects with a wink on its own alterity, lest it become an inadvertent dupe to the ruses that underlie and belie its textual "book of lief." Joyce's jabberwocky has rendered this self-punishing de-authorization, betraying his writing persona and his writing, letting us in on the spectacle as he "bespilled himself from his foundingpen as illspent from inkinghorn" (*FW* 563.5).

"This is vile work," admits poor Tristram, not without some wile, "—For which reason, from the beginning of this, you see, I have constructed the main work and the adventitious parts of it with such intersections, and have so complicated and involved the digressive and progressive movements, one wheel within another, that the whole machine, in general, has been kept a-going" (1.2.95). "Okay," says Christopher Unborn, going along with Jacques Le Fataliste to talk about something else. "[T]he limit to what a person can read is not the same as the limit to what that person can say, nor is the limitation of what is sayable a limit to the doable: this last possibility is the possibility of literature" (133; 151). Well,

CHAPTER FIVE

this is not exactly talking about something else, but the congenital something else, of course, is writing's alterity, which opens multifarious paths (always forking) that proscribe, with circumspection, the possibility of circumscribing scripture into paralytic territory. That would curtail its Heraclitan flux into authorized stasis—deprive it of its seeking motion, Socrates would say—that would take the truth out of its "lief," privileging it thereby, with the still life of falsehood. A good portion of Fuentes's novel is dedicated to chronicling and subverting such authoritative ideological and institutional mystification in Mexico's history (past and future). The passage I have cited here comes from one of *Christopher Unborn*'s recapitulatory turns, one of the "wheels within wheels" described by Tristram, except that in the case of this novel we do not have a wheel but an *ovum* within the novel that originates ostensibly *ab ovum* along with its protagonist in our much-discussed prologue. I say *ostensibly* for two reasons. First, because it is entirely likely that, like most prologues, this one too has been written after the fact, that is, after the novel's and its protagonist's birth, as I suggested earlier in my discussion of the novel's catachrestic title. In that case, of course, the entire enterprise is a *post-partum* conception. So much for the "sincerity" of parabastic ruses! Secondly, this twisted possibility is itself harbored, albeit deviously, even as the novel's ovoid recapitulation traverses and is traversed by the prologue. In that travesty, the text gives the lie to any claims of *ab oval* origination or *ab nihilo* etym, as Joyce would say, or even oceanic genesis, foamy, lapidary, or aquatic. This occurs most explicitly in part three, chapter seven (129–38; 147–56). There the narrative has us reading as the Cratylistically-named Huevo writes the novel he is writing the novel *in*, locked in a metal sarcophagus and uterine *ovum* (his "allwombing tomb," Joyce would have it):

> a novel seeks out its novels, the ascent and descent of its spermatozoon black ink: like the child, the novel is no orphan, it did not spring from nothingness; it needs a tradition just as the child needs a family tree: no one exists without something, there is no creation without tradition, no descent without ascent: CHRISTOPHER UNBORN philadelphically seeks its novelistic brothers and sisters: it extends its paper arms to convoke and receive them, just as the recently conceived child misses its lost brothers and sisters (he even misses the girl he might have been, which I give him straightaway: the girl named Baby Ba). (151–52)

FUENTES AND THE PROFANE SUBLIME

The graphic spermatozoon of black ink seminal to this genealogy has its figural symbolization, and is described here as "a spurt of black sperm, a spark of sinuous ink: life and opinions" (133; 151). The "life and opinions" are recognizably those of Tristram Shandy, Gentleman, and the sinuous stroke that flashes in Fuentes as ink sperm is unmistakably the flourish of Corporal Trim's walking stick that accompanies his declaration of celibacy's virtues:

> "Whilst a man is free,—cried the corporal, giving a flourish with his stick thus—

"A thousand of my father's most subtle syllogisms could not have said more for celibacy" (9.4.576. The flourish itself is brandished on page 132 of *Christopher Unborn;* 150 in the original). Corporal Trim, Uncle Toby Shandy's servant, is pleased with himself and satisfied enough with the flourish that becomes his declaration of independence from the advances of Bridget. As for Uncle Toby, he is content with gently laying down his pipe as Corporal Trim disabuses him of the underlying motives in the solicitude of Widow Wadman's attentive concern about Uncle Toby's groin wound. There is certainly very little of Fuentes's Mexican fire in these English gentlemen. And the irony of misappropriating a flourish declarative of celibacy's virtues as a spermatozoid whip is, of course, not lost on Fuentes. He compensates with vehemence for the twirl's gelded origin. His whole novel, after all, is a scriptive gesture of a spermatozoon's flourishing loquacity, whether testicular, *phallopaean,* or intrauterine.

Among Fuentes's greatest tributes to Sterne is one by way of avuncular Shandyism. I refer to the two avuncular characters who surpass even

CHAPTER FIVE

Tristram's Uncle Toby in their hobby-horsical hyperbole, Christopher Palomar's uncles, Fernando Benítez and Homero Fagoaga. The first is forgiven his critical and chronic irascibility because he is the Defender of the Indians in a country where Indians are vanishing and, at the same time, the territory of the nation is being decimated into parcels of "Indian territory," which makes it fair game for predatory multinationals and conglomerates. They invade with all manner of initials and babelian acronyms emanating from New York, California, Texas, or from Savannah, Georgia, as is the case with the Reverend Royall Payne and his evangelical Rambowar, directed personally by his devoted supporter, Rambold Ranger, also known as Arnold Anger, Dumble Danger, and the mastermind of the Gulf of Campeche Resolution. But Uncle Fernando and his obsessions are far outweighed by the gargantuan Uncle Homero, whose appetites are matched only by his exaggerated zeal for the preservation of the purity of the Spanish language and its defense from the constant threats "from the language of the Perfidious Albion and its perverse transatlantic colonies that contaminates the purity of our Castillian verbal inheritance" (103 in the original; part 2, section 5, to which this passage corresponds, has been excised in the translation. New Albion may rest in peace!). The only revenge is the countercontamination already well underway along with the "Mexican Reconquest from the Southwest." Unmistakably, Uncle Homero has earned the title of "Cid Lenguador," as well as his presidency of the Academia Mexicana de la Lengua Correspondiente de la Real Academia de Madrid.

Homero Fagoaga is endowed by Fuentes with the corporeality to adequately ballast the weight of tradition and with the necessary gravity of authority with which to champion the order of things as they were and as they were meant to be. James Joyce would have certainly seen in Uncle Homero his "Adipose Rex" (*FW* 499.16). And the illustrious Dr. Johnson, who quipped about *Tristram Shandy,* "Nothing odd will do long," would find him his own worthy counterballast in weight and in prophetic acuity. Homero Fagoaga's preservationist, conservative impulse shades into the cannibalistic, as his suggestive last name—"the admirable devourer"—etymologically avers. His appetites are, indeed, not only linguistic or oral but much more encompassing. And Fuentes takes every opportunity to display and deride this hypermetric and hypermetropic figure with a ravaging Greek last name and an oedipal Greek first name. On this account, Uncle Homero is stripped of his avuncular mask to expose his role as devouring father, Father Homer, the primal King Laius of the literary tradition. On Joyce's abacus, these hobby-horsical brothers echo Shem and Shaun Earwicker of *Finnegans Wake*, the perennial siblings who dialectically, antithetically, and often fratricidally keep human history on its circuitous course, or, as Joyce would have it, on its "vicous circles" (*FW* 134.16), or, as Fuentes twists it, on a course of "viciosos vicos: estrechos vícolos" ("vicious vicos: narrow straits" [551]). This is the vicarious spiral traced by the narrative of *Finnegans Wake*, modeled as it is on the periodic itinerary of Vico's *Scienza Nuova*. And this, too, is the current that carries the parabolic circularity of *Christopher Unborn*, conflating Joyce's wake and its own prenatal gestation in a continuous flow with Heraclitan circulation. And that is why the incipit of *Christopher Unborn*'s first chapter echoes the streaming current of the *Wake*'s primal headwaters:

> riverrun, past Eve & Adam's, from swerve of shore to bend of
> bay, brings us by a commodious vicus of recirculation back...
> (*FW* 4.1)

The "vicus of recirculation" resonates with Vico's name and notion of history, and the Latin *vicus* (alley, strait) of Joyce becomes the Italian/Spanish "vícolo estrecho" in Fuentes, as cited above. Joyce's "commodious" adjective—as always with Joyce—is too resonant for comfort (solely), and the scatological association is what Fuentes dilates, particularly in the prologue's "swerve of shore" and "bend of bay" of Edenic "Cacapulco" (220; 240). The streaming, midsentence first word, "riverrun" (according to some it continues the novel's last sentence), of *Finnegans Wake* transmutes into a current with weightier flotsam in *Christopher Unborn*, whose first chapter opens with "El Niño comes running up from Easter Island, tepid and sickly, the offspring of death by water" (15; 23). This opening mediates between the end of the prologue ("Homer, oh mère, oh mer, oh madre, oh merde origin of the gods: Thalassa, Thalassa....WELCOME TO LIFE, CHRISTOPHER PALOMAR") and the rest of the novel, which ironically begins with a deadly visitation from an island, coincidentally enough named after the Resurrection. It is an

Chapter Five

ominous influx washing the "Suave Patria" of Angel's Mexican poet that occupies the rest of the novel. The arrival of the child Christopher and the con-current arrival of the deadly warm Niño, which wreaked havoc with hemispheric climates and atmospheric conditions and, according to the novel, will have done the same ten years later in 1992, are conflated by Fuentes as a cycle of life and death from the very beginning (of the novel and of America's history). Fuentes plays on Columbus's etymological role and first name as *Christopherens,* the Christ-bearer, the bringer of the Christ across time and history's oceanic stream paralleled here with the Niño, the stream of death and destruction. We have, then, a rush of tides whose confluence precipitates the flow from "foetal sleep to fatal slip" (*FW* 563.10) into concurrent simultaneity. The "foetal sleep," of course, is the WAKEfulness whose memorial pronouncement echoes in the performance that is the novel we read. It is an immemorial wake and tide within yet without time, a gestation whose gesture recapitulates generic memory and genealogical history, all compressed into the congenital program of the embryo. Fuentes clearly subscribes to the idea that with birth all this memory reverts to a *tabula rasa* so that human history may recapitulate us in its Vichian spirals and circuitous course, and recourse, as the newborn begins the "fatal slip" that is the falling into life and onto the road out. And that is the tumble that Christopher Palomar will have taken, falling into life's profane sublimity and primal amnesia, slipping into inarticulate dis(re)membering at the end of his term and at the end of the original novel:

olvida todo olvida todo, o

l

v

i

d

a...............

In the Spanish verb "to forget," Socrates and Cratylus would be delighted to know, vibrates life.

CHAPTER SIX

INTERSTITIAL GARCÍA MÁRQUEZ

Between Milton and Tasso

*The World was all before them, where to choose
Their place of rest, and Providence their guide:
They hand in hand with wandering steps and slow
Through Eden took their solitary way.*

I begin with the closing lines of Milton's *Paradise Lost* by way of suggesting that *One Hundred Years of Solitude* is a catastrophe creation, that it is a postlapsarian topography through which an agonistic race wends its "solitary way." My invocation of the Miltonic coda does not originate in the caprices of strong reading. I take a cue from García Márquez and the locus of a writing scene whose interpretive key is identified in the novel as one that lies between Torquato Tasso and John Milton. Here is that disclosure as the García Márquez text phrases it:

CHAPTER SIX

> Melquiades revealed to him that his opportunities to return to the room were limited. But he would go in peace to the meadows of the ultimate death because Aureliano would have time to learn Sanskrit during the years remaining until the parchments became one hundred years old, when they could be deciphered. It was he who indicated to Aureliano that on the narrow street going down to the river, where dreams had been interpreted during the time of the banana company, a wise Catalonian had a bookstore where there was a Sanskrit primer, which would be eaten by the moths within six years if he did not hurry to buy it. For the first time in her long life Santa Sofía de la Piedad let a feeling show through, and it was a feeling of wonderment, when Aureliano asked her to bring him the book that could be found between *Jerusalem Delivered* and Milton's poems on the extreme right-hand side of the second shelf of the bookcases.[1]

A primal scene of transgression, *One Hundred Years of Solitude* also aspires to a primal scene of writing. Its reckoning is a millenarian arithmetic with a reduction by a factor of ten. An apocalyptic work that consumes its world, it is itself consumed by that consummation and, yet, perdures as graphic trace, as surplus of its cataclysm. The would-be paradox in this fate, however, becomes highly mitigated by tradition-bound mediations that conventionalize its strategic ploy. It has its franchise in a tradition of books that extend their lifeline(s) by being consumed. To that end, García Márquez appropriates certain writing strategies that convert two of the most notable figures of the Western canon into unmistakable precursors. Both Milton and Tasso are subsumed by his work as paraphs, by name and in procedure. They are privileged by the Colombian novelist as aleatory signatures that the text of *One Hundred Years of Solitude* would have us utilize for hermeneutical purposes against its own cipher. But the García Márquez text tropes these canonical giants into a *prosopopoeia*, into a *masked poesis* of its own poetic and rhetorical performance. In giving us a double key to his text and then twisting its skeleton, García Márquez introduces the necessity of our oscillation or shuttling between allegory and irony, between an other place, literally, and the misdirections of a cue that belies its own gesture. It is in the light of this elaborate turn that I venture to pursue a reading of this García Márquez on that problematic continuum which we call the prophetic tradition. Before turning to their tropical use by

García Márquez, I should like to rehearse selectively and in broad strokes a number of relevant commonplaces that pertain to our traditional characterizations of Milton and Tasso, after which I shall pursue, elliptically, their problematic subsumption by the Colombian Nobel laureate's ruses.

Our post-Romantic critical discourse has made abundantly clear that Milton's is a transdiscursive *oeuvre*. While the same claims may have not been made as elaborately for Tasso, his *Gerusalemme Liberata* (1581) might be as undeniably pivotal. Oscillating between the conventions of pagan antiquity and Christianity, between a Renaissance ethos and the radical ideology of the Counter-Reformation, and in problematically fusing the heroic epic to the romance of chivalry, Tasso may well figure as one of the most blatant examples of transdiscursiveness. His personal fate on that shifting and shiftless cusp took on indeterminate and often infelicitous turns, as has his reputation in posterity's ledger. He has been alternately viewed as heroic and religious or as superstitious and amorous. Like his ambivalent patron Duke Alfonso, many have seen him as a madman. His bouts of melancholia, his contrite effusions, his repeated confessions before the Inquisition, finally would prove so threatening to Duke Alfonso that he had Tasso chained at St. Anne's for as long as seven years. Caught between double paradigms that he could neither escape nor reconcile, he would become the howling prey of his ambiguous visions. Undaunted in his faith and in his faith in a "new science," he often would yield to a fascination with supernatural and magic forces. And yet, he would firmly believe that what escaped the explanations of the natural science must have the force of diabolical mystery. His implacable ambivalence would lead him at one point to the conviction that he was irreparably bewitched.

Those who recall García Márquez's archpatriarch José Arcadio Buendía will no doubt recognize in Tasso's baneful fate a prototype for the founding father of Macondo, whose indomitable fascination with nature and magic spanned the sciences of alchemy, warfare, and planetary cosmology. His heterologous obsession would end in his being chained to a chestnut tree where he spent his life's final years. And those who recall García Márquez's magical machinery and hyperbolic marvels, thematic and rhetorical, will not fail to remember the most frequently recurring lexis and praxis in the *Gerusalemme Liberata: meraviglia.* Tasso, who in his *Arte Poetica* insists on the poet's *licenza del fingere,* takes as his precedent the classical

Chapter Six

mirabilia with the self-convinced and self-doubting claim that he is even more eminently *meraviglioso* than Homer himself by dint of having infused the marvels of pagan antiquity with the supernatural spirit and structure of Christianity.

Tasso may well follow the formulaic overture of the classical epic, but even that departure point *in medias res* as prescribed becomes a baptismal parting of ways with antiquity. For Tasso's tempo is an *annus mirabilis,* the year 1099, and his paean takes Christian deliverance and the providential Second Coming as the subject of its song. The liberation of Jerusalem is, after all, the unmistakable signal for the apocalyptic parousia and the passing of this world into the next, as Scripture and its tradition have incontrovertibly fixed it. As in the mysteries of time, Tasso fuses, and in turn anoints, the mysteries of the pastoral, its enchantments of love and its psychology of eros. He appropriates the precedents of this waylaying melancholy in his epic figuration, subsuming the cast of chivalric romance and classical pastoral at once: Homer's Circe, Virgil's Dido, as well as Ariostos's Alcina and Trissino's Faleria. They all find their accommodation in the enchanted entanglements and the "soave licor" that befall a string of haplessly love-struck passions in the *Gerusalemme:* Sofronia and Olindo, Tancredi and Clorinda, Ermina and Tancredi, Rinaldo and Armida. Eventually, however, all these enchantments are duly purified, rehabilitated, and redeemed in keeping with Inquisitorial precepts and Tasso's contrite obsessions. In all, enchantment and disenchantment function as a *divertissement* of the pastoral's dilatory textual power, much in the tradition of Odysseus and, even more pointedly, of Achilles, who withdraws to brood after his argument with Agamemnon. And these dilatory ploys of textuality's self-deferment are also Christianized, e.g., Rinaldo is delivered from Armida's enchantment by the reflection he sees in his shield—an Augustinian speculum, a mirror of St. James.

One Hundred Years of Solitude exacerbates these enchantments with ironic wryness. For it is love's impulsiveness and unbridled possession that lead to Macondo's founding and apocalyptic demise. And the redeeming speculum becomes emptied out here, leaving, instead of a saving analogue, a solipsistic solitude of centurial duration, with no hope for a second opportunity, in which reflection as seconding assurance becomes irrevocably interdicted.

INTERSTITIAL GARCÍA MÁRQUEZ

García Márquez's novel subsumes and twists Milton's millenarian program as well. Historical soteriology and revolutionary zeal in its service find their mocking echo here. The grandeur of Milton's ideological dream prior to disenchantment finds its disconcertedness in a Rabelaisian irony: the Gargantuan ferocity of revolutionary commitment that leads Aureliano Buendía to launch over thirty wars and lose them each in turn. Like Tasso, Milton is animated by the impetus of the prophetic. It is an animation bedeviled by human contingencies that unceremoniously thwart the programmatic anticipation of providential history and its orderly unfolding. The vicissitudes of this startling peripeteia would lead Milton, who started out justifying men's ways to God, to confess that he ended by "justifying God's ways to men." It was after his 1638–39 sojourn in Italy, where he spent some time with Manso, Torquato Tasso's biographer, that Milton declared his intention to write a heroic epic based on some transcendental event in England's history. Before he could do so, however, England's history overtook him instead. *Paradise Lost* became the fruit of those waylaid intentions and their frustrated project, fortunately for literature. Prophecy's apocalyptic ethos, which so moved Tasso in the structuring of his epic, would infuse Milton's opus too with its determinations.

Milton knew well the lesson of Virgil's fourth *Eclogue,* the "messianic" Eclogue, that makes bards of old and prophets identical. But Milton was also well aware, or historical contingencies forced him to be, that prophecy was in good measure other than poetry. His role in the Puritan Revolution and its apocalyptics would impose a political agenda on his prophetic voice. As one of the prophets of Cromwell's Fifth Monarchy Men, Milton saw his times as the end time implied in that regime whose order was founded on the New Order announced in the prophet Daniel's apocalyptic book. And both in his *Defensio Secunda* of 1654 and in his earlier *Eikonoklastes* of 1649, Milton offers an apologia for the beheading of Charles Stuart in unmistakable Danielic tones. As the Revolution played itself out and Milton went from being minister of foreign tongues for the council of state to a prisoner of the revolution within the Revolution, he would sadly observe that the Puritan pilgrimage to the end time was "back to a second wandering over that horrid Wilderness of distraction and civil slaughter." Chastened by historical contingencies, Milton, now a true Tiresias in his uncanny vision, turns to the heroic epic he had planned to write on his return from Tasso's Italy.

Chapter Six

Truly a Christian epic after Tasso's, *Paradise Lost* more than pays obeisance to the *Gerusalemme Liberata*. Milton was well versed in the lessons of Tasso's *Discorsi del Poema Eroico* and its theoretical debates on the epic genre. The basic epic structure remains intact in Milton's opus. Certainly the plunge *in medias res* and the spiritualized centrality of the *medio tempo* are unmistakably present. Like Tasso, Milton baptizes the *in medias res* gambit of the *Iliad* and the *Aenead*. This baptismal accommodation of the pagan classical epos has one of its most significant transmutations in the temporal schema of these Christian epics. Christian temporality, unlike antiquity's tempo, emanates from the center of time toward both directions. Time is marked typologically backward and forward from the central event of the Incarnation, which, being the middle of time, is also the beginning of time. Reflecting the Christian spiritualization of the pagan epic's gambit, Milton opens his poem at a point that is central and whose centrality itself becomes divulged between the fourth and sixth books, or at the central point, of *Paradise Lost*. The beginning, then, is centric both as prolepsis and retrospective, as is the bifrontal linearity of Christian time. It is also antithetical in its specular inversions, and, since Milton deals with the Fall, Christ is mirrored by Satan at this centric beginning. In this regard, Tasso too was fully imbued with the belief that the End itself was also a beginning and, in choosing a millenarian year and an apocalyptic event, he too pointed clearly to a providentialist and prophetic vision of history and history's unfolding.

Here, then, between our poetic history beginning with lapsarian pathos (Milton) and the epic redemption of this history with the deliverance of Zion (Tasso), lies *One Hundred Years of Solitude*'s interpretive key, as the novel's own script would have it. In the suggestive placement of the interpretive codebook, the *Sanskrit Primer*, which will allow the last pro-creating Buendía to decipher the parchments that contain the history of his genealogy and the story of our novel, we are beckoned to a writing scene where writing betrays a vocation for scripture's vatic discourse. In heeding our text's beckoning, my focus is not on the world in the book but on the book of that world. I aim to discuss not the way stations of this peregrination on its "solitary way" but the graphic figuration of its itinerary. In doing so, I wish to imply that García Márquez is not a catastrophist but a strophist; for creation by catastrophe, as in the Miltonic paradigm, is not an end but a turn, or as the phraseology of the philosophical rhetor might put it, catastrophe creation is not entailed by an onto-teleology; rather it entails a trope. It is in the sense of this deliberately tropical implication that I make of García Márquez a pilgrim and master of the strophe. And in doing so, I mean to differentiate him from the master strophist of the Pindaric ode, who moves from strophe through antistrophe to culminate in an epode, as, for example, is the paradigmatic case in Archilocus's *epoidos* as after-song. Analogously, I mean to differentiate García Márquez from the topical paradigms of peregrination such as the Hegelian pilgrimage of trinitarian flight, as well as the Marxian progress of dialectical joust. Nor do I wish to identify him with Manichean schemata such as the one willed to us by Augustine, i.e., the cyclicalism that bedevils the *civitas terrena* with fated entrapment in doleful repetition vis-à-vis the blessed linearity of soteriological progress that blesses the *civitas dei* of the angelic redeemed.

García Márquez's strophe tracks a more circuitous itinerary, so circumvoluted that it justifies the epithet of *epistrophe,* that is, a figure that turns upon itself, a graphic play feasting on its specular and alterior display. In this sense alone, Augustine could find relevancy in this scene of writing through the venue of this speculum, the connection being his terse apothegm that mirror historicizes cipher or number. (We saw that mirror deployed by Tasso in Rinaldo's demystification, or "disenchantment" from Armida's charm in the reflecting surface of his otherwise vulnerable shield.) This is a mirror that lies between, but one that is also permeable, like Alice's looking glass, like the code transparency of the *Sanskrit Primer* lodged between Milton and Tasso. It is there, in the middle, where the number and the numbering begin, *in medias res:* in the Aurelian memory, the glacial mirror, and the often-invoked opening sentence of *One Hundred Years of Solitude:* "Many years later, as he faced the firing squad, Colonel Aureliano Buendía was to remember that distant afternoon when his father took him to discover ice." This proemial cipher is echoed reciprocally in the specular final scene, where the last Aureliano reads and deciphers his genealogy as "in a spoken mirror." What intercedes between the mnemonic mirror of overture and the apocalyptic speculum of coda is the graphic heliotrope that traces the epistrophe of the book's differential self-fulfillment. In that prophetic predication, the book becomes central to its story, not unlike the central bead on the abacus of providential history. And this,

CHAPTER SIX

principally, is why the book privileges Melquíades with genitive proprietorship, after the Danielic tradition and the prophetic mode. And I hark back to the tale of family romance in the grapheme of Scripture because that ancestral heirloom, so compelling for Milton and for Tasso, begins in the middle and ends in the beginning. I refer to Milton the Christologist, the salvationist chronicler and historiographer of grace for whom historical arithmetic scans in both directions, on either side of that momentous occasion in the middle of time when God became a spectacle in earthly guise and pathos. My aim is not to baptize García Márquez or to anoint any Buendía. I merely wish to illustrate that the design of *One Hundred Years of Solitude,* opening as it does with recursive memory *and* with proleptic omen, closes with a cosmic cataclysm that disposes of the world, leading from the kingdom of this world's history to the realm of the book's own story. The book, of course, survives as the only remainder (and reminder) of its world's catastrophe. That turn, that peristrophic transference, is precisely what I should like to discuss briefly.

By casting itself as the graphic surplus of catastrophe, García Márquez's writing turns us toward a tradition of writings that seek to assure their own protracted continuity by encoding it into their scripture. We encounter that strategy in looking back from the "latest" canonized scripture where John the Divine, a decidedly self-proclaimed last book, guarantees its own lasting status by including terrible admonitions against increments or emendations (Revelation 22:18), back through Daniel (12:9–10), where divine injunction defers the book's disclosures, thereby extending the book's perdurability, "until the time of the end," and back to one of the earliest strong moves for self-preservation through self-deferral, the Book of Enoch, whose opening lines guarantee its longevity by declaring itself "not for this generation, but for a remote one which is for to come" (1:2). I read in these scriptural ploys for survival the textual precedents for abortively repeated interpretive forays by generations of Buendías into the parchments of Melquíades, hermeneutical attempts that are invariably thwarted because the time is not nigh, and more significantly, because the book refuses to open up to premature foreclosure through preemptive yielding of its encoded scripture. Traditionally we assign to writings in this self-preservationist mode the epithets of "prophetic" and "apocalyptic," and many of our historical and philosophical notions of cosmic eschatology can be traced to this tradition. *One Hundred Years of Solitude* echoes citationally the emplotment strategies of this prophetic mode, and I would venture that it does so intentionally by dint of persistent allusion to thematic and structural precedents of the prophetic genre. Inadvertent allusion would be a solecism, as, Quintilian (*Institutes,* 1.5.53) reminds us, is the fate of all unintentional figuration. Surely the encounter of millions of readers with a scene of recognition when engaged in reading this novel should convince us that García Márquez's enterprise is far from solecism. As crafted artifact and emplotted structure, then, *One Hundred Years of Solitude* displays precursor strategies that our historical canon has turned into characteristic attributes of prophetic discourse. How García Márquez epistrophizes these ploys in the writerly bookishness of his book, as much as, if not more than, the thematics of this novel, is what joins him to the prophetic mode.

To instantiate these claims further, I refer back to Daniel and the Book of Daniel already mentioned. As a canonized book, Daniel offers the first sanctioned precedent for a textualizing strategy appropriated by García Márquez, a ploy that leads us to accept the proprietorship of *One Hundred Years of Solitude* as ascribed to Melquíades by García Márquez. Just as we have no idea as to who may have authored the book of Daniel, someday, especially if the post-Heideggerian disappearance predicted for the authoring subject should become a reality—as some fancy such an eventuality to be inevitable—that day we may not know who authored *One Hundred Years of Solitude* either, an inevitable eventuality that is already well underway through the "monumentalization" of the Colombian author. A *monumentum,* of course, is by definition an inexorable displacement, a receding into problematic memorial time-space that obliterates identity and propitiates difference. Daniel's authorial function is imputed to him because the book in which he figures casts him as voice and authoring persona. Likewise, some distant community of exegetes in an as yet indeterminate epoch may well consider Melquíades the author proper. García Márquez will have been responsible in good part for that divestiture of his authorship by virtue of having deployed an authoring persona designed to supplant him. The textualizing strategy I am describing here is called "pseudonymity" and, as a structuring principle, it has framed every prophetic book known since Daniel with the notable exception of the Book of Revelation by John the Divine. Of course, pseudonymous attribution has

Chapter Six

a long and distinguished tradition in secular scripture as well, its most obvious instance in the Hispanic canon being Cervantes. But in attributing the original text of the *Quijote* to a "heathenish tongue" and an "infidel" author, Cide Hamet Benengeli, Cervantes secularizes the strategy with a vengeance characteristic of his Renaissance epoch. I do not know that we live in a less profane era. Nonetheless, the prophetic ploy of pseudonymity has reverted to a more "sacral" figuration, perhaps as an ironic romancing of eschatology. We note this penchant in works of our own time such as *One Hundred Years of Solitude* and, more recently, as already discussed in our previous chapter, in Umberto Eco's *The Name of the Rose,* where, with paradoxical naturalness, the winking epigraph of Eco's novel reads, "Naturally, a manuscript."[2]

More than (or as much as) the secular scripture of Cervantes or, more contemporaneously, of a Borges, it is the precedent of the prophetic mode that finds its avatar as scriptive strategy in García Márquez. His invocation of Tasso and Milton would confirm as much. Even if we should overlook the eschatological schema and thematics of the novel, the attribution of its scripture to the pseudonym of a Melquíades suffices to suggest the biblical connection in the resonance of a near-homonym in Melquíades's name. Melquíades, our ostensible scriptor, harks back to the Melchisedek of Genesis (14:18–20) and his typological antitype in the Psalms and Hebrews. The intertestamental peregrinations of this tireless journeyman may well reach to Macondo's secular scripture, where he repeatedly surfaces bearing gifts, as did his prototype, with the most momentous of his bequests being the scripture of the novel itself. It would be in character, certainly, and the plot of tradition in this family romance of texts construes, at least insofar as the depiction of Melquíades is concerned, with the depiction of the mysterious, gift-bearing Melchisedek of Scripture.

It should be sufficiently obvious by now that García Márquez is neither ignorant of, nor averse to, the deployment of textual techniques that tradition has taught us to associate with sacred scripture, apocryphal or canonical. What remains for us to speculate is how and to what ends are these strategies put in a secular work that carnivalizes sacrality with iconoclastic flourish and irreverent irony. Pseudonymous attribution in the Danielic vein had very serious and, perhaps, very high-minded motives. Even though Hebraic prophecies of apocalyptical bent, for example, are penned in a period that extends roughly between 200 B.C. and A.D. 100, they are attributed to such venerable forefathers as Enoch, Abraham, the Twelve Patriarchs, Moses, Solomon, Ezra, and Baruch. These are commanding voices already legitimated by tradition who are now called upon to legitimate, in turn, the latest prophecies ascribed to them. Whatever the constellation of motives for such attribution may have been, one motivating factor most likely was linked to a revisionist and revisionary strategy for recasting history and the historical present as future and as yet unrealized objects of prophecy. This way the seer guaranteed some measure of self-assurance to the infallibility of his prophetic visions. This procedure—of envisioning and narrating as future what already has come to pass by removing oneself to a distant past and assuming pseudonymously the authority of an earlier discourse—comprises what we refer to as *vaticinia post eventum* and is an exercise in prophesying after the fact or foreseeing in hindsight.

When hindsight becomes vision, of course, what will be already is; to be good visionaries and accurate seers, all we need do is diligently decode what has been encoded by virtue of having been already. It may sound like it should be a cinch, but any good historian can tell us that "prophesying" the past is no less arduous a task than prophesying the future. Likewise, any conscientious textual exegete would admit to the difficulties of interpretation and decipherment of what scripture has already encoded. We could appreciate, in this regard, the temptation of some historians and literary interpreters to present their exegeses, not unlike the prophets of the intertestamental period, as though dictated by the voice of a Moses or a Solomon, when not by God himself, and I am sure we can all think of a few who have succumbed to that temptation. But the woes of our professional state of the art aside, it should be clear to us that in deploying a strategy of pseudonymous attribution, García Márquez is concurrently engaging the concomitant procedure of the *vaticinia post eventum*. And the inexorable unfolding of the novel as the interpretation of a hidden scripture that is a family history leaves little room for doubt that this might well be the case. Accordingly, we could say that the scripture and cipher of *One Hundred Years of Solitude* already preexists the novel *One Hundred Years of Solitude*, which *we read* and are given to cataloguing under García Márquez's name.

Chapter Six

As readers, and with García Márquez as titular writer, then, we are engaged in a belated activity of reconstituting in revisionist, i.e., prophetic, fashion what has already been constituted by the scriptive process described in the book and ascribed to Melquíades. Thus, any reading of *One Hundred Years of Solitude* is necessarily a re-reading, just as any living out of the plot of family history by any Buendía is a reliving of *what is* already, and already historicized by the inscription of the text, including the abortive attempts at deciphering the code which constitutes that history as scripture and pre-vision. As pro-visional acts, those ill-fated decipherments are themselves enciphered, as is the successful decoding of the script by the penultimate Aureliano Buendía. That is why this Aureliano sees himself in his targumic activity as through a "speaking mirror." I say *through* and not *in* that mirror, for this is the Pauline speculum of I Corinthians 13:12, only now the *aenigmata* have dissipated and the onlooker sees not through a glass darkly. One's self-perception no longer has any impedimenta. And just as Paul anticipated, such an unimpeded encounter face-to-face, and knowing just as one is known, can only come when the time is nigh and the day is done and a second opportunity in this world is only academic. The race of the Buendía genealogy has already had its second chance, which was the living out of "prophecy's" inscription. The genealogical history has already been a specular image, a redoubled peregrination on its "solitary way," reflecting its itinerary in secular scripture's mirror. As the graphic record of the *vaticinia post eventum,* including the event of its catastrophe, then, the book *One Hundred Years of Solitude* remains, and as remainder it constantly harkens to the prophetic fact that it is a post-Macondo phenomenon, an always differentially surviving trace of a catastrophe that it antedated in its proleptic scripture and survived by dint of a peristrophic ruse of deferential self-preservation inscribed in its code.

In this sense, *One Hundred Years of Solitude* is a post-script to *One Hundred Years of Solitude* that relentlessly prophesies *One Hundred Years of Solitude* after the manner of the grammatical verb conjugations that epistrophize a triple-faced mirror of temporality in the opening sentence of its writing scene. And, while the novel does image unmistakably certain thematic and figural topoi that it self-admittedly inherits from Milton and from Tasso, it does not naively appropriate or obeisantly acquiesce to that inheritance. Rather, as we have seen, it subsumes and twists its procedures as enabling strategy, as structuring frame and competency for its own scene of writing that harks back to a primal scene of transgression, after which the telltale sign is the novel itself. That is why I turn to that scriptural and scribal landscape and, in doing so, we perennially begin where Milton's epic "ends."

Between Inevitability and Life

The Cipher of Love

Henceforth, our rereadings of *One Hundred Years of Solitude* will yield sharper sensations. Macondo's sempiternal almond trees will flower with the poignancy of a more bitter fragrance. Their early blossoming will be interlaced with the aroma of cyanuric pungency. The alchemy of love and solitude in *Love in the Time of Cholera*[3] offers a piquant unction to the obstinate melancholy that irremediably plagues the solitary lovelorn of the García Márquez corpus. Between the "inevitable" in the novel's proemial words and the "life" in its coda, there is a sublime irony that mediates as threshold. That passageway has its focus in what is aptly named El Portal de los Escribanos (The Arcade of the Scribes). There love finds its graphic figuration, becomes committed to writing as talisman and incantation. As thresholds are always wont to do, this gateway of writing leads into ambiguous crossings, into equivocal junctures, bi-ways more given to simultaneity and mutual interchange than to mutual exclusiveness. At once redemptive and damning, curative and malignant, love's nostrum as scribal alchemy serves as an auspicious elixir and as a pernicious bane. And García Márquez's choleric love takes a franchise in Robert Burton's *Anatomy of Melancholy*. The melanoid pigment of love's body traces the graphic figurations incarnated as writing. In writing's ink and tincture flows the bittersweet pharmacopeia that heals and wounds with diligent simultaneity.

In this redoubled convergence, love is always allegory; it is always other (*allos*), already pre-occupying another space (*agora*) whose recesses and receding leave their inscription as bereaved pertinacity, as insistent *re-venant* whose symptoms function as a sign that signals unredeemable

CHAPTER SIX

and implacable otherness: the art of love become love of (as) art, the death of life become enlivening holy spirit, epidemic cholera become choleric eros with chronic acuity and unremitting hope. That is why García Márquez's novel begins with an inevitability that is not imminently inevitable (it is, after all, a calculated alchemic suicide) and ends in a life "after" life "unbounded" by inevitability's threatening. The toponym, the place and name of that boundless space—a river named Magdalena—is a graphic personification, a limitless estuary in whose confluence converge spaces of time and the timelessness of graphic spaces to dissolve and recombine.

Love in the Time of Cholera is an elegy of love that masks its own genitives, a love story that has love as its prophylactic, a story whose safeguard, or phylactery, is writing. It is a melancholy writing, even when most ironic, that sanctifies love as proleptic jeremiad in name, in the name of the self-sentenced Jeremiah de Saint-Amour, but a writing that also labors in a labor of love to breach that dubious sanctity and its elegiac aura. It is a melancholy writing as a breaching iconoclasm when tracing love's vacuity in the pertinacious loyalties of an unloving marriage, masked by youthful urbaneness and firm constancy: the lifelong connubium of Juvenal Urbino and Fermina Daza cemented by civic fealty and mulish stubbornness. And it is melancholy writing, too, as love's sterile flourish in overblown florescence: Florentino Ariza's erotic profligacy that proves to be an impossible compensation for an impossible love's ferocity in unyielding forbearance. And last, but not least, García Márquez's is a melancholy writing that edifies its ironies with the melodramatic building blocks of the penny-a-tear love story and its cloying sentiment.

A mirror to its world, *Love in the Time of Cholera* is a cholic cipher composed of love gone awry in a decomposing world plagued by the pestilence of cholera. Splenetic love and epidemic-ridden world coexist in specular juxtaposition, as mutually reflected allegories that have their final convergence on a wayward love-boat flying the yellow flag of choleric contagion, wandering timelessly on the third bank of the river, beyond life and death. That confluence, in turn, has its echo and spectral other in the very materiality of the novel and its writing—an act against time that survives to tell repeatedly with each unrepeatable reading its own graphic story. And this itinerary, too, is foreshadowed as iteration in the novel's opening gesture. Jeremiah de Saint-Amour's alchemical self-demise on

Pentecost Sunday becomes a spitting in the face of time, which had transfigured him. Jeremiah's enigmatic last words to the woman he loved become less enigmatic as the novel unfolds: "'Remember me with a rose,' he said" (16). That self-identification in testamental memory transforms the fated Saint-Amour into a Yeatsian "rose upon the rood of time," and through that memorialized wish of his final hour, Jeremiah finds a way to live beyond his own time. The invariable presence of evocation of the rose in subsequent amours, an evocation that culminates in Florentino's white and thornless rose for Fermina Daza, converts the flower into Jeremiah's constant melancholy reminder. Nowhere does that florid memento blossom with as much intensity as in the fated paramours of the aptly named Florentino, who loses his virginity to a woman named Rosalba under mysterious circumstances. And it flourishes, too, as writerly resonance in the poetry festivals designated as "juegos florales."

If *One Hundred Years of Solitude* comprises the residue of a writerly performance through Melquíades's Sanskrit manuscripts, *Love in the Time of Cholera* comprehends the scriptural with an éclat at once more subtle and more ironically banal. Its composition runs the gamut of the human register by virtue of being filtered through what is most divine and also most pathetic: the alchemy of love. And perhaps that is why the novel's opening sentence inextricably yokes inevitability to impossibility: inevitable memory and impossible love ("It was inevitable: the scent of bitter almonds always reminded him of the fate of unrequited love"). The inevitable is also what is often written with a capital "I," Dr. Juvenal Urbino's own unsuspected death, which will comically overtake him by the end of this same day. And the reminder evoked by the bitter almond trees may well hark back to the only real love which he could have possibly experienced but which became instead a bitter episode and an impossible memory with an accusing odor.

The olfactory sensation of bitter almond blossoms, which suffices to awaken the knowledge of impossible loves in Juvenal Urbino, becomes strangely proleptic and ironically commemorative at the same time. On this, the last day of his life, any prolepsis, or anticipatory promise, rings peculiar. And yet the unfolding of his life story still awaits the rest of the text's skein to unwind, after the fact, almost posthumously, since his end is only hours away. In the posthumous memorandum that is the rest of the

CHAPTER SIX

novel, we shall have discovered the irony of his own love's having been betrayed and interdicted, made into an impossible love, that is, by the smell of a woman named Miss Barbara Lynch, which permeates his body and clothing and leads to his detection by the canny sense of smell of his ambivalently (un)loved and (un)loving wife. And it is ironic, too, because in a peculiar way all love that is more than a firefly's copulatory blinking is either unrequited or posthumous here, except for love contracted by writing, by the abyssed writing in the novel. The notable exception in this regard may be Jeremiah de Saint-Amour's, but this love also becomes too nostalgic and desperate to brook life's melancholy. In this sense, *Love in the Time of Cholera* serves as a mirrored inversion of the author's *Chronicle of a Death Foretold,*[4] where death must ensue inexorably from love's prior consummation. In *Love in the Time of Cholera,* death becomes love's necessary precondition. Within this interchange between *eros* and *thanatos,* love only becomes possible at the far end of memory, as a retrieved or recollected realization in a second coming, or as an awaited resurrection after a season of loss. That recuperation is both graphic and redemptive. And it may be restorative, but not always assuaging. In this sense it conjoins the pharmacy of writing and the remedial effects of curative practice. And it is especially suggestive in this regard that the ravages of the cholera epidemic should be controlled by Juvenal Urbino, successor to his dead father's primitive medical practice and former apprentice to the great epidemiologist Professor Adrien Proust (114). In the graphic art of memory, García Márquez himself has clearly partaken of the lesson of Marcel Proust, the great doctor's progeny. Memorial recouping and valetudinarian recuperating, then, function correlatively in this pharmacal convergence.

The foregrounding of Jeremiah de Saint-Amour and his suicidal gesture takes on a highly textured significance in the light of these conjunctures. In privileging Jeremiah by making him the threshold to his novel, García Márquez points clearly to the commemorative powers of writing as recovery, as an unending recovery and lie against time. From that liminal overture, the novel remarks its own fate, troped as an ironic paragraph in Jeremiah's self-salvaging from the torments of memory ("se había puesto a salvo de los tormentos de la memoria") that make him irrevocably memorable throughout and beyond the novel. Having foreclosed on his own remembrances, Jeremiah becomes living memory after his alchemical death. That passage from liminality to sublimity, from writing's threshold to its perdurence as re-venant and unending recollection, is overtly staged in the novel on Pentecost Sunday under the emblematic aegis of a testamental rose: "'Remember me with a rose,' he said." In linking his own scripture's overture to Scripture's Pentecostal feast, García Márquez underscores, consciously or casually, the reclamatory and restorative character of his own writing and of all writing that reaps time's harvest in the perpetuity of temporal re-commencement. *Love in the Time of Cholera* is clearly a work that salvages writing from the plethora of banality proliferated in the name of love's pathos rendered trite. In that gesture, the author allusively remarks tradition's amatory genre of the bourgeois novel extending from Richardson's *Pamela* to *Madame Bovary* and *Anna Karenina*. García Márquez's scribal gesture becomes a recuperative act that rehabilitates writing on love's behalf as love's body for love's perilous sublimity.

Like the Pentecost celebration, García Márquez's is a harvest feast and a feast of weeks, that is, a gathering in and a reckoning of time(s) that makes its obligatory first offering of two loaves/two lambs in the Pentecostal deaths of Jeremiah de Saint-Amour and Juvenal Urbino. If Pentecost is reckoned as the birthday of the Jewish nation and of the Christian Church (Acts 2), the author's sacrifice of Jeremiah and Juvenal in the first part of the work spells a generic offering that engenders the life of his novel. This may well be why Jeremiah's "untimely" death is rendered inevitable, and Juvenal's demise patiently anticipated with dogged obstinacy by Florentino Ariza. In this sense, then, both love and love's body as writing become commemorative acts, re-venants in a life after life, as in an innumerable second coming, not unlike the divinity's second visitation to pour forth the holy spirit fifty days after the paschal sacrifice, or fifty days after Israel's deliverance from Egypt (Ex. 12; 19). This term of pertinacious time is troped with ironic exactitude by García Márquez into fifty-one years, nine months, and four days. That time stands for Florentino Ariza's arid wanderings in the exotic wilderness of loveless loving. The chronicle of this pilgrimage is diligently recorded, patiently strung and counted like beads on an endless rosary that keeps and dispels time. And it begins, suggestively enough, with a woman called the Widow [of] Nazareth:

Chapter Six

> he joined in historic battles of absolute secrecy, which he recorded with the rigor of a notary in a coded book, recognizable among many others by the title that said everything: *Women*. His first notation was the widow Nazareth. Fifty years later, when Fermina Daza was freed from her sacramental sentence, he had some twenty-five notebooks, with six hundred twenty-two entries of long-term liaisons, apart from the countless fleeting adventures that did not even deserve a charitable note. (152)

Florentino Ariza's mathematical diligence in the recording of peripatetic love with enciphered notation has its prefigured antecedent in the Pentecostal spirit of Jeremiah de Saint-Amour. This war veteran's final and deadly gesture is immediately preceded by another defiant act in the face of time: writing. Jeremiah's epistolary bequest in the form of a last letter, a letter of death transumpted, like himself, into a spirit of the letter, is itself the culmination of a series of graphic opuscules by way of mercurial and minimal insurgencies in a war against time, a war he knew to be losing. Jeremiah passed from the vocation of political insurrectionist, which left its stigmata on his invalid's body, to become a "most compassionate adversary" in the game of chess and a passionate rebel in the game of life. The hours he did not spend contesting on the chessboard he devoted to his avid task of children's photographer. Dr. Juvenal Urbino, his adversary in the game of chess and counterpart in so many other ways, appreciated profoundly Jeremiah's calling in the art of photographing children. Those photographic plates, he observed, conserved the images of a whole generation that might never know happiness again outside of its photographs (38). And while he would sign his friend's death certificate with a compassion that attributed his self-demise to natural causes, he knew full well what those causes signified. He reduced them, with clinical exactitude and trembling self-betrayal, to the economy of a single word: *gerontofobia.*

Juvenal was the repository of Jeremiah's unspoken secrets. He was also the addressee of his friend's final letter, whose contents he would jealously guard with sacred fealty. Dr. Urbino diagnoses his friend's final act through the symptoms of the unfinished chess game, interrupted but not scattered. Only a few moves from being checkmated by a masterful strategy, Jeremiah, as the doctor is informed, moved his pieces without love in a last match with the woman he loved for over twenty years; a love he unnecessarily and incomprehensibly kept clandestine. Adversaries in the game of chess understood as "a dialogue of reason and not a science," Jeremiah and Juvenal contend in a dialectical counterpoint whose contestation transcends well beyond their game. They are, in fact, deployed in the novel with almost Manichean clarity: one a revolutionary idealist, the other an establishmentarian pragmatist; the first a reclusive stranger with a clouded past, the second a favorite native son of revered pedigree; Jeremiah a jetsam derelict of life's tides mysteriously favored by love's constellations, Juvenal a pillar of success and respectability confounded in the barrenness of love's ambivalences. The urbane worldliness of Juvenal Urbino becomes decidedly inverted in the mirror of Jeremiah de Saint-Amour's enigmatic other-worldliness. And in the mirror of his friend's death and letter, the octogenarian Juvenal reads his own mortal fate on this Pentecost Sunday. And while the remains of Juvenal find their final resting place in the town's most hallowed ground, the "unbelieving Saint," as Jeremiah was knowingly dubbed, is planted in the common grave outside the cemetery gates reserved for those who preempted God in an untimely time.

The "timeliness" of Juvenal's own death endures fate's mockery with ironic derision, dying as he does in pursuit of a parrot that learned to speak French like an academician and faithfully parroted his master's cosmopolitan culture. While his obsessive adherence to a dietetic regimen of pharmacal and herbal potions may have extended his life to eighty-one years, love, that enigmatic alchemy which always dwells in this novel at the far end of memory, would inexorably escape Juvenal as his memory waned into sundry fragments of paper whose whereabouts were invariably forgotten. For while he did recall a hallowed truth from one of his medical-school mentors, Dr. Proust more than likely, "The man who has no memory makes one out of paper" (40), he more often would draw a blank in graphic recollection. And he would die, significantly, without having read through the two volumes at his bedside, books that contained the meditations and enigmatic dreams of two of his medical colleagues who dared confront the mysteries of life: Alexis Carrell's *Man the Unknown* (1935) and Axel Munthe's *The Story of San Michele* (1929).

If Jeremiah de Saint-Amour is Juvenal's "most compassionate adversary in the game of chess," Florentino Ariza is his passionate antagonist in love's melancholy. In the end, Florentino is the inheritor of and successor

Chapter Six

to Jeremiah and Juvenal respectively. Misbegotten fruit of a transitory love, Florentino devotes his life to love's legitimation. Already imbued with what will have become Jeremiah's Pentecostal spirit of love's defiant mercy (on at least five key occasions he is said to be possessed by the holy spirit, pages 50, 66, 82, 299, and 348), he consecrates love's youthful loss to steadfast obstinacy, doggedly waiting for Juvenal's death to free his love's merciless object.

Florentino's love story is a ghostly paragraph. Its genesis is in writing as trauma and as unction. And, like writing's open-endedness, his wound never scars but is always scarified. Rampantly unrequited, his love translates into rampant writing, a psyche in relentless pursuit of an elusive eros.

The Enchantments of Writing

Love in the Time of Cholera unfolds by dint of an association between eros and poesis, between erotic possession and writing's inflammatory incitation. Love and writing merge into a quantum echo that proliferates as autoleptic, or self-seizing, figuration, a resonant blend that clearly remarks a narcissistic seizure. In this latter-day romance of the rose, García Márquez proffers a figurative mirror that re-renders writing subtle and recoups love's sublimity through ironic harmony and celebratory plaint. Love's moan becomes writing's echo in textuality's contestatory iterations. This is another way of saying that in García Márquez textuality's constitutive performance turns on writing answering writing, and that the aleatory conduit and impossible inevitability of this dialogue is love's enchanted impulse. It is certainly no accident in this sense that those who seek love find it through or in writing and, conversely, the unread who would spurn writing go unloved and spurned by eros (e.g., Lorenzo Daza, tía Escolástica). I have already indicated how the novel privileges this yoking of love and writing in its opening gambit and how, for example, Juvenal Urbino, that fetishistic reader who made it his civic duty to read for fashionable ends and "love" for social means, in reading Jeremiah de Saint-Amour's last testament is moved for the first time in his life by a love that is not expedient, but rather one that even leads him to engage in certain acts and advocacies on his dead friend's behalf that go counter to his habitual sense of civic duty. The novel's most protracted love story, however, is Florentino

Ariza's, and his is a story born and experienced through the spectacle of writing. And that is why the lovelorn Florentino becomes the inheritor and chief executive officer of a commercial navigation "empire," and yet he cannot write a business letter that is not a love letter.

Conceived and born in the urgency of a furtive love affair, Florentino's life of love begins through the auspices of a most urgent scene of writing, the local telegraph office; and eros strikes him with flashing conflagration as he witnesses a reading lesson. As a mercurial messenger of writing's tradition, he is fulfilling his duty as telegraphic delivery boy when he calls on the house of Daza and steals a glance at Fermina Daza as she tutors her aunt and surrogate mother, Escolástica, who, in spite of her name, is neither schooled nor literate. In the allusive irony of that paronomasia, elusive love will find its ill-fated ally and implacable phylactery. Implacable because tía Escolástica, as guardian of her niece's maidenhood, comes to her new skill in reading and writing concurrently with the possibility of vicariously remedying her own loveless life through the opportunity of love that beckons to her surrogate daughter. And ill-fated because her daring earns her a banishment from the fraternal home that sends her into wandering and inimical oblivion. Fermina Daza will internalize that fate and make it emotionally her own. Her eventual marriage with Juvenal Urbino and consequent social elevation will serve as but a meager palliative for that traumatic destiny. It is also this implacable loss and the disproportionate expectations it engenders that lead Fermina Daza to reject Florentino Ariza's ardent love with dismissive disillusion. The measure of that disillusionment is diametrically proportionate to the intensity of love's illusion heightened by writing's fervency and promissory enchantment. It is all too appropriate, then, that her fated *dis*enchantment should occur in the *agora* of scripture, The Arcade of the Scribes (102).

But Florentino Ariza's awakening to love occurs in and through the locus of writing in a still more immediate and a more graphic fashion. Ever since his mother taught him to read, "reading had become his insatiable vice" (74). By age five, Florentino would recite from memory, and at every turn, the illustrated children's books of Nordic authors, which in reality, the novel tells us, were the cruelest and most perverse books one could read at any age; and his familiarity with those books, instead of assuaging his terror, made it even more acute. The passage from those terrors to poetry came with natural ease, and he devoured volumes with indiscriminate voracity, committing all love poems, the genre of his predilections, to memory with the second reading:

> Even during his adolescence he had devoured, in the order of their appearance, all the volumes of the Popular Library that Tránsito Ariza bought from the bargain booksellers at the Arcade of the Scribes, where one could find everything from Homer to the least meritorious of the local poets. But he made no distinctions: he read whatever came his way, as if it had been ordained by fate, and despite his many years of reading, he still could not judge what was good and what was not in all that he had read. . . . He had learned to cry with his mother as they read the pamphlets by local poets that were sold in plazas and arcades for two centavos each. But at the same time he was able to recite from memory the most exquisite Castilian poetry of the Golden Age. In general, he read everything that fell into his hands in the order in which it fell. (75)

Having consumed voraciously writing's graphic body, Florentino would be possessed, in turn, with concomitant ferocity by love's graphic enchantment. Florentino's amorous consummation is more than love experienced through the spectacles of writing. It is love *as* a spectacle of writing, where the conjunctive preposition "as" does not merely suggest a simile but figures an ironic identity, a copula that engenders and consumes its subject and its predicate with immediate fervency. Writing, in other words, does not function as a mediate instrument that enjoins two psyches in sentiment through its instrumentality. Rather, love is writing and writing is love in mutual propagation. And by extension, the novel's recitation, its *recit* of an amorous history, becomes a labor of love in/on love's laboring. The rites of its elaboration are highly autoleptic, that is, an arduous self-seizure that comprises and is comprised by the ardent ceremonies of a most writerly courtship, a graphic ritual that is always courting but never reaches the attainment of closure through courting's consummation. Only in that ever-withheld terminus does writing differentiate itself from love's consummatory impulse. And insofar as love and writing forge an identity, writing differentiates itself from writing, sundering the copula into otherness, into graphic difference and amatory disjunction. Thus, love as writing is left to pursue writing as love with unrequited fervor. And García Márquez's own writing as a love's body that constitutes the novel differentiates itself from the corpus of writings that have possessed his hero by turning on that enchantment with mocking irony.

As a result, Florentino Ariza comes off as the ironic personification and melodramatic hyperbole of the literary canon's amatory tradition, thrashing in love's possession, pouring forth interminable love letters with uncontrolled profligacy, regurgitating his voluminous consumption as fervently as he devoured it in the voracities of reading: the readings of his childhood and adolescence, the ostensible readings on a park bench by way of stalking his burning love's object, the readings in claustrophobic cubicles in the hotel of transients and marketplace of love's commerce, where he discovered the mysteries of love without love (75). And love's labor did not confine itself to love letters that filled every secret corner of the city and the trunks of Fermina Daza. Florentino Ariza also became the calligrapher of the maritime company he would one day inherit, where his business letters always ended by being love letters. So possessed was he by elusive love's enchantment that he would volunteer his services to the unlettered lovestruck in The Arcade of the Scribes, where he ended up answering his own letters on behalf of lovers who had been recipients of letters he had written.

Thus, as love finds its compensation in graphic correspondence, writing literally answers writing in narcissistic self-seizure—"and so it was that he became involved in a feverish correspondence with himself" (172). When the lovers so conjoined in matrimony have their first child and casually discover their union's instrumentality, they seek out the agent of their writerly alliance to name him the godfather of their love's first-born. So enthused was Florentino with his natural vocation as love's scribe that he would find time where he had none to compose a "Lover's Companion" (*Secretario de los Enamorados*), more extensive and more poetic than the one available to the lovelorn then for the price of twenty centavos: "When he finished, he had some thousand letters in three volumes as complete as the Covarrubias Dictionary, but no printer in the city would take the risk of publishing them, and they ended up in an attic along with other papers from the past" (172). By the time Florentino had the means to publish the

Chapter Six

amatory enchiridion at his own expense, he reluctantly had to realize that love letters had gone out of fashion, and, thus, love was spared from further proliferation as a graphic banality, and writing was mercifully saved from added derogation as an insipid handmaiden to cloying sentiment. In fact, the barb of García Márquez's mocking irony becomes scatologically truculent with Florentino's first letter. As his trembling hand reaches to deposit the initial love letters on Fermina's extended embroidery hoop, an inauspiciously perched bird in the bitter almond tree drops its ill-timed shit on Fermina's virginal needlework. And then, too, Florentino Ariza's incontinent pen in the service of love is matched by his lifelong necessity to administer suppositories in order to alleviate his chronic constipation.

García Márquez's novel forces the question of writing in writing, and it does so on writing's liminal gateway, that threshold where scriveners rendered their services since time immemorial, The Arcade of the Scribes. It is there, in that heterogeneous bazaar and motley *agora,* where it becomes another desultory item among diverse commodities, that writing works its assorted charms and carries out its multifarious commerce. And it is there, precisely, as I have already noted, that García Márquez ironically locates writerly love's disenchantment. Having endured the protracted vicissitudes of an impossible love's fervor engendered in and by writing, the lovelorn come face to face. In that ill-starred encounter between Florentino Ariza and the obdurate Fermina Daza, writing's charm becomes undone in shattering disillusion:

> She turned her head and saw, a hand's breadth away from her eyes, those other glacial eyes, that livid face, those lips petrified with fear . . . but . . . instead of the commotion of love, she felt the abyss of disenchantment. In an instant the magnitude of her own mistake was revealed to her, and she asked herself, appalled, how she could have nurtured such a chimera in her heart for so long with so much ferocity. (102)

Florentino would never have the opportunity to see Fermina Daza alone or speak alone with her until the first night of her widowhood—fifty-one years, nine months, and four days later.

On that unpredictable threshold of The Arcade of the Scribes, García Márquez presses as well the problematic caprices of writing's boundary in allegorical terms, in terms, that is, of writing's mercurial vocation for becoming other than the intended medium, for functioning as dysfunction, for withstanding determinacy as errant volatility. Writing, in other words, retains its putative character as a mediate commodity but it does so capriciously, for it can be ameliorative and damning with unpredictable charm. As an allegorical extreme in the mutant otherness (*allos*) of its diverse *agora* (and I use the term "allegory" in this ever-liminal and permutating sense of its etymology), writing intercedes with a random variability that can only lead to melancholy perplexity for those who would seek to employ it as a determinate instrument with firm constancy. And that is why that frontier space is off-limits to "decent girls" of the *burgesía*, such as Fermina Daza, lest its lubricious heterodoxy lead them into perdition—" "Fermina Daza shared with her schoolmates the singular idea that the Arcade of the Scribes was a place of perdition that was forbidden, of course, to decent young ladies" (100). Having dared to enter there, either through inadvertence or excess self-assurance, Fermina Daza discovers the panoply of writing's multifarious coloration of

> magic inks, red inks with an ambience of blood, inks of sad aspect for messages of condolence, phosphorescent inks for reading in the dark, invisible inks that revealed themselves in the light. She wanted all of them so she could amuse Florentino Ariza and astound him with her wit, but after several trials she decided on a bottle of gold ink. (101)

But having run the gamut of writing's alchemy and reached its golden tint (ironically reminiscent of the terminal cyanuric of gold in Jeremiah de Saint-Amour's fatal alchemy), Fermina has reached the threshold of writing's *dis*-enchantment, the *desencanto* of an ardent love that had been wrought in and by writing. The novel does not specify whether it was with the "tinta de oro" that she wrote to Florentino: "Today, when I saw you, I realized that what is between us is nothing more than an illusion" (102). Thus, writing as love's genitive also becomes love's prophylactic, and for the next half-century in Florentino's life of graphic melancholy it serves as love's phylactery, as an unrequited safeguard. Until, that is, impossibility and inevitability converge, and impossible love is rendered inevitable love in a protracted alchemy of melancholic loving. And then, too, at the far end

Chapter Six

of that long-drawn depuration, as during its process, the conjunction of complementaries—impossibility and inevitability, inevitability and autumnal life—is achieved through writing's intercession (Florentino's pertinacious letters to Fermina, now typed on the writing machine, technology's latest graphic invention). The corollary consequence of this, as of all previous graphic mediations, is the book entitled *Love in the Time of Cholera*. That book "ends" with the unending love-boat voyage of Florentino and Fermina aboard the aptly named *New Fidelity*. In the book's Magdalene estuary that is also Proust's diluvial tea-cup-run-over, we read, interminably, a spectral and melancholy scripture, writing's allegory in endless, and often ironic, re-formation.

CHAPTER SEVEN

SCATOLOGY, ESCHATOLOGY, PALIMPSEST
Vargas Llosa and the History of a Parricide

> *In vain would future narrators attempt to veil it in glorious descriptions. On each page they would have those indestructible and outrageous palimpsests.*
>
> —Euclides da Cunha, *Rebellion in the Backlands*

Mario Vargas Llosa's *The War of the End of the World*[1] is not the end of the world. Rather, it constitutes a "war" on those who would appropriate the world to their own ends. In its own appropriative move, the Peruvian novelist's enterprise partakes of the "violence" that it condemns, condemning itself, in the process, to the perennial predicament of incarnating, as narrative, the lie of its own truth. Self-belying truths, Vargas Llosa appears to be telling us, are as endemic to histories as they are to stories, whether in writing or in the telling, and the telltale signs of this self-betrayal comprise the outrage of a palimpsestuous mirror that scowls back with hilarity. Vargas Llosa's speculum takes Euclides da Cunha's as its mirror, fulfilling, in the process, the augural provisions that resonate in the above-cited epigrammatic admonition.[2] Thus, Euclides da Cunha, precursor and pretext, is also vindicated as prophet. Prophecies, of course, find their inevitable confirmation in the fact that they traditionally comprise *vaticinia ex eventu*, divinatory provisions after the fact. Vargas Llosa's project gives the lie to this hallowed truth as well in the corroboration of his Brazilian precursor's foresight some three-quarters of a century later. But, of course, this too is a graphic collusion of scripture's strategies that turn to confront,

Chapter Seven

with irony's grimace, the authorial project of both precursor and successor, as we shall see in due course.

As "outrageous palimpsest," *The War of the End of the World* imparts the graphic violence writing visits on writing. It partakes, too, of the echoic outrage that its opaque transparency lures us to read, through it, in its textual antecedent. The particular passage that serves as our epigraph in this respect is the scatological graffiti that can only be etched by the ire of men at war who know themselves to be condemned to certain death, a scatology born of an eschatological senselessness that can only make sense in the spectral abstractions of fanaticism's ideologies. Although Euclides da Cunha's perspicacity betrays an undeniable insight into the significance of that scatological record, the force of that presentiment is not sufficient for him to discern that his own chronicling enterprise labors under the illusion of a fanaticism. By virtue of this blindness, da Cunha occupies the dubious place of honor as ironically venerated precursor and as target of iconoclasm within Vargas Llosa's irreverent enterprise.

Derision, hilarity, ironic farce, and tragicomic grimace are sundry faces of the parodic mask that Vargas Llosa's scripture has deployed from the very beginning. The decade of the seventies particularly, a decade that sees the publication of the author's *Captain Pantoja and the Special Service*[3] and *Aunt Julia and the Script Writer*,[4] has come to represent a farcical phase in Vargas Llosa's itinerary. In contrast to the previous decade—*The Time of the Hero*,[5] *The Green House*,[6] *Conversation in the Cathedral*[7]—the seventies, according to the same critics, privilege a parodic tendency in which serious creative impulse cedes to the levity of a prolonged *divertissement*.[8] Mordant irony as well as the intellectual's self-parody are traceable to the author's first novel. Satiric play, or "diversion," as Vargas Llosa calls it, is no less demanding or any less serious. And as he confesses in a later interview,[9] the production of novels such as *Captain Pantoja* and *Aunt Julia* entails as arduous a task (and, perhaps, one of greater risk) as the more "realistic" works of his corpus. I rehearse this trajectory as a backdrop to the writing strategies employed by Vargas Llosa in *The War of the End of the World,* a work that transcends his earlier production even as it reiterates the technical stock of the author's repertoire. In this regard, this novel is a re-inscription, a re-writing in more than one sense.

As much as an appropriation and re-rendering of an earlier work from the Latin American canon, *The War of the End of the World* represents

SCATOLOGY, ESCHATOLOGY, PALIMPSEST

a self-revisionary undertaking by the Peruvian author, one that remands the reader to the whole trajectory of the author's own literary project. Nonetheless, in both cases—appropriative revision and self-revisionism—the significance of the "repetition" is not in constancy but in deviation, not in identity but in difference, the difference that re-marks the recurrence as other(ness), as novelty in iteration.[10] In the case of self-visitation, Vargas Llosa returns, as his countryman Cornejo Polar aptly points out, to the project he has pursued for years, what he calls "la novela total."[11] More than another sally after a "total novel," however, *The War of the End of the World* becomes the dramatization of this constant obsession. In this dramatic rendering, Vargas Llosa's diligent enterprise ends up as the implacable nemesis of everything that implies totalization, be it ideological mystification or teleological transcendentalism. In the vehemence of this turn, the only totalization in the novel concerns gastronomic movement that culminates, significantly, in the excremental. *Scatology,* in its ambiguous Spanish version—*"escatología"*—is an equivocal term that means both scatology and eschatology at once, and Vargas Llosa ingeniously exploits the ambiguity to all ends. The metabolic figure is not gratuitous, either as a naturalistic process or as a rhetorical move. We are dealing, after all, with a deliberate and flagrant case of literary cannibalization, a *literarofagia,* as the Spanish neologism would have it. Vargas Llosa himself refers to the metabolic process through the metaphor of cannibalization when he speaks of a work that he considers exemplary of "la novela total," *One Hundred Years of Solitude.* I translate from his book-length essay on Gabriel García Márquez:

> The themes and motifs of previous fictions are assimilated by fictive reality in this novel, at times through unfolding and amplification, at others through the simple mention or recollection of occurrences. This process is, literally, a cannibalization: those materials are simply digested by the new reality, transformed into a distinct and homogeneous substance.[12]

Obviously, Vargas Llosa is referring to a process of self-cannibalization: the Pantagruelian process loosed by García Márquez against his own sundry production that antedates *One Hundred Years of Solitude.* Nevertheless, the procedure in the Colombian Nobel laureate's work is analogous to

Chapter Seven

Vargas Llosa's own appropriative tactic loosed against the work of the Brazilian Euclides da Cunha. At this level of textual domestication, Vargas Llosa inverts another commonplace, Marx's revision of Hegel on repetition and recurrence. If, as Marx claims, repetition tropes the tragic occurrence into farcical recurrence, Vargas Llosa's *The War of the End of the World* not only seeks to controvert the Marxian apothegm but also attempts a conversion that would render the precursor into farce and his own revisionary repetition into tragedy. Such a strong move is not altogether innocent. Vargas Llosa's is clearly an antithetical posture toward a canonical text and canonized author whom he appropriates as precursor and frame for his own project. The great admiration professed for Euclides da Cunha, even the dedication of the novel to him, does not palliate the measure of contention, of agonistic confrontation between a canonical precursor and a deliberate and willful successor.

Vargas Llosa diligently engages Euclides da Cunha for purposes of a revisionary re-reading. Like all strong readings worthy of the designation, Vargas Llosa's also ends up as an enterprise of displacement, that is, as an intervention whose consequences interpose themselves between the read work and the modes of that work's acceptance and reception as defined and established by the canonical tradition and its evaluative norms. To the extent that these norms are shaken by the subsequent intervention of a reading, the work sustains that reading's revisionary performance. If a reading be truly revisionary, its consequences are inevitably disconcerting, since the canonical consensus must sustain the commotion of reevaluation. Such is the case with Vargas Llosa's appropriation of Euclides da Cunha and his classic *Rebellion in the Backlands,* a work that comes as close to being Brazil's national epic as any other.

The strategy of Vargas Llosa's enterprise is as ingenious as it is simple: the transformation of a document into a monument.[13] His procedure is a well-trod path: he stoops to conquer. The outcome is strictly predictable: consecration that turns, inexorably, into profanation. It is an all-too-familiar topos, the commonplace plot of succession. But the execution of the plot is not so pat, its motivations even less transparent. Latin America's literary tradition already confers a status of monumentality to da Cunha's opus. But Vargas Llosa is not after a monumentalization that this work does not already enjoy. His ambivalent diligence labors, rather, at privileging the precursor work as frame and as target, an ambiguity suggestively expressed in the Spanish equivoque *marco*. Vargas Llosa's is at once an embracing and an aggressive move that converts *Rebellion in the Backlands* into frame and framework for his narrative project and, simultaneously, into a significant target of canonical consequence. Unlike a *document,* which serves to elucidate phenomena or events other than itself, and whose importance lies in what it can proffer with respect to something else, a *monument* is important for itself, in its own existence. Vargas Llosa targets da Cunha's work in this latter sense. What interests him is the density, the historical opacity of the work itself and not its (or his own) novel interpretation of Brazil's or, for that matter, the rest of Latin America's sociopolitical and historical canon. Such a novelty or revision is, of course, an inevitable consequence of any critical intervention.

Vargas Llosa's interest in da Cunha has aesthetic origins. It is founded in the film script he was originally commissioned to render from the Brazilian's work. From that moment the Brazilian master's opus has fascinated the Peruvian novelist. Within that fascination, no doubt, figures Vargas Llosa's longtime preoccupation with the "total novel," a preoccupation not only traceable in his prose fiction, but one that dominates his critical and theoretical formulations as well in the decade of the seventies, that is, just prior to his encounter with Euclides da Cunha's work. Predictably enough, Vargas Llosa's theoretical preoccupations and critical essays on the works of Gabriel García Márquez and Gustave Flaubert have their repercussions in that encounter. The Brazilian's work offers Vargas Llosa an insight into the possibilities of what a "total novel" might be. *The War of the End of the World* may well be the reaction, or, more accurately, the contestation, to that insight. In the end, the novel stands as an act of exorcism that might have cured the author of the impulse to achieve "la novela total." Euclides da Cunha, then, serves as an instrument and a pretext for confronting that inherited or self-engendered daemon. This may explain, in part, the ludicrously twisted and aberrant nature of scriptorial creatures that parade through his novel.

"Totality" and "monumentality" are spectral synonyms. In terms of Michel Foucault's already-mentioned essay,[14] the constitutive process of a monument reflects the procedure of constituting a total history, fictive or factual. The monumentality that Vargas Llosa concedes to the work of

CHAPTER SEVEN

Euclides da Cunha is commensurate to the totalization the work displays as its essential characteristic. Vargas Llosa parodically exacerbates this defining trait in the mirror—his own novel—that he holds up to Euclides da Cunha. I shall elaborate on how he carries out this subterfuge shortly.

In his introduction to *The Archaeology of Knowledge,* Michel Foucault characterizes the process of monumentalization as a collation and integration of sundry elements (disparate documents) with the purpose of forging a totality. A "total history," Foucault notes, is the search for a governing principle, a law that gives history coherence. The monumentalist impulse presupposes the possibility of a system of homogeneous relations, a network of causality that links all events and phenomena so that all of these mutually imply and symbolize each other. Above all, a total history as monument presupposes a magnetic center, an ideological axis—principle, belief, myth, spirit—that connects discrete phenomena. In the seventh chapter of his study on García Márquez (*Historia de un deicidio*), published two years after Foucault's essay, Vargas Llosa describes the process of totalization in the Colombian novelist's masterpiece in unmistakable Foucaultian terms:

> The integration of new and old material is so perfect that the stock of themes and characters retrieved from previous work gives a remote idea of what the verbal in itself is: the description of a "total" reality. . . . The genius of the author resides in his having found an axis or nucleus . . . in which is reflected, as in a mirror, the individual and the collective, the concrete persons and the entire society, that abstraction.[15]

As in their constitutive processes, *monument* and *document* share yet another synonymy, a semantic one that sheds light on Vargas Llosa's fascination with Foucault's concept, with García Márquez's narrative strategy and with the Euclides da Cunha phenomenon. That convergence is centered on a superannuation implicit in the notion of monument and in the process of totalization. The monument is, by definition, reminiscence, an entity recollecting the departed and the disappeared. *Monumentum* is memorialization but also notification, admonition, advertence—connotative significations that take on pressing importance, as we shall see, in

SCATOLOGY, ESCHATOLOGY, PALIMPSEST

Vargas Llosa's enterprise. The monument as a sign of the displaced and memorially recouped, on the one hand, and as a self-referring sign, on the other, entails a juncture where the treatment of García Márquez and the treatment of Euclides da Cunha coincide. Vargas Llosa repeatedly attributes the totality of *One Hundred Years of Solitude* to the fact that this novel "exhausts a world" ("agota un mundo" [496]). "The vocation of 'totality,'" he tells us, resides in "that peculiar attempt to devour the narrator himself, to lose itself within him; it reaffirms, in the dimension of space, that desire for self-sufficiency and an absolute present in the material of the book . . . and, thus, as its life is *all* life, its death is also the extinction of *all*" (542). In other words, essential or ontological plenitude (of *being*) becomes a reflection of plenary and total inexistence. The generative totality is simultaneously eschatological/scatological totalization. Monument and totality, then, share a common fate that is, at once, displacement into inexistence and affirmation in the recuperative power of memory. Both phenomena, monument and totality, are products of *recollection* in the dual sense of the term that simultaneously implies recovery and displacement, recouping and withdrawal. In this ineluctable ambiguity, Vargas Llosa already becomes aware of the paradoxical impasse inherent to a "total" work. Thus, in his essay on García Márquez he notes with respect to the totalizing vocation of *One Hundred Years of Solitude:*

> The novel thus perpetrates the same deicide that the novelist wishes to perpetrate in the exercise of his vocation, the one ambition is reflected in the other. But, in both cases, that attempt only achieves an appearance, a mirage. (542)

The repercussions of this insight become much more explicit and much more accessible in Vargas Llosa's critical study of Flaubert and *Madame Bovary* from a few years later.[16] The linkage between Vargas Llosa's critical evaluation of Flaubert and *The War of the End of the World* with its monumental domestication of da Cunha's project becomes quite clear when the Peruvian author judges Jean-Paul Sartre's "exhaustive" attempt at a mastery, at a "total" evaluation of Flaubert.[17] Vargas Llosa equates the Existentialist philosopher's effort to the equally total encyclopedic project of Flaubert in *Bouvard et Pécuchet*. Vargas Llosa's sentence reads:

Chapter Seven

> Could there be a greater likeness, a failure so equally admirable and for so identical a set of reasons as that of *L'Idiot de la famille* and *Bouvard et Pécuchet?* Both are impossible attempts, enterprises destined to fail, because both fixed themselves beforehand on an unattainable goal; they are weighted by an ambition which in a way is inhuman: the total. (58–59)

Clearly, by the mid-seventies Vargas Llosa discerns, on a theoretical plane, the problematic nature of striving for a "total" enterprise, whether it be in critical valuation or in the composing of fiction. *The War of the End of the World* is the concrete application of that theoretical discernment. The fortuitous, but highly opportune, encounter with *Rebellion in the Backlands* at this juncture, then, offers Vargas Llosa the opportunity to essay his theoretical postulations in his own novel. And what continues in the just-cited passage on Sartre clearly reveals just how opportune that encounter with Euclides da Cunha was at this moment. For those familiar with the Brazilian writer's work, Vargas Llosa's observation sounds even more apt for *Rebellion in the Backlands* than for *Bouvard et Pécuchet* or for *L'Idiot de la famille*. And this is, indeed, what the narrative plot of *The War of the End of the World* dramatizes when it undertakes a problematic monumentalization of da Cunha's work.

> The idea of representing in a novel the totality of what is human—or, if you wish, the totality of stupidity, but for Flaubert both terms express almost the same thing—was a utopia analogous to capturing in an essay the totality of a life, explaining a man by reconstructing all sources—social, familial, historical, cultural, psychological, biological, linguistic—of his history, all of the tributaries of his visible and secret personality. (59)

In this characterization of the drive for totality one reads not only the portrayal of Euclides da Cunha's enterprise; one also finds Vargas Llosa's own project in *The War of the End of the World*. More than that, really, since Vargas Llosa does not limit himself to the material-historical but also embellishes, weaves, invents, augments "the totality of what is human," that is, all that he appropriates from his precursor in order to recoup an even greater totality than the received (or taken) patrimony of his Latin American tradition. How, then, are we to construe this exacerbated compounding

SCATOLOGY, ESCHATOLOGY, PALIMPSEST

of a totality judged by Vargas Llosa as "impossible attempt," "enterprise destined to failure," "unattainable goal," "inhuman ambition"? Vargas Llosa himself offers us a rejoinder, and with this I should like to return to my earlier observation that *The War of the End of the World* does not constitute an attempt to achieve the "total novel" but, instead, the dramatization of this overreaching impulse that necessarily includes its impossibility, its negation, so that the inevitable failure ends up as a "type of triumph" ("una suerte de victoria," in the author's words). I translate, once more, after which I shall elaborate:

> But it is evident that in both cases [i.e., Flaubert and Sartre, and of Euclides da Cunha and Vargas Llosa, one could add] in the flaw resides the virtue, that the failure constitutes a type of triumph, that in both cases the corroboration of failure is suitable only in the admission to the grandeur that explains and that makes failure inevitable. Because, having undertaken such a venture—having incurred in Lucifer's transgression to want to break the limits, to transcend what is possible—is tantamount to having fixed a greater highpoint for the novel and for criticism. (59)

With this anticipatory judgment of Euclides da Cunha, a valuation through the misdirection of Sartre and Flaubert, Mario Vargas Llosa is not exonerating da Cunha but indicting him. His differential "repetition" of da Cunha emphatically discloses the fact that the Brazilian precursor never evinces or admits to a recognition of "the grandeur that explains and that makes failure inevitable" in reaching after totalization, although da Cunha does incarnate in his own biography, in the historical events that determine his melodramatic life, the human paradoxes that contradict the positivities of his ideological and scientific convictions. Euclides da Cunha, in other words, betrays no consciousness of the fact that in his "flaw resides the virtue," even though he incarnates the paradox. Life's unreason humanizes him in spite of the orthodoxy of "infallible reason" that nourished his ideological fanaticism and hobby-horsical mystifications founded, primarily, in totalizing schemas of Spencerian evolutionism and Comtean scientificism. Da Cunha does, indeed, partake of "Lucifer's transgression," as Vargas Llosa would have it, but Lucifer's is a conscious and knowing infraction with full awareness of its possible consequences. And it is, of

Chapter Seven

course, still a breach at a divine and transcendental plane. The transgression of da Cunha consists in aspiring to the transcendent. While Lucifer, then, commits his (mis)deed knowingly, da Cunha transgresses blindly, convinced of his own and of his actions' virtue. That is why Lucifer's fate spells tragedy and da Cunha's a farce. Tragedy issues from confronting the uncompromising force of implacable virtue. Farce ensues from the conviction of believing oneself infallibly virtuous. Convinced of his reason, da Cunha ends up as unreason's dupe, even to his dramatic death, so elaborately dramatized by Vargas Llosa in one of the most prolonged scenes of his novel, as we shall see in due course.

Marx's dictum notwithstanding, then, da Cunha's enterprise is not tragedy for being primal, but rather farce. The tragedy is ironically "staged" by his successor, Vargas Llosa, who repeats that project, cognizant of its inevitable failure, once more, in order to corroborate the fact that salvaging is in human contingency, that "in the flaw resides the virtue" and not in the mystified perfection of an ideological, which is to say illusory, totality. Obviously this cannot be classical tragedy. That is already circumscribed by, and pertains to, its antiquity. Vargas Llosa's modern tragedy displaces austere credulity or belief, replacing it with irony. Thus, faith is transformed into conscience, good or bad, and the mask of tragedy betrays a superimposed grimace of derision that overlays it as "outrageous palimpsest."

The War of the End of the World is a *roman à clef*. The fact that it found its reflection, its repeated inverse image, in a precursor work that betrays so patently its social and intellectual context leads us forcibly to reflect on the context that has engendered this latter "repetition." If the *roman à clef* is an allusive mirror that turns reality into/within its poetic reflection, Vargas Llosa's speculum must reflect, no doubt, more than its ostensible appropriation—Euclides da Cunha's enterprise. That spectral impermeability must also reflect the reality of the author's historical present. Each work, Mikhail Bakhtin's legacy teaches us, has a *generic spaciotemporal dimension,* that is, it engenders specific significance with respect to the problem of appropriating and being appropriated by a particular time and space and by the historical personages that inhabit that dimension. Bakhtin's term for this problematic dimension of literature is *chronotope,*[18] a mathematical term he borrowed from Einstein, who introduced it in the theory of relativity—that nemesis of absolutes and "total histories" in another phase of our cultural life. Bakhtin's focus is on the encounter between literary work and historical reality, "the world." He does not theorize on the problem of a literary work's appropriation and "repetition," or "reflection" of another literary work. Perhaps he does not do so because such an occurrence is implausible; because given the discrete time and space of each occurrence, such reflecting is not possible, even when one work "repeats" another. Borges's Pierre Menard would surely second that insight, amplifying that the repeated or appropriated work figures as yet one more element among those that comprise the *chronotope* of the latter work. In this sense, within Bakhtin's scheme of things every novel would be a *roman à clef.* And in this respect, too, Vargas Llosa's novel is doubly a *roman à clef* because, upon undertaking one textual enterprise based on another, the author has conjugated two *chronotope* into one.

Although the focus of the present essay is on the act of appropriation and domestication of a precursor text rather than on that act's underlying motives, we should remember that such a project is not gratuitous, nor is the particular target of appropriation purely accidental. We should remember, too, that a mode of assimilation has its determinations within the concrete situation of the successor author. Motivations, like intentions, remain a mystery within the process and a matter of critical speculation. Without aiming to privilege any such objects of speculation as exclusive determinants, it should be noted that the conception and execution of *The War of the End of the World* coincides chronologically with a historical juncture where one totalizing ideology is being supplanted by another, both profoundly noxious to Vargas Llosa, at least at that historical juncture. At that transitional crossing, the author himself happens to be subjecting his own intellectual itinerary to close scrutiny with respect to the ethos of totality.

Two dominant ideological postures seem to dominate that temporal threshold between the decade of the seventies and that of the eighties. One, the new scientificism of technobureaucracy, evangelized principally by economists (as, for example, the vaudeville of the Chicago Boys in Chile following the military coup of 1973) and by technocratic regimes, military for the most part, that may not be totalitarian initially but end up that way (as in the author's home country). The other, a renewed zeal of ideological orthodoxy, spearheaded primarily by geriatric pharisees, symptomatic of what we might call the "ayatollah syndrome" that spread during the eighties in the North and in the South, in East and West, in the "Third World" as in

CHAPTER SEVEN

what used to be the other two before the "Second World" collapsed into the "Third." Vargas Llosa's encounter with da Cunha's *Rebellion in the Backlands* at that juncture proved opportune inasmuch as this Latin American classic offers an exemplary conjunction of these two modes of mystification and their totalizing fanaticisms. For *Rebellion in the Backlands* is at once story and history, "scientific" treatise and symptom of mystifying ideologies that range from apocalyptic messianism to scientific evolutionism, from economic and environmental determinism to progressivist positivism. Such reading was an opportune occasion for Vargas Llosa, and he availed himself of that opportunity. Thus, the profound irony and scurrilous parody, which often border on vitriolic truculence, unleashed by Vargas Llosa against da Cunha and his work, must be read as an index to the intensity and vehemence with which Vargas Llosa viewed his own historical present at the time. (I keep stressing the qualifying clause "at that time" in view of Vargas Llosa's own conversion to a mimetic form of neocolonialist "Thatcherism" by the end of the 1980s when he would seek the presidency of his country.) The precursor and *his* historical moment become targets of antithetical displacement. But they are, also, and above all, referential frames and allegorized figurae of the decade of the 1970s and its illusive and deluded zealotries:

> Perhaps there is a whole symbology, entirely a disguise in that story of Canudos, at least in the history of my novel, that has to do with very personal things. At one level I do realize concretely that this is true—at a political plane. That is, I think that the whole problematic that I have lived and that many of us have lived in the seventies is very much reflected in that history. . . . But the problematic of Canudos, that problem of national misunderstandings, of internal civil wars, of ideological fanaticisms . . . well, that is a problem which is absolutely current and that in the seventies I lived it very intimately, very personally. (O'Hara and Niño de Guzmán, 17)

Clearly then, in this sense, the turn-of-the-century Brazilian work finds currency in the penultimate decade of this same century. The intellectual and ideological environment symptomatically represented by da Cunha's project is converted into a monumental mirror in which Vargas Llosa recognizes altogether too much of the 1970s and 1980s not to feel com-

SCATOLOGY, ESCHATOLOGY, PALIMPSEST

pelled to confront its reflections. The author and protagonist of that enterprise also becomes a most signaled target of this confrontation and its subterfuge because Euclides da Cunha himself is unmistakably the greatest protagonist of *Rebellion in the Backlands*. He occupies that role by virtue of the imperiousness of his method and by dint of convictions with which his work is constituted. An ideologically overdetermined work, *Rebellion in the Backlands* is intended as history and ends up as novel, despite the author's prefatory declarations in which he invokes Taine (another mythographer of totality) on the veracity of historical narration, and in spite of the author's first note to the third edition (1905) where, this time, no less a historical narrator than Thucydides and his protestations on the veracity of his history of the Peloponnesian Wars are called upon to sanction the facticity of da Cunha's historical enterprise.

This permutation of history into novel occurs because historical narrative succumbs to the weight and ponderous determinacies of emplotment as well as to the ideological orthodoxies that condition historical fact. Facts and events as such dissolve to become absorbed into the framework, the scaffolding of the "science" that observes and constitutes them as narrative. Thus, *Rebellion in the Backlands* transmutes from an intended historical document into an autobiographical rehearsal. The work, then, betrays more the intellectual conception of the author himself than his conceiving of a work that might be other than the history of his own ideological formation. Precisely for this reason, da Cunha's project lends itself so naturally to monumentalization, to its treatment as an object with its own impermeable semantic and historical density.

Da Cunha undertakes a "total" enterprise inspired by Taine's fundamental and foundational triangulation: race, historical moment, environment. In da Cunha's positivist reshuffling, this triune schema becomes land, man, struggle, with Taine's environmental determinism displaced by a Spencerian evolutionist determinism of inheritance. But what really emerges is another triangle that incorporates and subsumes its author as one of its integers: event, narration, narrator. Or, in another version, occurrence, historicization, historian. This is a turn that befalls da Cunha's enterprise rather than a turn that is deliberately or knowingly wrought by him. And this is why Stefan Zweig, as cited by da Cunha's English translator in his prologue, consigns *Rebellion in the Backlands* to the category of "national epic." Zweig notes, "it was created purely by chance." Da Cunha's work

Chapter Seven

takes on its epic character, indeed, when it leaves behind the positivities of its author's declared intentions; when, that is, the author is transformed from the "entrepreneur" to yet one more symptom of his enterprise. Like the classical and medieval epic, *Rebellion in the Backlands* arrives at the category of epic upon losing awareness of itself, upon losing consciousness of itself as intended epic. Da Cunha's declared intention is prosaic. When his work ceases to be "prose," that is, when it can no longer function as enunciation with "scientific certainty," to paraphrase Hegel, then it becomes epic poetry.

But this, too, is an inversion of Hegel, an inversion of the sequence of things as Hegel orders them in his *Aesthetics,* his lectures on the history of art. Once Renaissance consciousness supplants poetic "innocence," Hegel had noted, prose displaces poetry. The unfolding of a work of "science," that is, of "prose" into poetic epos, as is the case with da Cunha's work, if we accept Zweig's characterization, wreaks a reversal on Hegelian succession. In keeping with this process of inversion and reversibility, Vargas Llosa exacerbates the subversion of progressive schemas of succession that lead, with teleological inevitability, to totalization, be it apocalyptic/eschatological, materialistic, or metaphysical. As an efficacious strategy for this subterfuge that reverts da Cunha's prosaic enterprise into poetic gesture, Vargas Llosa has opted for novelistic "repetition." In turning that "scientific" project into a poetic genre, Vargas Llosa achieves not only the subversion of da Cunha's progressivist ideology, but he manages as well to subvert and invert the metaphysical-transcendentalist enterprise of Hegel and the materialist-historical project of Marx through this antiteleological and antithetical appropriation and "repetition."

Rebellion in the Backlands, then, transmutes into a poetic phenomenon when it unwarily functions as the unintended aberration of its self-declared project. Euclides da Cunha is an epic poet when, unwittingly, he becomes self-distorted into the inverse figure of his enterprise. In light of these reversals and inverse repetitions, perhaps we could appreciate better the anachronisms insinuated in the recounting of da Cunha's story by Vargas Llosa, as, for example, the medieval *leitmotif* figured as the dwarf vaudeville singer, fated to repeat the heroic deeds of the knight errant Roberto the Devil throughout the forsaken desert of the backlands. In the same vein of iconoclastic demystification, we could read the ridiculous figure of the myopic journalist as the laughable personification of da Cunha. That characterization is undertaken with a parodic irreverence that transforms the nearsighted precursor into a blind man destined to witness and report the historical events in Canudos, a seer who looks on but can only "see" through the distorting fragments of his shattered spectacles. This prosopopoeia, furthermore, is subjected to uncontrollable sneezing fits whenever confronted with events he is incapable of comprehending. In his interview with Edgar O'Hara and Guillermo Niño de Guzmán, Vargas Llosa draws the connection between Euclides da Cunha and the myopic journalist in his novel:

> Euclides da Cunha . . . a sick man, a man with great physical shortcomings, but, on the other hand, the intellectual in that story is a totally diminished human being. If there is anyone who cannot see what is happening there, it's the intellectual; he is greatly responsible for all the confusion created around Canudos. They are the ones who write in the newspapers. . . . They are the intellectuals. They are the ones whose vision of reality is really *obnebulated*. The myopic journalist represents all that. (35)

(Vargas Llosa is speaking, in this 1982 interview, at a time when he himself had not as yet arrived at his decision to become a candidate for the presidency of his country.) I refrain from Anglicizing and italicize the Latinate term *obnebulated* because it is a key term in the cultural and historiographic discourse of Brazil's national self-diagnosis at the turn of the century. *Obnibulação brasílica* is an ideologically charged code term that connotes an elaborate theory of racial and ethnic origin and miscegenation, most thoroughly elaborated by T. A. Araripe Junior, a turn-of-the-century nativist whose treatises on the Brazilian race as *sui generis* were very influential in Euclides da Cunha's scientific formation and racist praxis.[19] Thus, Vargas Llosa's use of the term—which, by the way, goes totally unnoticed by his journalist interlocutors in the interview cited above—is a coded barb with a *clef* launched against a whole system of social thought and its originators.

But the figures of the dwarf, of the myopic journalist, and even of the monstrously deformed Lion of Natuba are less scurrilous figurations *à clef* of the Brazilian precursor and of the ideological orthodoxies that underwrite *Rebellion in the Backlands*. Among the most pointed personifications deployed against da Cunha by Vargas Llosa is a figure that the novelist

CHAPTER SEVEN

considers his most original, purely his own invention. "For example," he tells José Miguel Oviedo, "I was fascinated by one of the central characters (that I still believe to be so in the novel) who is totally fictitious, a European anarchist who is in Brazil when the rebellion of Canudos breaks out" (Oviedo, 84). The character Vargas Llosa referred to is Galileo Gall, but, far from being entirely his own invention and "totally fictitious," he figures among the characters with the most concrete antecedent, from his physical appearance to his scientific notions and mystified ideologies. His visionary prototype is none other than Euclides da Cunha, the precursor himself. And, in the final part of *Rebellion in the Backlands*—chapter ten, section five of the "Last Days," dedicated to the "Death of the Counselor"—we have Galileo Gall's physiological model. I cite from the Putnam translation of da Cunha's work:

> Here for the first time our men had an opportunity to see a jagunço who looked well fed and who stood out from the uniform type of sertanejo. His name was Bernabé José de Carvalho, and he was a second-line leader. He gave the impression of being Flemish, and it is no exaggerated conjecture to say that he put one in mind of the fact that the Dutch for long years had roamed those northern territories, trading with natives. His big manly blue eyes shone, and his flat, energetic-looking head was covered with a thick mop of straw-colored hair. These features were by way of being his credentials, as coming from a higher racial stock. (470)

Here, then, is Galileo Gall's racially *un-obnebulated* prototype. Gall's fanatical insistence on ideological purity and on the virtues of "science," as well as his histrionic epistolary notations destined for a European journal of doubtful existence, figure unmistakably as a parodic allusion to Euclides da Cunha and his mystified attachment to European Enlightenment ideologies. No less pointed in this sense are references to da Cunha's faithful adherence to a science of anthropometry and its racial conclusions, a science troped by Vargas Llosa into Galileo Gall's uncontrollable mania for phrenology.[20]

The parodic rendering of da Cunha's scientific positivism through the figure of Galileo Gall is too patent to insist upon. More compelling is what the critics of Vargas Llosa's novel have overlooked for the most part, an oversight for which the author is largely responsible through his already-cited commentary on the genesis of this particular character. I am referring to the parallel between the death of Galileo Gall in the novel and the circumstances of Euclides da Cunha's own demise. In response to a query on the inordinately protracted struggle to the death between Gall and Rufino, whose wife Gall has raped (patent resonances of Cortés/Malinche and Captain Smith/Pocahontas, of Europe in America), Vargas Llosa refers his interviewers to a duel in a romance of chivalry, *Tirante le Blanc,* that lasts a whole night and that he wanted to emulate. In the film script of *Rebellion in the Backlands,* he says, "it was not going to be a long heroic duel, but pathetic, as such a combat surely must be" (O'Hara and Niño de Guzmán, 34). There is, of course, no reason to doubt the existence of such a scene in the author's favorite chivalric romance. His response to the question, however, is a smoke screen, an evasive move that achieves its goal of throwing his journalist interviewers off track. But this scene in Vargas Llosa's novel has an unmistakably pointed *clef.* The episode is deployed with incisive irony against the evolutionist mystification and progressivist mythology of Euclides da Cunha himself. Its aim is directed in particular against what da Cunha's "science" holds as the sertanejo's, the backwoodsman's, "retrograde atavisms," a retrogression by which the Brazilian of the backlands reverts to a medieval ethos, according to the ethnocultural theories of the previously mentioned intellectual *obnibulados.* Euclides da Cunha himself died a melodramatic death in a duel of honor with a colonel he had challenged. Da Cunha's wife had betrayed him in an affair with the military officer. The tragedy repeats itself with implacable irony, since da Cunha's melodramatic son encounters his father's fate against the same colonel as he tries to save the family honor and avenge his father's death.

The da Cunhas' fate finds its allegorical figuration in that protracted and ironically pathetic scene involving Galileo Gall, a "medieval duel" founded on a code of honor and also found in a medieval romance of chivalry. Vargas Llosa clearly cannot resist targeting derisively the paradox offered by da Cunha's biography and scientific convictions. Turning the "retrograde atavisms" that da Cunha imputes to the Brazilian peasant back on da Cunha, Vargas Llosa gleefully points up how an *obnebulated* intellectual mystification such as da Cunha's is capable of engendering and harboring simultaneously the orthodox positivities of scientific modernity and the inviolable normativities of a medieval code.

Chapter Seven

Vargas Llosa's iconoclastic fervor reaches beyond his primary target to debunk a number of myths, dogmas, fanaticisms, and cultural-racial commonplaces. Any system that succumbs to the programmatic convictions engendered by its totalizing mythomania draws Vargas Llosa's subversive ridicule, at times with vehement truculence. In such allegories of demystification, a number of other characters are cast with studied deliberation as instruments of irreverent subterfuge: João Grande, a human thoroughbred, offspring of an "eugenics" program of slave breeding, turns against his mistress-programmer with sexual and mortal violence. The eschatological high priest, the Counselor, finds his scatological end in his own diarrhea. His mystified acolytes take their sacramental communion in that excremental effluence. In this apocalyptic and metabolic totalization, the ambiguity of the equivoque *escaton* becomes reduced to a univocal totalization. Mystified orthodoxy can privilege equally the scatological or the eschatological, the divine or the excremental, the transcendental or the descendental. Where *identity* eradicates difference, even god and the excremental can be homologized into the totalization of *the same.* Within the context of absolutes, differential valuation and relative gradation are inadmissible because value is arbitrarily unique, authoritatively singular and exclusive, and exclusively normative in its determinacies. The system of ideological dogma and its social structures achieve and legitimate totalization beyond human contingency and, therefore, beyond ethics or morality. This is how Vargas Llosa portrays in his novel Moreira César's Republican Jacobinism, Epimonandes Gonçalves's amoral politics, Galileo Gall's scientifico-anarchist fanaticism, and the sanguinary zeal of the cutthroat Alférez Maranhão.

By way of conclusion, I should like to point to two particular episodes in the final part of the novel where Vargas Llosa converts his characters into instrumental figures deployed against ideological structures that most obviously undergird the positivities of da Cunha's work and the programmatic works of other would-be saviors, whether they be operatives of a colonial or a postcolonial era. In the first instance, Vargas Llosa's target is religious fanaticism; in the second, positivistic evolutionism and its concomitant racist "science." The first has the Baron of Cañabrava as its central figure. His name is a homonymic pun alluding to his virility (*varón de caña brava,* literally, "male with fierce bamboo stalk"). Given the part he plays in this episode, his name becomes descriptively mimetic, and the intended pun is unmistakable. The second episode is protagonized by Coronel Geraldo Macedo, a Bahian bounty hunter scorned for his activities by other officers and looked on with contempt by those officers native to less tropical geographies and, thus, racially less "refined." Given Coronel Macedo's role in the culminating scene of the novel, it is important that he be Bahian, from the outback, and racially *obnibulado*. I shall take these two episodes in turn.

In the first episode, the Baron of Cañabrava violently assails religious fanaticism and messianic fervor, epitomized in the Luso-Brazilian tradition by the Moor-slayer King Sebastian and the rise of Sebastianism, an apocalyptic expectation of his eschatological return. The iconoclastic assault is figured by Vargas Llosa as the baron's sexual violation of Sebastiana, woman-servant and lover of his deranged wife, while his wife looks on. What Vargas Llosa has scripted for Coronel Macedo in the novel's closing episode is only slightly less truculent. He is to avenge himself and his race of *sertanejos* for the "obnebulation" to which da Cunha's science and scientific tribe has condemned them. Vargas Llosa emplots this retribution scene as a confrontational spectacle between Coronel Macedo and Alférez Maranhão, "white skinned, blond, closely cropped whiskers, and bluish eyes" (529), clearly a specimen of "superior" racial stock, man of military science, cutthroat political acuity, and ever present in Latin America's history. The Coronel slaps Maranhão to the ground and pisses on him, as the phantasmal eyes of Maranhão's victims look on.

"Truculence," Vargas Llosa asserts, "is a fundamental ingredient of reality on the one hand, and of literature on the other" (O'Hara and Niño de Guzmán, 32). In the reality and the literature of his work, in the conjugation of the two as *chronotope* of the novel, Vargas Llosa corroborates Euclides da Cunha's scriptural prophecy regarding the vanity of a narrative or historiography that might glorify the historical moment he had been destined to live, witness, and die in. His scientific obnebulation veiled from him the prevision that he himself would end up as eschatological/ scatological and outrageous object of succeeding palimpsests.

CHAPTER EIGHT

WRITING BEYOND THE BOOK
José Donoso Elsewhere

That obscene bird is not there for nothing.
—Emerson, "Compensation"

Ghost House

José Donoso's *Obscene Bird*[1] dwells in a house of writing, a house at once fairer and more perilous than prose. Its many windows and numerous doors, walled up and papered over with the desultory scripture of hybrid genres, become passageways of writing's indwelling. The book of the House transmutes into the house of the Book through a scripture that shuttles incessantly, obsessively, between the two. In the repeated crossings of that scribal threshold, writing becomes an ostentation of its own margins: a display of the writing in the book as the writing of the book in the process of writerly performance. When the novel draws toward closure with an apocalyptic conflagration in which the book itself succumbs to incendiary consummation, writing's process outlives that end by crossing its own threshold into the world of literature as canon's novelty. The reading of Donoso's novel reiterates these processes of writing's endlessly (re)current itinerary. Its writerly obsession fires our consumer's curiosity, implicating us in the infernal desire of writing's possession. The novel we

CHAPTER EIGHT

read is an unending postscript to the world of the novel's script. We thus become accessories to writing's survival beyond the pyrotechnic fate of the book and its world. That ultimate and extreme form of the book's self-curtailment as an incendiary act that propitiates writing's continuity echoes its myriad and minute correlatives of abnegation. This congeries of dilapidation becomes at once an essential and supernumerary cumulus that feeds the scripture's fire, a fire as "redemptive" as it is ravaging. For Donoso's novel is a heterocosm of sundry refuse, a desultoriness that finds another life beyond life's utility and operative convention. In this heterogeneity, all that is socially valued becomes mercilessly subjected to transvaluation, not least of all the institution of literature and the civil acts of writing. *The Obscene Bird of Night* is most fundamentally the novel's redactional autobiography, and it is this compelling facet of Donoso's narrative that I should like to remark here.

Our entry into the novel is a threshold of death, Brígida's dead awakening into a new dawn ("Brígida había amanecido muerta"). Our "exit" from the novel's story is an apocalyptic finality swept into the inexorable river of an ashen night. Between these two points of ultimacy, of dawn's death and night's nullity, lies the *jornada,* the work and day of limbo, the novel's writing in a space and a time beyond life's chronology and this side of nothingness, a twilight of suggestion where the bird chatters, the wolf howls, and writing does its job. That endeavor consists in the mortification of the letter, of writing's literal character and literariness, troped as the endless mortifications of society's human detritus, gathered in and shrouded by the "House of the Incarnation" and its ironically dubbed "Spiritual Exercises." While the irony is shrill within its incongruities, the allegorical personification as writing's obsession unfolds with methodically controlled rhetorical equanimity.

There is order in this wasteland, and its chaotic madness has an intricate decorum in narrative emplotment. Irony and metaphor emerge as governing figures through which writing finds its allegory in the world it wrights, and that world, in turn, allegorically reflects writing's compulsive process. The project of this obsessive task consists in unremitting caducity, a vertiginous (re)collection of outcasts and castoffs, spun into skeins of worthlessness, wrapped up as a cryptic cumulus waiting to expire. The outcome is wholly other, of course, as in irony's self-belying gesture. For in its anarchic

Writing beyond the Book

dissolution a desultory heap is generative, its evanescence assertive. Powerlessness in this novel exerts a more emphatic puissance, decrepitude a more arresting vigor; and in its mysterious ironies muteness compels with eloquent garrulity. The nameless has many names as the unnameable, just as the lie is many truths in the guise of fiction. The novel's language is metaphorically declarative, its predications elliptical and ironically self-belying in their obliquity. Nothing is what it appears to be, nothing means what it says, not because of the figurative character of literature's poetic language but because "literariness" itself is figured in a manner that deliberately undermines poetic figuration. In the process, literary composition, the act of writing, turns into a problem that finds no adequate relief or resolution but rather unremitting multiplications. These accretions, in turn, become enveloped by scriptural frames, equally problematic, that they generate as their own provisional displacements.

In this proliferation through self-abnegation and diminishment—a form of "metastasis," as the novel itself terms it at one point (401)—writing becomes writing's allegory, and the novel as a self-consuming package is the ultimate allegory for the process of its own (de)constructions, its own multiple (un)making. This allegorical periphrasis is thematized in the novel's story. The novel's plot, in other words, mirrors in problematic fashion the strategies of its emplotment. At the "culminating" point, when the two (thematic plot and emplotment strategy) coincide in that mirror and threaten to become identical or fuse into one, the novel as book "ends" and puts an end to itself by burning in the fire beneath the bridge and at the edge of the river. It thus forecloses on that closure in which writing would become identical to itself and the novel one with its history, leaving open, instead, the temporal possibility and textual potential of our own repeated and innumerable readings that trace writing's iterative process, endlessly "new" and self-displacing with each reading.

The locus of this thematization is ternary, with the three focal points being the House of Spiritual Exercises of the Incarnation, the Rinconada, and the Bridge. As spatial and metaphorical foci, however, their discrete and individual existences become breached by writing's agency, that is, by the authorial prosopopoeia figured as the "mute" narrator and scrivener in the novel. Himself a problematic entity in multiple refractions, he is referred to variously as El Mudito—the Deaf-mute—Humberto, Humberto

Chapter Eight

Peñaloza, the Seventh Hag, the Miraculous Child, the Witness, the Secretary, and, finally, "the package" that is consumed. The multiple appellation of this graphic figure forms a polyphony, a polyphony that clearly clashes with its most frequent cognomen: El Mudito, the Mute. This deliberate paronomasia echoes, in turn, the most blatant irony devised by Donoso: the loquacity of silence, the garrulity of muteness, the eloquence of quietism. As prosopopoeia of authorial obsession, as personification and mask of writing's enterprise, this oxymoronic figuration speaks to that nagging paroxysm that has assailed every writer since Plato and his troubled Phaedrus: the orphaned exercise of writing, the destitute predicament of writing's graphic discourse as unvoiced but not wordless, as speechless but declarative, as silent but proclamatory, self-sufficient yet as desirous as the howling wolf, decorous and laconic yet as prolix as the chattering bird of night.

The depth of this authorial anxiety in Donoso is a measure of the extremes of abandonment inflicted on his scripture, the dire ferocity with which the package that is the novel is *exposed* in the inexorable end to the inclement fortuities of night, wind, and fire. It is a measure of the disquietude with which the novel is wrought and of the self-immolation that this writing perpetrates on its personae. It is also a measure of the intensity with which it cries out to the reader for its writerly recovery. Not least, the pitch of this scribal anxiety is a measure of the vehemence that confronts oral paraphrasis and proliferating hearsay through the utterance of tyrannical speech that would have writing succumb to an *histoire on dit.* I refer to the most insistent reiteration in the novel: "dicen . . . dicen . . . dicen/they say . . . they say . . . they say," against which the aphoneous utterance of the Mute's scribal gesture is vehemently deployed. Writing's dispossession, in short, acutely prepossesses the constituting of Donoso's work. And it is not surprising that the novel should be constituted by the dispossessed, the orphaned, the discarded, the martyred *pharmakos* as an expiative witness and a monstrous outcast. Donoso, however, is masterfully awake to the fact that such derogation is a double-edged matter. And so, writing's pharmacal duplicity as baneful and as healing, as affirmative gesture and *via negationis,* as articulate muteness, is deployed with an ironic tact that derives and maintains its tenacious potency through the ruse of abdication.

That powerful pertinacity of writing's undying doggedness inscribes itself indomitably as an illegitimate and vexatious bitch, as legend's indelible scrawl: "The yellow bitch is a mere scrawl ("un garabato flaco"), capable of eating anything whatever, even the most disgusting things" (153). That voracious scrawl's obstinacy, like the salvaging hound (*"il veltro"*) of Dante's *Inferno,* at once prurient and famished, is a survival mechanism. Writing's self-negation affirms with rage. For writing negates itself so that it may survive better. And it survives best on residue and relic, as does the limitlessly capacious House of Incarnation, where mounds of cultural and political history's rubbish find their innumerable reincarnations as edifice of writing:

> broken statues of saints that can't be thrown out because they're religious objects and must be treated with respect; mountains of magazines and old newspapers that clutter room after room with dead news items that have turned into food for mice, additions to my library of incomplete encyclopedias, of bound collections of *Zig-Zag, Life, La Esfera,* of books by authors no one reads anymore, such as Gyp, Concha Espina, Hoyos y Vinent, Carrere, Villaespesa; truckloads of assorted objects such as clocks, burlap sacks for wrapping heaven knows what; pieces of worn-out rugs and hangings; armchairs without a bottom—all things that fill the endless cells and yet seem to always leave room for more. (40)

This desultory agglomeration of piety's disposal heap and literature's detritus forms the bookish reliquary in which writing attains to its reincarnations beyond, yet in juxtaposition to, time and its conventions—timelessly temporal because even the clocks accompanying these canonical castoffs, having succumbed to time, are no longer functional; and unconventional because the heap of scripture is no longer suitable to literature's institutional criteria:

> we find Mudito in one of the rooms where the old newspapers and magazines and old books have been stored, in hideaways he fixes up for himself in the middle of all that useless paper . . . sometimes we find him reading, because they say Mudito read all the books and newspapers in the Casa, that's why he is not strong anymore, and yet, when we catch him in those coverts, buried away in those caverns of useless literature, he tears off again . . . but we . . . scramble after him up the mountain of

Chapter Eight

> bound, moldy copies of *Zig-Zag* and *La Esfera* and *Je Sais Tout*
> that I know by heart, trapping me like an animal screaming for
> more old women to come and help, till at last they catch me. . . .
> They begin to wrap me up, swaddling me in bandages made
> with strips of old rags. (266–67)

The expired yet potent scripture and truncated encyclopedism of magazines and newspapers that can only haunt as temporal ghosts outside their time capsules and that form Mudito's diet consume, in turn, this writing's ghostly omnivore. And the anacoluthon that wrenches this cited sentence from the third to the first person finds that unseemly library's curator and consumer analogously bundled, gathered in rags no more decorous than the wrappings of this scribal cumulus or the packages of useless objects heaped under the old women's cots. His writerly consumption, by now consisting exclusively of scribal detritus ("but shadows don't eat until they dare become somebody, and the nameless shadow that feels no hunger wants to melt into the other shadows in the room, to shrink to newspaper size" [358]), augurs this writing subject's disappearance into writing, and the disappearance of his disappearance as his book's scriptive trace consumed in conflagration and transformed into literature and literature's own fiction.

As a literary exemplum, Donoso's textual heterocosm is willfully antithetical, monstrous, ephemeral, eccentric vis-à-vis the canon. In having attained to literary canonicity as a masterful exemplar, it achieves a corroboration of its descriptive statement of writing's masterpieces, a corroboration of the institution of literature as a deliberate or accidental paralogism, as a congeries of incorrigible (per)mutants in adversary militancy against the very canonical status they seek and that may well be conferred upon them. (Donoso articulates discursively, essayistically, the issue of writing's dire predicament when canonized by institutional respectability, when it ceases to be other and marginal to the institution to which it nonetheless aspires, in his essay *The Boom in Spanish American Literature: A Personal History*.)[2]

The Obscene Bird of Night evinces the unmistakable trademarks of a would-be supreme-fiction with a superlative awareness of itself as writing's self-contrariety that willfully proscribes for itself a totalization or transcendence to that "supremacy." As such, its most characteristic ruse is to demure, to give itself over to writing's most fundamental traits: defenselessness, ephemerality, muteness, otherness—paradoxical traits, of course, since writing's defenselessness, as ascribed to it since Plato, constitutes a stance of power, as attested to by the perdurability of the *written Phaedrus* itself. Writing's ephemerality comprises endurance through multifariousness; and as for its muteness, mutability itself becomes its strength as a dialogical polyphony that refuses to yield to logos's formal, ideological reduction or immutable representation.

Mute, mutable, and mythic: this is the story of writing, its fiction as a history and antimyth in *The Obscene Bird of Night,* its writing subject a mute scrivener whose self-characterization pointedly ascribes writing's plaintive predicament to his own fate: "I am used to eyes sliding over me without finding anything to fix on. Why did you follow me, then, if you didn't mean to acknowledge my existence by so much as a glance?" (58). Mudito then amplifies on this graphic lament of being looked through but not seen, seen only as transparency, as medium, as nothing of substantive density: "¿Quién era yo? Nada, nadie, no soy nada ni nadie" (77). I cite from the original Spanish edition here for two reasons, both illustrative of the ontological ambiguities that undergird the novel. First, because the response to the question "Who was I?" equivocates suggestively in Spanish. Depending on the inflection of the first person copula "soy," the statement affirms *and* contradicts itself, especially since double negatives are perfectly grammatical in Spanish. Accordingly, "Nada, nadie, no soy nada ni nadie" could be read as "Nothing, nobody, I am not anything or anybody," with the second clause as emphatic redundant. The statement could as well be read, however, as "Nothing, nobody, I am not nothing or nobody," with the mute scribe at once equivocally stating the negation and affirmation of his ontological status. Secondly, I cite from the original Spanish edition for the simple reason that the passage has been deleted by Donoso when he amended the original somewhat for the English translation, rendering, in the process, writing's equivocal otherness into haunted and haunting other space. This excision, so telling in itself, also reflects suggestively the ambiguous equivocation of the deleted passage. In that passage, writing, as a graphic affirmation of its own differential, deferential, and equivocal role, confronts, via the prosopopoeia of Mudito, what would banish its claims as nontransparent, nonmimetic density.

Chapter Eight

Writing confronts, in other words, the terror of ideology. Given the traditional part assigned to writing as translucent medium or faithful mirror, its self-problematizing assertion implies a revolutionary stance. This becomes especially significant in the case of Donoso, who, until the publication of *The Obscene Bird* in 1970, was generally regarded as a bourgeois writer remarking the sociology of the Chilean bourgeoisie. Writing's defiance in this instance, however, confronts, with an "ideological" obstinacy of its own ambiguous denial, the epitome of ideology, Che Guevara—ideology's martyred and most visible persona at the time of the novel's composition in the late sixties. This ideological figura too becomes incarnate to haunt with its own fury in the House of Incarnation:

> Where did I know him from, could it be from the news of outdated newspaper . . . the newspapers and magazines and books that as old as they may be are always good for something? What did that apocalyptic figure that filled the Casa demand from me? In the night he did not leave me in peace in galleries, shouting insults at me, coward, asslicker, effeminate, sellout, dragging his whole retinue that chanted the litanies of the world's tragedies through my passageways, invading my solitude, cornering me, convoking a turbulent multitude that burst into my world intending to tear it to pieces. (77, my translation)

The passage may well betray a besieged writer's unhappy consciousness or writing's graphic social conscience. Writing, nonetheless, must press its own claims as pertinacity in a less-than-ideal world, and it does so with ironic vehemence. Yesterday's newspaper that incarnates in its tableau the bearded revolutionary ideologue is shaped into a dunce's bonnet worn by the nubile harlot, Iris, and finally committed to the fire, the inevitable conflagration that is the fate of all scripture, including, proleptically here, that of the novel itself. Even (especially) ideological writing must endure alchemical burning, timely depuration: "I found the paper bonnet discarded in the mud of the patio and I burned it. The stench of singed whiskers soon dissipated in the breeze" (79, my translation). The original Spanish reads, "El olor a barbas chamuscadas pronto se disipó en la brisa." Now, the adjective *chamuscado(a)* metaphorically connotes a "taint," ideology's untenable taint on writing's mutable body in this instance, and the phrase "oler a chamusquina" (542) idiomatically figures what in English would be rendered as "to come from hot words to hard blows." The summary banishment of this railing revolutionary persona and the overweening contentions of ideology through the excision of the passage from the 1973 English version of the novel is, indeed, a coming to hard blows that spells a literal knockout. This is a strong move on behalf of a writing's persona that characterizes itself as "nothing" and as "nobody." The stalwart other face of this ambiguity is not unaware of its own puissance as writing's voiceless but deadly sentence that can dispatch or embrace its object.

Mudito as the mute scrawl, the "soundless words" that compel, the faceless "nobody" in the typefaces of writing, the nameless "nothing" that can name all things and call all things names, would have everything devolve to incipient limits of possibility, to full potential poised on the verge of inception. Thus, his very first voiced utterance: "Nada" (86), "Nothing" (64), an ontological nullity, a mute's fabula in which everything is virtually comprised as tantalizing possibility. It is also a frightful event, an awesome howl that shatters the night's emptiness with the echoing presence of "nothing" that betrays ontology as fabulation's fictions, the secret and secreted life of writing's desire:

> Frightened to death, covering my mouth with one hand and holding my throat with the other, I ran down streets that my voice had turned into an abyss filled with the faces of people who all resembled Don Jerónimo, Emperatriz, Peta—cruel people who are going to report me to Mother Benita, who'd tell Father Azócar that my whole life was just a story . . . Mudito can talk, he has desires, his eyes have extraordinary power, he knows things, he can hear, he's a scoundrel, a dangerous person . . . and they'd take away my keys, the ones I use to lock myself in here . . . nothing, nothing. The accusing word had escaped from me and now it was burning my throat. (64–65)

"Nothing," this predicative affirmation of/as a fiction, as declaration of nonbeing, Mudito's life as "just a story," constitutes a haven whose graphic "keys" allow him to take refuge in its soundless words, in the voiceless

CHAPTER EIGHT

worlds of writing. The utterance and fabulation as the essential inversion of plenitude and being transforms his world into an abyssed constellation that brings his "facelessness" face-to-face with the haunting figures that populate his fiction and incarnate his own writing. This abysmal compounding of writing's borders, of graphic frames and scribal thresholds, these junctures of self-belying nullity where incipient and ultimate edges verge as interstitial vibrancies of writing's articulations, function as indices that betray writing's own process and the novel's redactional story. On this front, *The Obscene Bird of Night* displays its writing's autograph and its scriptor's autobiography. The conjugation of writing and self-writing (the implied identity between the two), however, is relentlessly undermined. This differential subversion issues from the fact that the ploy of *mise en abîme,* of writing framed by writing, entails more than autography, because the writing "con-tained" by writing is deliberately untenable and untenably "main-tained."

Writing, in other words, ostentatiously engenders its alterity; writing becomes other than what is already written in the materiality of the novel. It emerges as what is being written or what is about to be written through the pretext of the novel as book. The notion of autograph, or abyssed writing, then, is a truly problematic proposition, a compounded fiction. Likewise, the scriptor's autobiography, the writing subject in the novel in coincidence with his enterprise—in what is technically referred to as "authorial parabasis"—becomes equally problematic. It does so deliberately in this novel because Mudito as writer and as writing's personification obsessively eludes a self-identity. In fact, he eludes a "self," not to speak of an identity to it, by self-effacement, defacement, and multiplication into compulsive and compelling otherness. This self-problematizing strategy of negation takes on many guises. It others its "self" into its differential alterities in and into other words with unremitting obsession and paroxysmic paradox, giving way to antithetical paralogisms and figural oxymorons: garrulous muteness, omnipotent impotence, youthful senectitude, prepossessing dispossession, nonideological ideology, civic/institutional wolfishness—all summed up by the novel's most painstakingly wrought figura: the *imbunche,* a paralogism that literally translates as "confusing subject with an impossible solution."

As an interstitial non sequitur that oscillates between affirmation and negation, between self and other, between mask and transparency, *The Ob-*

scene Bird of Night, then, serves as a threshold to Donoso's subsequent major novels. Henceforth, Donoso's authoring agon and his scriptive corpus will haunt the ghostly demarcations of this writing's frontiers. I should like to move along now, next door, to one such visitation of these scribal revenants.

Next Door

Next door is always in an other space, another yearned-for place of the other yearning in the perpetual unsituatedness of u-topia. Writing's difficulty must be brooked in the writing, inevitably. The predicament finds no necessary and sufficient conditions of absolution or amelioration in its protocols. The assuasive salve does not reside in what is written but in what writing does not give up, in what and where writing does not yield, in the indomitable and untenable otherness that writing insinuates only as a trace and never as a presence or outright representation. The only hope is a partial and borderline suggestion, a promise that reverberates at the far and always further end(-lessness) of writing's unpredictable alterities. Thus, the passage from the "unsubdued forest where the wolf howls and the obscene bird of night chatters" (Henry James, Sr.) next door to "the laughter in the garden [of] echoed ecstasy / Not lost, but requiring" (T. S. Eliot) is no less an attempt to indemnify the scriptor's damned project, to recoup the light in the darkness, the dancing in the stillness, the hope in the enervation of hope, the scrawl in the blankness of the page.

Donoso's peregrination from the *locus damnificus* of *The Obscene Bird of Night,* epigraphized by Henry James, Sr., to *El jardín de al lado*[3] ("The Garden Next Door"), punctuated at its pivotal turning point by T. S. Eliot, does not figure a felicitous pilgrimage to a *locus amoenus* that lies beyond the howl of requirements or the unrequited need for ragged salvaging. Writing's prosopopoeia, as authorial persona or as hapless scribe, is always already circumscribed by a yearning world of writing that will never yet relinquish its differential otherness to the writer's solicitation. Thus, whether walled in, wrapped up, and packaged tightly—as is the case of Mudito the

Chapter Eight

scrivener—or shut out, exiled, kept at voyeuristic distance—as is the writer and would-be novelist Julio Méndez in *El jardín de al lado*—there is a breach to be brooked, an impossibility to be countenanced, a divide to be negotiated. Traversing from here to there always figures a stray travesty that suspends the goal, extenuates distance, and attenuates direct bearing. The trajectory, then, becomes inexorably elliptical, the path unpredictably misleading.

This is Donoso's itinerary through *El jardín de al lado*. And his pilgrimage echoes in the citations of its epigraphs the circuitous journey of two wayfarers, Cavafis and James Joyce, two whose Virgilian services Donoso engages with allusive pathos throughout his peregrination. For launching as he does from the nightmarish port of his wakeful history, his exilic wanderings will have taken him by the end of the novel to the *mare nostrum's* enchanted other shore, "next door" to the indigent home of the Alexandrian poet and its haunted geography. And Donoso's scriptor will have been baptismally immersed and metamorphosed in Ovidian fashion in the mysteries of the Kasbah of Tangier, leaving behind the trace of his impossible novel, the chronicle of its impossibility that elicits the sanction of an ambiguous and androgynous writing as coincidental script, the published novel of the "Glorious" other we retrace in readerly consumption. But if the antipodic mirrors of Joyce and Cavafis open as a double door to the antechamber of Donoso's dark wood-become-a-garden-next-door, it is T. S. Eliot's Dante that serves as mirrored lamp and supple guidepost in steadying the wayward voyage through a shadowed forest and a sinuous path. And as the enervation courses through *Néant,* through writing degree zero and blankness of the page, the recourse for the energy to salvage the journey citationally harks back to the third part of the second quadrivium from Eliot's *Four Quartets*. It is here, where the infernal whiteness ogling the scribe darkens to an infernal shadow with triple intensity in its incipit and enjambs its first verse with a Stygian verve: "O dark, dark, dark. They all go into the dark"—there, where the opened abyss of the ensuing verse proffers its ineluctable promise to be won and its unhurried challenge to be vanquished: "The vacant interstellar spaces, the vacant into the vacant."

Donoso's self-conscious evocation of Dante's Eliot in this "middle way" —at the midpoint of his novel (111) and in midcareer—enjoins his exilic itinerary to one of exile's most emphatic poets, who, banished from his native Florence, would begin "Nel mezzo del camin" (*Inferno* 1.1) to explore the byways of the wayward path ("la via smarrita" [*Inferno* 1.3]) in the human comedy's divine way stations, or in "the divine comedy's human leaps and lapses" (the phrasing here belongs to Dante's inimitable translator Allen Mandelbaum), as he went on enduring the salt taste of exile's bread and the vicissitudes of the path that descends and ascends the stairs of others (*Paradiso* 17.57–60). Eliot's *Four Quartets,* certainly its "East Coker" evoked by Donoso, is a polyphonous lament in which authorial predicament, historical circumstance, and epigonic anxiety converge into a scribal threnody with incorrigible hope:

> So here I am, in the middle way, having had twenty years—
> Twenty years largely wasted, the years of *l'entre deux guerres*—
> Trying to learn to use words, and every attempt
> Is a wholly new start, and a different kind of failure
> Because one has only learnt to get the better of words
> For the thing one no longer has to say, or the way in which
> One is no longer disposed to say it. And so each venture
> Is a new beginning, a raid on the inarticulate
> With shabby equipment always deteriorating
> In the general mess of imprecision and feeling,
> Undisciplined squads of emotion. And what there is to conquer
> By strength and submission, has already been discovered . . .
> ("East Coker," V)

Eliot goes on to end "East Coker" in an encyclical tone whose anaphoric tempo and driving cadenza leave Dante behind to echo in Ecclesiastes. But Eliot's intonation too has a decidedly historical precedent that resounds with the baneful circumstances of exilic experience and political trials that perennially haunt the dispossessed other among others' prepossessions. I refer to Eliot's coda here, which gives voice to the motto of Mary Queen of Scots in the Tower of London: "In my end is my beginning."

Donoso's circuitous harking back to the beleaguered Dante and the woeful Mary Stuart through this Eliotic incorporation into the midsection of his novel underscores the emphatically political character of his writing. And by political here we are to understand a highly textured site whose map includes, at once, the politics of writing, the politics of gender, the politics of historical torsions, and the ideological distortions of political power

Chapter Eight

whose self-serving claims displace and ostracize even would-be alterities as an insufferable threat. Donoso's *The Obscene Bird of Night* has already dramatized this allegory of power in the juxtapositions of oligarchical privilege to the desultory discards of social dispossession. In *El jardín de al lado,* he rends the allegorical mask, baring the *clef* of his *roman-fleuve* to the point that more than likely proves unbearable for some, not only for politicians and petty dictators but for stalwart church wardens of our literary institutions, as well as for homophobic *machos.* A writerly text that confronts its world and worldly circumstance, *El jardín de al lado* indeed unfolds within the reckoning of history's nightmare from which Stephen Dedalus, transposed to the epigrammatic head of Donoso's novel, is still trying to awake. And it unfolds, too, with the almost fateful inexorableness of ancient tragedy which that other Greek, Cavafis, at the epigraphic gateway of this Donoso script stoically embodies as Necessity. Donoso is not oblivious to this political constancy, to the allusive byways plotted by his novels that on the abacus of some might come up redundant. His response lies at the threshold of his Eliotic citation; just where Donoso stops citing, Eliot continues with studied and insistent re-iteration:

> You say I am repeating
> Something I have said before. I shall say it again.
> Shall I say it again? In order to arrive there,
> To arrive where you are, to get from where you are not,
> You must go by a way wherein there is no ecstasy.
> In order to arrive at what you do not know
> You must go by a way which is the way of ignorance.
> In order to possess what you do not possess
> You must go by the way of dispossession.
> In order to arrive at what you are not
> You must go the way in which you are not.
> And what you do not know is the only thing you know
> And what you own is what you do not own
> And where you are is where you are not.
> ("East Coker," III)

Eliot's antithetical enigmas undergo a transformation in Donoso. *El jardín de al lado* elevates this counterpoint to a high order of desperate intensity, to an instrument of cultural and historical diagnosis, to an austere device of authorial confession, to a severe measure for probing the somber intensities of writing's vocation. The soundings of this scrutiny figure an echoic discourse, a heterocosm of crossed antitheses that resound in a mirror: splenetic yet compassionate, melancholy yet desiring, despairing yet auspicious, desolate yet expectant. As a more extended antithesis, disconsolate pathos finds its antidote in the manifold otherness of juxtaposition. Disbelieving in the possibility of an apocalyptic absolution, shunning the univocal word of the self-convinced, suspicious of the ideological talisman, the orthodox emblem, the canonical cameo, and the unproblematic deliverance they would proffer, Donoso's scripture is hell-bent *not* on resolution but on rummaging, *not* on hierophantic salvation but on heterodox salvaging. As such, the site of this writing is a shifting ground, a mobile locus for the *convivio* of alterities. And the problematic mutability of this restive seeking that always devolves upon exilic shiftlessness finds its animation on the edgy and exercised marginalities of the dispossessed, the contiguities of otherness that, instead of converging, engage in a compensatory exchange of their histories, in a conversative trade in sundry versions of their otherness and its unremitting difference.

Thus, the garden next door in the Old-World city in the heart of Spain is also the garden at home in the exilic memory of the New-World city in Spanish America's Santiago, Chile. "Home is where one starts from," Eliot avers. But in the beginning is also the end, and in the end is the beginning. Eliot knew the atopicality of the predicament quite well, born as he was in Saint Louis, Missouri, a New-World home, traveling as he was to "East Coker," Somerset Village, England, an Old-World home of the Eliots' birth. The alterities are confounded and confounding. Antipodic (mirrored) symmetry implodes problematically into the disjunctions of a filiation that refuses to cohere; the antistrophe denies being rendered into harmonized epode; the antithesis that stubbornly tries to cling to its adjacency comes up against its indomitableness. The garden next door scurries unremittingly next door; the home garden is no more at home and the next-door garden never has been home. Both are elsewhere, in antithetical filiation through mind's eye and memory's recollection. And the amenity of the genial garden now turns to "unsubdued forest" and "dark wood" where the wolf still howls, and the obscene bird chatters once again. Thus, the neat antitheses derail from the straight path, Euclidian parallels flee into random ellipses,

Chapter Eight

ordered dichotomies crisscross helter-skelter, opening up to exponential increments of contingency.

Within this complex, this novel's Stephen Dedalus—Julio Méndez's uncomprehended and unassimilable son—wanders off into his own creative exile only to haunt his parents' homeless home-front as a deracinated and dispossessed supplement, as an androgynous ephebe, as an ambivalent hermaphrodite and scatological jewel out of Cavafis. Bijou, Méndez's substitute son of ambivalent gender and unpredictable acts, of fathomless yet unassailable vulnerability and invisible resources, floats in randomness and contingency. He bursts on the scene as a wayward waif and exile's scapegoat and ends as a Virgilian father to his would-be paternal substitute. It is (s)he whom Julio Méndez invokes as a psychopomp to guide him in his transformational passage through the infernal other world of the multifarious Kasbah of Tangier, just as he had done previously through the kasbah of Madrid, the multitudinous Rastro. Intrusively mercurial, like his kleptomaniac prototype Hermes, Bijou serves as a catalyst in Julio Méndez's transvaluation of his bourgeois values to the unveiling of the *faux-semblants* that dissimulate the sanctioned little criminalities of bourgeois decency. It is through this hermaphroditic adolescent, this generational other to the middle-aged Julio Méndez, that the latter begins the arduous and often painfully hysterical process of demythologizing the foundational myths in which his middle-class ethos and neuroses find their legitimation. And in a more profound and cataclysmic sense, it is this would-be Rimbaud of the Verlaine-Mathilde triangle, this *angelo musicante*, as Julio dubs him, who sends a seismic shudder to the complacently self-centered sexuality of Julio and Gloria Méndez's droll marriage (78).

Though peremptorily repressed and dismissed, this awakening may well have been, nonetheless, the spark that would lead to Julio's acceptance of his own ambivalent and ambiguous sexuality, as well as to his recognition of the rightful claims of the generic other, of Gloria as legitimate alterity, as real other and superior scriptorial talent. Any recognition of one's creative limitations as a writer figures an agonistic trial, especially exacerbated when coupled with the concession of primacy to the creative powers of the "weaker gender" on the part of a phallocentric agonist at midlife plagued by the insecurities and ambiguities of his own sexuality, as is the case here with Julio Méndez. On this reckoning, the antithetical stress within sexuality and scripture, gender and engendering, writing and authorial potency, serves as the animating force that propels the itinerary of Donoso's novel through the embattled way stations of its cathartic and purgatorial plot.

El jardín de al lado is a chastening scene of writing become a scene of recognition that, in turn, transmutes again through reincorporation into a scene of writing. It figures a writer's self-recognition in a trial by fire, the threat of failing potency. At the far end of this alchemical trial, however, Donoso's plot offers no orthodox purities in the depuration. One finds, instead, a heterology, a heterodox intermingling of differential multiplicity, of "unnatural" ruptures that transgress received hierarchies of domesticity. And the exercise of writing falls to the subservient other; it devolves upon the dispossessed alterity, as it did once before in the case of Mudito the secretary, amanuensis and general domestic in the institutional hierarchies of Latin America's oligarchic order. And, as was the case in *The Obscene Bird of Night,* institutional order(ing) in *El jardín de al lado* becomes subjected to a politics of substitution through the mediate pressures of writing's agency—the agency of scriptor and of scripture as diverse pharmakos: expiatory sacrifice and witness, martyr and attester, dependent and scribal deponent. In the earlier work, the institution of power traces a clearer dialectic of antitheticality, rooted, as it is, in the destitution of those who would confer its privilege. Potency, whether sexual, generative, or scriptive, is not a possession but the consequent by-product of dispossession, and, as such, its authority lies in the "powerless" other. In *The Obscene Bird,* the politics of this order find their dramatic foregrounding, now as a discursive predication, now as an apostrophe: "[W]itnesses are the ones who have power" (205); "don't leave the room, Humberto, watch me . . . lend me your envy to make me potent . . . you're the owner of my potency, Humberto, you took it just as I took the wound on your arm, you can never leave me, I need your envious eyes beside me if I am to go on being a man" (185). And while the privileged apprehend the indispensable nature of the "dispensable" other, the latter is no less cognizant of the authorizing necessity of his otherness: "[S]tripped of everything of the Humberto I used to be, except the still active principle of my eyes. I am just another old woman, Don Jerónimo, I'm Iris's dog, let me rest . . . I've already served you, being a witness is the same as being a servant" (62); "sew me all up, not only my

Chapter Eight

parched mouth, but also my eyes, *especially* my eyes, so their power will be buried deep under my eyelids . . . sew them up, old women, in that way I'll make Don Jerónimo impotent forever" (65).

Now, in *El jardín de al lado,* the antithesis moves beyond a linear dialectic, or, one could say, it becomes truly dialectical in transumpting to a reversible scripture whose politics of substitution entails a mutuality of implication, a capability of the pharmakos (writing and scriptor) to author(ize) *and* usurp the other as the other, to privilege the other through a self-effacement that is simultaneously a self-privileging of one's own position. In short, a typical strategy of the ironic turn. Within the reversibility of this scriptive *convivio,* otherness attains to a domesticity of unpredictable (and unpredicative) exchange that proscribes the possibility of domestication. The scribing "domestic" could well be, through the ruse of indeterminacy, the purveyor of the script for a master(ing) narrative. And what ultimately salvages Donoso's novel from the dirge of splenetic monody is precisely this indeterminate surprise, the irony of a Jamesian turn (Henry, Jr., this time) that catapults the narrative and its history into the "echoed ecstasy" of this oscillation within as well as between otherness. In this emphatically conversative economy of writerly compensation, a diacritical process, or interrelation, constantly (re)capitulates writing to its otherness, the novel of the writing and the writing of the novel apprehending each other without monitory apprehensions.

I do not mean to imply by this "capitulation" that writing crystallizes into totalization through self-seizure—an endomorphic autolepsis, with the novel in the writing and the writing in the novel mutually gripping with inextricable and solipsistic stricture. Much to the contrary, the process I describe is indeterminately apprehensive, one in which every instance of attained security or privilege engenders a dispossession not only of the other but within the "secured" position, within the authorized and authored privilege itself. For, if this scriptive autolepsis figures a self-writing of writing—an "autograph"—then autography, as with autobiography, ultimately figures a critique, a diacritical enterprise, and, as such, it is always bent on critical apprehension, always on a course of decision, adjudication, and evaluation that does not run, cannot run out its course. The diagnostic project is always that, a dia-gnostic that inscriptively proscribes a definitive gnosis. By virtue of its analytic task, diagnosis works as anacalypsis rather than as apocalypsis. As diagnosis, in other words, the critical examination is always augmentative rather than subtractive. It figures a parting discernment that necessarily compounds rather than one that renders a reduction. And as writing, it is by its very nature redactive rather than reductive. In this sense, writing as autograph engenders not only the transgressive frames of the provisional diagnoses it inevitably must transgress; it becomes generative, too, of a problematic and nonreductionist synonym between critique and eros because writing is a desperate demand for love. Certainly so in Donoso and unmistakably in *El jardín de al lado,* where exilic writing clamors for acceptance by and of the other. ("No necesito su amor para terminar mi novela," Julio Méndez cloyingly protests at one point [215].)

Writing is always exilic by virtue of necessity. Necessarily exilic because it is engendered by an irredressable plaint, an insecure insufficiency with an unrequited necessity to become necessary. Destined to founder in this seeking, writing invariably encounters the greatest necessity of all, impossibility—the impossibility born of betrayal and self-betrayal, the impossibility of decisively and decidably breaching otherness, of comprehending and being comprehended by "next door" into home. If indemnifying acceptance is an impossibility, there is, of course, the venue of surreptitious usurpation. And this is the recourse adopted by Donoso in *El jardín de al lado.* But, in the end, this hermetic strategy proves no less treacherous. (Gloria must write a second novel that "confirms" the present surreptitious first one. Does a writer ever know which is the "second" novel of confirmation? Is not each one a furtive first novel?) Thus, writing must go on seeking conciliation and indemnity in desultory versions of its own production, a production in which betrayal itself becomes scripted, embedded as a curse on the wandering exile in exile's multifarious contingencies. *El jardín de al lado* dwells precisely in/on this adversative site of writing's adversity, rehearsing the writer's betrayal by writing's insurmountable demands in the rendering of experience to scripture. Scribing itself entails more than sufficient indomitable adversity to allow for its domestication into instrumentality, into a tractable medium for chronicling experience.

In the end, as a novel *El jardín de al lado* does not comprise or circumscribe the novel being rewritten in the novel by the beset Julio Méndez. It is comprised, instead, by the (other) scripture of the other, the writing "next door" inside one's own borrowed home, if you will, that chronicles

Chapter Eight

the vicissitudes of the novel's impossible writing, its pre-cluded completion. We are left, in fact, with the incompletion and the impossibility of the novel being written, with the unbreachableness of Julio Méndez's re-vision and revisions as he goes on to essay endlessly revisionary versions of writing as a professor of literature, as a professor of writing's insatiable desire that knows no closures and admits of no indemnity. In this sense, Julio Méndez, the former political prisoner and exiled writer, recapitulates to writing's sententious sentence; he becomes "reconciled" to writing's irreconcilable corpus as yet another reading and writing grapheme. The story he leaves behind is a surreptitious production that displaces him as authorial persona, as will the indomitable turns and twists of textuality that inevitably will have undermined the proprietary authority of his professional/professorial illusions of mastery, turning him out, yet again, into exile's nowhere.

If writing be a demand for love, reading is no less a desperate clamoring to brook exclusion, to breach unbreachable otherness in unrequited yearning. As a professor of literature, Julio Méndez cannot escape this insight. It becomes doubly poignant, then, that he should be reading out loud to Gloria (214–15) the revised versions of his impossible, would-be novel while she, in fact, as it turns out, is the one authoring the novel of his enterprise's impossibility and is the graphic voice of his own narrative throughout our reading.

Within the conversative economy of this reversible scripture, the novel we read is the consequent difference—as in the above-cited enigmas of Eliot's antithetical way stations—that issues from the other's ineluctable intrusion to salvage writing's enterprise. Like Julio Méndez, like his most significant other, like Donoso, we oscillate between writing's novel and the would-be novel in the writing. Rather than an endomorphic ruse on the part of a self-privileging authority—authorial or prosopopoeic—this differential situation of unsituatedness translates into the fact that we all inhabit (and are inhabited by) an itinerant predicament, a predicament of interstitiality —between alterities but also betwixt the manifold otherness within. It is a volatile habitation, its predicament subject to the contingencies of unpredictable commutation. Donoso's *El jardín de al lado* allegorically dramatizes the allegory of this predicament. And, of course, I consciously emphasize "allegory" in the reiteration, lest we forget the otherness of atopicality that its radical etymons connote. Need I repeat Donoso's Eliot? I shall repeat Donoso's Eliot:

> In order to arrive at what you are not
>   You must go through the way in which you are not.
> And what you do not know is the only thing you know
> And what you own is what you do not own
> And where you are is where you are not.

In Donoso's text, this Eliotic allegory of scurrying unsituatedness finds its echoic parentheses in George Eliot and in Henry James, for Donoso situates the internal displacements of his novel between *Middlemarch* and *The Spoils of Poynton*. And what sustains, literally and materially, his *tandem* scriptors—the would-be novelist, Julio, and the novelist, Gloria—of his novel is a "tedious translation of George Eliot's *Middlemarch,* done *in tandem* with Gloria, a task that seemed eternal, but one which provided a modest but sure income" (13). When, finally, at long length, the reversible significance of this scriptive tandem is revealed by dint of a Jamesian twist, and Gloria's writing, which gives voice to Julio's narration, displaces the latter altogether from the ruse of narrative performance, then we read: "And while I [Gloria] read and write, he puts the final touches to his translation of *The Spoils of Poynton.*" And then, in tandem, a parabastic reflection, an autographic-exegetical moment of reflexivity:

> Some relationship to the sold Roma home [the family home in Santiago, Chile], whose sale allows us to live a bit better, with the auctioning and dispersal of its furnishings that might be Poynton's? I have read Julio's translation: it is daring, creative, a masterpiece.
>   While I write this, I see him totally absorbed in its revision. (215)

Sustained by a version of *Middlemarch* in the beginning, "totally absorbed" into a revision of *The Spoils of Poynton* in the end, Donoso's ostensible scriptor and his ostensible script straddle in oscillation the vicissitudes, on the one hand, of a family romance of Torys and Reformers in political strife and, on the other, of the dispersal and dispossession of a

Chapter Eight

homefront and its heirlooms. The first, authored by a woman writer, Mary Ann Evans, with a male persona, George Eliot, becomes subsumed into *El jardín de al lado,* a novel with a male author and an ostensibly male narrator but with a female scriptor. The second is an equally androgynous script, scripted by a Henry James, whose own gender has its animus in the mesomorphic ambiguities of an equivocating otherness. This, too, becomes subsumed by Donoso into the equivocal ruse of his graphic figurae and into the transanimation of Donoso's/Gloria's revising and "revised" scriptor. *El jardín de al lado,* the garden next door itself, comprises a daring embrace equally of the other and of its parentheses, allowing a multifarious suggestion of the other to situate itself in parenthetic relation. In that hospitable relation, its problematic, internal otherness inverts its parentheses, turning its parenthetical bookends outward, opening up and up to a writing that endlessly seeks to unveil what may lie next door, and beyond the next, infinitely.

CHAPTER NINE

A WOMAN'S PLACE
Gendered Histories of the Subaltern

I have no theory to offer of Third World female psychology in America.... As a white woman, I am reluctant and unable to construct theories about experiences I haven't had.

— Patricia Meyer Spacks, *The Female Imagination*, 1976

Spacks never lived in nineteenth-century Yorkshire, so why theorize about the Brontës.

— Alice Walker, "One Child of One's Own—An Essay on Creativity," 1979

I find the above juxtaposition of Patricia Meyer Spacks and Alice Walker particularly instructive.[1] The lesson I derive from this counterpoint leads me to the conclusion that, in my own critical practice, between neglect and intrusion I must opt for intruding. I follow the more hazardous path of intervention, keenly aware that all of our acts may inevitably be as interventionist as they are exclusionary. I find the risks of intervention preferable to the safety of supervention. Supervening, in the final analysis, is a supreme form of willful neglect, if not righteous ignorance. By "supervention" I understand a self-removal to the security of a superior venue, to a self-serving higher ground.

Persuaded, then, by the wisdom of Alice Walker's riposte to Patricia Meyer Spacks, I have sallied into the perilous terrain of the other, as I now venture into the critical minefield that feminist discourse, as articulated by Spack's apologia in our epigraph, has reprovingly disciplined as women's domain.[2] In this undertaking, I shall trace the steps of a particular woman, Diamela Eltit, a writer who makes "a woman's place" the problematic locus of her writing as "literature" and as her own life's writing practice. I am not a woman. But, then again, I have not limited myself to writing my

CHAPTER NINE

autobiography in the exclusive sense of that circumscription. I am not a Latin American man, either. Certainly I am no Latin, and my marginal Americanness is due only to that unnatural act which the U. S. Immigration and Naturalization Service, in its denatured causticity, designates as "naturalization." My own critical sense of cultural ethos dictates that who we are not is infinitely greater than whoever we may be; that any self-salvaging from solipsistic self-aggrandizement resides in our capacity to countenance the possibilities of who and what we are not. Thus, to ignore the resonances that Alice Walker's contestation finds within me would mean succumbing to the logic that spawns ghettos—ghettos of mind, of socioeconomic practice, and of institutional subdivisions. Such self-empowering and self-serving logic exerts its unmitigated virulence to no lesser degree in the confines of academic institutions and critical practices, as our disciplinary divisions and tribal animadversions clearly attest.

Diamela Eltit is a Chilean writer who subjects the question of gender and gender constructs to a radical disambiguation.[3] In her work, generic ambivalence becomes exacerbated into a rending critique that scorches the historical commonplaces—sociopolitical givens that sanction exclusions and oppression of the nonconforming and the exploitable. In the process, the Spanish language, itself the patron of a cultural discourse that has maintained everything in its "proper place," is wrenched from its authoritative procedures, grammatical protocols, and rhetorical graces, as is the genre of the novel that serves Eltit as generic venue. Eltit's is an all-out confrontation, not mere resistance, that assails the institutional foundations of Latin American culture and political structures. As the titles of the two works under question proclaim, they are cast in the forge of a hemispheric allegory, searingly conscious and implacably combative. The first title is a resonant neologism, *Lumpérica,* the second a strident irony, *Por la patria.*[4]

The conditions of production and publication of these works are equally telling. Eltit's novels form part of the publishing venture of CADA, *Colectivo de Acciones de Arte,* a collective whose founders, in addition to Eltit, include the poet Raúl Zurita and the artist Lotty Rosenfeld. Founded within the first decade of Chile's post-Allende military dictatorship, the collective alludes to its mission of salvaging and survival in one of the darker times of the country's history. That suggestive allusion is expressed by the logo of the Collective's imprint as it appears on its publications' copyright page:

A Woman's Place

En un perdido rincón del planeta los ornitorrincos se extinguen. Con seguridad, no hay en toda la Tierra seres que luchen con más empeño por sobrevivir en ella (In a lost corner of the planet, the platypuses are becoming extinct. Surely, there is not in all the Earth beings that struggle with more determination to survive). *Lumpérica* initiates the imprint's series in new prose fiction. By the time Eltit's second novel is published three years later, Ediciones del Ornitorrinco counts a number of key intellectuals on its list, some of whom—Ariel Dorfman, for example—enjoy international reputations. In addition to its title, *Por la patria,* Eltit's second novel embodies yet another peculiar irony, an all too often ironic fate that befalls "Third-World" writers, whether male or female. The novel was written with the patronage of a Guggenheim Fellowship (1985). The Guggenheim Foundation is founded, of course, on the fortunes of the Guggenheim family, made in good measure through the operations of its Anaconda Mining Company in Chile. Anaconda has extracted more than copper from the terrain and human geography of Diamela Eltit's baneful "Fatherland." The irradiated, skeletal hand with the superimposed map of the Western Hemisphere that graces the book's cover beckons the reader to glimpse more than might have been intended. The cover was conceived, according to the credits of the copyright page, by CADA's cofounder Lotty Rosenfeld.

Diamela Eltit negotiates the distance between irony and paradox with inconsolable austerity. Her agon is woman situated at the center. Central to her novel's story as she is to her culture's history, Eltit's female agonist endures the paradoxical fate of the center's marginality, of being at the center yet peripheralized. Her protagonists occupy society's symbolic and spatial common place: the agora, the central square, the city plaza in *Lumpérica,* and, in *Por la patria,* the pivotal centrality of familial lines and linkages that weave the tribal and national network, a web that turns into a cruel trap for its central female figure. The two novels offer a continuity that spans the historical predicament of Latin American women from the technological, postmodern present of mechanical simulation to a modern allegory of a pre-Hispanic indigenous world in which women's role was no less a form of institutional dissimulation within whose roles women had to forge their precarious existence. In both worlds, woman serves as a mediate social and political commodity and as an intermediary conscience. And though in *Lumpérica* the protagonist woman's place is in the public

CHAPTER NINE

square, the collective commonplace, and in *Por la patria* she is situated in the conjunctive sanctum where filial lines converge, in both instances the female is circumscribed by and meshed into a social and political order in and through which she has to negotiate her own survival, as well as the corporate well-being of the community she comes to personify as a political allegory.

In *Lumpérica,* the female protagonist becomes a ghostly echo, a shadowed mirror of a modern urban society's dispossessed. These are the faceless phantom masses whose precarious existence haunts the institutional, national, and international center from the periphery. As America's lumpen, this peripheral nebula is a subculture, an opaque and denied nimbus that envelopes the legitimate and visibly licit order. The female protagonist as reflector and reflection of modern society's marginal otherness haunts in Diamela Eltit's novel as compelling specter and spectacle. The author's experience as filmmaker and cinematic documenter of mass culture gives her novel a dimension of political immediacy. Her first novel in this sense is a multimedium whose language narrates and reflects at once the human world it brings into focus. *Lumpérica,* as a mixed medium, reads now as discursive narration, now as filmic script and as video recording. The novel's world, then, is multiply echoic, reflective of a shadowy world of humanity alienated from the "real" social order. It is a peripheral world that emanates as a hallucinated projection from the visions and language of a feminine conscience acutely aware of having been derogated herself from the sanctioned social order. Her participation is relegated to a negative reflection, an obverse alterity whose aberrant existence gives normalcy its normality. Her sole interaction with the dominant order consists in the Kafkaesque interrogations she is subjected to by the state's police in the municipal plaza. An earlier era's madwoman has now been resituated from the dark corners of the attic to the ghostly visibility of the central square and the penetrating scrutiny of its spotlights.

From her paradoxical predicament as a "Third-World" woman writer under the patriarchy of a military dictatorship and the patronage of a foundation built with the lifeblood of her people, Diamela Eltit reflects and reflects upon the circumstance of her marginated world, now symptomatically, now discursively. The most dazzling of human paradoxes tend to be those closest to reality, and in Eltit's work and practice we are confronted with the paradox of irreality that issues from an unmitigated focusing on the

A Woman's Place

hyperreal. The lumpen of America in Eltit's *Lumpérica* has its personification, its ironically and paradoxically *unmasked* prosopopoeia, in the female figure of the novel's protagonist, L. Iluminada. A glaring figure that in turn glares, she is illumined starkness that sheds her *institutional* vestments so that by her light the *destitutional* remnants might come to life, take on discursive weight and political visibility, breach their ghostliness, reclaim their banished reality, and do so at the spatial and symbolic center of society's habitat—the town square, now become the permanent home of the homeless at strictly sanctioned hours of the day and spotlighted hours of the night.

The fate of the dispossessed commands an urgency in the conscience of *Lumpérica*'s protagonist and in the art of its author. Inasmuch as that conscience devises a literal and metaphorical relationship between the fate of the disenfranchised and the condition of the woman protagonist, the work is a consciously feminist political novel. Within that feminist perspective, Eltit's novel takes on an even broader dimension of sociopolitical concern and ideological significance. The mode of discourse and the artistic devices deployed by the author within the context of such concerns reflect the urgency of the human predicament portrayed in the novel. Neither shrill nor theatrically emphatic, the austere urgency in the novel's language and modes of depiction relentlessly question the authoritative discourses employed by the dominant sociopolitical order for its own self-empowerment and, concomitantly, for the disenfranchisement of the other and for the exclusion of the marginalized others' would-be claims that might compete with the reigning order's prerogatives.

In this vein, Eltit's novelistic procedures exacerbate the scriptive otherness that we have explored already in the works of the male authors in the preceding chapters of this study. If those masculine writers betray an awareness in their writing that writing itself is a process and an instrument that opens itself and its cultural context to heterodox and heterologous otherness, Eltit's writing forges headlong into exploring, positing, and demonstrating what that otherness might consist of when it would focus on the question of gender and the politics of dispossession. Accordingly, Eltit populates her novelistic world with the human obverse of socioeconomic and political power, with those cast by society's privileged hierarchy to the marginal obscurity, with the wretched who come back to haunt society's "civility" at its symbolic and spatial civic center. In technical terms, Eltit's

CHAPTER NINE

art of urgency violates with impunity the sanctioned norms of the novelistic genre as the masculinist tradition has willed it to posterity. While the male writers we have already discussed also question that tradition, as we have seen, Eltit's work engages in a more radical and more radically revisionary form of reinscription, breaking with even a self-problematizing linear narrative, giving us instead disembodied sequences, syncopated scenes, kinetic (cinematic) "takes." The emphasis shifts, then, from tale telling and the self-betrayal of its telltale ruses to visual representation, still in/through language, but a language whose visual immediacy often shades into the visionary, into hypnogogic, hallucinatory visions that are no less immediate and real for being visionary. Because those visions divulge the ghastly realities of the periphery, a content that the discursive protocols of the novel, as canonical genre, all too often have swept into the unseen margins or skewed to accommodate the vested interests of a dominant discourse.

Like most visionary writing, then, Eltit's has the political urgency that comes with the immediacy of vision. The result is a novel that by traditional expectations might be deemed "unreadable," or resistant at best. I have already referred to Eltit's work as a literature of confrontation rather than a literature of resistance. Any such forced encounter requires that those doing the confronting meet with open eyes. As a sensitive cinematographer, Eltit is fully aware of the potential, as well as of the hazards, of our unavoidable or deliberate blinking. And lest in the process we blink at the reality of what her tableau would have us perceive, the novel is segmented into attention-retaining portions, the typeface is varied, the page space diversified, the sentence structure shifts, the syntax is inflected, and the rhetorical gesture fluctuates.

From scripting directions destined for the production of cinematic scenes to first-person reminiscence and detached third-person narratives, the language that constitutes the novel spins its tale and spins about the site of communal space that its gaze has fixed upon: the central plaza. That locus is, at once, the dramatic stage of a society's passion play, the passionate synecdoche of the protagonist's conscience, and the receptacle of modern society's human detritus. In that choreographed space, the lights and shadows of dominant society's commercial and self-promoting technological talismans blare and blink from promotional billboards, objectifying the human masses on which they reflect into so many more consumable and expendable commodities. The neon alphabets of vested interest and political power brand their luminous stamp on the bedraggled throng, turning the disinherited into a procession of mobile graffiti. In this passion play, the female agon echoes as afflicted conscience. She moves and *acts* as body, as the spurned embodiment of what the social order and its hierarchy would excise from its body politic, from the social corpus and its officially sanctioned organs. The woman, then, emerges as the mediate instrument of articulation, remembering the dismembered, reflecting on what membership means in a society that would mutilate itself, that would sever so much of its own, casting it into shunted otherness as silenced alterity and disappeared difference. (I use *disappeared* in the previous sentence as a transitive verb, a verbal permutation that the baneful history of Chile and other countries has given the verb in the recent past.)

Lumpérica is a ten-chapter novel, an inverse *decameron,* if you will, compressed into the vigil of an abysmal night. It begins as a nocturnal procession of shadows and light, a chiaroscuro that captures silhouetted human forms and the formative social grids that array those ragged ghosts into the recesses of society's symbolic civil space. The convention of shadows, however, is anything but conventional. The disheveled outcasts turn into the surreal cast of a macabre dance under the artificial and inquisitorial lights that the social order trains on its public square in order to dissipate the night and banish its ragged shadows. Into the midst of this phantom space, the symbolic negative image of the civic and civil arena, the ghostly forms of society's closet skeletons burst forth. There they become defined and identified as society's pallid and insubstantial otherness. The "rhythmic ritual" of baptismal lights palliate these figures into inexistence, thus cleansing society of its human detritus. At the center of this ghostly squalor is L. Iluminada, the novel's protagonist, illumined into a revenant of perspicuity as embodied consciousness and allegorical sensor, as fictitious as a novel's protagonist, as real as the hyperreality of the human desolation that society's powers-that-be would fictionalize into luminous and bedazzled inexistence. The novel ironically calls this the "fiction in the city" (7),[5] a fiction that is as "fictional" as Eltit's own predicament in a dictatorial regime and patriarchal domain.

From passion play of illumined specters, the novel moves into the shadowy realm of police interrogation. The object of questioning is not the protagonist solely, but the very right of human communing and social interaction. Having transformed the town square into the locus and symbolic

CHAPTER NINE

object of interrogation, the inquisitorial instruments of political power in effect permeate all human exchange with the ill-logic and circular reasoning of power. Kafka's interrogation room becomes generalized into ubiquity. In the process, the very existence of civic life and the foundations of civilization are put into question. The interrogation ominously begins with, "What is the use of the public square?" (37). It is a loaded question, of course, an explosive charge ignited at both ends that threatens to undo the edifice of human civility on the one hand, while on the other, human civilization itself is deemed questionable in the face of so little humanity and civility so mooted by the exercise of unmitigated power. That foreboding reality takes on a further allegorical transformation in the thirty-one segments that comprise the novel's third chapter. The allegorized persona of the female protagonist confronts the squalid mass of the dispossessed as the embodiment of irrepressible desire and the dark forces of necessity. The imagery of this transformation is unmistakably reminiscent of Picasso's war mural, the *Guernica,* with the protagonist transformed into "animal lumpérico," into beast of deliverance and perdition, a mare of damnation and indemnity, a night-mare in heat that pounds the plaza's public ground at the center of the ghostly mob.

Unlike the first three chapters, the fourth carries a title, "Para la formulación de una imagen en la literatura." Divided into six subsections, the chapter is headed by a cast of literary figures whose roll call resonates in the *imagenes* formulated here. The chapter begins as a foregone conclusion that echoes with Mallarmé's *Igitur* ("Entonces/") and continues as a stanzaic enumeration:

> Entonces/
> Los chilenos esperamos los mensajes
> L. Iluminada, toda ella
> Piensa en Lezama y se las frota
> Con James Joyce se las frota
> Con Neruda Pablo se las frota
> Con Juan Rulfo se las frota
> Con E. Pound se las frota
> Con Robbe Grillet se las frota
> Con cualquier fulano se frota las antenas. (69)

187

A WOMAN'S PLACE

(Therefore/
We Chileans wait for messages
L. Iluminada, all of her
Thinks of Lezama and she rubs them
With James Joyce she rubs them
With Neruda Pablo she rubs them
With Juan Rulfo she rubs them
With E. Pound she rubs them
With Robbe Grillet she rubs them
With any Tom, Dick, and Harry she rubs her antennae.)

I read this fourth chapter as a key to Diamela Eltit's novel. I do so because this is where the author confronts the nagging problem of how to construe and justify literary vocation with social commitment, particularly when the vocation in this case is that of an author whose gender as a class and political phenomenon must endure the repercussions of society's hierarchical order and exclusions. The "formulation of an image in literature" is the perennial concern of every writer, whether male or female. In the context of Latin American culture and literary history, the question of "image" has provoked an acute and elaborate debate. The continent's history has been, in good measure, a dialectical counterpoint between image and reality, spectacle and spectator, imagism and imagination, appropriative reign and proprietary revenant, each pressing its claims on the terrain of geography and on the ledger of history. José Lezama Lima, the Cuban polymath who heads the list in the above enumeration, has been most articulate and most dazzling in his treatment of this dialectic.[6] The "formulation of an image" is the formulation of a reality, and it is no less real for being a "formulation of an image in literature." Much to the contrary, by dint of the pleonasm and tautology implicit in the convocation of image and literature into a common space, reality is subjected to the scrutiny of a redoubled focus. The compounded force of that conjugation compels us to countenance a reality more real than what the sanction of authoritative privilege and official declaration *would deem to be real.* Anyone minimally familiar with Latin America's, or, for that matter, any other region's history, and with the formations of any official story, knows full well that reality inevitably lies elsewhere. And that "elsewhere" in the context of

CHAPTER NINE

Latin America's cultural debate hovers in the image, in the alterior periphery, the spectral otherness to what authorized reality claims as its own.

For a marginalized writer such as Diamela Eltit, cast as alterity by patriarchal hegemony's political travesty and by the happenstance of gender, this predicament of otherness is a given. Therefore, her point of departure is already a locus set apart. She casts off from a place already cast out. Her enterprise is perforce a parting of ways from the commonality of society's commonplace. As "one child of one's own," in Alice Walker's apt phrase, Diamela Eltit, as a woman writer in a decidedly men's world, has no salvaging alternative but to engage in an "essay on creativity," to essay a generative and engendering process that she calls "the formulation of an image in literature." Borne to the edge already by social circumstance and political predicament, her breaking away, like the point of her departure, is a foregone conclusion. It should not be surprising, therefore, that her enterprise should begin adverbially, with the force of the resolute adverb *therefore* and its altereffect: *Entonces/.*

The irrevocable consequence of this afterclap is the recitation of a male canon's hagiography with which this key fourth chapter begins. What ensues is an act of self-submersion into the dark recesses of the foregone and of forgetting. Eltit thus subjects her male precursors to the vicissitudes of nullity and recuperation, of denial and indemnity. The chapter begins in catatonic lapse, passes through memorial relapse, and ends in the recovery of self as one's spectral twin, a retrieval in which the author and her protagonist emerge as mirrored identities. The itinerary is suggestive of the vicissitudes of Chile's most recent unhappy history, allegorically personified in the female agon and her self-disfiguring. It is significant, at the same time, as a trial of curtailment and negation to which these preponderant figures from canon's sacred roster are subjected, attenuated into so many "Tom, Dick, and Harrys." This is because the pantheon of gray eminences that range from the magnetic and dazzling fragments of a baroque image (Lezama Lima) to the still-life snapshots of a hyperreality (Robbe-Grillet) comprises an ancestral catacomb and a scribal catechumen whose scripture conjures a sorcerer's book to be lit by reading and snuffed out by iconoclastic altercation. This, too, is yet another familiar scene, a *graphic* commonplace where venerable lights and their riven shadows perform the macabre dance of the possessed and the dispossessed.

A Woman's Place

In this theater of crisis, the shrillest resonance is in the adverbial declaration itself: *Entonces*. Read in its Latinate lexis, it echoes as the palpable presence of *Igitur,* its unnamed author become the revenant high priest of this ancestral tomb and its deadmen's roll. Though Eltit's novel is in good measure a national/hemispheric allegory of a crisis that involves her inexorably in its historic catastrophe, her vocation as a writer is not separable from that predicament. On the contrary, her writer's vocation compels her to countenance that calamity as a *personal* literary event. The "formulation of an image in literature" is a task of extremity, a labor of personal survival subsumed as a particular instance of a national struggle for self-salvaging. For an individual testament, for an instantiated infrahistory that involves her as a writer, Eltit turns to writing's history for a defining context. In doing so, she betrays her ambivalences as a woman reaching into a gallery of precedents, a gallery whose images are preponderantly male. Hers, then, is a critical predicament as a woman and as a writer. And the most apt exemplum of crisis-bound authorial dilemma that might correspond to hers also happens to be that of a man. She appropriates that crisis chronicle as precedent, nonetheless, translating the title and protagonist's name and, ironically, translating, too, the individual plight of a beleaguered poet into the axiomatic echo of her own struggle against the real threat of nullification. *Igitur,* therefore, becomes *Entonces,* and Mallarmé's confrontation with *Néant* transmutes into Eltit's encounter with patriarchal specters: a male-dominated canon of precursor images and a dictatorial patriarchy engaged in the fratricidal decimation of its own people.

Mallarmé's "dark night of the soul," then, echoes as the literary correlative to the social reality and personal predicament that Eltit seeks to formulate as "an image in literature." The profound sense of crisis and impotence that besieged Mallarmé between 1867 and 1870 when he wrote *Igitur* was a self-submersion into an ancestral tomb where light and shadow weave a tenebrous rite and a tenuous passage to the farther side of nothingness and despair. That "ceremony" is replayed, *mutatis mutandis,* in the fate of Eltit's own agonic Arachne called L. Iluminada, her self-immersion into darkness, mutilation, and resurfacing as the identical twin of her authorial persona. Only, Mallarmé's ironic "rêve pur d'un Minuit"[7] transmutes by historical necessity into Midnight's nightmare, and Eltit's female agon becomes the very embodiment of her ancestral and national tomb. As

CHAPTER NINE

a tomb of one's own, the author and her agonic persona pass through Mallarmé's *rêve* into a haunting *revenant,* disembodied from the body politic's national history and its nightmare, phantasmally other to the very existence they are fated to embody in history's reality and in reality's formulated literary image:

> Su alma es material.
> Su alma es establecerse en un banco de la plaza y
> elegir como único paisaje verdadero el falsificado de
> esa misma plaza. . . .
> Su alma es este mundo y nada más en la plaza
> encendida.
> Su alma es ser L. Iluminada y ofrecerse como otra
> Su alma es no llamarse diamela eltit /sábanas
> blancas/cadáver.
> Su alma es a la mía gemela. (80–81)
>
> (Her soul is material.
> Her soul is settling in on a park bench of the plaza and
> choosing as sole true landscape the falsified landscape of
> the very same plaza. . . .
> Her soul is this world and nothing more in the lit plaza.
> Her soul is to be L. Iluminada and offer herself as an other.
> Her soul is not to be called diamela eltit/white sheets/corpse.
> Her soul is identical to mine.)

Having thus fused into the nightmare of her story and the history that she allegorically personifies, the author and her protagonist wander into the squalid whiteness of national history and private autobiography where one charts a course as one traverses the uncharted topography of a phantom space. *Quo Vadis?* is the fitting title of the novel's subsequent middle chapter, and the town plaza becomes the ghastly emptiness to be mapped as human geography and agonistic chronicle: "Ella no era un adorno para la plaza sino a la inversa: la plaza era su página" (92. She was not a decoration for the plaza; on the contrary. The plaza was her page). In that civic common place, human destiny and a committed writer's literary destination converge. The traces and metaphoric lines imprint themselves as indelible figures of a collective history, its characters drifting as stray graffiti. The human scrawl of the disinherited and writing's lines conflate most overtly in the novel's next chapter. Its major second section is indeed entitled "Los grafitis de la plaza," and here the pages divide into stanzaic form, each headed by a titular description of its own writing, with a running narrative gloss at the foot of the page. A coded manifesto with an allusive political message, the section's headers would have writing function as proclamation, extravagance, fiction, seduction, gearing, sentence, rub, evasion, objective, enlightenment, joke, abandon(ment), and erosion. These are the terms that are strung at the head of each page as the second part of a binomial phrase whose first term is "writing as." All these writing functions are indeed rehearsed, and, in the eighth chapter—one of the most recondite in the novel, entitled "Ensayo General"—writing and language are subjected to the greatest test, pushed to the farthest limits of intelligibility. The text's self-mutilation becomes concomitant to the de-formations performed on the Spanish language, on the master narratives it sustains. All of this scribal and institutional disfiguration devolves upon the highly symbolic and protracted act of shearing that the protagonist perpetrates upon herself. In this respect, the end of this chapter becomes a rehearsal for the concluding scene of the novel, in which the protagonist, coarsely shorn and a "bag lady," becomes invisible to the bustling good folk hurrying by.

The act of chopping off hair is traditionally an act of humiliation, of contrition, mourning, excommunication, and social exclusion. This cutting gesture in Eltit's novel also becomes a link that articulates this first work to the author's second and also binds the contemporary predicament of women to their past history, as we shall see presently. The novel's final scene is drab, a scene in which the woman, dressed in gray, sits on a park bench holding her paper bag. From it, she pulls a pair of scissors and proceeds to chop off her hair in disheveled bunches, a process that comes to an end with the break of dawn. Unperceived by the growing number of people going by, her nocturnal drama too has become invisible. By the light of day, the city is utterly oblivious to the sacrificial figure that propitiates its survival through the darkest night of its history.

When it haunts as *no-man's land,* society's common space become's a *woman's place.* Hollowed out by anonymity, the heart of the nation's capital is a ghastly quarter at the center of the commonwealth. Relegated to the margin at the specious center, the disinherited can be better circumscribed. For Diamela Eltit, that disinheritance is best personified as woman because,

CHAPTER NINE

in the master narratives of Latin America, historically woman is doubly entitled to that role, by dint of gender and, secondly, for embodying the privileged patrimony's political and economic subservient other.

The female protagonist's self-disfigurement comprises the single most emphatic and most often repeated action in *Lumpérica*. The coarse shearing of her hair becomes the climactic act that reiterates the ignominy of national self-mutilation under the aegis of one of the bloodiest military dictatorships in Chile's history. That baleful history's embodiment and symbolic enactment by Eltit's female protagonist is a melancholy reminder that history writes itself sempiternally on and through woman's body. The author monumentalizes that historiographic document by placing her protagonist into the ironic centrality of the capital's central square. There, she becomes an unreadable text, a paradoxical national autobiography that goes unnoticed and, when perceived, remains unrecognizable except as alterior and aberrant (per)version of a master narrative's history and body politic. The fate of Eltit's own work is consonant with the fate of the feminine body as history poignantly dramatized. Women's writing as social discourse is, after (and before) all, part and parcel of national history. As such, it is not immune to the conditions of the disinherited and of society's invisible specters. Nevertheless, history perdures, and Diamela Eltit persists. She does so, with her second novel, aiming still at the heart of the city, the symbolic and spatial nucleus of society. And the female agon serves, once more, as the nation's matrix and its history's incarnation.

Por la patria conjures a temporal reversal. Its allegory is just as timely in its urgent relevance to contemporary history. But its historical reach goes back far enough to recoup a woman's place and its paradoxical centrality, to write, once more, history's commonplace as female embodiment, as collective biography written on/in woman's body. The historical precedents of history as female incarnation and woman as history's matrix for Diamela Eltit's second novel are twofold. Both are family histories. In both, woman serves as memorial, as repository, as tomb of one's own—quite literally in the first of these precedents, in the case of the second, not as figuratively as it might appear.

In book two of the *Rerum familiarum libri*, Petrarch includes "A letter of consolation on the misfortunes of a dead and unburied friend and some thoughts concerning the rites of burial."[8] There, we read about Artemisia II

A Woman's Place

of Caria, a woman whose embodiment of her family history makes the phrase "a tomb of one's own" more than a boutade glinted off Virginia Woolf. Artemisia was quite literally a primal mausoleum. As sister *and* wife of King Mausolus in life, she became the matrix and repository of Caria's history through the dual filiation to the patriarchal monarch at a time when the king was considered the absolute head of the body politic, the incarnation of the social corpus and of his people's genealogy. Upon King Mausolus's death, Artemisia not only succeeded her brother-husband to become queen of Caria (353–52 B.C.); she also drank his ashes, stirring them little by little into her cup, incorporating his material and symbolic existence, thereby arriving at a complete embodiment of her family and national history.

Writing in the first decade of the seventeenth century on the Iberian peninsula, Inca Garcilaso de la Vega, progeny of a conquistador (Captain Garci-Laso de la Vega) and an Inca princess (Isabel Chimpu Ocllo, daughter of Huallpa Tupac Inca and granddaughter of the Inca Yupanqui), may well have had some familiarity with Petrarch's *Rerum familiarum libri,* as he did with his *Canzioneri.* He was familiar with the genre, having translated León Hebreo's *Diálogos de amor* from the Italian before completing his *Comentarios Reales* in 1609. The *Royal Commentaries,* as the work is known in English, is Inca Garcilaso's own maternal family history, chronicling as it does the history of Peru's indigenous empire. The work was dedicated to Catherine, princess of Portugal and duchess of Braganza, whose matronage for this maternal genealogy was being courted by the Peruvian author. Written across an ocean and an unbreachable time whose vicissitudes rendered a glorious past even more glorious because irrevocable, Inca Garcilaso's history has an unmistakable elegiac tone. The Spanish imperial authorities viewed it as a dangerous encomium to a people and a geography that proved more valuable in subjugation than in elegy and commemoration. By the time of the most serious threat to Spanish hegemony in colonial Peru (the rebellion of Tupac Amaru in 1780–81), the Spaniards became truly convinced of the dangers that lurked in the free circulation of a history such as the *Comentarios Reales.* Thus, on 21 April 1782 a royal decree ordered the withdrawal of all copies of the book, and the Holy Inquisition placed it on its Index alongside all heretical works. It would not resurface until the postcolonial period, actually during the struggle for independence, when the liberator José de San Martín proposed

CHAPTER NINE

in 1814 the republication of the work by subscription, claiming this precolonial history as the primal book of postcolonial America.

In part one, book four, chapter nine of the *Comentarios Reales,* Garcilaso relates how the Incas "married the prince and heir to his own sister, and the reasons advanced for this."[9] As in other instances of mores and customs that the cross-culturally sensitized Inca Garcilaso felt might prove troublesome to the Spanish sensibilities and to the Inquisition, he goes to great lengths to explain the genesis of this particular institution, referring primarily to a cosmological explanation. The Inca's solar genealogy naturally dictated a parallel relationship between the corresponding sun and moon in the institutional life of the royal family. Genealogical purity in the hereditary ascendancy to imperial power was the more earthly and equally significant rationale for the marriage of the heir apparent to his eldest sister. In seventeenth-century Iberia, the precedent of Artemisia and Mausoleus in Petrarch's *Rerum familiarum libri* more than likely cushioned Inca Garcilaso's explanation of the "et soror et conjux" practice as an indigenous institution.

In *Por la patria,* Diamela Eltit makes clear that she is abundantly informed of the Incas' family practices as described by Inca Garcilaso de la Vega. She may well be familiar too with the precedent of Artemisia of Caria and Petrarch's family history. The most overt detail that links Eltit's second novel to Latin America's indigenous antecedents is the protagonist's name: Coya. This titular name designates the sister-wife-queen of the Inca emperor. In Eltit's work, the Coya becomes the mirror and echoic response to the female figure as political institution and historical embodiment.

Blunted by familiarity, political sensibility in a region like Latin America, and in a military dictatorship such as Chile's between 1973 and 1990, would not be moved by yet another literary indictment of fratricidal violence. Commonplace enough to be institutionalized and state-sponsored, the violence of fratricide as a political practice is too much a part of the male-dominated political process and, therefore, rather ordinary to the inured patriarchies of power. As the title of her novel indicates, Eltit's *Por la patria* is an urgent memorandum to the dictatorial patriarchy and to the "Fatherland." It is an excoriating message to an order that devours its progeny with systematic savagery and virulent exercise of power. In a masculinist context where such brutality has become banal and an integral part of "civil order," Eltit has sought a pressure point to which a relentless

A WOMAN'S PLACE

machismo might still be susceptible. Incest and sexual violence trained on the "weaker gender" is still a taboo, and the "fairer sex" is a fetishistic commodity in the most hardened patriarchies. In such a context, Eltit has found a literary venue in the reinscription and allegorical updating of certain royal family practices in European and indigenous American imperial courts. As was the case in those ancient contexts, woman has a central role in such institutions. But hers is a recondite centrality. She serves as the mediate instrument for the engendering and maintenance of a world order—a male-dominated order, naturally—and for the perpetuation of a national/imperial history through her body, literally. Eltit's novel is quite graphic in its dramatization of this historical tangle. And the novel begins with a family entanglement in which the female intrauterine fetus endures the phallographic intrusion of paternal thrusts into maternal body. The novel will end with literal conflagration and with the metaphorical conflagration of "epic" history whose holocaust liberates the female body to find its solidarity, to feel "nearly human."

> El fuego, el fuego, el fuego y la épica.
> Volví a sentir: volví a sentir sobre el erial,
> superpuesto a mi niñez.
> Todas soltamos el cuerpo y las manos
> móviles y diestras.
> Vimos el continente y fuimos otra vez
> combatientes y hermanas, humanas casi. (279)

> (The fire, fire, fire and the epic. / I felt once more: once more I was able to feel / upon the barren ground superimposed on my childhood. / We all loosed our bodies and hands / mobile and skillful. / We saw the continent and we were again / combatants and sisters, human almost.)

Between the beginning and ending of the novel, we are treated to a chronicle of power and the repercussions of power's exercise upon the female body as physiology, as political institution, and as historical field. This entire institutional complex reverberates with a number of subversive dislocations wrought by a juxtaposition of antithetical terms, terms of gender and of language. The most prevalent and most intense antithesis resonates in the onomastic representations of the female protagonist, designations

CHAPTER NINE

that come laden with semantic and sociohistorical connotations: "Esa noche de la tragedia, alguien acabó en mi nombre y desde entonces respondo dual y bilingüe si me nombran Coa y Coya también" (22. That night of the tragedy someone hit on my name and, since then, I respond doubly and bilingually, whether they call me Coa or Coya just the same). If the protagonist's name, *Coya,* suggests the woman's intricate role in the institutional history of Europe and indigenous America, as chronicled for us by Petrarch and Inca Garcilaso respectively, Coya's antonym and onomastic mirror connotes a volatile semantic wilderness that threatens with undoing the "epic order" of history: "Coya, yo, perdida en el ancestro, en el siniestro cargo y nobleza Coa" (253. I, Coya, lost in ancestry, Coa in sinister duty and nobility). Thus, *Coya* is also *Coa.* And whereas *Coya* is shorthand for imperial and cosmogonic orderliness founded on woman's role, *Coa* is repercussive. It functions as an improvisational cursive for all that dismantles normative order, grammatical tidiness, institutional regimen, cosmic symmetry, and, of course, sexual practice. Coya undermines the infrastructure implied by her name by progressively taking on the character implicit in the name of Coa.

Whereas Coya signifies institutional decorum and discursive manageability, Coa is the sign of the indecorous, the haywire, and the indeterminate. This transgressive name that disconcerts institutionally concerted investments in disciplined politesse derives semantically from the counter-extreme of Coya's social genealogy. *Coa* is most literally an improvised hoe. In today's Chilean society, it refers to the street language of the subaltern culture. Such a lowly instrument could not be further from the imperial family's royal accouterments and social practices. From its earthly etymology, the word *coa* has come to mean anything that resonates outside of the institutionally sanctioned and grammatically lawful. At the end of the novel, on the penultimate page, the text itself parses the word into its sundry synonyms and multifarious renditions throughout the American hemisphere: "Se levanta el coa, el lunfardo, el giria, el pachuco, el caló, caliche, slang, calao, replana. El argot se dispara y yo" (278. The *coa,* the *lunfardo,* the *giria,* the *pachuco,* the *caló, caliche,* slang, *calao, replana* rise up. The argot is fired off and so am I). This is a transition from the sacred to the profane, from the lordly to the demotic, from the royal to the common. In trespassing from the imperial to the marginal, language takes with it the corresponding sociohistorical contents. The shift from Coya to

A WOMAN'S PLACE

Coa sweeps along with it the phenomenon named. The woman signified moves from the embodiment of order and historical edifice to the disembodied materiality of language and of social institutions, all consigned to the conflagration at the end of the novel. And the female body now moves with liberated agility and skill in solidarity with its feminine multiplicity in a communion that makes her feel "almost human."

The narrative of *Por la patria,* then, foregrounds a long series of social rituals and institutional protocols, all susceptible to the female agon's noncompliance and apostasy:

> Mi insurrección es total. Quiero mi casa, mi cama
> y yacer autóctona con otro nombre y rango.
> Cedo mi cargo.
> Ya no Coya incesto e hibridez.
> Renazco Coa y mi maldad me subyuga. (260–61)

> (My insurrection is total. I want my home, my bed, and to lie autochthonous with another name and rank. I yield my position. No more Coya, incest, and hybridism. I am reborn Coa and my evil subjugates me.)

The novel's language and the narrative's tale rehearse a series of rituals of dis-integration that culminate in the protagonist's disembodiment of all that she embodies as corporeal materiality of the historical record. The first unit to disintegrate is the nuclear family, and its narration makes that dispersal simultaneous to the entropy of the language in which it is narrated. The tale begins with the first utterance of acquired language. The novel's opening paragraph comprises a bleating descant on the syllable "ma," at once a searching elegy to (m)amorous maternity and a plaintive prick song. The melodic cacophony will in fact shift into maternal abjuring and paternal abdication:

> No veo a mi mamá.
> No veo a mi papá.
> Los veo cada vez más seguido en las confusiones que tengo y
> las ganas que se eleven y leviten a mi alrededor. Por eso
> cuando camino, miro hacia los lados y para arriba, por si acaso
> andan cuidando que nada me vaya pasar. Nada más. Nunca.
> No están. (13)

Chapter Nine

(I don't see my mother. / I don't see my father. / I see them more and more in the confusions and in the desires that rise and levitate around me. Therefore, when I walk, I look on every side and upwards, just in case they are taking care that nothing should happen to me. Nothing more. Never. / They are not there.)

Displaced ("disappeared") by political cataclysm in a night whose events have the unmistakable mark of a military coup and ensuing roundup, Coya's parents are supplanted by a paradigmatic male figure generically named Juan. An archetypal figure of patriarchal history, Juan could well be Petrarch's Mausoleus or Garcilaso's Inca emperor. He could be, as well, modernity's military satrap and postmodernity's perennial warden of the fraternal order. His peroration on the woman he has appropriated distills the role of the female figura as cast by the male epic since time immemorial— time immemorial, that is, except for time's *via dolorosa* as incorporated by woman and indelibly inscribed in woman's memory. Through this male character's enunciation, then, Eltit recapitulates woman's male-determined place in the epic scheme of history, a centrality, or common place, yet again, upon which society's generic responsibility devolves, including the responsibility for the fate meted out to her and for the role she has been assigned:

> Eres mi madre, mi padre, mi familia.
> Eres todo lo que tengo.
> Exclusiva en mí, traicionando por el desconocimiento y el error
> confuso que hiciste con parientes, con corrientes seres que te
> engendraron. Eres Coa mi memoria. Coya raza. No te amo, eres
> el descampado que me rige y la memoria de mi origen.
> Esa es la forma de mi búsqueda incipiente, constante, enferma.
> Aquí liberada en el rapto te poseo íntegra en mi particular
> nacionalidad: mi necesaria traición para evitar la matanza.
> Todo mi humanismo como dote a ti, cuando te protejo del
> afuera que está corrupto y agarrotado. . . .
> Tú que eres todas las cosas, toda mi familia y la humillación,
> mantienes viva mi lucidez y en cuanto viva seremos los
> sobrevivientes, los tejedores que más, mucho más adelante se
> van a destacar, saliendo de la oscuridad, del frío miserable que
> nos invade. . . . (271)

A WOMAN'S PLACE

(You are my mother, my father, my family. / You are all I have. / Exclusive in me, betraying out of ignorance and out of the confused mix-up of relatives, of ordinary beings that bore you. You are Coa, my memory. Coya race. I don't love you; you are the clearing that rules me and the memory of my origin. / That is the form of my incipient, constant, infirm quest. / Here, liberated in rapture, I possess you entirely in my particular nationality: my necessary treason for avoiding the slaughter. All my humanism as dowry for you; when I protect you from the outside that is corrupt and garroted. . . . / You who are all things, all my family and humiliation, you keep alive my lucidity that inasmuch as it is alive we will be the survivors, the weavers that in the most distant future will rise out of obscurity, out of the miserable cold that invades us.)

Coya's/Coa's reaction to a speech that may well have been pronounced by the Inca himself is one of astonishment. She is awed by the chronic exactitude of the unchanging portrayal, by the immutable destiny allotted to women and the inescapable danger such abiding constancy implies: "Lo miro asombrada. Pienso que ha dado con el término exacto. La peligrosidad se yergue: El ha sido, va seguir siendo mi contramemoria" (272. I look at him astonished. I think he has hit the mark. Danger lurks: He has been, he will continue to be my counter-memory).

Incorporate memory forced to countenance her spectral counterpart, Coya/Coa remands her eternal cross to the ghostly otherness of memory's weight. If he be her "counter-memory," what better way to alleviate history's burden than to consign counter-memory to its own? Accordingly, the male figure's peroration is followed in the novel by the metamorphosis and re(in)surrection of the female agon as a disembodied figure, as liquidation of the corporate structure she has been fated to sustain in her own corporal materiality:

> Tan mojada, traspasada de agua, retorno a la androginia.
> Retorno, digo, en la carencia y el exceso, habitada de
> muchachos expertos, de mujeres insurrectas y me desahogo.
> Pierdo pubis y carne, pierdo mis bienes corporales.
> Así ensayo posición y respuesta.
> COYA—COA
> (despejada, despojada, ardiente)
> Memoria

CHAPTER NINE

(So wet, so soaked with water, I return to androgyny. I return, I say, in scarcity and in excess, inhabited by expert boys, by insurgent women and I unburden myself. I lose pubis and flesh, I lose corporeal goods. / Thus I essay posture and response. / COYA—COA / [clear-headed, despoiled, burning] / Memory)

What ensues is, at once, memory, counter-memory, but, as well, memory's radical otherness: forgetting. And in that forgetting what is bequeathed to oblivion most emphatically is the corporate, the instrument of concretion that serves to bond with binding terms of a perennial narrative whose master plot defines her role and refines his privilege:

> Hay una hazaña que no puedes ni podrás con nada desmentir.
> Hay una épica.
> Surgido de la opresión y destello del linchaco.
> Yo para ti madre y padre en cuanto insurgente y diestra, en tanto reina y el poder de resistencia a tu vacío.
> Olvidé.
> Olvidé aquello lo cual te aferras y tras lo cual te prevaleces:
> Olvidé tu cuerpo.
> ... Olvidé mi ansia y la necesidad de las tocaciones.
> Olvido aquello a lo que te aferras para contenerme. (273–74)

(There is a deed you never can and never will be able to deny. / There is an epic. / Risen from oppression and from the blandishment of the club. / I, mother and father for you inasmuch as insurgent and able, as the queen and the power of resistance to your emptiness. / I have forgotten. / I have forgotten whatever you persist in and by whatever you prevail: I forgot your body ... / I forgot my anxiety and the need of fondling. / I am forgetting whatever you hold onto to contain me.)

The response culminates in the unequivocal declaration: "From vanquished, I shall be a victorious species" ("Seré de vencida en vencedora especie" [275]). An invincible determination punctuates the female agon's proclamation. In the vehemence of that sanguine conviction, one might read resilience, incorruptible hope, or an abiding rhetorical ruse. Diamela Eltit, in any case, does not succumb to the naivete of a Pollyanna or to the cheerful sanguinity of a utopian future. Her female protagonist finds herself, at the end of the day, in the same pub, the symbolic place of the populus, the public space violently invaded by the strongmen of a patriarchal dictatorship in the opening scene. Only now, that common locus is to be administered by women, still hierarchically ("lo administramos con jerarquía") and under the aegis of desire, a thirst to which the surviving women succumb at the far side of epic history's conflagration.

To relegate the highly political writing of Diamela Eltit to the comfortable remove of a "Third-World," female otherness, thereby absolving oneself from the discomfiting responsibility to breach that distance, would mean to turn a blind eye to the multiple worlds breached by the polemical commitment of this author. As we have seen, Eltit's writing allusively ranges from Eurocentric antiquity to imperial Peru to a street culture of modern society's darker side. In ranging so broadly across the geopolitical and historical spectrum, Eltit is far from abstracting the predicament of woman and the politics of gender into timeless mythos and irreality. On the contrary, the author historicizes with reiterative force the question of gender and a woman's place as a political and historical figure in the institutional order of things across the span of time and of cultural specificity. The constant in this gamut resides where dominant orders and their patriarchal master narratives have invariably demanded that the burden of constancy lie: in women and in the conservatory role prescribed for woman as the vital but shunted repository of historical claims. In this sense, Eltit's enterprise functions as an irrefutable demonstration that the position of the subaltern other, woman in this case, should not be relegated to an otherworldly alterity or to exotic and forbidding otherness. Any reading tinged by the slightest ethical commitment will find an obligation to breach the gap between self and other, between one's own and the other's cultural boundary, not for self-confirmation or for appropriative ends, but out of the necessity to understand and for the genuine sake of solidarity.

Epilogue

To conclude, as I have with the previous chapter, by pressing the claims of a woman writer in the context of what is clearly a masculinist writing scene might seem as futile and incongruous as the woman writer's own enterprise in a writing and publishing context that has been historically male-dominated and canonically male-centered. Yet, in endeavoring to read the other and the otherness that resides within them, we have seen how the preceding male writings are susceptible to giving ground, to yielding up a graphic and discursive space to what *prima facie* literalist readings collude in hiding. After all, such readings and their critical practices themselves, as well as the institutional contexts that abet them, have been traditionally as male-dominated and male-centered as the conditions of production that engender the writings we read. Read as cultural other to the dominant Western tradition and as otherness in their own writing, however, we have seen how even the most politically intractable of these male scriptures could be limned and teased out of the exclusionary confines of self-empowerment. In a political anachronism as cavalierly reactionary as Borges's, for example, we can learn that the value of any reasoned argument or orthodox conviction ultimately resides in its capacity to include its antithesis, its ability to resonate with, and potentially yield to, its difference and alterity, lest the identity of self-reiteration succumb to the self-demise that logically and inexorably awaits. From the doxologies of "The Theologians" to the deductive calculus of "Death in the Compass," Borges has elaborately dramatized that fate. Our reading of "The Mirror of Ink" reconfirms that the Borges corpus as the privileged embodiment of a canonical authority belies its own self-privileging status.

Epilogue

Octavio Paz is considered no less a political conservative, albeit of a different stripe, than Borges. Yet, in what may well be the most autobiographical (and, therefore, self-centered) of his works, we have been able to read the relentless signature of a deference to uncompromised otherness. We see how, in encoding difference, Paz generously poeticizes alterity, yielding to the other within, the other without, and the resonant other between the verses which he would not banish into blankness, but which he would have us cultivate, instead, as the furrow that nurtures the lives of poetry we read in his poems.

Allegorically in the hymeneal role of *Terra Nostra*'s Celestina, parodically in the generic and engendering persona of Angeles in *Christopher Unborn*, Carlos Fuentes dramatizes the indispensable nature of the feminine other. In the scripture of a writer so hilariously close to embodying the playboy of the Western world, one can read how the feminine other underwrites culture, even as the phallocentric privilege of that tradition writes its feminine otherness under into the invisible bias of its cultural tapestry. And as traditionally masculinist a writer as García Márquez is often considered to be, his *Love in the Time of Cholera* targets with irony, and even with truculence, the displacement of the feminine and her humanity by the banal "femininity" contrived in the amorous tradition. In that banality, García Márquez points out—for the reader who would see it—how our literary tradition has dehumanized the feminine into an "amorous" object.

In the patricidal enterprise of Vargas Llosa's *War of the End of the World,* one could still glimpse the chagrin of a decidedly masculinist and anxiously macho author before the ideological determination of a religion of progress. Vargas Llosa's novel, as we have seen, targets equally the secular and the theistic, both projects that would eradicate a people by subsuming its life and history into their own determined program of apocalyptic and eschatological melioration. History offers a shrill irony here because, in spite of his dramatic allegorization of a perennial encounter between a hegemonic European ideology and a supine America, Vargas Llosa's critique of this endemic historical condition in Latin America founders on its own hard rock of reality. The belated Thatcherite and unsuccessful presidential candidate Vargas Llosa has had to endure personally the chastisement of the failure reserved for such programmatic missions

Epilogue

and for those with designs on/for a historically ravaged people's own particular history.

Diamela Eltit's compatriot José Donoso, as we have seen, dramatizes in *El jardín de al lado* the inevitable, and not always surmountable, politics of gender that form part of any writing enterprise, regardless of the writer's own gender. Donoso engages the question of gender and sexuality in the hierarchical forms of Chile's socioeconomic history, as in his *Obscene Bird of Night*. He focuses, as well, on the politics of writing and displacement, whether in the fate of political exile or in the problematic ambivalence of sexually and generically ambiguous authors such as George Eliot, Henry James, and Constantinos Cavafis, all of whom he incorporates into his novelistic world and writing practices. In as reactionary a writer as T. S. Eliot on the politics of gender, Donoso manages to map for us the inescapable alterities that bedevil Eliot's own itinerary, an itinerary on which the ambivalently American writer found himself always swept to a locus other than where he sought to be.

The intense light Donoso focuses on the question of graphic dislocation and political unsituatedness becomes more intense still, because more acutely focused, in the first two novels of Diamela Eltit, where we see the question of otherness permeate the most sacred and inviolable constructs of alterity. This is the exacerbated locus where the political and cultural entailments of the other confront us at this moment. The ways in which these implications are countenanced ultimately translates into how we read and write. The writing of this book itself should be read as a symptom of this inevitability.

NOTES

INTRODUCTION: *OTHERWISE READING AND WRITING*

1. Gilles Deleuze and Félix Guattari, *Kafka: Toward a Minor Literature,* translated by Dana Polan (Minneapolis: University of Minnesota Press, 1986).
2. For an epitome of culture by prescription see E. D. Hirsch, *Cultural Literacy: What Every American Needs to Know* (New York: Houghton Mifflin, 1987).
3. For a suggestive discussion of this whole issue of authenticity and privilege to discourse, see Henry Louis Gates, Jr., "'Authenticity,' or the Lesson of Little Tree," *New York Times Book Review,* 24 November 1991, 1ff.

CHAPTER ONE: *ORBIS TERTIUS*

1. Raymond Williams, *Key Words: A Vocabulary of Culture and Society* (New York: Oxford University Press, 1976).
2. Michel de Certeau, *Heterologies: Discourse on the Other* (Minneapolis: University of Minnesota Press, 1986).
3. Samuel Weber, *Institution and Interpretation* (Minneapolis: University of Minnesota Press, 1987).
4. Fredric Jameson, *The Political Unconscious* (Ithaca, N.Y.: Cornell University Press, 1980).
5. Cornelius Castoriadis, *L'Institution imaginaire de la société* (Paris: Editions de Seuil, 1975).

CHAPTER TWO: *SURVIVING THEORY*

1. Walter Benjamin, "Unpacking my Library: A Talk about Book Collection," in *Illuminations,* translated by Harry Zohn, edited and introduced by Hannah Arendt (New York: Schoken Books, 1969), 59–67.

NOTES TO PAGES 20-63

2. Jorge Luis Borges, "Tlön, Uqbar, Orbis Tertius," in *Ficciones,* translated by Alastair Reid, edited by Anthony Kerrigan (New York: Grove Press, 1962), 17-35.
3. Paul de Man, *Resistance to Theory* (Minneapolis: University of Minnesota Press, 1986), 3-20.
4. Plato, *Collected Dialogues,* edited by Edith Hamilton and Huntington Cairns (New York: Pantheon, 1961).
5. Tzvetan Todorov, *The Conquest of America,* translated by Richard Howard (New York: Harper and Row, 1985).
6. Octavio Paz, "A Literature of Foundations," in *The Tri-Quarterly Anthology of Contemporary Latin American Literature,* edited by José Donoso and William A. Henkin (New York: Dutton, 1969), 2-8. See also "Anxious Foundations," chapter 1 of my *Columbus and the Ends of the Earth* (Berkeley and Los Angeles: University of California Press, 1992).

CHAPTER THREE: *A SHORT PARABLE*

1. Jorge Luis Borges, *Historia universal de la infamia* (Buenos Aires: Emecé Editores, 1954; *editio princeps,* 1935).
2. "Borges's Infamy: A Chronology and a Guide," *Review* (Spring, 1973): 6-12, particularly p. 11.

CHAPTER FOUR: *ARBORESCENT PAZ, INTERLINEAL POETRY*

1. Octavio Paz, *Posdata* (Mexico: Siglo XXI Editores, 1970), 111. Here and henceforth translations are my own, unless indicated otherwise.
2. Octavio Paz, *Pasión crítica,* edited and introduced by Hugo Verani (Barcelona: Seix Barral, 1985), 221.
3. Octavio Paz, *El ogro filantrópico* (Mexico: Joaquín Mortiz, 1979), 149.
4. Rita Guibert, *Seven Voices* (New York: Random House, Vintage Books, 1973; A. A. Knopf, 1972), 186-88.
5. Martin Heidegger, "...Poetically Dwells Man...," in *Poetry, Language, Thought,* translated by Albert Hofstadter (New York: Harper and Row, 1971), 211-29.
6. Octavio Paz, *In/mediaciones* (Barcelona: Seix Barral, 1979), 243.
7. Octavio Paz, *Blanco* (Mexico: Joaquín Mortiz, 1967).
8. In an edition of Paz's earliest writings, ably prepared and introduced by Enrico Mario Santí, we can see the emphatic moral force that has always undergirded Paz's literary career and political commitment from the very beginning. See *Primeras Letras (1931-1943),* edited, introduced, and annotated by Enrico Mario Santí (Mexico: Editorial Vuelta, 1988).
9. Octavio Paz, *Arbol adentro* (Barcelona: Seix Barral, 1987). Translations are from Eliot Weinberger's rendering, *A Tree Within* (New York: New Directions, 1988) unless indicated otherwise.

10. Paz's memorial address at the MIT ceremony honoring Roman Jakobson on 12 November 1982 is included in the author's endnotes to *Arbol adentro,* 178–80. It does not appear in the English translation.

11. The final quartet of the collection's last poem leaves no doubt in this regard. It reads:

> Tu mirada es sembradora.
> Plantó un árbol.
> Yo hablo
> porque tú meces los follajes. (174)

("Your glance scatters seeds. / It planted a tree. / I talk / because you shake its leaves." [155])

CHAPTER FIVE: *FUENTES AND THE PROFANE SUBLIME*

1. Mexico: Editorial Joaquín Mortiz, 1975.

2. See, for example, the "Bibliografía conjunta" that Fuentes appends to his essay *Cervantes o la crítica de la lectura* (Mexico: Editorial Joaquín Mortiz, 1976), 111–14. This *joint* bibliography refers to readings that served the author in the writing of this essay and the novel *Terra Nostra.*

3. Mexico: Editorial Joaquín Mortiz, 1976.

4. Mexico: Editorial Joaquín Mortiz, 1978.

5. See Neil Hertz, "Lecture de Longin," *Poétique* 15 (1973): 292–306. The present discussion also relies on a lucid synoptic treatment by John Logan, "Longinus," in *Ancient Writers: Greece and Rome,* edited by T. J. Luce (New York: Scribners, 1982), 2:1063–80. My preferred text of the Longinus treatment is the D. A. Russell translation in *Ancient Literary Criticism: The Principal Texts in New Translations,* edited by D. A. Russell and M. Winterbottom (Oxford: Clarendon Press, 1972).

6. On the Olympian personification of "kairos" see H[erbert] J[ennings] R[ose], "Kairos," in *The Oxford Classical Dictionary,* edited by N. G. L. Hammond and H. H. Scullard, 2nd edition (Oxford: Clarendon Press, 1970), 573.

7. For an informative discussion of this technique, see Kristine Gilmartine, "A Rhetorical Figure in Latin Historical Style: The Imaginary Second Person Singular," *Transactions of the American Philological Association* 105 (1975): 99–121.

8. I am citing from Margaret Sayers Peden's translation of *Terra Nostra* with the same title (New York: Farrar, Strauss and Giroux, 1976), 688.

9. For a synopsis of Stoicism see K[urt] von F[ritz], "Stoa (1)," *The Oxford Classical Dictionary,* 1015–16. For a more extensive treatment see John M. Rist, *Stoic Philosophy* (London: Cambridge University Press, 1969). A model study for the examination of Stoic philosophy in Hispanic letters is Henry Ettinghausen's *Francisco de Quevedo and the Neostoic Movement* (Oxford: Oxford University Press, 1972).

10. Lucius Annaeus Seneca, *The Stoic Philosophy of Seneca: Essays and Letters of Seneca,* translated and introduced by Moses Hadas (Garden City, N.Y.: Doubleday, 1958).

11. The words of Fuentes's narrator resound with the echo of the oft-quoted opening comment on Hegel in Karl Marx's *The Eighteenth Brumaire of Louis Bonaparte* (New York: International Publishers Co., Inc, 1963), 15: "Hegel remarks somewhere that all facts and personages of great importance in world history occur, as it were, twice. He forgot to add: the first time as tragedy, the second as farce." Those immutable structures that may inhere in the Marxist ideological program are obviously not spared by Fuentes's time-bound iconoclasms, *pace* Fuentes's readings in Marxism.

12. Carlos Fuentes, *Cristóbal Nonato* (Mexico: Fondo de Cultura Económica, 1987). I cite in English from *Christopher Unborn,* translated by Alfred J. MacAdam and the author. (New York: Vintage Books, Random House, Inc., 1990). References in the text by page number refer to this translation, followed by the page number in the original after a semicolon.

13. Deleuze and Guattari, *Kafka: Toward a Minor Literature,* 16.

14. James Joyce, *Finnegans Wake* (New York: The Viking Press, 1969). References in parentheses are to page and line number from this standard edition.

15. Laurence Sterne, *The Life and Opinions of Tristram Shandy, Gentleman,* edited by Graham Petrie, introduced by Christopher Ricks (Harmondsworth: Penguin Books, 1967), 9.33.615. Subsequent references in parentheses are to volume, chapter, and page number.

16. The term is from Gianni Vattimo, "The Crises of Subjectivity from Nietzsche to Heidegger," *Differentia: review of italian thought* 1.1 (1986): 5–21. The notion of *de-founding* is discussed on page 12. See related discussion in *Il pensiero debole,* edited by Giovanni Vattimo and Aldo Rovatti (Milan: Giangiacomo Feltrinelli Editore, 1983).

17. Italo Calvino, *Six Memos for the Next Millennium* (Cambridge, Mass.: Harvard University Press, 1988).

18. Italo Calvino, *Palomar* (Turin: Guilio Einaudi Editore, 1983).

19. Plato, "Cratylus" in *Collected Dialogues,* 421–74.

20. Homer, *The Iliad,* translated by Robert Fitzgerald (New York: Anchor Press/Doubleday, 1974), 14.201.

21. James Joyce, *Ulysses,* the corrected text, edited by Hans Walter Gabler et al. (New York: Random House, 1986), 4–5.

CHAPTER SIX: *INTERSTITIAL GARCÍA MÁRQUEZ*

1. Gabriel García Márquez, *One Hundred Years of Solitude,* translated by Gregory Rabassa (New York: Harper and Row, 1970; Avon Edition, 1971), 329.

2. Umberto Eco, *The Name of the Rose,* translated by William Weaver (New York: Harcourt Brace Jovanovich, Inc., 1983).

3. Gabriel García Márquez, *Love in the Time of Cholera,* translated by Edith Grossman (New York: Alfred A. Knopf, 1988).

4. Gabriel García Márquez, *Chronicle of a Death Foretold,* translated by Gregory Rabassa (New York: Alfred A. Knopf, 1982).

NOTES TO PAGES 137–52

CHAPTER SEVEN: *SCATOLOGY, ESCHATOLOGY, PALIMPSEST*

1. Mario Vargas Llosa, *The War of the End of the World,* translated by Helen R. Lane (New York: Farrar, Strauss and Giroux, 1984).
2. Euclides da Cunha, *Rebellion in the Backlands,* translated by Samuel Putnam (Chicago, Ill.: University of Chicago Press, 1944; first edition, *Os Sertões,* 1902).
3. Translated by Ronald Christ and Gregory Kolovakos (New York: Harper and Row, 1978).
4. Translated by Helen R. Lane (New York: Avon Books, 1983).
5. Translated by Lysander Kemp (New York: Grove Press, 1966).
6. Translated by Gregory Rabassa (New York: Avon Books, 1973).
7. Translated by Gregory Rabassa (New York: Harper and Row, 1975).
8. The author himself contributed to such facile schematizations. See his interview with José Miguel Oviedo, "Historia de la historia de la historia: Conversación en Lima," *Escandalar* 3.1 (January–March 1980): 82–87.
9. Edgar O'Hara and Guillermo Niño de Guzmán, "La guerra victoriosa de Vargas Llosa," *Revista Peruana de Cultura* 1 (July 1982): 9–36.
10. See Gilles Deleuze, *Différence et répétition* (Paris: Presse Universitaire, 1969).
11. Antonio Cornejo Polar, "*La guerra del fin del mundo:* Sentido (y sinsentido) de la historia," *Hispamérica* 11.31 (1982): 3–14.
12. Mario Vargas Llosa, *Gabriel García Márquez: Historia de un deicidio* (Barcelona: Seix Barral Editores, 1971), 481. All translations are my own.
13. My discussion of the binomial antithesis document/monument parts from Michel Foucault, *The Archaeology of Knowledge,* translated by A. M. Sheridan Smith (New York: Harper and Row, 1976).
14. See previous note.
15. Page 496. The passage occurs in a chapter entitled "Realidad total, novela total."
16. Mario Vargas Llosa, *La orgía perpetua: Flaubert y Madame Bovary* (Barcelona: Seix Barral Editores, 1975), 58–59. Translations are my own.
17. Jean-Paul Sartre, *L'Idiot de la famille. Gustave Flaubert de 1821 à 1857* (Paris: Editions Gallimard, vols. 1–2, 1971; vol. 3, 1972).
18. Mikhail Bakhtin, "Forms of Time and the Chronotope in the Novel: Notes toward a Historical Poetics," in *The Dialogic Imagination,* translated by Caryl Emerson and Michael Holquist (Austin: University of Texas Press, 1981), 84–258.
19. Araripe Junior, *Obra crítica de Araripe Junior,* edited by Afrânio Coutinho (Rio de Janeiro: Casa de Rui Barbosa, 1958, 1960–62); see volume 2 in particular.
20. The question of Euclides da Cunha's racism has always been a delicate matter in Brazilian cultural discourse and has received broad critical attention. For a cross section see Gilberto Freyre, *Actualidade de Euclides da Cunha* (Rio de Janeiro: Edição da Casa do Estudante do Brasil, 1941); Waldo Frank, *South American Journey* (New York: Duell, Sloan and Pearce, 1943), 339; and Clovis Moura, *Introdução ao pensamento de Euclides da Cunha* (Rio de Janeiro: Editôra Civilização Brasileira, 1964), especially the chapter entitled "Uma questão incômoda."

CHAPTER EIGHT: *WRITING BEYOND THE BOOK*

1. José Donoso, *The Obscene Bird of Night*, translated by Leonard Mades and Hardie St. Martin (New York: Alfred A. Knopf, 1973).
2. José Donoso, *The Boom in Spanish-American Literature: A Personal History*, translated by Gregory Kolovakos (New York: Columbia University Press, 1977).
3. José Donoso, *El jardín de al lado* (Barcelona: Seix Barral Editores, 1981). Translations are my own.

CHAPTER NINE: *A WOMAN'S PLACE*

1. I am grateful for this telling juxtaposition of Spacks and Walker to my former colleague Deborah E. McDowell. See her "New Directions for Black Feminist Criticism," in *The New Feminist Criticism: Essays on Women, Literature, and Theory*, ed. Elaine Showalter (New York: Pantheon Books, 1985), 186.
2. Annette Kolodny, "Dancing Through the Minefield: Some Observations on the Theory, Practice, and Politics of Feminist Literary Criticism," *Feminist Studies* 6 (1980). The "minefield" Kolodny referred to a decade ago was the critical establishment, then male-dominated, canonically self-empowering, and exclusionary.
3. Lest some pharisaic numerologist impute political motives to the sequence in which I discuss these writers, and thereby interpret the fact that I discuss Diamela Eltit's work last as a token afterthought for the sake of political correctness, I should say that Eltit's work does indeed come (and go) after thought, as does all good literature and literary commentary. I should say too that my focus on the question of a woman's place in what is traditionally a masculinist writing scene is not an afterthought. In fact, this chapter was written before some of the others, and my dialogue with Eltit dates from 1988, when we coincided at the Woodrow Wilson International Center for Scholars. I am merely following the dictates of chronology. Born in 1949, Eltit is the youngest of the authors treated here. Her novels are the most recent, and the thematization of the issues that her writing raises is done in a manner that makes hers a fairly recent discursive phenomenon in the Latin American tradition. This is not to say that there have not previously been voices and pens that broached the subject of a woman's place in the tradition. On the contrary, there are venerable precedents in this regard that date from the seventeenth century. But the nature of the politicization is qualitatively new, and the contextual entailments are indeed recent enough to be contemporary with this writing.
4. Diamela Eltit, *Lumpérica* (Santiago, Chile: Ediciones del Ornitorrinco, 1983); *Por la patria* (Santiago, Chile: Ediciones del Ornitorrinco, 1986).
5. All translations are my own.
6. I have dealt with this issue, particularly as it pertains to the work of Lezama Lima elsewhere. See my *Questing Fictions: Latin America's Family Romance* (Minneapolis: University of Minnesota Press, 1986), particularly chapter 1.

NOTES TO PAGES 189-94

7. Stéphane Mallarmé, *Igitur ou la Folie d'Elbehnon,* in *Œuvres,* ed. Yves-Alain Favre (Paris: Éditions Garnier, 1985), 378.
8. Francesco Petrarca, *Rerum familiarum libri I–VIII,* trans. Aldo S. Bernardo (Albany: State University of New York Press, 1975), 2.2, pp. 57–69.
9. Inca Garcilaso de la Vega, *Comentarios Reales de los Incas,* ed. Angel Rosenblat (Buenos Aires: Emecé Editores, 1943), 1.4.9, p. 196

INDEX

Aesthetic ideology, 37, 38, 95, 96
Agnosticism, as religion, 56
Alchemy, 53
Altereffect, 16, 87
Anna Karenina, 127
Anomie, 25
Apollodorus of Pergamum, 78
Apostrophe, 74, 77, 79, 82
Arabian Nights, 52
Araripe Junior, T. A., 151
Archilocus, 117
Arendt, Hannah, 32
Ariosto, Ludovico, 114
Aristotle: *Constitution of Athens,* 36; *Nichomachean Ethics,* 35
Arnold, Matthew, "Culture and Anarchy," 18
Ars moriendi, in Paz, 64
Ars vivendi, in Paz, 64
Augustine, Saint, 117
Authenticity, 2, 4, 7, 49, 207n. 3
Authority, 5, 6, 11, 17, 18, 45
Autobiography, authorial, 180, 190; as autograph, 166, 174; national, 192
Ayatollah syndrome, 147

Bakhtin, Mikhail, 146, 147
Barbarians, 1, 2, 3
Basho, Matsuo, 63
Baumgarten, Alexander Gottlieb, 37

Benjamin, Walter, 32–34
Bergson, Henri, 92, 93
Biography, and language, 94
Borges, Jorge Luis, 13, 33, **45–54**, 55, 120, 147, 203, 204; *Historia universal de la infamia,* 47; "The Mirror of Ink," 47–54
Browne, Sir Thomas, 33
Burke, Edmund, *Reflections on the Revolution in France,* 26
Burke, Kenneth, 20
Burton, Captain Richard F., 47, 49, 50, 51, 52
Burton, Robert, *Anatomy of Melancholy,* 123

Cabrera Infante, Guillermo, 7
Calvino, Italo, 92
Canonicity, 3, 104, 162; as male hagiography, 188–89
Carrell, Alexis, *Man the Unknown,* 129
Castoriadis, Cornelius, 23, 26
Castro, Américo, 75, 76, 77, 81, 83, 85
Catachresis, 89
Cavafis, Constantinos, 16, 168, 170, 172, 205
Censorship, 47
Certeau, Michel de, 20, 21
Cervantes Saavedra, Miguel de, 85, 87; *Don Quijote,* 120

215

INDEX

Civility, 1, 4, 183
Colonial subject, displacement of, 91
Colonization, 8
Colony, and culture, 20, 29
Columbus, Christopher, 40, 110; *Book of Prophecies,* 42
Complexity, 24, 26
Contingency, 34, 78, 80, 81, 84, 91, 146, 154, 175
Cornejo Polar, Antonio, 139
Cotton, John, 42
Cultural criticism, 27
Culture, 1, 2, 6, 17, 18, 19; and colony, 20, 21, 29; postcolonial, 31; and rhetoric, 28

Da Cunha, Euclides, 15, 137, 138, 142, 154, 155; death of, 153; and positivism, 152; and race, 151, 211n. 20; *Rebellion in the Backlands,* 140, 141, 144, 148—as national epic, 149–50
Dante (Alighieri), 168; *Inferno,* 161, 169; *Paradiso,* 169
De la Cruz, San Juan, 63
De la Cruz, Sor Juana Inés, 63
De las Casas, Bartolomé, 77
De Man, Paul, 34, 37, 38
Deixis, 19
Deleuze, Gilles, 5, 87
Deliberation, on the other, 21
Derrida, Jacques, 77
Desire, and language, 93, 96
Deterritorialization, 6, 87, 89, 91, 96
Diagnosis, as epistemology, 175
Dickens, Charles, *David Copperfield,* 88
Dickinson, Emily, 15, 71
Difference, xii, 4, 11, 21, 34; in Borges, 203; and identity, 59–60; and otherness, 185; in Paz, 58–59, 204; and repetition, 139; self-differentiation, 87; and writing, 176

Di Giovanni, Norman Thomas, 49, 50, 51
Dilthey, Wilhelm, 76
Discourse, 19; colonial, 87; critical, 23; cultural, 21, 22, 28, 39; dominant, 29; feminist, 179; historical, 78; and ideology, 20, 87; literary, 38; neocolonialist, 10, 43
Displacement, 22
Donne, John, 63
Donoso, José, 8, 15, 16, **157–78**; *The Boom in Spanish American Literature,* 162; irony in, 160; *El jardín de al lado,* 15, 157, 167–78, 205; *The Obscene Bird of Night,* 15, 42, 157–67, 170, 173, 205
Duchamp, Marcel, 63
Durkheim, Emile, 25

Eco, Umberto, 77, 96; *The Name of the Rose,* 92, 93, 120
Economy, 12
Einstein, Albert, 146
Eliot, George (Mary Ann Evans), *Middlemarch,* 177, 178, 205
Eliot, T. S., 16, 167, 205; *Four Quartets,* 168–72, 177
Eltit, Diamela, 8, 16, **179–201**, 205; *Lumpérica,* 180, 181, 182–92; *Por la patria,* 180, 181, 182, 192–201
Emergence, in the sciences, 24
Emergency, 17
Emergent: cultures, 17, 19, 22, 23, 25, 26, 29; literatures, xiii, 17, 19, 25, 26, 30, 42; properties, 25, 27, 30; state, 23, 29
Emerson, Ralph Waldo, 24
Entropy, 24
Epistemology, 14, 27, 37, 39
Erasmus, Desiderius, 104
Etcetera, 47, 48
Ethnic cleansing, 7
Ethnicity, 5, 7

INDEX

Ethnocentrism, 7
Eurocentric: criteria, 39; discourse, 26, 29
Eurocentrism, 23
Excentricity, 76
Exile, 8, 175; in Dante, 169

Faulkner, William, 102
Fiction, 40
First World, 42
Flaubert, Gustave, 141, 145; *Bouvard et Pécuchet*, 143–44
Foucault, Michel, 47, 141; *The Archaeology of Knowledge*, 142
Fuentes, Carlos, 8, 13, 14, **73–110**; *Cervantes o la crítica de la lectura*, 77; *Christopher Unborn*, 14, 86–110, 204; on history, 84–85; *La nueva novela hispanoamericana*, 76; *Terra Nostra*, 14, 42, 73–86, 204; *Tiempo mexicano*, 77
Fundamentalism, 41

García Márquez, Gabriel, 14, 15, 90, **111–36**, 141, 142; allegory and irony in, 112, 123; *Chronicle of a Death Foretold*, 126; *Love in the Time of Cholera*, 14, 123–36, 204; *One Hundred Years of Solitude*, 14, 40, 42, 111–23, 125, 139
Garcilaso de la Vega, Inca, 196, 198; *Comentarios Reales*, 193–94
Gates, Henry Louis, 207n. 3
Gender, 5, 6, 7, 8, 16, 58; constructs of, 180
Genealogy, 12
Girard, René, 31
Godzich, Wlad, 23, 29
Gödel, Kurt, 24
Goytisolo, Juan, 76
Graham, Fred, 2
Great American novel, 41

Greek Old Comedy, 74, 105
Guattari, Félix, 5, 87
Guevara, Che, 164
Guibert, Rita, 58

Hebreo, León, *Dialogos de amor*, 193
Hegel, G. W. F., 86, 95, 117, 140, 150
Heidegger, Martin, 59, 75, 77
Heisenberg, Werner, 96
Heraclitus, 90
Hermes, 49
Herodotus, 79
Hirsch, E. D., 207n. 2
History: in Fuentes, 80–83, 89; and genealogy, 110; and historicity, 80, 82; idealization of, 97; and metaphysics, 62; and narration, 73–75, 83; as national allegory, 190; and poetics, 77; prophetic, 116, 121; and truth, 104; in Vico, 109; and woman's body, 192, 193
Hobbes, Thomas, *Leviathan*, 19
Hölderlin, Friedrich, 59
Homer, 98, 102, 109, 114; *The Iliad*, 101, 116; *The Odyssey*, 100
Horace, 32
Hortus conclusus, 13
Hsieh Lin-Yün, 63
Humboldt, Alexander von, 41

Identity, xii, xiii, 4, 16, 21, 22, 28, 30, 34, 53; Cratylian, 38; and difference, 58–60, 154; mimetic, 38; and monument, 119; and national history, 96, 97; as self-reiteration, 203; and writing, 132, 159, 166
Ideology, 20, 36, 58, 62, 69, 86, 87, 164–65
Incorporation, xiii, 28
Irony: and allegory, 158; and otherness, 55; and writing, 105

INDEX

Jacobins, 58
Jakobson, Roman, 63, 65
James, Henry, Jr., 174, 178, 205; *The Spoils of Poynton,* 177
James, Henry, Sr., 167
Jameson, Fredric, 20, 27
Johnson, Samuel, 108
Joyce, James, 14, 16, 87, 89, 98, 101, 106; *Finnegans Wake,* 88, 89–90, 100, 105, 108, 109–10; *Ulysses,* 100

Kafka, Franz, 5, 87, 186
Kant, Emmanuel, 37, 100; *Critique,* 27, 28; *On History,* 19; "The Strife of the Faculties," 19
Kolodny, Annette, 212n. 2

Lacerda, Alberto, 63
Lane, Edward William, 49, 50, 51, 52
Lezama Lima, José, 63, 68–71, 187, 188; *Fragmentos a su imán,* 69
Longinus, 14, 78, 79, 80
López Velarde, Ramón, 96, 97, 98
Love, and writing/reading, 176

McDowell, Deborah E., 212n. 1
Madame Bovary, 127, 143
Magical realism, 26, 41
Mallarmé, Stéphane, 60, 91; *Igitur,* 186, 189, 190
Mandelbaum, Allen, 169
Mann, Thomas, 16
Marginality, 43
Marx, Karl, 86, 117, 140, 146, 150
Marxists, in Paz, 58
Mastery, 5, 6, 13, 34, 37, 39, 42, 43, 54, 143
Maternity: and nature, 97; and writing, 97
Matta, Roberto Sebastian, 63
Memory, and history, 94
Metalanguage, 38

Milton, John, 14, 117, 118, 120, 122; *Defensio Secunda,* 115; *Eikonoklastes,* 115; *Paradise Lost,* 111, 115–16, 123; and Puritan Revolution, 115
Mimesis, 23
Minority, 5
Minor literature, 87, 96
Miró, Joan, 63
Monumentalization, 119, in Foucault, 141; in Vargas Llosa, 144
Munthe, Axel, *The Story of San Michele,* 129
Mythologie blanche, 77

Nature, 26
Necessity, 81, 96
Neocolonial, 13, 14, 22; discourse, 43
Nero, 82
New World, 15, 40, 42, 76
Nietzsche, Friedrich, 76; *Genealogy of Morals,* 19
Niño de Guzmán, Guillermo, 151, 153, 155
Nomadism, 6
Novel, 41

O'Hara, Edgar, 151, 153, 155
Ontology, 92, 165
Ortega y Gasset, José, 75; *Invertebrate Spain,* 76
Othering, 28, 29
Otherness: and allegory, 135; in A. Castro, 75; as commonality, 4; and cultural discourse, 21, 22, 24; and difference, 185; in Donoso, 174; economy of, 12; and ethnocentrism, 7; and gender, 188, 201, 205; and identity, 43, 53, 55, 166; in Paz, 57; politics of, 5, 6; and representation, 10, 11; and rhetoric, 19; and theory, 34, 38, 39; and writing, 8, 9, 53, 132,

Index

163, 167, 176, 178, 183, 203
Other World, 40, 41
Oviedo, José Miguel, 152

Papaioannou, Kostas, 63
Parabasis, 74, 80, 104
Paradox, 10, 28, 56, 166
Partiality, 31
Paz, Octavio, 13, 42, **55–71**, 204; *Blanco,* 60; *In/Mediaciones,* 61; and mortality, 58; *El ogro filantrópico,* 62; otherness in, 204; *A Tree Within,* 63–71; *via negativa,* 61
Pericles, 35
Petrarch (Francesco Petrarca), 196, 198; *Canzioneri,* 193; *Rerum familiarum libri,* 192–94
Pharisees, xi, 56, 147
Pharmakos, 50–53, 83, 160, 174
Phenomenalism, 36
Picasso, Pablo, *Guernica,* 186
Plato, 23, 37, 55, 98; *Cratylus,* 93, 94, 96, 97, 98, 101; *Laws,* 36, 103; *Phaedrus,* 50–52, 160, 163; *Theaetetus,* 50
Pluralism, 4
Poesis, 61, 68
Poetics, and history, 77
Political correctness, 5, 212n. 3
Politics, 5, 10, 15, 22, 56; and interpretation, 19, 23, 45; and representation, 69; rhetoric of, 20
Positivism, 41, 43
Postcolonialism, 1, 13, 14, 22; and magical realism, 26
Power, 29, 173; authorial, 48; and gender, 195; and reason, 186
PRI (Partido Revolucionario Institucional), 95
Prigogine, Ilya, 24
Proust, Adrien, 126
Proust, Marcel, 126

Pseudonimity, as narrative strategy, 119–21

Quevedo, Francisco de, 33
Quintilian, 79; *Institutes,* 119

Renan, Ernest, 76
Representation, 9, 11, 13, 17, 23, 29, 31, 38, 39, 43, 54
Revolution, and paradox, 95
Reyes, Alfonso, 78
Rhetoric, 19; politics of, 20
Richardson, Samuel, *Pamela,* 127
Ricoeur, Paul, 78
Robbe-Grillet, Alain, 188
Rosenfeld, Lotty, 180

San Martín, José de, 193
Sartre, Jean-Paul, 75, 143, 145; *L'Idiot de la famille,* 144
Schlegel, Friedrich, 85
Science, and interpretation, 19
Sebastianism, 155
Seneca, Lucius Anneus, 83, 84; *Epistulae morales,* 82; Pisonian conspiracy, 83
Shakespeare, William, 99
Socrates, 55
Sophists, 55
Spacks, Patricia Meyer, 179
State, 17, 21
Stein, Gertrude, 96
Sterne, Laurence, 14, 87, 90, 98, 103; *Tristram Shandy,* 94, 107, 108
Stoa, 81, 82
Sublime, 26; cultural, 26; in Kant, 28
Sublimity, 14; politicization of, 27; and postcolonialism, 26
Supreme fiction, 39, 162

Tacitus, *Annals,* 83
Taine, Hippolyte, 149
Tasso, Torquato, 14, 111, 120, 122; *Arte*

Index

Poetica, 113; *Discorsi del Poema Eroico,* 116; *Gerusalemme Liberata,* 113–15, 116, 117
Temple, Shirley, 90
Theodorus of Gadara, 78, 79, 80, 81, 82
Theoroi, 32, 35–39
Theory, 10, 13, 22, 31; and aesthetics, 35–39; Athenian, 34–39; poetics of, 34; and praxis, 34; reader-reception, 54
Third World, 22, 39, 179, 201
Thucydides, 149
Tiberius Caesar, 78, 82
Tirante le Blanc, 153
Translators, 49
Transvaluation, 6
Tupac Amaru, 193
Tzu Chuang, 63

Unamuno, Miguel de, 75
Utopia, xiii, 88, 167

Vargas Llosa, Mario, 8, **137–55**; *Historia de un deicidio,* 142; historical irony in, 204; Thatcherism of, 148, 204; and total history, 142, 146; and total novel, 139–45; *The War of the End of the World,* 15, 137–55, 204—as *roman à clef,* 146

Vasconcelos, José, 94–95
Vattimo, Gianni, 210n. 16
Vers de circonstance, in Paz, 68
Vico, Giambattista, 103; *Scienza Nuova,* 109–10
Virgil, 114, 115
Von Neuman, John, 24

Walker, Alice, 179, 180, 188
Weber, Max, 23; "Science and Vocation," 19
Weber, Samuel, 20, 21, 23, 27, 29
Williams, Raymond, 19, 23; "Culture and Society," 18; *Key Words,* 18
Woman: and counter-memory, 199–200; and history, 93, 192–201; and memory, 94
Woolf, Virginia, 193

Xenophon, 98, 101, 104; *Anabasis,* 100, 102, 103; *Cyropaedia,* 103; as primal novelist, 103
Xipe Totec, 90

Yeats, W. B., 86, 125

Zurita, Raúl, 180
Zweig, Stefan, 149, 150